Praise for

The Flamenco Academy

"The pulse and passion of flamenco take center stage in [this] tale of love and longing and transformation."
—Veronique de Turenne, NPR

"Fascinating . . . a tale of friendship and betrayal with powerful glimpses into the legacy of flamenco, its mysteries and power." —*Santa Fe Reporter*

"In the monolithic culture of flamenco, Bird finds a remarkable landscape for transforming the inaccessible whims of an obsessive, lonely teenager into the epic saga of self-acceptance, loyalty and love to which no one is immune."
—Austin *Chronicle*

"A heady brew of a novel, lushly romantic at one turn, wryly and wittily observant at the next." —*San Jose Mercury News*

"A perfect book club read." —*Palm Beach Post*

"Sarah Bird writes fiction with such energy and snap, her novels seem to be in motion." —*The Dallas Morning News*

"Bird . . . delivers a story brimming with romance and visceral details of flamenco, its music and its history."
—*Publishers Weekly*

The
FLAMENCO
ACADEMY

A NOVEL

Sarah Bird

Ballantine Books · New York

To Greg Case, editor of *The Journal of Flamenco Artistry,*
August 23, 1945–July 11, 1998.
And to all true *flamencos,* past and present.

2007 Ballantine Books Trade Paperback Edition

Published in the United States by Ballantine Books, an imprint of The Random House Publishing Group, a division of Random House, Inc., New York.

BALLANTINE and colophon are registered trademarks of Random House, Inc.
READER'S CIRCLE and colophon are trademarks of Random House, Inc.

Originally published in hardcover in the United States by Alfred A. Knopf, a division of Random House, Inc., New York, in 2006.

Grateful acknowledgment is made to Farrar, Straus, and Giroux, LLC for permission to reprint "Ditty of First Desire" from "Love" from *Selected Verse: Revised Bilingual Edition* by Federico García Lorca. Translation copyright © 1994, 2004 by Catherine Brown, Cola Franzen, Angela Jaffray, Galway Kinnell, Will Kirkland, Christopher Maurer, Jerome Rothenberg, Greg Simon, Alan S. Trueblood, and Steven F. White. Reprinted by permission of Farrar, Straus, and Giroux, LLC.

Library of Congress Cataloging-in-Publication Data
Bird, Sarah.
The Flamenco Academy : a novel / by Sarah Bird.
p.   cm.
ISBN 978-0-345-46238-1
1. Young women—Fiction.   2. Flamenco dancers—Fiction.
3. Female friendship—Fiction.   4. Albuquerque (N.M.)—Fiction.
5. Flamenco—Study and teaching—Fiction.   I. Title.

PS3552.I74F55 2006
813'.54—dc22   2005044418

Printed in the United States of America

www.thereaderscircle.com

2 4 6 8 9 7 5 3 1

Ditty of First Desire	*Cancioncilla del Primer Deseo*
In the green morning I wanted to be a heart. A heart.	*En la mañana verde,* *quería ser corazón.* *Corazón.*
And in the ripe evening I wanted to be a nightingale. A nightingale.	*Y en la tarde madura* *quería ser ruiseñor.* *Ruiseñor.*
(Soul, turn orange-colored. Soul, turn the color of love.)	*(Alma,* *ponte color de naranja.* *Alma,* *ponte color de amor.)*
In the vivid morning I wanted to be myself. A heart.	*En la mañana viva* *yo quería ser yo.* *Corazón.*
And at evening's end I wanted to be my voice. A nightingale.	*Y en la tarde caída* *quería ser mi voz.* *Ruiseñor.*
Soul, turn orange-colored! Soul, turn the color of love!	*¡Alma,* *ponte color de naranja!* *¡Alma,* *ponte color de amor!*

—*Federico García Lorca* (1898–1936)

The Flamenco Academy

Chapter One

Flamenco has Ten Commandments. The first one is: Dame la verdad, *Give me the truth. The second is: Do it* en compás, *in time. The third one is: Don't tell outsiders the rest of the commandments. I come here, to the edge of the continent, to honor the first commandment, to give myself the truth.*

Waves, sparkling with phosphorescence in the darkness, crash on the shore just beyond my safe square of blanket. I cup my chilly hands around a mug of tea that smells of oranges and clove and search for that first streak of salmon to crack the far horizon. There might be one or two early risers, insomniacs, troubled sleepers, who will see the light of a new day before me. But not many. I am alone with my tea and my thoughts.

The waves roll in all the way from Asia and slam against the shore. Their roar comforts me. It almost drowns out the sound of heels, a dozen, two dozen, pounding on a wooden floor, turning a dance studio into a factory manufacturing rhythm. That is the ocean I hear. It is broadcast by the surge of my own blood, pulsing en compás, *in time, to a flamenco beat. My heart beats and its coded rhythms force me to remember.*

Once upon a time, I stepped into a story I thought was my own. It was not, though I became a character in it and gave the story all the years it demanded from my life. The story began long before I entered it, long before any of the living and most of the dead entered it.

I start on the night that I saw the greatest flamenco dancer of all time perform. That night I had to decide whose story my life would be about.

Chapter Two

It was early summer in Albuquerque, when the city rests between the sandblasting of spring winds and the bludgeoning of serious summer heat to come. New foliage made a green lace against the sky. The tallest trees were cottonwoods and they spangled tender chartreuse hearts across the clouds. It was the opening evening of the Flamenco Festival Internacional. A documentary about Carmen Amaya, the greatest flamenco dancer ever, dead now for forty years, was to be premiered at Rodey Theater on the University of New Mexico campus.

I dawdled as I crossed the campus. The air smelled like scorched newspaper. The worst forest fires in half a century had been blazing out of control in the northern part of the state. Four firefighters had already been killed and still the fires moved south. That morning, the Archbishop of Santa Fe announced that he would start saying a novena the next morning to lead all the citizens of New Mexico in prayers for the rain needed to save the state, to save our beloved *Tierra del Encanto.*

I slowed my pace even more. I wanted to reach the theater after the houselights were out so that I could see as much of Carmen Amaya and as little of "the community" as possible. I dreaded being plunged again into the hothouse world of New Mexico's flamenco scene. Tomorrow, when I started teaching, I would have no choice. Tonight was optional and only the promise of glimpsing the greatest flamenco dancer ever could have dragged me out.

Although we, all us dancers, had studied every detail of Carmen's mythic life, although we had pored over still photos and read descriptions of her technique, none of us had ever seen her dance. Film footage of her dancing was so rare and so expensive that we'd had to content ourselves with listening to the legendary recordings she made with Sabicas. We memorized the sublime hammer of her footwork, but hearing was a poor substitute for seeing.

Only the news that the documentary contained footage of Carmen Amaya performing could have gotten me out of my bed and into the shower. The shower had removed the musty odor of rumpled sheets and unwashed hair I'd wrapped myself in for the past several weeks since I'd taken to wearing my own stink as protection, as a way to mark the only territory I had left: myself. I wouldn't have been able to face the humiliation of seeing "the community" at all if I hadn't had my newly acquired secret to lean on.

When I was certain that Rodey Theater would be dark, I slipped in the back and grasped the first empty seat. Only there, alone and unseen, was it safe to take the secret out and examine it. It strengthened me enough that I corrected my slumped posture. I'd leaned on my new knowledge to get this far; tomorrow, somehow, some way, the secret would guide me to what I needed, what I had to have. Of course, tonight it changed nothing. To everyone in the theater, which was every flamenco dancer, singer, and guitarist in New Mexico, I was still the most pathetic creature imaginable: the third leg of a love triangle.

The credits flickered; then Carmen Amaya's tough Gypsy face filled the screen, momentarily obliterating all thoughts. It was brutal, devouring, the face of a little bull on a compact body that never grew any larger or curvier than a young boy's. As taut with muscle as a python's, that body had made Carmen Amaya the dancer she was. A title beneath her face noted that the year was 1935. She was only twenty-two, but had been dancing for two decades.

She oscillated in luminous whites and inky blacks, gathering herself in a moment of stillness, a jaguar coiling into itself before exploding. A few chords from an unseen guitarist announced an *alegrías,* Carmen's famous *alegrías.* The audience, mostly dancers as avid as I, leaned forward in their seats. Hiding from random gazes, I burrowed more deeply into my chair, considered sneaking out. Even armed with my secret, I wasn't strong enough yet for this. There would be questions, condolences, sympathy moistened with a toxic soup of schadenfreude. I wasn't ready to be a cautionary tale, the ultra-pale Anglo girl who'd dared to fly too close to the flamenco sun.

I was pushing out of my seat, about to leave; then Carmen moved.

A clip from one of her early Spanish movies played. The camera crouched low. Her full skirt whirled into roller-coaster arcs that rose and plunged as those bewitched feet hammered more rhythm into the world than any pair of feet before or since. I dropped back into my seat, poleaxed by beauty as Carmen told her people's hard history in the sinuous twine of her hands, the perfectly calibrated arch of her back, the effortless syncopation of her feet.

I tore my eyes from the screen long enough to pick out the profiles of other dancers, girls I'd studied with for years, women who'd instructed us. They were rapt, mesmerized by the jubilant recognition that Carmen Amaya was as good as her legend. No, better. That not only was she the best back then, but if she were dancing today none of us, forty years after her death, could have touched her. I wished then that I were sitting with those other pilgrims who'd made flamenco's long journey, who understood as I did just how good Carmen was.

I joined in the muttered benediction of *óle*s, accent as always on the first syllable, that whispered through the theater; then I surrendered and let Carmen Amaya's heels tap flamenco's intricate Morse code into my brain. Though I had willed it to never do so again, my heart fell back into flamenco time and beat out the pulses with her. Flamenco flowed through my veins once more. From the first, flamenco had been a drug for me, an escape from who I was, as total as any narcotic, and Carmen Amaya hit that vein immediately, obliterating despair, rage, all emotion other than ecstasy at the perfection of her dancing.

The brief clip ended. We all exhaled the held breath and sagged back into our seats. An old-timer, white shirt buttoned up to the top and hanging loosely about a corded neck, no tie, battered, black suit jacket, appeared onscreen. A subtitle informed us that he had once played guitar in Carmen's troupe.

"Tell us about Carmen's family," an offscreen interviewer asked.

"Gitana por cuatro costaos," the guitarist answered. "Gypsy on four sides." The translation of this, the ultimate flamenco encomium, made my secret come alive and beat within me. Blood, it was all about blood in flamenco.

The withered guitarist went on. "Carmen Amaya was Gypsy on all four sides. We used to say that she had the blood of the pharaohs in her veins back in the days when we still believed that we Gypsies came from Egypt. We don't believe that anymore, but I still say it. Carmen Amaya had the blood of the pharaohs in her veins. That blood gave her her life, but it also killed her."

"What do you mean?"

"Her kidneys. The doctor called it infantile kidneys. They never grew any bigger than a little baby's. La Capitana only lived as long as she did because she sweated so much when she danced. That was how her body cleansed itself. Otherwise, she would have died when she was a child. Her costumes at the end of a performance? Drenched. You could pour sweat out of her shoes. She had to dance or die."

"Bailar o morir." As the guitar player pronounced the words, his lips stuck on his dentures, tugging them up, holding them rolled under so that he looked like a very sad, very old marionette. "Dance or die. Dancing was the only thing that kept her alive."

"Bailar o morir." He was right. I had to start dancing again. The last few weeks had brought me too close to the alternative. For the first time, I was happy I'd agreed to teach. But that was tomorrow. Tonight, it was essential that I be gone before the lights came up. I glanced at the exit and debated whether I should leave.

When I looked back, though, a clip from one of Carmen's glitzy Hollywood movies was playing. I settled into my seat; I would risk a few more scenes. Carmen was dancing in a nightclub in New York. She wore a short, cabin boy–style jacket and high-waisted white pants that jiggled about her legs as she pounded the wooden floor, creating an entire steel band's worth of percussion.

"Before Carmen Amaya," a narrator intoned, "flamenco dance was a languid, matronly twining of arms, legs rooted to the earth like oaks. Eighty years ago, Amaya's father, El Chino, put her in pants and Carmen broke the spell that had frozen the lower half of *las bailaoras'* bodies for all of flamenco's history."

The narrator pronounced *bailadoras* the cool Gypsy way, *bailaoras.* To show that we were insiders, we did the same, using Gypsy spelling and pronunciation whenever we could. Dancer, *bailadora,* became *bailaora;* guitarist, *tocador,* turned into *tocaor;* and once we'd gobbled the *d* in *cantador,* singer, it emerged as *cantaor.*

The guitarist returned and stated unequivocally, "She never rehearsed. Never, never, never." *Nunca, nunca, nunca.*

The other dancers in the theater snorted at that statement. We knew how ridiculous it was. It was like boasting about a Chinese child never rehearsing before speaking Chinese. We knew better. We'd read the biographies. Like all good Gypsy mothers, Carmen's had clapped *palmas* on her belly while she was pregnant so that her baby would be marinated in flamenco rhythms in utero. Carmen danced before she walked and was performing in cafés in Barcelona by the time she was six years old. As the other dancers leaned their heads together to whisper and laugh, I wished I were sitting with them. We would all share our favorite complaint, the near impossibility of a *payo,* a non-Gypsy, ever being truly accepted in flamenco. Compared to Carmen Amaya, Gypsy on four sides, even those Latinas who believed they had an inside track were outsiders.

I counted few of the dancers as friends. I knew this world too well. Friend or not, I would be the subject of hot gossip and, since I'd been asked to teach at the festival, envy. There were those who believed that the honor had been bestowed out of pity.

Pity—that was what would be the hardest of all to deal with. No, tomorrow would be soon enough to face them all. At least then, when I was teaching, I would have my flamenco armor on, my favorite long black skirt, my new Menke shoes from Spain with extra *claves*—tiny silver nails—tapped into the toes.

On the screen, home movie footage from the fifties played. The colors of the old film had faded to sepia tones. A much older Carmen sat on the concrete steps of a porch and held her arms out to a chubby-legged toddler in sandals who staggered toward her. Offscreen, an ancient voice recalled, "Carmen couldn't have any children of her own so she asked us for our son." That image, a little boy, just learning to walk, wobbling toward the most famous flamenco dancer ever, one who had earned her crown with blood, caused the polarity in the room to reverse. The air beside my head trembled as the secret beating in my chest recognized its double on that screen.

Carmen couldn't have any children of her own so she asked us for our son.

The home movie ended and the speaker, an elderly Gypsy man identified as Carmen's nephew, appeared. The harsh light glistened off his bald scalp, sweating beneath a few wisps of ash-colored hair.

His wife, portly and silent, nodded. Her husband continued speaking. He was as passionate as if he were pleading his case before a jury, though the incident had occurred half a century ago. "Why did she ask that of us? It was like he was hers anyway. We were all one family anyway. Why did she need to adopt him? Simply because she wanted a child who was of our blood?"

The old man finished and a rustling swept through the auditorium as heads steepled together and whispers hissed back and forth. A few dancers, those who knew the most, craned their necks searching the auditorium. Doña Carlota was who they really wanted to see, to search her face for a reaction. When the other dancers discovered that she wasn't in the theater, the glances sought me out. I ducked my head, hiding until the bat-wing skitter of attention had dissipated.

When I looked up again, Carmen Amaya's funeral procession was winding across the screen. It snaked for miles down through hills thick with rosemary, leading from Carmen's castle on a bluff above the Costa Brava to her burial plot in the town of Bagur. This home movie footage was old and jerky, but rather than fading out, the colors had intensified into a palette of cobalt blues and deepest emerald greens. The devastated faces of thousands of mourners were masks of grief as profound as if each one had lost a sister, a wife, a mother.

The documentary returned to Carmen in the last year of her life. A clip from a Spanish movie played. She was only fifty, but Carmen's ferocity had been blunted. The feral lines of her face were swollen with fluid her infantile kidneys could not eliminate. She sat at a rickety wooden table in a dusty neighborhood, a slum, like the one in Barcelona where she'd been born in a shack. She was surrounded by Gypsy children as dirty, ragged, and hungry as she once had been. She began to tap the table. One knock, two. Just enough to announce the *palo,* the style. Then in flamenco's code of rhythms, she rapped out a symphony that held the history of her people during their long exile from India. She told all the secrets her tribe kept from outsiders. All the secrets they had translated into rhythms so bewilderingly beautiful that they lured you in like the honeyed drops of nectar hidden in the throat of pitcher plants. You got the nectar, that's true, but you could never find your way back out again. You never *wanted* to find your way out again. All you wanted was to burrow even deeper, to break the code, to learn one more secret.

In that moment, watching Carmen, it was still all I wanted. Even after everything that had happened, all I wanted was one more sip of nectar.

"*Mi corazón,*" a singer wailed the start of a verse in the background behind Carmen's image fading into history, into legend. I knew the *letra,* had danced to it dozens of times, and my cheeks were wet before the translation appeared in subtitle: "My heart has been broken more than the Ten Commandments."

The line sung in flamenco's unearthly quaver stabbed straight into my chest because I realized then that my own heart was not broken so much as missing entirely and no secret, however carefully interpreted, would ever return it. I was groping in the dark, ready to escape, when the lights unexpectedly came up. I had missed my chance. I was scrubbing tears off my cheek when a hand grazed my shoulder. Thank God it was Blanca, universally recognized as the least bitchy of all the serious dancers. We'd started out together back when Doña Carlota had taught the introductory class.

"Rae, how are you doing?" Blanca patted my shoulder and stared with the damp sympathy I'd dreaded.

"Pretty good." I injected as much pep as I could into my answer, gesturing toward my reddened eyes. "Allergies are bothering me. All the smoke from the forest fires." There was no smoke in the air inside the theater.

Blanca nodded. "It's good to see you, Rae. Really good." She put too much emphasis on the last *good,* speaking to me as if I were a patient who doesn't know yet that she's terminal. But Blanca was nice. I'd discovered far too late that I should have put a much higher priority on nice. I should have been friends with someone like Blanca instead of Didi.

"Keep in touch, okay?" she said. Her solicitous question was drowned out by the thunder of applause that erupted when the incandescent Alma Hernandez-Luna, director of the flamenco program, bounded onstage. *"Bienvenido a todos nuestros estudiantes.* Welcome, welcome, welcome to the more than two hundred students who are with us this summer from China, Germany, England, Belarus, Tokyo, Canada, and nearly every state in the union. We welcome you all to the country that we will create for the next twelve days. The country of flamenco!"

The applause fell briefly into *compás* and the audience laughed at us all speaking the same language with our hands.

"It is strange to be welcoming you. For the past fifteen years our founder, Doña Carlota, has always opened the festival. She cannot be with us here tonight in body, but her spirit fills this hall! We are all here because of Doña Carlota Anaya. She created the first academic home for flamenco in the New World."

That part was true.

Alma continued, "The festival is her baby." That part wasn't true. *Alma* means soul, and Hernandez-Luna had been the soul of the program for years. The festival was entirely her baby. Through her connections, she was always able to lure *la crema del mundo flamenco* to our little sun-blasted campus. Whoever the reigning god or goddess of flamenco was, Alma would hunt them down and bring them to the festival to perform and teach. I was one of only a handful of locals on this year's faculty. The night should have been a triumph for me. I knew it wasn't going to be that, but, until the film, I had thought the festival would be an opportunity for me. An opportunity to learn where Tomás was. To start using my secret. The film, the image of the coveted child toddling toward the world's greatest dancer, had changed all that.

"I hope everyone has their tickets for Eva La Yerbabuena's show"—a burst of applause for the acclaimed dancer interrupted Alma—"because they're going fast. I would like to thank our visiting documentarian"—the maker of the Carmen film stood to a hearty round of applause—"for helping us to kick off this summer's festival with that astonishing film. Okay, gang, the fun is over."

Laughter erupted.

"Tomorrow we get down to work."

The loudest applause yet broke out.

"But before that could you, all you visitors, please, join us in a moment of silent prayer. Pray for rain, okay? Because if we don't get some rain *Dios* only knows what's going to happen to our poor state."

As the theater fell silent, Alma stared at her palm. When the moment of prayer was over, she read the note she'd written there. "Oh, big announcement, people. It's about Farruquito." A chorus of squeals greeted the name of the Elvis of flamenco, a young dancer with the talent and, more important, the right genes, to be crowned the Great Bronze Hope. Like Carmen Amaya, like all the members of the true inner circle, Farruquito was *gitano por cuatro costaos.*

Alma gestured for the squealing girls to calm down. "This is a good news–bad news sort of deal. We're not going to have time to publicize this, but I think we can probably fill the KiMo Theatre just with word of mouth. We have a last-minute change in the lineup."

For the second time that evening, my skin began to prickle and the air around me seemed to become denser, the molecules slowing down as if the barometric pressure had suddenly dropped the way it does before a storm. Because it was the worst thing I could imagine, I knew before Alma said the words what her announcement would be.

"The bad news is that Farruquito has had to cancel."

A wave of groans swept through the crowd at learning that the boy wonder of flamenco and heir apparent to the title of king of old-school flamenco, *flamenco puro,* was not coming. The deadened thud in my chest accelerated with a rhythm like horse hooves pounding nearer.

"But the good news is that our most famous alumna has agreed to fill in."

I prayed, I begged all the flamenco deities to, please, stop what I knew was coming. They ignored me.

"So let's spread the word. Ofelia is coming home!"

That name, those syllables, *Oh-fay-lee-yuh,* filled my head with a rushing like storm water surging down a drain. It blocked out the sound of clapping. I had to leave. Immediately. I staggered to my feet. Heads bobbed in front of me like a collection of people-shaped piñatas, a gauntlet I had to run.

Outside the theater, I tried to inhale, tried to make myself breathe. The scorched air chafed my lungs as I ran across the campus. I was coughing and my eyes were streaming by the time I jumped into my truck, which I'd left in the Frontier Restaurant parking lot. I pounded my hands on the steering wheel to drive that fraud of a name, Ofelia, *Oh-fay-lee-yuh,* out of my head. One name, that was her entire life's goal, to be a one-name celebrity. I refused to give her that, to think of her as Ofelia. To me she would always be Didi. Didi Steinberg.

A long time ago she had been my best friend. Not so long ago she stole the only man I will ever love.

Chapter Three

A triangle. The staple of opera, melodrama, romance novels, of flamenco. Odd how knowing something is a cliché actually makes it slightly more painful rather than less.

When I was a girl with hair turned white blond in the Texas sun, I used to squat beside tiny funnels of dust created by ant lions. I would carefully feed captured ants into the funnels. The ants would scrabble frantically, trying to escape, but all their clawing accomplished was to create microscopic avalanches that swept them inexorably down toward the predator that waited, hidden beneath the dry dirt.

A hot wind blew through the truck. The smoke drifting down from the north seemed to have sealed the day's heat in. Still my fingers on the steering wheel were stiff and I trembled with cold.

She was coming back. Which meant that he was coming back as well. I had to be ready. Before I ever faced Didi again, long before I ever faced Tomás, I had to decode the secret I'd been given, the long history that explained so much.

I started the truck, drove to Central Avenue, and turned right, heading east. I could have turned left and gone west, but the future lay that way. East to West. Old to new. That was the direction Americans took to move away from the past. I needed to move toward the past that night. My answers were back there, back in my history with Didi. With Tomás. Back before any of us, any of our parents, were even born.

I passed the old Lobo Theater. It had been converted into a Christian meeting place. I kept driving. Past Nob Hill Shopping Center. Past the Aztec Motel. I drove Route 66 back to where it all started. Back almost a decade to when I was still Cyndi Rae Hrncir from Houdek, Texas. Back to when all flamenco was to me was a big pink bird and the most exciting person ever to step into my life was Didi Steinberg.

Chapter Four

Naturally, Didi Steinberg had no idea on earth who I was that day she sat with her parents in the reception area at the oncologist's where I was waiting by myself while my parents consulted with the doctor. Even though Didi and I had several classes together, she was unaware of my existence. I was suffering through my senior year at Pueblo Heights High School in total anonymity. I had made one friend, Nita Carabajal. Nita had been assigned to be my physics lab partner. All we had in common was that neither one of us had any other friends. Everyone knew who Didi Steinberg was. She occupied a space that was a unique blend of legend and outcast.

Didi was the coolest person I could imagine because one look at her told you that she didn't give a shit about much of anything. Stories of her general wild-ass behavior had even reached me way out in my social Siberia. I'd heard about how she was sent to the principal for wearing a top that officially met dress code regulations because it wasn't spaghetti straps, but was so short the bottom half of her tits showed. I heard how she'd put on a tuxedo and taken herself to the prom the year before, then danced all night with the busboys. I'd heard that she called her car the Skankmobile and got stoned in it every day before school. That her father was a disc jockey and she'd had her own show on his station for a while. Mostly, though, I'd heard that Didi Steinberg was the Groupie Queen of Albuquerque.

That day, however, slumped in a chair next to her father, she looked like any teen trying to become invisible when she's with her parents. Mr. Steinberg reminded me of Daddy. His clothes, his skin, his eyes, they all looked borrowed from a bigger person, the person he'd been before he'd gotten sick. Even in the best of health, though, Mr. Steinberg would have been old enough to be Didi's grandfather.

A nurse in lilac scrubs with a bright aquarium print opened the door to the reception area and called out, "Mort Steinberg." Mr. Steinberg breathed heavily as Didi and her mother helped him up. He had a goatee, thick, gray muttonchops, with only a few strands of hair on top. A black turtleneck and a silver ankh around his neck completed the ancient hipster look.

I was surprised that Didi's mom stayed in the waiting room and let her husband go back alone with the nurse. My mother had not left my father's side in the past four months, ever since he'd developed the cough that wouldn't go away. Mrs. Steinberg was the most exotic woman I had ever seen. I couldn't decide if she was Mexican or Asian. She looked like an animé Natalie Wood with big eyes and a broad, doll-baby face. She gibbered away to Didi in rapid-fire Spanish.

Didi ignored her mother, pretending to be interested in an article in *Golf Digest*. This gave me a chance to study Didi Steinberg. She made me think of one of those celebrities who swear in *People* magazine that they were dorky and unpopular as teenagers and you don't believe them until you see the old yearbook photo and understand how out of place they would have been in a normal life. Didi was like that, bigger than life, at least normal life. The hard planes of her face, the harsh flare of her nostrils, her high, slanted cheeks and wide, ravenous mouth were too masculine for a girl, too unsettling. Not pretty, not ugly, something more compelling than either of those classifications. The word that popped into my mind was *arresting* because of the way she put your attention behind bars. Didi Steinberg was made to be looked at and not just because she wore more liner than a mime around her paisley-shaped eyes, and she had three diamond studs glittering in her right nostril, and she'd dyed her hair black then done the tips the color of a lime popsicle. You would have stared at Didi Steinberg even if she'd been wearing Chap Stick and jeans from Wal-Mart like me. Even back then, Didi always seemed like there should be a bank of footlights between her and the rest of the world.

If you'd taken a picture of Didi Steinberg and looked at the negative, what you would have seen would have been me, her exact opposite. My family had moved to Albuquerque from Houdek, Texas, at the start of my junior year. My mom had taken one look at the brilliant swoops of gang graffiti and metal detectors at Pueblo Heights High School and announced that no child of hers would ever set foot in such a place. She homeschooled me until Daddy got sick, so when I entered Pueblo

Heights at the start of my senior year, I didn't know a single person. In addition to not having one friend, I had two names, Cyndi Rae, and a Texas accent.

The first thing I had learned when we moved to Albuquerque was that pretty much everyone in New Mexico hates Texans. On top of that, I had a gruesome collection of consonants for a last name, Hrncir, so every time a teacher called on me, I had to conduct a little seminar in Czech pronunciation, HERN-SHUR. The best any of my teachers were ever able to do was make a sound like they had a chip stuck in the back of their throats, Hrr-KURR! Few teachers called on me more than once. I had more than the usual teen quota of reasons to do what came most naturally to me, which was keep my mouth shut and try never to be noticed.

Didi suddenly looked up from *Golf Digest* and caught me staring at her. She shot me a look that my mother would have said "coulda killed Aunt Katie." My mother had lots of country sayings that no one else understood. Except my father. Probably because they'd grown up on farms next to each other in Houdek, a little town north of San Antonio populated mostly by members of their two Czech families. Everyone back home had thought my father was a giant rebel when he took a job with Circuit City and drove forty miles into San Antonio every day and a complete extraterrestrial when he got a big promotion and moved us to Albuquerque.

It was a hard move for my mother. She'd never lived more than two miles from her parents her whole life and even after she was married always ate either breakfast or lunch with them every day of the week and dinner every Sunday. In Houdek everyone knew that my mom, Jerri, was high-strung. That was how she'd been her whole life. It was the reason she'd never finished high school in spite of having straight As and being a math genius. She couldn't sit still for an entire class. Sitting still made her so nervous, she took to plucking out, first, a big patch of hair above her right ear, then all her eyebrows. When she started in on her eyelashes, everyone agreed that Jerri would be better off at home.

In Houdek my mother's high-strung peculiarities were "just Jerri's way." No one ever asked my mother's parents if they'd thought about Ritalin or seeing a psychologist. People in Houdek tended more to say oddball behavior was just someone's "way" and let it go. Still, everyone agreed that it was a blessing when my mother married my father, easygoing Emil Hrncir. Daddy, all reddish blond hair and freckled from the sun, was the opposite of high-strung. Quite content to spend his days rumbling around on the back of a tractor and his weekends hunting dove or deer or whatever was in season, Daddy was so low-strung, in fact, that he verged sometimes on being unstrung. I always wondered what had brought two such different people together. Maybe Daddy thought my mother's relentless buzz of energy would rub off and energize him, that they'd balance each other out. Or maybe it was just because my mother was pretty, really, really pretty, with wavy, strawberry blond hair, delicate features, and skin like a baby's. Everyone said I favored her but had Daddy's height, though I never saw the resemblance.

I never questioned the world I was born into. That, in our house, the radio and television always had to be kept at a whisper-soft volume. That all dishes had to be removed from the table immediately upon finishing a meal. That friends were never allowed to visit. That when my mother's migraines struck, I would stay home from school to bring cups of flat 7Up to her. I never questioned it and never took it too seriously because Daddy didn't. Whenever Mom would tell me to stop turning the pages of my magazine so loud, or insist that she couldn't stand to even look at any food that wasn't white, or when she'd get so wound up, her hands balled into tight fists that oscillated beside her head, Daddy would always catch my eye and wink. Then we'd lay low together. I'd take my magazine and sit up in the cab of the tractor with him and we'd pretend to plow until we saw the light in my mom's bedroom go out. Or we'd take off early in the morning and leave a note saying we'd gone to fish or hunt snipes, then we'd sit all day in the Dairy Queen in Helotes and drink coffee and Cokes. We had great times together. His favorite thing was teasing me by asking how "Sometimes Y" was. Sometimes Y was his name for the pretend boyfriend he claimed I had. It came out of his joke that I would fall in love with the first boy with a lot of vowels in his name. "A, E, I, O, U, and Sometimes Y, right?" he'd say. I told him to stop it. I was too shy to even talk to a boy, much less ever have a boyfriend.

We were all right in Houdek where everyone accepted that Jerri Hrncir was a little too tightly wound and that Emil Hrncir was the best thing that could have ever happened to her. We were a small-town family, designed to do what generations of Hrncirs before us had done: farm, raise soybeans, sorghum, a little cotton. After Granddad's stroke, Daddy took over and might have made it if the price of diesel along with everything else hadn't kept rising. After Mom's nerves got too bad for her to handle the bookkeeping, I was the one who itemized all the expenditures. Like my mother, I was good with numbers. It was never anything I worked at, just something I was born with. It was my "way."

When I told Daddy the bad news the numbers had for us, he got a job with Circuit City. At first it was just to tide us over. But the numbers told another story: he'd never go back to farming. The transfer to Albuquerque was a shock to Jerri that she never recovered from. We left Houdek right after the last day of my sophomore year, when the creeks were still running and the fields were still green and succulent. We drove a U-Haul truck loaded with our stuff to Albuquerque and parked it in front of a house Daddy had flown out earlier to rent for us. It was flat on top and squared off as a shoe box with red lava rocks where a lawn should have been and one spindly desert willow out front that didn't cast enough shade to cool off an ant. Mom took one look at the shoe-box house and burst into tears. She folded her arms across her chest and locked Albuquerque out as much as she possibly could. Everything about the city frightened her, annoyed her, or dried her skin out.

Daddy got a giant-screen TV as a return from Circuit City and Mom kept it turned on night and day. Every time there was anything on the news about someone being taken to the West Mesa and raped or a drive-by shooting in the south valley, Mom stepped up our home security system. She had bars put on all the windows, triple dead bolts on the doors, and an alarm system wired to a special private security service. I think she'd decided to homeschool me before she even saw Pueblo Heights, but the armed cop at the entrance and the sight of more brown than white faces sealed the deal for her.

The one good thing for me about homeschooling was that I discovered an incredible online math program that let me go as far and as fast as I wanted in calculus, trig, some statistics. The only people I met my junior year were other homeschoolers and the geeks I competed against in Math Olympiad. It was through the homeschooler group that Mom connected with HeartLand, the weirdo church she ended up joining. The major emphasis of HeartLand seemed to be to remind women that they were "subject" to their husbands and to try to return to what they imagined was a simpler time. None of the women from Mom's new church cut their hair and they all wore clothes that they thought small-town people wore. But no one I ever knew back in Houdek would have been caught dead in a long denim skirt and high-buttoned blouse like a five-year-old would wear to a piano recital.

All the burglar bars and buttons in the world, though, couldn't keep out the one thing Mom should have been afraid of. Daddy had the cough for months before he finally went to the doctor. It was cancer. Daddy acted like it was no big deal. Still, it was decided that homeschooling on top of taking care of Daddy was too much for Mom's weak nerves, and for my senior year I was enrolled at Pueblo Heights.

Daddy joked about the chemo and radiation, said he was doing it just to "humor the tumor." Even when he got so weak he had to use a wheelchair, he was still able to convince Mom and me that the thing growing inside of him was merely a passing annoyance. The day I met Didi was the day even Daddy had to stop pretending.

When my parents came back out to the oncologist's waiting room where I sat watching Didi Steinberg act like she was reading *Golf Digest,* the expression on my mom's face scared me. The way the nurse in her tropical fish smock held the door open for her to push the wheelchair through scared me even more. It was too kind, too solicitous. My eyes met my father's and everything he'd tried to hide from me for the past four months was there. The fear and panic were so big that they made him a little boy who just wanted someone to rescue him. My mom looked at me in the same lost, scared way. But there was nothing I could do for her, for either one of them. When Mom realized that no one would be coming to rescue her, that nothing would change what the doctor had just told her back in his office, her face started squirming around. At first, it didn't seem she was about to cry, more like she was going to say something but couldn't remember the words. All I cared about in that moment was that she was going to do something embarrassing in front of Didi Steinberg. Like talk.

She did something worse, though. My mother fainted. One instant she was standing behind the wheelchair, pushing my father toward me, the next she went down so fast I thought she'd stepped into a hole.

Didi, who only truly came to life when the adrenaline was flowing, reacted faster than anyone, even the nurse. She was helping Mom to a chair before I could figure out what had happened. My father tried to hoist himself up to help her, but Didi was already in charge.

"Make sure he stays put," she ordered me, pointing to my father as she helped my mother bend forward to put her head between her knees. She looked at the nurse and barked at her, "Get us some water. Stat."

Everyone followed her orders. Her calm, authoritative manner combined with using the medical word, *stat,* made us all believe that, in spite of the lime-popsicle-colored hair, she just might be an intern, a medical student, someone who had answers and could help us. That, I would later learn, was Didi's greatest gift. When she wanted to, she could read your deepest needs and turn herself into whoever could fill them.

"Cyndi. Rae. Honey." My father huffed out one word on each laborious exhalation. "Get. The. Keys."

I picked the car keys up from the floor where Mom had dropped them. "I'll. Drive. Home." He held out his palm.

"Are you tripping?" Didi asked my father, plucking the keys from my hand.

Mom didn't object. Whatever unimaginable news the doctor had given my parents had stolen the little bit of fight she had left.

"You"—she pointed to my father—"need to get into bed. Stat. You"— she pointed to my mother, who was staring at the cup of water the nurse had put into her hand as if she were trying to figure out how to work it— "should not be behind the wheel of a car. You"—my turn—"need to be in the backseat of the car monitoring your father. I"—she thumped her chest with an open hand—"will drive."

Didi blurted something in Spanish to her mother. She used the word *papi* a lot so I assumed she was telling her mother to take her father home. All Mrs. Steinberg did was shrug and nod vaguely. Then Didi took the handles of my father's chair and propelled him forward. I helped my mother get up. Her body was damp and clammy against my own. Didi seemed so crisp and strong marching ahead of us, so dark and well defined. Mom and I with our identical wispy, strawberry blond hair, blue-veined skin, invisible eyelashes and eyebrows, had always run together like two underdone cookies melting into one blob on the baking sheet. I hated the touch of my mother's doughy body.

Didi drove us home, helped Daddy into bed, then refused Mom's half-hearted offer of a ride home. Instead, she said she needed the exercise and ran off.

The next morning, without any plan being made, Didi pulled her dad's Mustang into our carport and honked until Mom gasped, "Well, I mean, that is the rudest thing I've ever heard. Go make her stop before the neighbors call the police."

I crunched across the rocks that were our front yard, wishing I had a pair of the cool low-rise jeans Mom had forbidden instead of the dorky ones with a waist she insisted on. Didi yelled out her open window, "You going to school today?" Just like it was optional. Just like I might be considering not going that day.

"Uh, yeah," I answered. "Give me a second." I rushed into the house, certain that if I gave Didi more than ten seconds to consider what she was doing, she'd be gone. I grabbed my books and the box of animal crackers I took every day to eat on a bench in the patio so I wouldn't have to sit alone in the cafeteria at lunch. I ran back to the car pretending I didn't hear Mom yelling that she didn't approve and that I was to get back into the house this instant.

The Mustang, fingernail-polish red with white leather upholstery, rumbled as we roared down Carlisle Avenue. I wondered what it would be like to have parents cool enough to buy a red Mustang with white leather interior. On the back window, written in swirly script, was SKANKMOBILE. Didi smoked Eve cigarettes, occasionally waving the smoke out the tiny slit she opened in her window. Piercings had appeared in her lip and eyebrow that I didn't recall being there just the day before.

"You have a theme song?" she asked.

"Am I supposed to?"

"Here's mine. Check it out." She shoved in a CD and an oldie blared out: "Dirty Deeds." I looked at the case to find out that the band was AC/DC, some guys dressed up like British schoolboys.

"I know what you're thinking," she said. "You're thinking, No rap? No hip-hop? Where's Snoop? Why's she like this old-school shit?"

That wasn't remotely what I was thinking, but I loved having a conversation with Didi Steinberg that didn't require my participation.

"Well, old school still rules! There's a reason it's called rock. Cuz it rocks!" Didi sang along with the CD, hitting the chorus hard, yelling about doing dirty deeds dirt cheap. She turned to me as if I were sitting on a stool next to her at a bar instead of careening down a road and explained, "That's how I got my nickname, Deeds."

We headed east, toward the mountains, toward the rising sun, which was turning the Sandias the watermelon color they were named for. Morning light flooded into the car. Didi had the visor down so only the bottom half of her face was illuminated. Her mouth was golden as she sang.

With a screech, she opened the ashtray, snuffed the cigarette, and plucked out a half-smoked joint. I knew what it was only because back in

Houdek Sheriff Zigal had visited our class in seventh grade with a brief-case filled with drug paraphernalia. He'd told us a joint could be called a blunt, a spliff, a number, a nail, a stick, a stake, a spike, a rod. I think Sheriff Zigal made up some of the names. Didi pinched the joint between her lips as she fumbled through her purse until she dug out a box of matches.

"Take the Skank," she said, nodding toward the steering wheel as she removed both hands to strike a match. It took me a split second to process the fact that there were no hands on the wheel before I lunged over and grabbed it as we bumped onto the median. Didi laughed when we side-swiped a newly planted catalpa tree. She got the joint lit and sucked in a long hit before holding it out to me.

I waved it away and tried to keep the Skankmobile in its own lane.

Didi shrugged. "How does anyone do Pweb straight?" she asked. Pweb. I liked her name for Pueblo Heights. "Gotta keep consensual real-ity at bay." She inhaled until there was nothing left to burn, then popped the still-smoldering roach into her mouth and took the steering wheel from my death grip. "You're not a bad wheelman."

I made myself lean back, but lunged forward the instant Didi closed both eyes and joined AC/DC singing, "Call me anytime. I lead a life of crime!" She laughed when I grabbed the wheel again. "Wow, someone who's interested in keeping me alive. You could be just what the doctor ordered." She giggled a giggle that made me remember another one of Sheriff Zigal's names for a joint, giggle stick.

Didi's new piercings, dozens of tiny silver rings, glinted in the sun. "When did you get the piercings?" I yelled over the music, keeping my hands on the wheel.

She ripped one of the rings out. It was a fake clip-on. "No tattoos, no piercings. That's the rule. Have to be ready to change at a moment's no-tice. If it'll grow out or wash off, fine, but I'm not gonna be sitting in the old folks' home covered in saggy ink and Ubangi piercing holes." Even the diamond studs in her nose were fake. "Nothing permanent. I'm not into permanent."

Not into permanent. That was the first line in the manual I started composing that day on how to be Didi Steinberg's friend.

She took the wheel. "Hey, you study for the test in Mith Myth?"

Mith Myth was what everyone called world cultures since the teacher,

Ms. Smith, even more than most teachers, taught what she liked best and that was Greek and Roman mythology. Hence her nickname, Mith Myth.

"Yeah?" I said, cautiously, not knowing how dorky she would think studying for a world cultures or any test was.

"Brilliant! I'll sit next to you. I'm not into the whole test-regurgitation thing."

Not into the whole test-regurgitation thing.

She pulled into the Pueblo Heights High School parking lot. It was guarded by the school mascot, a giant hornet painted on the wall of the gym. The Pueblo Heights Hornet was a snarling bully with a sailor cap pulled down palooka-style over one eye, his hornet dukes up waiting to sting all comers into the next century. Students milled around beneath our hostile hornet.

"Well," said Didi, popping down the visor and tugging her eyelid tight so she could outline it in black pencil. "I see all the Whore-nut cliques are out in force. You've got your skate punks in their traditional place, east side of the gym, all properly scabbed and stoned, recounting face plants and road rashes for their skuts."

As Didi moved on to the lower lids, I checked out the skate punks in their black knit caps and giant shorts that hung off their butts and below their knees. Skuts, I guessed, were skate sluts, the girls in spiky pigtails, striped tube socks, and shredded camou cutoffs who revolved around the punks, pretending to care about skateboarding.

"Next farther out, the gamers."

This was an all-male group that didn't really have any uniform fashion look other than pasty skin and slumped shoulders. All they cared about was what level they'd gotten to on Doom and what the new cheats were for Quake.

"And even sadder and more pathetic, our Goth friends, who all, somehow, have the exact same desire to express their really intense individuality through dyed black hair, creepy flowing black clothes, blue lipstick, devil horn implants, and goat's-eye contact lenses."

The Goth kids congregated the farthest of any group from the bellicose bee. They seemed nervous and, Didi was right, sad.

"But the scariest of all the groups? The Abercrombies." She pointed her eyeliner toward the clique who occupied the area directly in front of the hornet as if by divine right. They looked like they belonged front center—cheerleaders, football players. All the popular kids, the ones who could afford to buy stuff from Abercrombie & Fitch.

"Ew, backward caps? Cargo pants and fleece?" Didi pretended to shudder in horror. "Give me a Goth anytime over those Whore-nuts."

I snuggled more deeply into the white leather. The Mustang had come to feel like a cave to me with us on the inside, all snug and dry, and everyone else on the outside being drenched in the downpour of Didi's caustic comments. I noticed that, for the first time, the knot that had tied in my stomach when we left Houdek, then tightened when Daddy got sick, had loosened so much that I could actually take a full breath. I took one, then another, marveling in the simple pleasure of breathing. I never wanted Didi to stop talking about everyone who wasn't us. I never wanted to leave the Skankmobile.

"Hey," she said. "I just thought of something. How are you in math?"

"Sort of, well, brilliant?"

The bells on the rings Didi wore tinkled as she slapped her hands together like she was praying. "Thank you, Jesus!" Then to me, "You are *so* what the doctor ordered. Depew would just stroke out if I actually turned in an assignment." She reached back, fished an algebra book from the pile scattered on the floor, and opened it to the homework assignment she hadn't done.

"Cool beans, factoring polynomials! I haven't gotten to do that for years." The words, unbelievable in their dorkiness, popped out before I could stop them.

"Hey, knock yourself out."

While Didi worked on her hair, getting the lime popsicle tips to stick up in a cunning way, I zipped through her assignment. Dorky as it was, it was true, I did love factoring polynomials. We both finished a few minutes later. Didi snapped the visor back up, tipped her head back, squeezed one drop of Visine into each eye, and turned to me. "So, how do I look?"

She didn't look like anyone else under the hornet. She didn't look like anyone I'd ever known before. The word whispered out of me before I could worry about how dorky I would sound. "Beautiful."

Didi smiled. It was the right answer.

Chapter Five

After that first morning, Didi showed up at my carport every school morning. It was my own personal miracle. At school, I took over all note-taking in the classes we had together like world cultures and English, advanced placement classes that Didi could have aced if she'd wanted to. But she didn't want to. Instead, I fed her answers when she got called on and sat next to her during tests so she could copy off of me. We even developed a vast language of hand signals for me to use to flash her test answers. In spite of the fact that she was naturally better in world cultures and English than I was and it would have taken less time and work for her to actually study, she insisted on cheating. After school, we went to her house, where I did her homework in the classes we didn't have together, like science and her slow-boat math.

I loved our division of labor, the fact that I did all the labor. It helped me and everyone else understand why Deeds Steinberg would be friends with Cyndi Rae Hrncir. While I worked, Didi jumped on the Net to research the only subjects she was truly interested in: bands, astrology, and weirdo diets. She would always fire up a joint. She said it helped her concentrate.

A couple of times in those first weeks, Didi got me to take a few hits. Maybe it kept "consensual reality at bay" for her, not for me. When I smoked all I thought about was my dad waiting to get on the lung transplant list. Mom had started telling me to be thankful that I'd had him for as long as I had and to stop always thinking of myself. I had my whole life ahead of me plus I was lucky and had inherited Daddy's steady nerves. What did she have, she asked me?

I tried not to make things any harder on her than they already were. Mostly, I made myself not think about what was happening to Daddy and that had been impossible the few times I'd smoked. Then his face would bob up in my mind like a balloon that I couldn't press down, swollen from all the steroids he took to fight off infections.

Numbers, though—numbers took me away. At night when I lay in bed trying to go to sleep, the only thing that could block the sound of the ventilator pushing air into my father's ruined lungs was numbers. I'd hoard the extra-credit problems from my AP calculus class to work at night. I'd start trying to figure out what the area underneath a soccer ball would be if it followed a path defined by the curve $y = 20 \sin x$ over 2 yards and a vast calm would flood me.

The one good thing about Daddy getting sick was that he absorbed all Mom's attention and she didn't have any left over to scrutinize my new friend. If she had, Mom would have forbidden me from ever seeing Didi again.

Every morning, though, the miracle of Didi pulling the Skankmobile into our driveway repeated itself and I would jump in, devouring air, avid for the first real breath I'd been able to inhale since Didi had dropped me off the night before. Maybe it was sympathy, my breathing problems. Like when my uncle Anton gained fifty pounds when Aunt Geneva got pregnant. Because Daddy's lungs were getting worse. Pretty soon he had an oxygen line clamped to his nose all the time and hardly ever got out of bed.

Didi's father, on the other hand, still got around fairly well. He even managed to tape his radio shows from the studio he'd set up in their garage. Mr. Steinberg always treated Didi more like a grandchild than a child. Like there was a real father somewhere doing all the hard stuff like discipline and all he had to do was the indulgent, grandfather stuff like hand over the keys to his Mustang and never check what time she came home at night or whether she'd done her homework or brushed her teeth. He'd converted their garage into a studio and Didi and I helped him tape his shows there. He let us pull the old vinyl records, black and shiny as a cockroach's back, out of their covers and cue them up on one of the three turntables he used. I loved the names of the albums: *I Sing the Body Electric, Bitches Brew, Pithecanthropus Erectus, Black Pastels, Ezz-thetics, Descent into the Maelstrom.*

Nobody else had ever talked to me the way he did. "Cue up this side for me, babe. Mingus in Stuttgart."

"Which cut, Mr. Steinberg?"

"Mr. Steinberg? Who let my father in here? I told you Mort. Mort!"

"I'm sorry. Mort."

"Okay, third cut. Now, listen to this. It will freak your bird."

All I knew about Mr. Steinberg—Mort—was that he was the black sheep of a wealthy Jewish family somewhere back in Chicago and had a small trust fund that allowed him to do what he wanted: to be a disc jockey at a failing radio station and play the jazz records he loved so much. I knew that he called Didi babe and she called him Mort and that he believed and taught Didi to believe that, against all evidence to the contrary, her shit did not stink.

There was nothing Didi could do that Mr. Steinberg wouldn't find charming and cute and forgivable, from getting in a fender bender with his beloved 'Stang ("It's only money, babe. It can be fixed. Thank God you weren't hurt.") to flunking English ("I met that teacher of yours and she's a real chromosome case. Don't sweat it, babe.") to getting expelled for skipping ("You can learn more hanging out at the mall, or wherever it is you go, than that factory for bureaucrats will ever teach you. Assholes.").

When Mr. Steinberg got too weak to tape his show, Didi knew it was the end. That's when she got even more hard-core about "keeping consensual reality at bay." Her mother always had lots of pills around the house and Didi started dipping into them. Percocet, Ativan—she especially liked "the floaty ones." She stopped asking me about my father and I stopped asking about hers. Talk was for things you could change. When all the "sharing" and "feelings" in the world wouldn't stop one cough from being wrenched from one pair of ruined lungs, talk was worthless. Didi and I knew that. She knew I had her back just like she had mine and talking about it only made it worse.

Didi's parents dealt with their fear like bears, each Steinberg denning up in his or her own pain. Mr. and Mrs. Steinberg never had much in common to begin with. They just didn't fit together. Him: bald, glasses, a vinyl nerd with no interest in humans unless they had recorded on Blue Note before the Second World War. Her: twenty, thirty years younger, beautiful as Natalie Wood, barely speaking English and always vaguely pissed off in a petulant way that made her look like a Pekinese dog. They, literally, didn't even speak the same language. They were an even less likely couple than my parents. One day, I overheard Didi and her mom arguing and out of the jumble of furious Spanish, Didi hissed the phrase "mail-order bride." I never asked Didi about it and she never brought it up, but suddenly her parents made a little more sense.

It was a surprise when Mr. Steinberg died before Daddy. After the funeral, there was a reception at Didi's house. A few neighbors dropped by. Some of the other oncology patients and the nice nurse who wore the fish smock showed up. None of Mr. or Mrs. Steinberg's family came. No friends. There was no one to wrap their arms around Mrs. Steinberg and make her feel safe enough to cry. Instead, Mrs. Steinberg opened Mr. Steinberg's liquor cabinet, took out a bottle of Chivas, filled a snifter, and never faced life without a glass in her hand from that moment forward.

When Mrs. Steinberg finished the Chivas, she bought a white plastic bucket of margaritas and kept it in the freezer. She scooped a frozen margarita out for every meal and several snacks during the day. Overnight, her fragile, doll-like beauty disappeared and she developed the poochy gut and spindly legs of the serious boozer.

Didi unhinged a little less dramatically. For the next few weeks, I walked to Pueblo Heights because I never knew when, or if, Didi would be going to school. Even though I'd barely spoken five words to any of my teachers, I went to all of Didi's and told them about Mr. Steinberg. I begged them to cut Didi some slack, to give her special assignments she could do at home. My workload got pretty intense finishing my work, Didi's normal assignments, and all of her special makeup projects. But I was actually happy to have extra stuff to do since Didi was immersing herself in two activities: groupieing and getting wasted on the West Mesa. I don't know why I had faith that in time she'd come back. Maybe because I could no longer imagine my life without her.

I didn't mind being stuck at my house since it gave me more of a chance to be with Daddy. That was when I noticed how my mother's peculiarities had blossomed. The sicker Daddy got, the worse her nerves were. The only time she left the house was to go to her new church. When she wasn't at HeartLand, she was on the phone talking to other members whom she called "sister" and "brother." She ended all her conversations with them by saying, "Bless you." She had taken to telling me things like "Give Satan an inch and he'll become your ruler." And "What you weave in this world, you wear for eternity."

She was happy when the Skankmobile stopped appearing in our driveway every morning. I'd spent my whole life catering to my mother's peculiarities. So, when she insisted that I start wearing one of the long denim skirts with an elastic waist that all the women at her church wore, I just put it on. Right over the jeans that I rolled up so they didn't show.

Then, as soon as I was out of her sight, I'd yank the skirt off and stuff it in my backpack. When she informed me that Didi was "an agent of Satan," all I did was nod. There was no point in arguing. There never had been.

Seeing me leaving the house in the long skirt and not riding with Didi made my mother hum with righteous joy. She relaxed and one night, about a month after Mr. Steinberg's funeral, she went out for groceries and left me alone with Daddy to watch the History Channel. Right in the middle of the Battle of the Bulge, he huffed out one word, "Stars." My father loved looking at the sky. His favorite thing about Albuquerque had been how clear the sky was, how many more stars he could see here than in Texas.

"I don't know, Daddy," I said. "Mom'll get mad."

Daddy didn't waste any more of his breath arguing. Instead, he just raised his hand and pointed his finger toward the window where a bit of night sky, a few of the stars he wanted to see, were visible. His skin seemed stained by grape juice. When I pressed his purplish fingers, a dead white spot remained for minutes.

I bundled him up in the quilted camouflage jumpsuit he used to wear when he went hunting back in Texas. He hadn't had it on once since we'd left Houdek. I tried not to notice how the suit drooped on him like a little boy in his father's clothes. I disconnected him from the big tank of oxygen that stood in the corner and hooked him up to the little portable canister he used on the rare times when he left the bedroom.

"Your chariot, sir," I said, pushing the wheelchair up to where he sat on the edge of the bed, breathing hard from the exertion of getting dressed. He waved the chair away and tried to stand on his own. When he started wobbling, I angled the chair under him and he half-fell into it.

When I pushed him outside into the cold night air, he closed his eyes so that even the lids could drink in the wild, free feeling. Then he opened them, pointed his finger to the sky, and, one word at a time, exhaled the names of the stars. Big. Dipper. Little. Dipper. Ursa. Major. Ursa. Minor. North. Star. When he finished, he said, "Can. Always. Find. Your. Way. Home."

Because there was a little smile on his face, I laughed as if he'd made a joke and said, "Yeah, Daddy, now I can always find my way home." Then, exhausted, he fell asleep and I pushed him back into the house.

Chapter Six

Around that time, my mother officially went off the rails and plowed headlong into HeartLand. The sisters began coming to our house, bringing gigantic bags of old clothes that Mom washed, then cut up into squares of fabric for the church's quilting operation. Her hair had grown long and she was wearing it in a bun that skinned all the hair back off her face, then rested like a dowager's hump on her neck. She switched from the long denim skirt to pioneer dresses. She wore kneesocks to cover the little bit of calf that showed and bought special shoes that looked like they'd been cobbled a hundred years ago. Actually, they had just been manufactured at HomeTown, HeartLand's headquarters, and cost a fortune.

The literal cap came when Mom was awarded a "prayer covering," a kind of bonnet that all the HeartLand females wore. There was a special ceremony, a "consecration," when she was awarded her "covering." It usually took place at the church but my mother got a special dispensation so they could hold it in Daddy's room. I watched my father's face as they placed the white lace hat on her head. He looked over at me and did what he used to do when we hid out at the Dairy Queen: he winked. But the sparkle in his eyes now was from tears. I knew he was thinking about what was going to happen to me when he was gone, and that, combined with the fear that Didi might not come back, made me start crying, too. The sisters hugged me and said not to worry, my mother had told them that I had chosen to walk God's path, and, if I stayed on it, I too might be consecrated in less than a year.

The HeartLanders really started swarming over us after my mother was consecrated. They promoted her to making quilt tops. While I waited for Didi to come back, I started quilting with my mother so I could spend as much time as possible with Daddy. That's what I told myself anyway.

Actually, it scared me not only how good I was at quilting but how much pecking out stitches as small as a sprinkling of salt soothed me. Even the sisters noticed how fine my handiwork was. When they came over to pick up the finished work and made a fuss about it, my mother pouted like a little kid. I didn't care. I tried to make my stitches microscopic just to hear someone tell me I was doing a good job.

Who knows? Maybe I would have gotten completely hooked if Didi hadn't reappeared. But she did. One morning when I was gathering up the report I'd written for her about McKinley and the Tariff of 1890 so she wouldn't flunk American history and I already had the long denim skirt on over my jeans, she honked. My mother and I both identified the honk immediately. We stared at each other as we worked through a long series of lightning calculations that yielded the same answer: my mother was not big enough to stop me. I walked through the door and out to Didi.

All she said as I jumped in the front seat was, "Nice skirt."

I ripped the denim skirt off and stuffed it under the front seat.

"You have that history report?" she asked, backing out of the driveway.

I plucked the neatly typed paper out of my backpack and held it up for her to see. She smiled and nodded, her eyelids drooping like a cat's in the sun, then held her fist up. I tapped it with mine. Didi put the Skank in first, revved the engine, and we peeled out in a spray of gravel.

I knew I would pay, but I didn't care. Didi was back.

Chapter Seven

Didi returned with a new mantra that we both followed: Stay distracted. We never talked about our mothers, about how things were at home. School became an afterthought. We put most of our energy into the jobs we both got at Pup y Taco, a take-out place based on a marketing strategy that reasoned, if you don't like Mexican food, there's always hot dogs. The only other thing we put any energy into was groupieing. Actually, Didi did the groupieing. I tagged along for logistical support, taking care of the details the way I always did.

I was the one who made sure that the tank of the Skankmobile was filled so we could get to the airport where Didi could flirt with the car rental guy enough to weasel the name of the hotel where R.E.M. or Everclear or whoever was in town was staying. I was the one who installed the extra memory in her computer so she could run her astrology program and do charts for whichever band member she was currently obsessed with. Didi was the one who played the roadies and got the all-access backstage passes. She was the one cool and sexy enough to get chosen from the pack of skinny girl groupies. She was the one the stars would point to as they whispered to a flunky to make sure she—that one there with the lips, the mouth, the jeans lower than anyone else's—was at the party. After.

I didn't like thinking about the After part. The part when the doors closed and Didi was one of the throwaway girls with the band or a pack of roadies. She called them missions and that was the part I liked, the part that was like a spy mission. Scouring the city for glimpses of tour buses, getting gullible hotel clerks to reveal room numbers, raiding maids' uniforms from unguarded hampers, swiping tiny bottles of shampoo and conditioner. The last had nothing to do with getting to the band; it was just my own little vice. I liked everything up to meeting the band. The actual band, the stars, held no interest for me whatsoever. That was when I would leave.

We established our groupie division of labor the first time I went with her on a mission. Limp Bizkit was playing at Tingley Coliseum. Built on the state fairgrounds to host rodeos, Tingley looked and smelled like a big barn. Didi loved it since security was impossible there. I followed her through the chutes usually used to herd livestock into the ring that had been covered with a fake floor and turned into a mosh pit. The roadies picked her out as soon as she appeared. When the show was over, they herded her toward the tour bus.

She turned my way and asked, "You coming?"

The prospect utterly panicked me, but I'd already learned enough from her to give something resembling a cool reply and answered, "You have your own compulsions to answer to, but, as for me, just because a sweaty hillbilly in a black T-shirt with thirty tour dates printed on it has carried Fred Durst's amp is never going to be enough reason to let him stick his tongue in *my* ear, much less anything else anywhere else. Period. Nonnegotiable."

Didi laughed. She loved my answer since she hadn't really wanted me to stay.

The day after a mission, she always gave me a vague report, which usually meant translating the evening into "coins of the realm." The coins of Didi's realm were blow jobs. I'd come to accept the blow job as Didi's standard unit of currency. But Didi didn't *give* blow jobs, she *deposited* them. In her own personal economy, every second she spent on her knees was another second that she banked in *her* future celebrity account. Another second that some future Didi groupie would spend on his or her knees in front of her. All that was incidental, though. Even meeting the stars was not the point. Sure, Didi would rather have been with someone famous than any of the boys who existed in our actual world. But Didi's secret, the secret that only I knew, was that the real reason she groupied was to learn how to be a celebrity. Because Didi knew, had always known, that she was going to be famous. She just had to hang out with enough famous people to learn how to become one herself. And if the price of lessons was a few blow jobs, she considered that a bargain.

We didn't yet know what she was going to be famous for. There were plans for the first truly kick-ass girl band that would make the world totally forget they'd ever heard of Courtney Love. One night, she'd returned from a mission with an old Fender that some roadie had given her. I bought a practice pad and some sticks so I could be her drummer. But the metal strings hurt Didi's fingers and I never got the money together to buy an actual drum set, so we ditched that idea. Didi switched to singer-songwriter and started working on her material.

That her voice wasn't all that good never really mattered. She had something more important than a good voice: she could put herself into every word she sang. I think there was just so much of Didi, so much personality, so much ambition, so many definite ideas about so many things, that it all flowed out when she opened her mouth. It wasn't ever pretty or even pleasant. But, right from the start, it was all her, all Didi.

We were lucky that we always wanted different prizes. She wanted to hang out with famous people and be famous herself. I just wanted to hang out with her. The biggest groupie prize Didi ever went after were the Strokes. She discovered the New York group before they were famous, and, as soon as she did, all other bands ceased to exist. She loved their aura of dissipation, the way they harkened back to a lost era of rock 'n' roll glamour and decadence that she was certain she would have ruled over had she not been born too late. Also, as she informed me about eighty-five times a day, the lead singer, Julian Casablancas, was "hotter than lava."

As for our jobs, Didi called Pup y Taco, Puppy Taco, but after the renaming she didn't have much to do with the take-out joint other than collecting a paycheck. I was the one who flipped the Mexi-burgers and shredded bales of lettuce for crispy tacos. She was the one who redid her makeup and stared in the mirror wondering if Julie would like her better with short hair. I was the one who pulled the baskets of fries out of hot grease and scrubbed counters with bleach at the end of our shift. She was the one who flirted with customers and blasted Strokes music and turned every shift we worked together into a party that I was happy to be invited to. My hair always smelled liked tacos, my forearms were speckled pink and white from grease burns; I did all the work, and I didn't care. The twisted, tweaked math nerd part of my brain loved nothing better than organizing complicated tasks, adding columns of numbers in my head, and doing the tax without a calculator. When I got into a perfect groove—five burgers working, a load of tots in the frier, and figuring tax on three Mexi-dogs, one Big Red grande, and two Sprites chico—I was as high as Didi ever got on weed, Ritalin, and Stoli.

Our boss and the owner of Puppy, Alejandro Trujillo, just shook his head when he found Didi slacking or sleeping. He was a good guy, always telling me I should look out for myself more. But Alejandro and everyone who thought Didi was using me were not getting the whole picture. The whole picture was that I was out of my house and I wasn't thinking about Daddy. The whole picture was that when I was with Didi I could breathe.

The highlight of senior year was the night the Strokes came to town. Through her Internet sources, Didi found out they were coming before the tour dates were even set. That gave her a long lead time to consult with other groupies online, like the Kumfort Gurlz in Phoenix, who told her that Julie had a thing for Japanese anime. With that information, she put together a killer Japanese schoolgirl outfit complete with pigtails, sailor-collared middy blouse, chunky Mary Janes, kneesocks, and a pleated skirt so short she had to bikini wax.

We already knew from chatting up the Hertz Rent-a-Car guy that the band was staying at the Hilton on University. My job when we got to the Hilton was to stand guard and watch for managerial types. Didi, holding the red vinyl zippered Domino's Pizza delivery case that she'd stolen for just such occasions, went up to the reception desk. Her Japanese schoolgirl pigtails were tucked under a red, gold, green, and black Rasta cap. Jeans and a schlubby T-shirt covered the rest.

As always, Deeds had done her homework and had the name of a roadie written on the Domino's order slip. Deeds gave the front desk clerk the guy's name, checking the order slip as if she couldn't remember what it was.

The clerk, who'd no doubt already parried teams of hyperventilating teen girls, balked. "The Strokes put a hold on all deliveries."

"Strobes?" Didi acted like she didn't recognize the name. "I don't know from Strobes." Maybe because of the pizza, maybe because the Strokes were from New York, Didi slipped into her best *Goodfellas* goombah impersonation. "This"—she paused to check the order slip where she'd written the roadie's name—"Justin Patterson, he ordered a pie. I'm delivering a pie. End of story." She rapped the reception desk with her knuckles. "You explain to him why he didn't get his pie, okay, pal?"

As she was pivoting away, the clerk, half realizing he was being tooled, but also half not wanting to risk infuriating a hungry roadie, called after her, "Five-twenty-six."

Didi never finagled the room number of the famous guys, the ones she was really after, which was anyone who got onstage. The clerks knew better than that. They might give her the number of a roadie or the chiropractor traveling with the band. But that small opening was always enough for Didi, who, once she got into fame's orbit, could always manage to home in on the celestial body with the heaviest gravity.

I casually joined Didi on the elevator. As soon as the doors closed and we were hidden from the clerk's view, we jumped up and down squealing a few times before she handed me the Domino's box, Rasta cap, and the jeans and T-shirt she stripped off. We got off at the fifth floor. Didi stopped at the mirror above a dried flower arrangement, fluffed up her pigtails, spritzed on some CK One, and spit her gum into the sand of the ashtray imprinted with the hotel's logo. We found room 526 and Didi collected herself before knocking.

As usual, a lank-haired roadie who looked as if he'd just gotten up answered the door. The room behind him was filled with roadies and soundmen who had the same stunned, hungover look. It was like the day room at a mental ward with everyone smoking—cigarettes, joints—and the room littered with hamburger wrappers and Big Gulp cups. Someone was watching *Reservoir Dogs* on cable. As always, it amazed me to see Didi turn on her high-wattage charm for these losers, angling for backstage passes and access to someone higher on the rock 'n' roll food chain. The guys beamed big as troops at a USO show as Didi stepped into the room.

"Where's Julie?" was her first question. She never had any problems getting what she wanted. I handed the princess to the rock plebeians who would deliver her to their aristocrats and then I left.

I remember everything about the next morning. Sunday morning when Mom went to worship services at the HeartLand compound was my only time to be alone with Daddy and I looked forward to it all week. Even though she never said it, my mom was punishing me for being friends with Didi by banning me from the sickroom. She shooed me out, saying that it upset Daddy for me to see how bad off he was. It didn't. She was the only who was upset. If I objected, though, she'd get even more twitchy and weird. She'd make her tiny hands into tiny fists that she'd shake beside her pink head until it turned red while she shrieked, "I can't take it! I can't take it!" louder and louder. I knew she was wrong, but what difference did that make? I'd tell her I was sorry and to, please, calm down. Then she would blubber and tell me I had to stop being so difficult, that she couldn't take any more. She told me that I was lucky, I had inherited Daddy's strong nerves and I had no idea what she was enduring. I had to be strong the way Daddy always had been or else.

Or else what? I wanted to ask because I didn't want to imagine how things could get worse than they were.

When Daddy and I were alone on Sunday, he tried to tell me not to let my mother bother me, but it was getting harder and harder for him to talk. I'd heard her on the phone the week before saying, "No! No hospice. We don't need hospice here and we don't need talk like that." I knew what hospice meant and it scared me. I was scared all the time except for when I was with Didi. Not that we ever talked much about our fathers. But, at odd times, like when we were in the middle of a burnfest on what goobers the Pueblo Heights Whore-nuts were, she'd stop, catch my eye, and ask, "You doing okay?" I never did much more than nod, but I didn't have to. That question was everything I needed. It said that she understood that about 99 percent of the time I was putting up a front and if I didn't, I'd start crying and never stop. That my life was horrible and we both knew it was going to get a lot worse.

That morning Daddy had seemed good. There wasn't much he liked to eat anymore, but I'd discovered the perfect mixture of Cream of Wheat and butter and melted ice cream and had helped him eat five spoonfuls before he fell back, exhausted. Then, huffing out one word on each breath, he asked, "How. Is. Old. Sometimes. Y?"

It had been a while since he'd teased me about my imaginary boyfriend with the last name full of vowels and I laughed too loud and too much when he did. Still, it made him happy and I joked back, "Oh, Sometimes Y and I are through. I'm dating a Hawaiian boy now. Ahahkahluauluau."

He wheezed out a laugh that was the equivalent of hysterics for him. The effort wore him out and he slid back into sleep. He was snoozing when the church van pulled up in front and dropped my mom off. I slipped out the back before she came in and walked to work.

At Puppy Taco, I clocked in for me and Didi and did the prep work, shredding the pale iceberg lettuce, slicing pulpy tomatoes, crying over the onions I had to chop up for the burgers. In addition to all the regular stuff, on Sundays it was Alejandro's tradition to add a few New Mexican specialties to the menu. He shopped the night before and left everything in the refrigerator. Nothing microwaved. On Sunday we actually cooked. I pulled out a couple of fifty-count bags of blue corn tortillas and dragged them through the red chile that Alejandro's mother made by soaking dried red chiles until she could scrape the pulp off the skins and cook that with pork shoulder.

I rolled up a batch of pork enchiladas, another of beef, some with just asadero cheese, covered them with sauce and cheese, and slid the pans into the industrial oven. I made another batch with green chile sauce. On Sundays Alejandro banished fries and tots in favor of sopaipillas. I had just lowered the first batch into the fryer and the shop was filling with the heavenly smell of yeast and flour they made as they puffed up when the high-pitched shriek of a transmission in its final days alerted me that the Skankmobile approached. I glanced out through the drive-up window in time to see Didi run the red light at Central and Monroe before cutting into the parking lot.

She squealed up in the 'Stang and jumped out, grabbing the hideous striped uniform shirt we were supposed to wear, and which Didi might occasionally drape over her real clothes. Her real clothes that day were the Japanese schoolgirl drag she'd been wearing last night when I'd left her at the Hilton. That morning, watching her dance through the parking lot, I was struck by how spindly, how vulnerable she looked. Her short skirt showed off the speed freak figure she attributed to ADD. Didi maintained that her attention deficit disorder kept her distracted from food. My theory was that she didn't have ADD. She only claimed to so she could get prescriptions for the Ritalin that kept her too speeded up to eat. Or sleep. Sleeping was something she clearly hadn't done much of last night.

She jerked the back door open, stepped in, and threw her arms open. "Ah, the smell of five-month-old fryer grease on a Sunday morning. Who needs church when we have Puppy Taco?" Didi grabbed a handful of the slurpy tomatoes I'd just sliced up, slid them into her mouth like oysters, and closed her eyes against what was obviously a monster hangover.

"Somewhere in the depths of my bowels today's tomatoes will meet last night's Stoli and create the perfect Bloody Mary."

"So did he show?"

She played it cool. "Who?"

"Who! Julie, of course."

"Ah, Julie." She imported a look of fond remembrance. "Dear, sweet, naughty Julie."

"Tell! Tell! Tell!"

"Hydrate! Hydrate! Hydrate!" She turned on the water in the giant, industrial-sized sink, stuck her hand under the flow, siphoned about a gallon into her mouth, then collapsed onto the upturned mop bucket, her skinny rear fitting perfectly between the wheels on the bottom, legs straight out in front with that Bambi-on-the-ice kind of sexy cuteness. She heaved a big sigh and leaned her head back against the wall. Being Didi Steinberg, Queen of Albuquerque Groupies, took a lot out of a person.

"So?" I prompted.

"So our Julie learned more than Swiss at that fancy boarding school, if you know what I mean. And I think you do."

"Uh, they don't actually speak Swiss in Switzerland. I mean, there isn't actually a Swiss language. They speak French and German and—"

"Don't nerd out on me, Rae, okay?"

"Sorry. Just keeping the details straight." That was my job in our friendship. Keeping the details straight.

"So he came back to the hotel? You met him?"

"Met him? Uh, yeah, I 'met' him." Didi rolled onto her right hip and hiked up her skirt to show me the bottom half of her left cheek. A red hickey, purpling at the edges, floated across it like an end-of-the-world sunset. Above the hickey were penned the initials J.C.

"No effing way!" I shrieked.

"Yes, fucking way."

"And . . ."

"You know how sublime and divine and scrumpo he is in videos?"

I nodded wildly to affirm the intense Casablancas scrumphood.

"Times, like, a thousand in person."

I was too engrossed to pay any attention to the pinging that signaled the arrival of our first customer of the day. Didi was singing a song about the dimples at the top of Julian Casablancas's butt in what she told me was the Strokes' New York/Velvet Underground style when Alejandro strolled in, fresh from Mass at Our Lady of Fatima.

"You gonna open anytime soon?" he asked, nodding toward the car waiting at the take-out window as he carefully hung up his brown suit jacket.

The reason Alejandro was so casual about us not working was that he knew Didi was our star. Her hours during the week were sporadic, but she was guaranteed to be there on Sunday. Over the months Didi had been in his employ, she'd built up a following until Sunday was the busiest day of the week for Puppy Taco. And Alejandro knew it wasn't all because of his *enchiladas verdes*. That day was no exception. I peeked out the window. The cars were already lined up around the store and spilling out onto Central. There was some form of male behind the wheel of every vehicle. Old geezer males getting lunch burgers for wifey back at home; young horny males yucking it up in Dad's borrowed Explorer; sad, lonely males who told themselves there was something special about Pup y Taco's tater tots and that was why they had to make a special trip there every Sunday, only to be reminded that Sunday was the one day we didn't sell tots. Just sopaipillas.

I spun around and pushed up the big, old-fashioned take-out window. I wished that Alejandro would install a high-tech speaker system so that customers could order into a scratchy box. But, if Pup y Taco had that instead of a window, Didi wouldn't have had a stage and Sunday morning was all about Didi being onstage.

The fryer dinged.

"Uh, Cyndi Rae . . ."

"Rae," I corrected him.

Alejandro still called me by the name he'd copied off my driver's license when he'd first hired us. My old name. The name I used to go by before Didi dubbed me Rae and I stopped answering to anything else. Even Daddy called me Rae. Mom was the only one who called me Cyndi Rae anymore. I liked it that she identified me as someone I had stopped being. That she was still calling a number that had been disconnected.

"Right, Rae, sorry. Listen, would you mind . . . ?" Alejandro's question trailed off as he nodded toward the fryer. What he didn't have to say was *Rae, you wanna get the fryer so Didi's fans can catch a glimpse of their queen and we can sell more hot dogs and chile cheeseburgers on Sunday morning than we do any other three days put together?*

"Didi? You ready?" he asked, sounding like a celebrity handler coaxing a star onstage.

Didi heaved herself to her feet, then paused a second, turning away from the window. When she turned back around, she'd done that thing she did where one second she looks completely beat to shit; then she gathers herself and uncorks some mysterious inner light and she's beaming a thousand watts. That was the face the males making their Sunday pilgrimage saw. The face of a girl who had something they only glimpsed on television, in movies. Not beauty, exactly, but something more exciting, more alive. Something that made them want to keep looking, keep coming back to a not-so-great taco place every Sunday morning.

"Hey, Key Biscayne," Didi greeted her first regular, an old guy still in his Sunday suit, smelling of Old Spice, ear hairs all nicely clipped, getting the lunch burgers. "Three number sevens, hold the green chile, right?"

"That's right, Didi," he chirped back.

"Hey, come on, man, what's a Fiesta Burger without the green chile? Live a little, try the green chile. My boss's mom makes it herself. You look like you could use a little spice in your life."

"Twist my arm," he said, holding a spindly limb out, which Didi pretended to wring. And so, Key Biscayne got the green chile along with the biggest thrill he would have all week.

"You got it under control, Cyndi Rae?" Alejandro asked, as I assembled the three Fiestas, all the way.

I nodded, already moving on to the next order that Didi had stuck on the clip in front of me. "Under control, Alejandro," I said, as he headed out the back door, smiling at the line of cars circling his business.

He stopped at the door and gestured for me to come closer. "Make her do *some* of the work."

"Yeah, that'll be the day."

Alejandro and I glanced at Didi who was leaning over so that a load of guys from Pueblo Heights High School, the driver with a newly minted learner's permit and his mom's Subaru Forester, could get a nice peek at the Steinberg mammaries.

"Hello, you wacky Whore-nuts." The guys' pimples flared red in excitement. "How many rocks of crack can I get you gentlemen today?"

One especially twerpy kid with the hair at the front of his head waxed into a fin yelled out of the back window. "Hey, where's the other Skankette?"

That was my signal to step forward and put my arm around Didi's shoulders while we yelled, "The hos are in the house!"

"Yo! Yo! Yo! Skankettes!" the boys shouted as I waved my greasy spatula.

I loved the psychological jujitsu Didi did on her bad-girl reputation, turning the snickers behind her back, the whispered "ho" and "skank," into our badges of honor. So that's who we were, the Skankettes in Didi's Scarlet Letter–red Skankmobile.

Alejandro snorted, shook his head, and walked out. Maybe neither Alejandro nor I was wearing a black T-shirt with thirty tour dates printed on it, but in our own way we were both happy to be carrying the amps, happy to be part of the show.

For the next few hours, I fried sopaipillas and boxed up enchiladas. I assembled tacos, burritos, and Mexi-dogs while Didi applied lip liner, tweezed her eyebrows, restyled her hair into a couple dozen twisted tufts of mini-dreadlocks, scribbled a few orders, raved about Julian Casablancas, whom she may or may not have actually met, and, mostly, worked the crowd. Like groupieing, working the crowd was also something Didi considered practice for when she became famous. She kept score of how many return fans she lured back to Puppy, giving herself extra bonus points for females.

After the initial rush of backed-up cars subsided, Didi handed the order pad to me and flopped back down on the mop bucket where she exhibited her extraterrestrial ability to fall asleep instantly, anywhere, any time.

I got into a steady rhythm of taking orders and slamming out the grub, not wasting any time playing up to latecomers who were disappointed because they'd missed Didi. After I told the last lonely loser who pulled up and asked if, by any chance, "that other girl" was working today that Didi was indisposed and would be appearing next Sunday as usual, I slid the drive-up window closed. I had snapped on the yellow latex gloves and was squirting bleach solution on the counters when Didi woke up.

"We almost through here?"

"Uh, yeah, *we're* almost through, bitch."

"You say that like it's a bad thing. Whore."

"Skank."

"Trollop."

"Strumpet."

"Harlot."

"Pox-ridden doxie."

"Doxie! All right, Hunker! The Hunker Woman goes Shakespearean on my ass! Doxie? You are one wild woman!"

I grinned. When I was with Didi I *was* one wild woman. She tugged on a pair of gloves and actually helped me clean the counters for a while but ended up pretending she was a proctologist and had to perform an emergency exam on me. I was swatting and threatening to squirt bleach all over her anime outfit when the phone rang. Didi answered the phone with one hand, "Allô! Allô! Le Poop ay La Taco ici!" while she dipped the index finger of the other hand in Crisco and poked it my way.

The yellow latex finger with a white glob of Crisco on the end froze, stuck out, pointing at mc for a long moment, while she listened. Then she handed the phone to me and said, "It's your mom."

Chapter Eight

It's your mom.

That was all I needed to hear. My mother never called me at work and there was only one reason why she would have done it that day.

As Didi said later, the funeral was "psychedically surreal" in its awfulness. The only thing that got me through it was having her by my side. My mother tiptoed close to full-on hysteria when she found out Didi was coming. But I just blanked out her face turning red and repeated over and over, "No Didi, no me." Mom and her cult hadn't totally given up on me at that time so, after lengthy consultations with her pastor and the sisters, who were directing her every move in life by that time, she agreed to allow my best friend to attend.

I didn't ask her permission to ride over with Didi to the HeartLand Compound, where she'd arranged for the funeral to be held. I just left. Nothing on earth could have gotten me to cram into the HeartLand van. Didi parked in the huge lot surrounding the complex of buildings— church, school, fellowship hall, crafts store—that was HeartLand's Albuquerque center. Neither one of us left the 'Stang, we just watched the SUVs and vans drive up and women in lace bonnets and men in suspenders pile out and parade into the church, the men leading, the women and children following behind, as if there were dangers ahead that the head of the house would have to deal with. Indians, crack dealers, who knew? I felt as if I were watching a movie that had nothing to do with any life I could have ever imagined living.

"Jesus, why don't they all just get buggies and be done with it?" Didi asked. "Bunch of Amish wannabes." Didi had dressed as conservatively as she could out of respect for Daddy. But even her most sedate skirt was still a foot above her knees and her hair was currently bleached white with pink stripes.

"Come on," Didi said, opening her door. "This will be a freak show and a half."

The church looked like a giant wooden barn with lots of big oak beams and wooden pegs holding everything together instead of nails. Inside, all the men and boys were sitting on one side and all the women and girls were on the other.

An usher with an Abraham Lincoln beard led us to the front row and seated us next to my mother. My right side prickled where it almost touched her. I leaned away from her and into Didi. The service was worse than I imagined it would be. Of course, it had all been arranged without anyone consulting me. Hearing strangers talk about Daddy was awful. My mother hadn't even asked if I wanted to speak. The brethren and what Didi called the sistern stood up and recounted stories that were supposed to illustrate what a good Christian Daddy was. I wanted to scream that none of them had the tiniest idea about who my father was. Daddy *was* a good Christian but not in the way they were talking about.

Their pastor, a tall man with broad shoulders whom the sistern all had crushes on, took the pulpit and made a big show of placing his Bible on the lectern and opening it reverently. He made a bigger show of starting to read, then looking up to show that he knew the passage by heart. "Let not your heart be troubled: ye believe in God, believe also in me. In my Father's house are many mansions: if it were not so, I would have told you. I go to prepare a place for you. And if I go and prepare a place for you, I will come again, and receive you unto myself; that where I am, there ye may be also."

My mother was sniffling beside me, dabbing at her eyes and nose with a balled-up Kleenex. The pastor looked straight at her and asked, "Sister, why do you weep? This should be a day of rejoicing, for your husband has gone before you to prepare a place just as Jesus did. If you truly believe, there should be a smile on your face."

The prickling on my side turned to waves of revulsion when Mom obeyed, stretching her mouth into a big puppet smile that made all the sisters beam at her.

Didi popped her eyes at me to show how strange she thought it was to be told you're not supposed to be sad at a funeral.

After the service, there was a reception in the fellowship hall next door. The HeartLanders walked into the afternoon sunshine with shoulders thrown back and satisfied looks on their faces as if they'd just cleared some pioneer land or churned a batch of butter. Some of them seemed kind and acted like they wanted to come over and say something to me. But I had shut down behind a wall of sullen hostility and glared warnings at them to keep their distance. They were happy to oblige since I was clinging to Didi, and she represented everything in the modern world they had arranged their lives around rejecting. For my mother, basking in the consolation and condolences and blessings that were being rained on her, the funeral was like a debutante ball, like her coming-out as a true Heart-Land sister. I wanted her to be my mother so badly that I momentarily considered breaking into the group clustered around her, but that would have been pointless. My mother was enjoying being mothered herself too much.

Didi drifted away and I followed her toward the big showpiece of the Compound, the HeartLand Crafts Center. A large display window was piled with quilts, baskets, decoupage, pottery, beeswax candles, hand-made brooms, and all manner of jams, jellies, and pickled things. In another window were manly items like handmade furniture and wrought-iron grilles. In the girl window, I recognized a quilt top I had worked on. A really intricate Double Wedding Ring pattern all in gorgeous, supersat-urated shades of periwinkle and lavender, violet and marine blue, it had a $1,200 price tag on it.

"Wow," Didi, who was also perusing some of the price tags, said, "the brethren and sistern aren't shy about asking for the big bucks. What kind of a cut does your mom get?"

"None that I know of. It's all supposed to go to support 'The' Work and 'The' HomeTown." I made quote marks in the air so Didi would know that they always capitalized the words.

"What is 'The' HomeTown?"

"It's their headquarters or something, somewhere down in Georgia or Mississippi. One of the hookworm states."

Didi shook her head. "Wow, and they think I'm weird. At least I'm not making a whole life out of pretending I'm living in another century. What a bunch of freaks."

"Nutcases," I added, feeling a guilty thrill.

"Lunatics."

"Psychos."

"Amish wannabe foot-sniffers."

I started laughing. Not good laughing either. Scary, gasping, hiccuping laughter that I couldn't stop.

Didi watched me for a few seconds, then put her arm over my shoulder and gently led me to the 'Stang. I fell into it, never more grateful for its refuge. I calmed down the instant the door closed.

"This reception? It's not going to work, is it?"

I shook my head no.

A few of the sisters still outside the fellowship hall stared as we pulled away.

We drove in silence over to Central, taking the street past Old Town, then up Nine Mile Hill toward the West Mesa. I watched the city shrink in the mirror on the visor until it was little more than a short streak of green winding through the high desert, the thinnest thread of life fed by the slender silver artery of the Rio Grande. On either side of the fragile city, desiccated plains waited to suck the life out of it. The Sandias loomed above, ready to crush whatever might survive. I flipped the visor back up.

We parked and hiked up toward the petroglyphs. Didi led me to a sheltered spot. "This is my compound, my church. This is where I came every day. After."

After her father died.

We squatted on the ancient volcanic rocks that marked the escarpment. Blue tail lizards skittered away through the snakeweed with their sulphur-yellow flowers. A desert millipede traced waves in the sand as it undulated past my feet. The black basaltic rocks, shadowed even in the bright sunlight, felt forlorn. Everywhere I looked petroglyphs thousands of years old had been scraped into the dark lava to reveal the lighter, tan rock beneath like chalk drawings on a blackboard. On the rocks just beneath us was a drawing of many tiny hands raised to the sky that made me think of HeartLanders when they were "receiving the Spirit." Farther on was a petroglyph that depicted strange, extraterrestrial lines resembling those at Nazca. Another featured a bloom of happy, square faces like Teletubbies. Contemporary graffiti on a nearby rock had the Teletubbie heads committing pornographic acts. On the path around the rocks the powdery dirt was imprinted with treads from hundreds of pairs of running shoes, the squiggles, waffles, and starbursts as mysterious as any of the petroglyph designs.

The sun edged low enough to shine golden through the papery seed heads of the chamisa. A breeze scented with sage and moist from the first exhalation of a cool evening wafted by. In the distance, pylons marched across the open rangeland, a line of silver kachinas that went on until they were out of sight.

Didi stared off and seemed to be talking to the pylons more than to me, as if she were continuing a conversation she'd been having with them that I'd interrupted. "What I really loved about my father was that he liked me. He didn't just love me, he really liked me. He got my jokes and I got his. Maybe I would have loved music without him, but he made sure that I loved it for the right reasons. That I knew it was a gift from the people who made it. I loved it that he never, ever said one negative thing about my mother even though she didn't like him. I loved it that I could talk to him about anything." She looked at me, the sunlight cutting into her eyes, glittering on the gold flecks there. "What about you? What did you love about your father?"

For one second, I didn't want to say anything. Not out loud. But the words flowed forth on their own. "I loved how, in his heart, I was still a little girl. How he thought my favorite food was corn dogs because I liked them when I was five. I loved how he sang along with the radio, even though he had a horrible voice, just because it made him happy. I loved how he treated waitresses like queens and always gave bums money and called them sir and wished them luck. I loved how much joy he could get out of a corny joke. He could barely get to the punch line, he was always cracking up so much. The jokes were never any good, but it was funnier than anything to hear him try to tell one."

The more I talked, the more important it became that I make one other person really understand who Daddy was. "We had this sort of like code phrase that we always used. 'Now what was that about?' He would whisper it to me or I would whisper it to him whenever something weird happened. It was the punch line to this really corny joke he told me when I was eight."

"Tell me."

"Naw, it's really stupid."

"It was your father's joke," Didi said. She meant, it didn't matter if it was a good joke or a bad joke, it was my father's joke.

"Yeah, okay. So, the doorbell rings and a guy answers his front door and finds a snail on the porch. He picks up the snail and tosses it out into the yard."

"And?"

"And two years later, the doorbell rings and the man answers the door and there is the same snail. And the snail says"—Didi helped me say the punch line—" 'Now, what was that about?' "

Halfway through the last line that Daddy had said to me or I had said to him so many times—when my mom was melting down, when I came home in a grumpy mood, when he started cursing and yelling at the TV set because the Cowboys had made a "bonehead" play, but mostly because my mom was melting down—I stopped dead. It was as if I'd awakened in the middle of a dream and discovered I was standing on the edge of a cliff that dropped off into infinity. That I was leaning out over the edge and could not step backward. That I was going to fall and never stop falling.

"He's gone."

Didi let me cry until a spot of powdery dirt between my knees had turned to mud, then she said, "Repeat this after me. 'As long as I keep my father in my heart, he is with me.' "

I raised my head. My face was glazed with tears and snot.

"Say it," Didi ordered. "Say, 'As long as I keep my father in my heart, he is with me.' "

I bent my neck into my shoulder like a bird and scrubbed my face against my blouse until it was streaked with black from mascara. "As long as I keep my father in my heart, he is with me."

" 'He will always be with me.' "

"He will always be with me."

" 'No one can ever take him away.' "

"No one can ever take him away."

"Okay, good," she concluded, relieved. "Keep saying that because it's true."

She was right. Daddy was with me and he always would be. I nodded and my stomach, which had traded places with my heart when I peered over the edge of the cliff, settled back enough that I could breathe. Not a full breath but enough to keep living. The shadows grew longer and deeper. I was hugging my knees and shivering before I realized the sun was down, it had gotten dark, and I was cold.

"I've got your back. You know that, don't you?" When I didn't say anything, Didi put her hand on my shoulder and asked, "You do know that, right?"

I nodded. Didi Steinberg had my back.

Chapter Nine

At Didi's house, Mrs. Steinberg quickly burned through the small savings Mr. Steinberg had left, then turned to eBay. She was using it to sell off all of Mr. Steinberg's jazz albums and memorabilia.

Didi had taken to calling her mother Catwoman since Mrs. Steinberg now barely spoke, slept most of the day, worked on her eBay sales during the night, lapped all her nutrition out of a bowl, and never showed any outward signs of affection toward human beings. Catwoman had turned the living room into eBay Central with two computers going all the time, tracking the progress of whatever auctions she had under way. She had economy rolls of clear tape on big gun-type dispensers and stacks of sturdy boxes scrounged from the liquor store for shipping out items that had been sold. Teetering piles of old albums, autographed publicity stills, yellowed copies of *DownBeat* magazine, and odd things like cuff links and bar napkins, all carefully labeled and stuck in ziplock bags sat around waiting to be sold or shipped.

We were looking through Mr. Steinberg's stuff one day a month after Daddy's funeral when a loud chiming came from one of the computers.

"Hey, Catwoman made a sale," Didi said, and went over to study the screen. "Shit! One thousand, two hundred and eighty-five dollars for a—" Didi read off the "Description of Item" that she had copied for her mother from the detailed labels Mr. Steinberg had affixed to the hundreds of archival sleeves he'd stored his jazz memorabilia in. " 'One 1941 cover of *DownBeat* magazine signed by Duke Ellington, two mint condition B&W, 8 ¥ 10s signed by Billie Holiday, one 1944 photo signed by Dizzy Gillespie with Juan Tizol on valve trombone.' " As she read, the nimbus of manic energy that always surrounded Didi like a cloud of bees sagged. Finally, she sucked in a deep breath. "Wonder what he'd think if he knew that all the stuff he loved most in life was getting turned into frozen margaritas?" She attempted a laugh, then decided to scoop us out a couple in his honor.

We locked ourselves in Didi's room and ate the margs out of bowls. Even though Didi's bedroom door was closed, we could still hear Mrs. Steinberg snoring in the next room. Didi rolled her eyes at the sound. "You know what we need?" she asked.

"What?"

"A lair!"

"A lair?"

"Yes, a lair! God, why didn't I think of this before?"

She grabbed her marg and rushed out. I followed her into the garage where Mr. Steinberg had had his studio. We hadn't been in it since he'd died. Mrs. Steinberg had cleared out most of his stuff. Didi stood at the door for a long time. What hit you first was Mr. Steinberg's smell, how strong it was, how much it seemed as if he should still be there. Before I even really had a chance to miss him, though, I was missing Daddy.

"Don't you fucking cry," Didi warned me. The muscles in her jaw tightened and she stepped into the empty studio like someone was behind her jabbing her in the back with a bayonet. Acoustic tiles covered all the walls and several layers of carpet had been laid on the concrete floor to absorb noise so that the garage was not only soundproof but had a cozy, hobbity feel to it. The old turntables and microphones were gone. Probably sold on eBay. Mr. Steinberg's battered headphones had been left lying on the floor. Didi picked them up and pressed them to her nose. When she turned around, she had the same expression on her face that I knew I'd had when I realized I was standing on the edge of a cliff, and if I fell, I would fall forever because there was no one to stop me. My face started squirming around. The tears she'd forbidden me to cry stung like vinegar under my skin.

Didi abruptly hurled the headphones down, stood in the middle of the old garage, and twirled around. "This is perfect! Can't you see how perfect this is? Are you going to be a total goober and not see how perfect this is?" Her voice started off wobbly, but got stronger as she got mad at me. I was glad to hear it. I didn't know what I would have done if Didi had started crying.

"We can be out here screaming our heads off and no one will ever know!" she yelled, twirling faster.

I threw my arms out and started spinning with her. "We can commit ax murders!"

"We can have giant parties with live bands!"

"And circus animals!"

Didi stopped, picked up her bowl of 'rita, handed me mine, and we clinked. "To the Lair." "To the Lair."

I loved the Lair; it was our clubhouse. Didi moved all the best stuff from her bedroom into the Lair, including her twin beds. I stripped the primo items from my room and brought them over. We bought a pair of really cute fifties lamps at the Disabled Veterans, some great madras bedspreads with lines of elephants marching across them, threw up some posters, and the Lair was ready. Pretty soon, I was spending more time at Didi's house than I was at my own, which suited Mom fine.

My mother, who had barely left the house at all while Daddy was sick, hardly came home once he was gone. Every morning, one of the sistern would stop by and pick her up, then she'd spend the day at the Compound stitching quilts and dipping candles or praying and testifying. I couldn't remember her ever being happier. She was always singing old-time hymns like "The Old Rugged Cross" when she came home but would stop when she saw me. Neither one of us was who the other wanted to see. So I spent more and more time at the Lair and she spent more and more time at the Compound.

I was home, though, getting foam board and my X-Acto knives for our world cultures class project, a scale model of the Temple of Dionysus we were constructing in the Lair, when my mom came home early. That day, she was so happy she didn't stop singing when she saw me, just looked my way and beamed. It had been so long since she'd smiled in my direction that it didn't bother me that her smile was for her goofy church, not me.

"What?" I asked, after she'd stood there grinning for so long I started smiling too. "What is it?"

"Oh, I don't know how to tell you. I don't know how to make you truly understand."

"Understand what?" I was still smiling but had started to worry.

"Understand what a glorious day this is for me. For us."

"Us?"

"Oh Cyndi Rae, we've been approved to move to HomeTown."

"You mean Houdek?"

"No, silly. Our real, true hometown. The home of our heart and spirit."

"You mean that place in Mississippi."

"Georgia. HomeTown is in Georgia and we're going to move there. I've already made all the arrangements. We could move right now, but you'll probably want to finish high school."

I wanted to say something snippy like *Yeah, finishing high school, that little detail.* But I knew I had to control myself. My mom's eyes were glittering. She was high, high on HeartLand, high on group approval, high on sanctimoniousness, high on subjecting herself to a higher will, high on goopy pieties, high on a dream of a simpler life, in a simpler time that never existed. All those things had given her a strength she'd never had before, a strength that made her dangerous. I had to be very careful.

"So, we'll move after you finish high school."

"We? We'll move?"

"Of course. You're my daughter. A mother would never think of abandoning her child unless the mother's very soul was under mortal threat of eternal damnation. We'll go together as soon as I make the rest of the arrangements."

As calmly as I could, I asked, "'The rest'? What, uh, 'arrangements' have you already made?"

"The usual. Finances, assets, shedding all the unnecessary complications of the modern world."

I felt sick but had to go on, had to get the answers. "So what happened to all these unnecessary complications?"

"The brethren are handling all of that. All of my finances and such."

"*Your* finances?" Panic crept into my voice. "You turned our money over to those people?"

My mother clicked back into full android mode as she parroted Scripture at me. "'For the husband is the head of the wife, even as Christ is the head of the church: and he is the savior of the body. Therefore as the church is subject unto Christ, so let the wives be to their own husbands in every thing.'"

"What are you saying? Those men, those brethren, aren't your husband. You don't have a—" I stopped myself.

"They are my brothers in Christ. You have never understood that. Never even tried. I put up with your willfulness, your lack of respect while your father was alive." The pink fragility that had encased my mother for as long as I could remember was gone. Self-righteousness pumped through her like steroids, giving her new muscles of determination and will. "I endured your abuse for his sake."

"Abuse? You're kidding, right? Tell me you're joking."

She wasn't listening to me. "For his sake, I allowed a friendship that has corrupted you to continue."

"Didi? Didi corrupted me? Didi saved me."

"This is my fault. I blame myself. You are lost. Unruly and spoiled children are among the most miserable of children. They are not the blessings that the Bible says they should be to parents. 'Withhold not discipline from the child, for if you strike and punish him with the rod, he will not die. Thou shalt beat him with the rod, and shalt deliver his soul from hell.' It was your father's decision to raise you without boundaries and I was subject to him in everything."

"This is insane. 'Subject?' You were 'subject' to Daddy? Daddy and I spent our entire lives tiptoeing around you and living in fear of your nervous fits and depressions and migraines—"

"It's true. I was lost. Lost without the light of Christ's love in my life just as you are lost. Just as you will always be lost unless you are consecrated. You can't understand now. Your heart is closed. You will never live a Christ-filled life until we get you away from bad influences. Until we are living in HomeTown."

"I can't talk about this anymore. I have to go."

"You're going to her, aren't you?"

Something in my mother's tone gave me the creeps. "What is that supposed to mean?"

"You people, so smart and witty. We'll see how smart and witty you are on Judgment Day."

"'You people'? I'm your daughter."

"Then honor thy mother!" She was starting to lose her HeartLand android cool. She'd balled her hands into tiny fists and was drawing them up toward her ears where they would vibrate in one of the nervous fits that had controlled Daddy and me for my whole life. For a second I was lost, ready to collapse in a sobbing blob. But Didi's voice spoke in my head telling me that if I caved in, I'd end up in Hookworm, Georgia, with a doily on my head.

"You want me to honor you as a mother? Then start acting like one!" For one second, she was so stunned by the sound of my raised voice that her fists dropped and she fell silent. "Start acting like you care about me! About my life, my future. You want to abandon me for that cult, just say it. Say it!"

All the toughness that lurked behind her baby-doll prettiness gathered itself up. "I have made provisions for you to come with me provided you accept the discipline of the brethren."

"What's that supposed to mean?"

"That you will renounce Satan and live a good Christian life."

"I don't have to renounce Satan. I do live a good Christian life and I am going to leave now because there is no point in talking to you." I slammed out of the house because I hated her so much at that moment I wanted to squash her puffy, bratty face in. Worse, the X-Acto knife in my hand had started to tingle. I ran all the way to Didi's house.

When I got there, she was in a pissy mood, PMSing wildly. Even though our cycles were synched up, she was the only one ever allowed to have PMS. She was playing the Strokes so loud it made my bones ache. I knew she wanted me to tell her to turn it down so she could bitch me out, but I'd had enough of being screamed at by crazy women for one day. Of course, she hadn't done anything on our group project, the scale model of the Temple of Dionysus and Altar of Zeus. So I just got out the foam board and graph paper and started making a pattern. Even though Mith Myth would never know the difference, I did a long series of calculations to translate the altar's original dimensions into a perfect scale rendering. I did it to keep the fidgety numbers synapses in my brain occupied. To block out Didi, my mother, HeartLand, everything.

After about an hour, Didi turned down the Strokes and started sniffing around the temple like a curious woodland creature. She decided we needed to cover the temple in a mosaic and started smashing up Catwoman's old liquor bottles. She sorted through the green, blue, and brown shards to find the perfect chips and slivers.

Didi liked ancient civ since she took all the doings on Mount Olympus as a sort of template for what life at the top was going to be like for her when she arrived. Zeus, Jupiter, Steven Tyler, Julian Casablancas. They were all the same in her book. Gods were gods as far as she was concerned.

Didi got so into the project that after we finished the temple and altar, she made tiny Sculpey sculptures of Apollo, Zeus, Athena, and Callisto, along with some satyrs and centaurs. We baked them in the oven and the house filled with the smell of burning plastic. It was four in the morning when we finally finished and went to bed.

I'd forgotten it was Easter until Didi woke me up and sent me to the backyard where she'd hidden speckled eggs and malted milk balls. It was more fun than you would have thought finding candy tucked into chinks in the patio wall, under the toe of the garden gnome, balanced on the limb of a desert willow. But that was Didi's gift. When she wanted to, she could turn anything into a party.

After we finished gluing the last pieces of glass onto the temple, Didi drove me home. The desert willow tree that had been a twig when we'd moved in had grown into a taller twig that had sprouted a fluff of lilac blossoms. A few lilac petals were scattered across the brick red lava rocks. Random stuff was strewn on top of the petals: my CD player, a couple of spaghetti-strap tops, the Swollen Members CD Didi had burned for me, my makeup kit, all the old copies of *Raw, Spin,* and *Crud* that Didi had passed along. Even a package of Summer's Eve douche and my Lady Epilator.

Didi surveyed the scene and figured out what it meant before I could. "Wow, an official wig snap." She nodded at the church van parked on the street. "Obviously, she needed her brethren and sistern around to do something like this."

I tried to open the front door, but it was locked. "Mom? Mom! Mom, are you in there! Could you open the door, please?"

Finally, the door opened. Mom stood there, not saying a word, backed up by half a dozen sisters and brothers, all in their best pioneer Easter finery. Even the pastor was there, his broad shoulders blocking the doorway.

The sight of them all there arrayed against me rattled me so much that my thoughts zoomed immediately to what I'd feared the most for so long that I almost asked, "What's wrong? Is something wrong with Daddy?" Then I remembered.

No one spoke. No one budged. They had obviously rehearsed this whole thing. It was a sort of intervention on my mother's behalf. She finally spoke. "In case you hadn't noticed, today is Easter. The day we celebrate the resurrection of the living Christ."

The pastor put his hand on my mother's shoulder and she touched it in a way that made me aware that she was the prettiest of the sistern. There was no wedding ring on the pastor's hand. He gave her shoulder an encouraging squeeze and she went on. "As your mother, I have to love you enough to save you. God did not bless me with a child to"—she glanced at the pastor, who nodded for her to go on with the approved message—"populate hell!"

The others nodded and muttered, "Amen."

"Don't be too hard on yourself. Go on, sister," the pastor prodded.

My mother gathered herself up like a child in a Christmas pageant about to recite her piece. "'A child left to himself bringeth his mother to shame.' I have left you too long to yourself and you have brought me to shame."

"Don't blame yourself, sister," the pastor said in his ultra manly rumbling voice. "God had two children in Eden and they both made wrong choices."

The others chuckled with nervous relief, then stiffened their spines again.

"Thank you, brother, but this is my fault and my responsibility to change." My mother turned to me. "My brothers and sisters have helped me to cast out those things that are abhorrent in the sight of the Lord and they stand beside me today as I fight to reclaim the soul of my child."

"Mom, my soul isn't lost so it doesn't need to be reclaimed."

"We knew you would say that, for Satan is a powerful deceiver." She glared at Didi and added, "And his agents are even more devious."

Didi's head started weaving from side to side like the black girls at school when they fought. That's how she sounded when she got up into my mother's face. "Uh-uh, bitch, I did *not* just hear you call me an agent of Satan!"

The sistern gasped as if they lived in a world where every other word wasn't *bitch*. My mom's eyes glittered with self-righteous vindication since Didi had just demonstrated for all the other androids how impossibly hard her life as a parent was.

The pastor's voice boomed out. "Be not deceived: neither fornicators, nor idolators, nor adulterers, nor effeminate, nor abusers of themselves with mankind, nor thieves, nor covetous, nor drunkards, nor revilers, nor extortioners, shall inherit the kingdom of God."

Didi snorted, "Oh, that's a big fucking tragedy. Like Rae and I would even want to spend eternity with a bunch of hypocritical, self-righteous, intolerant assholes like you. Give me the fornicators and idolators any day."

The pastor took his arm from my mother's shoulder, stepped in front, and squared off with Didi, glaring at her until the tendons in his neck jumped out as he thundered, " 'If a man also lie with mankind, as he lieth with a woman, both of them have committed an abomination: they shall surely be put to death; their blood shall be upon them!' "

Didi squeezed her eyes shut and shook her head, laughing as if the pastor had just made a joke. "Did you just call me gay?" She looked at me. "He thinks I'm gay. God, that's funny. Probably projecting, right? You got a secret boyfriend, pastor? Is that it? Little boys maybe? You guys do altar boys? Is that your deal? You like little boys?"

The pastor turned solid in front of my eyes, filling up with bottled rage until he was a slab of marble who intoned, " 'And my wrath shall wax hot, and I will kill you with the sword; and your wives shall be widows, and your children fatherless.' "

He scared me. Didi just shrugged. "Yeah, whatever." She turned from him and, already crunching across the rocks, asked me, "Rae, you coming?"

I glanced at my mother, but she wouldn't meet my gaze. She wailed and pretended to be heartbroken when I walked away with Didi. "Come back! Do not choose the path of iniquity for I will do anything for you but abandon my lord and Christ, Jesus. You are giving me no choice."

We both knew that what I was giving her was a way to do exactly what she wanted: run off to HeartLand without looking like a bad mother in front of her cult friends. It was my Easter present to her and it showed how endlessly ridiculous the human heart is because, even after everything, I was still crushed that she took it. That she chose those strangers over me.

While the sisters and brothers prayed and the pastor boomed out another Bible quote, " 'Then will I pluck them up by the roots out of my land which I have given them; and this house, which I have sanctified for my name, will I cast out of my sight, and will make it to be a proverb and a byword among all nations,' " Didi and I crammed as much of my stuff as we could grab into her trunk. Didi flipped the HeartLanders a giant bird and cackled wildly as we drove away. I was laughing with her when the glee caught in my throat and turned into sobs.

"Rae-rae, baby, don't stress. You lost her a long time ago."

"But why does she hate me? What did I ever do to make her hate me?"

"It's not you. She's, you know, troubled. Some people just weren't meant to be mothers and you and I got two prime candidates."

I tried to stop crying, but my life seemed ruined and meaningless and utterly ridiculous. I felt arbitrary and unnecessary. Someone a mother could leave with only some Bible verses and a few fake tears.

"'Children are for the motherly,' that's what Brecht says. Anyway, nothing we can do about it. I know you think we're friends because of our dads, but it's all about the moms. Face it, at this point neither one of us, technically, has 'rents. We have each other."

When Didi said, "We have each other," my heart filled my chest in a way that convinced me the pastor was probably right, I was a total lez. I slid a glance at Didi. She had on a white angora top that looked like cottonwood fluff floating on a pool of syrup against her dark skin. Did mom see something that I was hiding from myself? Is that why I had zero interest in the few guys who'd asked me out? Rodney Tatum, who occasionally worked the late shift at the Pup, had asked me to the state fair rodeo to see his sister ride in the barrel-racing finals and I'd turned him down flat. No, lesbian, straight, extraterrestrial, whatever I was, I don't think Rodney and I would have hooked up. Michael Debont? He'd asked me to Homecoming. But everyone except Michael knew he was gay. Was that a sign? Was I broadcasting my essence while being too blind to see it myself?

It was true, I wasn't attracted to the handful of loser guys who'd asked me out. I couldn't imagine choosing to be with any of the boys I knew over being anywhere with Didi. Didi dug a roach out of the ashtray and tried to light it and drive with the palms of her hands while I wondered if I was a lesbian. It was better than thinking about Mom. I was doing what Didi ordered; I was staying distracted.

Didi sucked in a lungful, then squinted at me while she held the smoke in, and said, "What?" inhaling the word so she sounded like a robot.

"What what?"

Didi exhaled, coughing. "That is some harsh bammer."

I patted her back until she stopped coughing, judging with every whack what effect touching her was having on me. Did I want to do more? I remembered the crush I'd had on Scooter, my counselor back at Camp Lajitas. But I'd read enough Judy Blume to know that such infatuations were common among prepube girls.

"You've got that look," Didi said, pinching the roach out between her fingers, then putting it into the pocket of her jeans. "You know, storm cloud brows."

I touched the space between my eyebrows where they were bunching up, trying to come together.

"I've got it! I know exactly what we need to do. I read this account of an actual Lakota Sioux ceremony for taking a blood sister. Blood sisters, what do you think? You wanna be my blood sister?"

Sister. The word shone in my mind pure as light from a full moon. I nodded.

"Okay then, let's do it!"

It was late afternoon as we cruised back down Nine Mile Hill. The sun had slipped below the horizon and the last slanting rays were turning the phone lines into sagging, golden spiderwebs as they looped along Central Avenue.

Didi sang/shouted along with AC/DC about all manner of dirty deeds involving cyanide and concrete shoes as we passed Old Town. She finished with a rousing accolade to all deeds dirty at the same moment that she screeched into the lot of Las Palmas Trading Post, where she parked and announced, "Of course, we have to have an exchange of ceremonial offerings. Wait here."

"Deeds, hold on, I don't know if—"

But Didi was already out of the car and sauntering into Las Palmas, which was not a trading post but a really good Indian jewelry store. The thought of all the valuables inside made me nervous, but Didi wasn't wearing the puffy parka or carrying the diaper bag she usually took along on her "five-finger discount" shopping expeditions. In fact, in her lace-up hip-huggers and skimpy top, she didn't have any place to stash items. Still, I didn't relax until she sauntered back out with nothing in her notoriously sticky hands.

My relief disappeared the instant she jumped in the car, reached between her breasts, fished around in her bra, and hauled up a silver chain with a turquoise cross dangling from it. "Sorry about the cross. It was only supposed to be my cover while I was trying on this really cool screaming eagle pendant, but the clerk turned around too quick and I unhooked the wrong one, so the cross dropped down instead of the eagle. Sorry. Thought that counts, right? I'll hang on to this until you get your offering." She hung the turquoise cross around her neck. "Okay, your turn, sister."

Sister. I repeated the word to myself as I crossed the parking lot and pushed open the door. There was no one in the store except a couple of women, tourists in shorts that showed more than most would care to see of their varicosed legs. A high school girl, Native American from the look of her apple-shaped body and sleek black hair, wearing matching glitter nail polish and eye shadow, was waiting on the tourist women. Two other clerks, hard-eyed, older women, gossiped by the far register. I was certain they all knew what I planned to do.

Harsh afternoon light sliced in the front windows and glinted off the silver and turquoise jewelry tucked into the black velvet trays filling the glass cases. One of the older women glared at me. "Can I help you with something?"

She knew. There was no question, she knew. I shook my head too quickly, answered, "No, just browsing," and tacked off into a side room filled with baskets and kachina dolls. I hid out there while I came up with a plan: I would ask Didi if we could postpone the ceremony. I'd tell her that it would be better to come back on a Saturday when the store was jammed and clerks were trying to wait on three customers at a time. But I caught a glimpse of her, sitting in her father's old Mustang, her elbow resting on the edge of the open window. She was singing along to the AC/DC tape. I thought about her driving away, just leaving me there in the store to find my way home by myself.

Home? What did that mean anymore? I turned back toward the glass cases filled with jewelry. Through the feathers hanging down from a row of ceremonial drums, I watched the young clerk with sparkly nail polish pull black velvet trays out of the case so that the tourist women could try on squash blossom necklaces. The women left without buying anything. While the young clerk was bent over, putting the trays back, I stepped out of the side room.

"Oh," she said, surprised when she stood back up and I was standing there. "I didn't see you come in. Can I help you?"

"Yes, I'm looking for a present for my mom. I want to get her something really special. My dad's sick."

"What were you looking for?" She pointed down at the cases and named what was in them. "Bracelet? Ring? Pendant?"

"I don't know. Just something really special. My father's not doing real well." I hadn't planned to say that, to have to look away because tears filled my eyes.

"Oh. Wow. Sorry, that sucks."

"Yeah." The look of sympathy made her baby face seem even younger and my courage returned.

"Bracelets are good," I said.

She swiveled over to the right section and pulled out a tray humped with rows of bracelets. With a glance at me to gauge what my taste would be, she plucked several delicate pieces set with pink mother-of-pearl in butterfly designs off the tray. "These are real popular."

She'd nailed me because I loved them, but Didi? Didi sneered at both pink and butterflies.

I searched the trays still behind the case until I spotted the perfect bracelet, Didi's bracelet. It was a band of beaten silver with a design that appeared abstract at first, but gradually revealed itself to be two stylized panthers coiled about each other, either fighting or mating. I asked the clerk if I could see the tray with the panther bracelet on it, then requested half a dozen others. She slid the trays onto the counter in front of me, before turning her attention to chipping the polish off her nails.

She had her middle finger in her mouth, gnawing at the nail, when one of the older clerks asked her, "Where did you put those small gift boxes?" Her peevish tone accused the younger clerk of putting the boxes in the wrong place.

"Right where they're supposed to be." The younger clerk pointed at a stack of boxes.

"Small, as in ring box small," the woman said, pretending to be patient but actually almost sneering.

"Like she couldn't have said that in the first place?" the clerk whispered to me.

"Really," I said, adding a snort of sympathy as the girl pivoted away from her post to locate the ring boxes. I probably wouldn't have done anything if she hadn't turned away. I probably would have walked out of the store empty-handed, but she did, she turned away. I plucked out the panther bracelet, clamped it onto my wrist, and slid it up under my sleeve. By the time the girl turned back around, I had returned all the bracelets to the tray. Maybe she would have counted them if the older clerk hadn't been mean to her or if I hadn't told her my father was sick.

"Thanks," I said, backing away from the counter. "I'll think about it."

"Cool," the clerk chirped, bending over to put the tray back in the counter. "Come again."

The older clerks eyed me suspiciously and didn't say "Come again" as I rushed out the door.

Didi was all over me the instant I opened the car door. "What did you get? What did you get?"

"Just drive!" I screamed. Thank God, Didi was at the wheel. Because she calmly backed out and pulled away. I would have been squealing rubber so bad, every shop owner for blocks would have taken down the license number.

Mrs. Steinberg was just waking up when we walked into Didi's house. Curled up in her husband's old recliner spooning frozen margarita out of a cereal bowl, she shot a question at Didi in staccato Spanish. I'd taken Spanish for all three years of my high school language requirement and, if I could have seen Mrs. Steinberg's question written down, I would have been able to conjugate every verb in the sentence, but as far as understanding the spoken language, that was Didi's department. Didi answered in even more rapid-fire Spanish but never made eye contact with her mother once as we both hurried through the living room.

Back in the Lair, Didi assembled everything she needed for our blood sister ritual. She got out the pricker thing from the kit her father used to use to test his blood sugar, lighted some patchouli incense, and read a passage from *Black Elk Speaks,* which didn't appear to have anything to do with sisterhood.

"This is going to hurt like hell," Didi promised when we got to the blood part of the blood sister ceremony. She jabbed my finger with the pricker and blood materialized in a perfect ruby bubble.

Didi turned her back to me and grunted when she stuck herself, then turned around, holding her finger hidden in the closed tunnel of her hand and captured my bleeding finger in it. We pressed our fingers together while she chanted her very own translation of the Lakota vow. "I take you as my sister. My heart now knows your heart. Your tears will flow if my blood ever falls. Your enemies' tears will flow if your blood ever falls."

Didi lifted the turquoise cross up from between her breasts, kissed it, and hung it around my neck. When I removed the bracelet from under my blouse, Didi squealed with delight, snatched it out of my hand, and put it on her wrist herself in a way that made me think of Napoleon crowning himself.

I didn't notice until she held my finger under the bathroom faucet that all the blood flowing had been mine; her skin wasn't broken. I didn't say anything when she put a Band-Aid printed with stars and smelling of rubber on my finger, then one on her own. I didn't even feel cheated. I accepted that that was the way the ceremony was supposed to go. That the price of having Didi for my sister was that I would be the one who bled.

Chapter Ten

Didi and I had survived our senior year. It was the last day of school. As seniors, we had the week off, but most of us, like animals set loose into the wild who keep coming back to the cage even though they're free, returned to Pueblo Heights.

The main hallway was jammed. Didi skipped away from me, jumped up, grabbed a big banner reading SENIORS RULE!!, ripped it from the wall, and ran outside with a pack of outraged Abercrombies trailing behind her. I started to follow, but someone behind me called out, "Cyndi Rae. Cyndi Rae!" No one called me Cyndi Rae anymore. Not since my mother had left.

It was Nita Carabajal, the girl who'd been assigned to be my lab partner when I first started at Pueblo Heights. Because we had absolutely no other friends, I had clumped with Nita in those lonely weeks before I met Didi. I say "clumped" because we sat next to each other at lunch and shared physics notes but were never actually friends. Nita was a Jehovah's Witness so she didn't do many "things of this world" like Christmas or pledging allegiance to the flag or shaving her legs or pits. She seemed to be a natural to hang with the Christians, but Nita alienated even them by informing anyone who wore a cross that Jesus had died on a stake.

She held her yearbook and a pen out to me. "Sign it, okay?"

I'd managed to avoid Nita since Didi entered my life, so of course she didn't know that my mom had gone off to live at HeartLand HomeTown, and I'd moved in with Didi.

I took the yearbook Nita offered to me. "How's your father doing?" Her eyes were two pits of gooey sympathy. She didn't know about Daddy either.

"Same. About the same," I mumbled as I scribbled *Have a great summer!!!!* My fingers had gone icy cold. I shoved the book back the instant I was done without even asking her if she'd like to sign mine. Nita darted away and was immediately swallowed up by the crowd, just another floater, one of the invisible ones who pass through high school as unnoticed as possible, bent beneath an overloaded Target backpack, hurrying to catch the bus, slipping through the halls like a wraith, scanning the cafeteria for a friendly or at least a tolerant face. Nita Carabajal was who I would have been if Didi hadn't saved me. I caught my breath and ran outside to find her.

Since Didi declared the few graduation parties we were invited to "major dorkfests," we had our own celebration that evening at Puppy Taco, where we spent most of our shift giving away tater tots to anyone who would yell, "Whore-nuts suck!" Between customers, Didi read the apartment-for-rent ads. Catwoman had sold most of Mr. Steinberg's albums and all of his memorabilia and Didi figured the house wouldn't be far behind. Didi's mom still didn't exactly speak to me. I wasn't even certain that she realized I was living in her house, but, like a cat, she'd gotten used to my presence.

"I mean," Didi asked me, "what does she have to stay in Albuquerque for?"

It was an odd gift that Didi never held any delusions about how important she was in her mother's life. It was harder for me. I actually missed my mom and, in spite of everything, was hurt that, in the few letters she wrote, she sounded so happy with her new 1890s life. That bothered me more than her little reminders that I'd be burning in hell for all eternity unless I renounced Satan. She did send small checks, enough for clothes and makeup and to contribute to groceries at Didi's house. She always ended her letters saying that whenever I put the Devil behind me, I would be welcome at HomeTown. She didn't make any other effort to convince me to come. Not that I ever would have.

To celebrate our last day of high school, Alejandro gave us two quarts of his mother's red chile and a short shift so I was Cloroxing Puppy Taco's counters by quarter of five when an old Econoline van pulled up to the closed take-out window and honked. I held up the yellow latex gloves to show Didi that I was occupied and she roused herself enough to shuffle to the window and shove it open. "When the light that says DRIVE-UP OPEN goes out, boys, that means it's closed. Okay, I know it's pretty complicated, but you all got that?"

I smiled at Didi's sarcasm imagining the carload of horny boys she was deflating. I waited for a high-pitched, honking answer from whatever puberty-ridden boy she was talking to. Instead an accent came over the loudspeaker that was the odd blend of English and hillbilly that people from places like North Carolina have.

"You're Dirty Deeds, right?" the voice asked. "The Black Crowes told us you were cool." The Crowes were some band Didi had groupied a few months back. "We're here with the Whatevs."

"Never heard of them."

"Wanna come to a party?"

"What kind of party?"

"An after party after the concert."

Didi joined the mechanical laughter that came over the loudspeaker. "Where's this party going to be?"

"Right across the street at the Ace High Motel."

"Ohmigod! I love the Ace High!" Didi said.

"So the Crowes told us."

Didi laughed. "I don't know," she said. "I'll think about it. But only if my friend will come."

A chorus of male voices implored me, "Friend, whoever you are! Come, okay? Come to the concert. Didi, we'll leave a plus one for you at will call."

"Whatev, Whatevs." Didi laughed and shut the window. The Whatevs honked wildly and roared off.

"Why did you say I had to come to their party? I never go with you to after parties. Besides, they're not even with a band you want to meet."

"I don't know. It's our last night of high school. We should stay together."

"Yeah, but—"

Didi cut off my objections with a quick, "Let's think about it over a trip to Le DAV."

I snapped off the gloves even though I wasn't completely finished with the counters. Most of our major great clothes scores had been made at the Disabled Veterans Store. At the thrift store, I always followed in Didi's wake since she could scan a twenty-foot rack of castoffs in hardly more than that many seconds, dismissing bales of career separates and zeroing in on the one garment with potential.

Le DAV was housed in a huge building that had once been a roller-skating rink. Still, some days it didn't hold a single garment worth looking at. But that day, our last as Whore-nuts, was a lucky one.

"Here, take this," Didi said, handing me what was clearly the prize find of the expedition: a scarlet, fitted ladies' Western shirt with collar points.

"Are you sure?" I asked, already putting it on over my clothes.

"It was made for you."

"But you saw it first."

"I always do," she said, moving on to a fabulous Mexican skirt with a matador swirling a red cape in front of a panting bull painted on it.

We each filled a large shopping bag, handed over a twenty for our combined finds, and got change back.

In the parking lot, we threw our bags into the trunk of the Skankmobile, paused to flip fingers in the general direction of what was now our alma mater, Pueblo Heights High School, then headed north. We took a left, and the instant the tires hit Central Avenue, Route 66, we started singing about getting our kicks on Route 66.

No matter how we goofed on the song, on the road's tackiness, we loved our stretch of Route 66 stretching out toward all the infinite possibilities our lives held. Though we pretended to believe that Central Avenue embodied everything that was most tacky about our hometown, we loved to drive it at the exact moment right after the sunset finished its warm-up act when the Sandias were fading from pink to granite and the neon started to vibrate against a darkening desert sky. That was when the tires of the Skankmobile soaked up every dream of every traveler who'd ever headed west to start a new life out where the slate was clean. For that moment, it was us, Didi and me, who were going to drive through the night and see the sun come up over the Pacific Ocean and do things so amazing that future generations of Whore-nuts would talk about them.

Didi sang words she made up and set to the irresistible "Route 66" beat. "Now you go through Puppy Taco. Get your Big Red and your nachos!"

I joined in. "And AlbuKooKay is mighty pretty."

"Don't forget Winona, Kingman, Barstow . . ." Didi started before seguing into a musical inventory of every cheesy store and flophouse motel we passed. "Round-up Motel. Pussycat Video. Winchester Ammunition. And, ohmigod!" Didi stopped singing. "The Ace High Motel!"

It was too early for the band to be back at the motel. I thought Didi would drive to the Journal Pavilion so we could watch the Whatevs' concert for free. But the only reason Didi ever went to concerts was to meet the bands and since she had already done that, she skipped the concert and we drove up Nine Mile Hill. Graduating seniors from every high school in town were there partying, stumbling around the West Mesa, bobbing in and out of the glare of headlights. When it was late enough to arrive in style, we drove back into town.

As we passed the Palms Trading Post, I asked, "Could you just drop me off at the Lair, please?"

"What? No. Rae-rae, you have to come. It's the night of our last day as Whore-nuts." Didi shifted gears and the panther bracelet on her wrist gleamed in the dim light reflected from the dashboard. She hadn't taken it off since the blood sister ceremony. I'd never taken the turquoise cross off either.

"Naw, I don't think I'm up for it tonight."

"Please, please, please."

"Since when did you ever need me?"

"Since when *didn't* I need you? Of course I need you. You take care of the details."

"Yeah, but why do you even want to go?"

"Uh, let's see? Number one, better than going home. Number two, better than going home. And number three, did I mention? Better than going home."

"Could I just go to your house and eat margs with Catwoman and you go without me like we always do?"

"No. Come on, Hunker. Come on, you wiener-happy woman, you."

There she'd done it, hit the fiction that I was a hot number always up for a good time.

I didn't actually agree, just stopped arguing. We stopped at Wendy's on Central, ordered Diet Cokes, and took our drinks and everything we'd bought at Le DAV into the ladies' room for a try-on party. Didi sorted through our bags and hauled out the primo vintage fiesta skirt painted with a bullfighting scene in fiery reds and blacks. The black tummy tee she already had on went perfectly with it. The skirt rode low on her hips and the tee stopped somewhere above her bottom ribs, showing Didi's navel ring and the perfectly flat stomach it was attached to. She painted on some red vinyl lipstick from her purse and looked like a stylist had spent hours on her.

"Now you," she said, rooting around in the bags.

"What about this?" I asked, tugging on the rockabilly shirt I was wearing. I felt safe in it, covered up.

"Oh, yeah, that's perfect." One beat. Two. "For a remake of *Deliverance*. Here, try this." She pushed a pair of late-eighties stone-washed jeans into my hands. I put them on. Didi circled her finger indicating that I should twirl around. I did and she shook her head. "No, definitely not. Serious case of No Assatall."

I peeked over my shoulder and saw that the jeans did indeed flatten my butt down like a sack of feed.

"This! This! This!" Didi shoved a flimsy skirt into my hands.

I held it up. "Uh, are you sure?" The skirt, a froth of lace and some slinky, slippery fabric, was one of those homemade creations you can find only in a thrift store, a flight of fancy that had found no place in its maker's real life.

"Uh, I don't think so. I didn't shave my legs."

"You need to shave your legs about as much as an albino. You have virtually no visible body hair."

"I'm not really a skirt person." I handed it back and started to put my jeans on.

Didi ripped the jeans out of my hands. "Cyndi Rae Hrncir, you are too young to be saying what kind of person you are and *way* too young to be saying what kind of person you are *not*. Put this on!" She held the skirt out and stared at me, not saying what was in both our minds: I could either put the skirt on or keep following a path that was starting out too narrow and would only get narrower.

I took the skirt. "Okay, but just to try on." The garment might not have worked for its creator, but it settled onto my hips as if made for me. A fantasy me who wore skirts that revealed her midriff.

"Don't say anything!" Didi ordered as I eyed myself dubiously. She tugged the skirt down until first my belly button, then the very top of my pubic hair showed.

"No way!" I yanked the skirt back up.

"You're right. Pubes are too hoochie mama. But you have to wear this." She plucked a cream silk camisole out of the bag.

"But that's underwear."

"Uh, yeah. Put it on! Put it on!"

I was surprised by how good the pale camisole looked against my skin, which had turned a rosy pink from all the hours we'd spent cruising with the top of the Skankmobile down.

Didi fluffed up my hair and painted my face as if I were her favorite doll. Then she spun me back around to face the mirror. "See how great I made you look!"

I studied not myself but Didi's handiwork, amazed at what she had done. My lips were plump, my eyes sparkled, my face was a palette of delicious creams and pinks and blues. Even in the buzzing fluorescent lights of Wendy's bathroom, I looked good. Didi had made me look good. "You're a genius," I whispered.

"And tits out!" Didi drilled a knuckle into my spine and I jerked my shoulders back. "Sexy mama," Didi said.

It was as if I had still been carrying a heavy backpack and had just dropped it. For that moment, that night, I was light, and free, and sexy.

The skirt felt like a cloud barely floating around my body as we walked outside. The parking lot was bathed in silver all the places where the gaudy neon colors didn't reach. Didi stopped dead and pointed up. "Hey, look. Have you ever seen a moon that full?"

I hadn't. It was as if the moon had graduated that day too and was shining more brightly than it ever had before. I tilted my head up to let the silvery light stream over me.

"Wow, I wish you could see yourself. Someone is going to fall in love with you tonight, sexy mama. Probably me."

I laughed along with Didi. The joke wasn't Didi falling in love with me. It was her falling in love with anyone.

The Whatevs' party had started by the time we pulled into the parking lot of the Ace High. The motel's sign, an ace of hearts, flipped over and over in blinking red neon. As soon as we stepped out of the car, we could hear the old ZZ Top song about how she's got legs and she knows how to use 'em blaring from an upstairs room. Didi was already bobbing her head to the music as we followed it upstairs. The matador on her Mexican skirt swung his red cape from side to side as we climbed the concrete stairs to the third, the top, floor. The music led us to the door of room 312. We pounded, but no one heard, so we walked into the front room of the suite. It was dark and felt tropical, the air overheated and dense. The only illumination came from a black light that turned Didi's smile into a phosphorescent zombie grin. We stumbled over a quilt of grease-ringed pizza boxes. The black light made a pyramid of Foster's beer cans stacked in one dark corner appear to be floating in midair.

The door to the back room where the real party was going on opened and a blast of ZZ Top and smoke poured out. A guy wearing a straw hat that drooped down in front and back, and a black T-shirt with tour dates printed on it, stumbled out, fixed his gaze blearily on Didi and me, and yelled, "New recruits! New recruits!" He could have been any of a hundred roadies or soundmen who'd waved Didi past security guards and welcomed her into hotel rooms. Didi beamed. She was home.

"Hey, come on back." He waved toward the open door. "Party's in here."

Didi turned to me and gave the shrug that guided most of her actions, the shrug that asked, *Why not?*

"Go on." I flagged her a wave of permission, wishing again that I was back at Didi's house spooning margaritas with Catwoman.

"I'll just hang out here for a while," I told Didi. Without any discussion, we'd reverted to our usual groupie MO where I left after the reconnaissance work was over. Didi danced away and I yelled after her, "I might walk home!"

"Yee-HAW!" The guy in the droopy hat led Didi away.

I flopped down on an abused couch covered in the brown tweed Herculon favored by low-end motel chains. The boom from a throbbing bass pulsed along my spine. I could barely make out the sound of a laugh that was Didi's before it was lost in the thundering music.

I had decided to leave when, drifting above the roar of the party, I heard another sound, a sound so pure and crystalline that even though it was barely audible, it cut through the cacophony with diamond-sharp clarity. As my eyes and ears adjusted, I realized that there was an alcove beside the Foster's pyramid and someone was sitting in it, playing guitar.

For a second, he was nothing but blurred streaks of ghostly white where the black light caught his nails rippling over the strings of his guitar. His head was bent down, resting on the neck of his guitar so that he could hear himself play, the sound resonating directly into his skull. The music was unearthly, like stumbling upon a fallen angel playing his harp on the floor of a steel mill. The party noise fell away and suddenly all I could hear was the cascade of notes pouring from his fingers. I didn't know enough about music to identify the style. It was too raw to be classical, too rarefied to be rock. Then I stopped trying to figure out what it was and just listened.

I'd read a theory in *Newsweek* once about why crack cocaine is so addictive. It said that some people have receptors in their brains like keyholes. That if you have such a keyhole in your head, the drug will slide into it, the drug will be the key that unlocks you. It is this unlocking of a true and essential self that dooms a person with this chemical quirk to addiction from the first pipe. I had a keyhole in my brain for the music this stranger was playing. From the first notes I heard, it seeped into me, filling an empty spot I hadn't known existed.

He was seated on a straight-backed chair. Invisible in the darkness, mesmerized by this angelic music, I was freed from self-consciousness. I sank to the ground beside him, hoping to keep that sound pouring into my head. He tilted his face toward me so that the black light picked up the whites of his eyes turning them into flashes of phosphorescence. His only acknowledgment of my presence was a small nod as if he'd been waiting for me to take my place at his feet. I was invisible in the black light, lost in darkness, nothing but a hopeful smile glowing in the dark above a lacy camisole floating disembodied as a cloud in the phosphorescent light.

My pulse fell into time with his playing as if it were the moon capturing my blood in a tide that surged, then fell away.

In the dim light I saw that he was as different from any of the guys I'd ever been this close to as a human could be and still belong to the same species. Where other guys were pink and embryonic, he was brown and fully formed. His black hair, brows, the black lashes shadowing his cheeks had an etched certainty missing in the tentative pastel fuzziness of the boys I knew. Those boys were poised to take everything about themselves back, to change it all if a better idea came along; this stranger was a finished product. He was a full-grown man in a way that the boys I knew never would be no matter how old they grew to be.

He didn't stop playing, barely looked up from the guitar, and asked, "What are you doing here?" A seam of white opened in his dark face as his lips formed the words, hiding then revealing his teeth so that they almost seemed to blink on and off like the neon sign that buzzed outside the window. He had a slight accent. Spanish, but not like the homeboys at Pueblo with their shorts that drooped to midcalf and wallets on chains. His accent made his words sound oddly formal and important.

"I came with—" I pointed toward the back room, then realized that he couldn't see my hand in the darkness and couldn't hear my soft voice over the deafening music. But I had heard my voice and what I heard was wrong. The sound of my words didn't fit this music, this room, this night. They didn't fit the person I suddenly wanted to be. In my head I heard Didi's voice, teasing, flirty, funny, nasty, challenging. That was who I wanted to be, so I echoed the memory of Didi's voice and said in a bold voice, "I came to hear you, of course."

The seam of white widened into a full smile. He stared at me, ignoring his hands flowing over the strings. A trail of white followed his nails as he took his left hand from the neck of the guitar and patted the side of his leg. "Come here." His right hand kept plucking music.

I edged closer until my shoulder nuzzled against his thigh.

"*Escuches.* Listen." He pressed my head against the polished body of the guitar, then stroked the strings with the tips of his nails, showing me how he coaxed the sound out. As the rush of soft notes resonated inside my brain, I studied the insect scurry of his fingertips across the strings. Each note was a minute collision of wire-wrapped string and the tender pad of finger flesh that launched an upward tug of nail on string. I focused on his right hand so intently that it became a creature separate from the body it was attached to. His knuckles rolled like marbles beneath the skin as fingers pulleyed up and down, floating over the strings, gently drawing sounds that made my head fill with stained-glass colors: cobalt blue, Prussian blue, emerald, ruby, colors so deep and saturated it hurt to even imagine them.

When he stopped playing and leaned over to pick up a can of beer, the colors shattered and I was dumped back into a seedy motel room that had, for a few seconds, been transformed into a cathedral.

I had to ask, "What are you doing here?"

He shrugged and nodded toward the din coming from the back bedroom. "I was hitching down from Santa Fe and they, those Whatevers, picked me up." He put the beer can down and started playing again as if the words he'd spoken had depleted him in some way and he needed to fill himself up with music in order to speak again. And then he sang so softly I was barely able to hear the Spanish words that stretched themselves out, rising and falling on the waves of rhythm rolling effortlessly from his guitar. The chords he plucked, the words he sang were both sadder and more thrilling than anything I'd ever heard in my life. They translated the state of gloom and exhilaration I lived in. I saw my father's bony shoulders heaving up toward his ears as he struggled to suck oxygen into his wrecked lungs. I saw my face golden in a setting sun, laughing until tears ran down my cheeks. I saw myself kissing the guitarist. He finished with a hail of notes and one quick, dismissive thump of his ring finger on the face of the guitar.

"I'm not a *cantaor,* not a singer. But I like that one."

"What does it mean? The song?"

"Mean? I'm not sure. Let me see." He nodded his head as he whispered the Spanish words to himself. "Okay, this isn't an exact translation but something like this."

> *By the light of a candle*
> *I wept without shame;*
> *The candle went out.*
> *The tear is greater than the flame.*

I couldn't be Didi, couldn't be cool. "It's beautiful," I whispered. "So beautiful. And so sad."

"Tragedy in the first person," he said, studying his hands. "That's the best definition I've ever come across for flamenco."

Flamenco. I'd heard the word before, but it hadn't had anything to do with me. Now, here it was, inside my head, presented to me by an angel prince enthroned next to a pyramid of beer cans.

He kept playing, not looking up. "This"—he pointed at the dried curls of pizza in greasy boxes, at the pile of beer cans, the noise bludgeoning us from the back room—"this is my tragedy." He played some more, each chord sadder, more wistful than the last. "Sorry, I'm not usually like this. Okay, I'm not *always* like this. You caught me on a bad night. A really bad night. Possibly the worst night of my life."

"What's wrong? What happened?" What I meant was *What can I do? Tell me. Anything. I will do anything for you. I will spend my life fixing whatever is wrong. Tell me what the problem is. I'm good with details. Just ask Didi. Tell me.*

"It's complicated," he answered.

"I'm good with complications. I got an A in calculus." For the first time, he smiled a real smile and stared at me for a long time. The smile and the stare were gone in the next instant when a blinding light filled the room. It bounced crazily off all the walls, exploding in flashes of blue and white. Before I could even figure out what the light meant, he was on his feet. An amplified bullet of static crackled, then a voice on a bullhorn in the fake country drawl of an airline pilot boomed out from the parking lot three floors below, "Come on down, boys. Party's over."

"Of course," he said, shaking his head wearily as if he'd been expecting the party to get busted.

The music was silenced and a barrage of voices coming from the other room followed. "Hey! What the fuck you—?"

"The fucking cops are outside, fuckhead!"

"Fuck! No!"

"Shit!"

"Get rid of the shit!"

The door to the back room burst open. The guy in the floppy straw hat ran out, emptied a ziplock bag of pot and a handful of pink, red, and blue pills into the toilet, then flushed. Band members, groupies, roadies followed him stampeding out of the bedroom heading for the bathroom. A fog of smoke enveloped the suite.

"Didi!" I screamed, but could barely make myself heard above the panicked voices. I tried to get back to the other room, but the fleeing revelers pushed me aside. "Didi!" I screamed again.

Suddenly, a hand grabbed me and I was dragged away from the back room, away from the frenzy of bodies. The stranger, his guitar slung over his shoulder by its strap, pulled me to the far corner of the room where mustard-colored thermal curtains hung over a set of sliding glass doors.

I pointed frantically to the bedroom. "My friend, Didi, is back there."

He jerked me away. "We've got to get out of here. Now." I hesitated and looked back at the door where pierced and tattooed heads churned through the smoke. He caught my eye and asked with a glance if I was coming or not. When I didn't move, he released my arm and, moving with the assurance of a cat burglar, flipped up the lock on the glass door.

"Move it on out, boys," the cop downstairs said in his amplified shit-kicker accent. "Don't make us come up there and drag you out. That'll put us in a real bad mood."

The stranger paused at the glass door and held out his hand to me. The gold-colored motel curtain was pushed back over his shoulders like a cape. The clang of heavy shoes pounding up the metal staircase rang through the room. "Now!"

"Didi! I have to find Didi!"

He shrugged, stepped outside, and let the curtain drop. I rushed into the back room. It was empty. A hand hammered at the front door. "Open up!" I ran back to the spot where the curtains had just closed over the open door and stepped through.

Outside, beyond the smoky room, the evening was cool, the air fresh. The balcony was lighted from the tubes of ruby, emerald, and topaz neon glowing on the motel sign. The lights, buzzing and popping, disoriented me. I couldn't see past them, into the dark night beyond. I was alone on the balcony. He had already left.

Inside the room, a voice, menacing, fake-friendly, asked, "And what do we have here. Not *drug paraphernalia*!"

It would be only a matter of seconds now before they found me hiding on the balcony. I wondered if the police would be able to track my mom down. If they would call HeartLand to tell her that I'd been arrested. I wondered what I would break if I jumped the three stories down to the asphalt parking lot below.

"Down here." The words were a strangled hiss.

I shielded my eyes from the neon glare and looked down. The guitarist hiked out from the balcony on the second story and opened his arms.

"Lower yourself down. I'll grab you."

"I can't. I'll never . . ."

"Do it. Now! I'm out of here in ten seconds."

I stepped over the black wrought-iron railing. In the ruby glow from the neon, I noticed puddles of rust stain around each of the iron pickets. As I lowered myself over the edge of the balcony, the concrete scraped against my leg and the railing gave slightly in my hand. I stretched my leg down into the darkness. No hands reached up to receive me. The neon swam around me in flashes, darting in and out like fish fleeing from a shark.

Up above me, the scary-friendly cop barked, "Trujillo, get the bedroom! I'm checking the balcony!"

I reached with my whole body toward the second-story balcony, but my feet found nothing but air. I heard the railing beneath me rattle and knew it was the sound of the stranger swinging easily from the balcony to the ground below. I had made a mistake. I had gone too far. I wasn't Didi after all.

I didn't have the strength to pull myself back onto the balcony. My arms quivered. I hoped he was gone, that he wouldn't see me fall and end up sprawled in a broken heap on the asphalt below. The fingers on my left hand gave way first. Next, the fingers on the right uncoiled. I started to slip. Hands grabbed me. Arms hugged my legs, guided me down, clasped me around the waist and set me down safely on the second-floor balcony.

"Ohmygodohmygodohmygod." My panicked whimper was silenced by his hand pressing against my mouth. The long nails of his right hand dug into my cheek as he drew me into the shadows.

Over our heads, the gold curtain covering the patio doors was pushed aside and light from the motel room spilled down through the railings. It striped the hand he pressed against my mouth. The cop stepped onto the balcony and a rain of rust flakes fell onto our upturned faces. He clamped his hand even more tightly against my mouth. It tasted of sweat and metal and smelled of marijuana.

The cop stood on the metal grating of the patio above us and turned on his flashlight. A beam of light spiked past. The beam wove about, illuminating the alley below, then slashing across the parking lot and up the side of the building until it fell straight down on my face. I was so convinced that the cop standing on the grating above could see us that I would have stepped forward and given myself up, but he held me back.

A second later, the cop turned the flashlight off and went inside. The gold curtain fell back and the light was blacked out. On the floor above our heads, footsteps moved from the bedroom to the living room, then out through the open door. A dozen or more heels clanged as the cops herded their captives down the metal stairs.

A rumble of voices reached us, band members and roadies protesting their arrest.

"Yeah, yeah," a cop sneered in reply. "We already heard all about your two Grammy nominations. Ah, yes, you did already mention that the governor's daughter is a 'giant, giant' fan. Come on, move it along. We don't want to have to cuff you."

I strained to pick out Didi's voice, but all I heard were harsh male intonations. Then there was a flash of movement at the far end of the alley and Didi appeared at the corner. Her face was in shadow but I recognized her skirt. I started to call out to her, but the guitarist pressed his hand against my lips, the long nails on his right hand furrowing the side of my nose and cheek. Didi clung to the edge of the alley and peeked around at the scene in front of the motel. Bursts of cop-car light strobed the dark alley. More cars pulled up. Radios broadcast static.

Didi backed away and the mercury vapor street light on Central Avenue painted the top of her head with a violet halo. A cop stepped into the alley and grinned as he caught Didi in the beam of his flashlight. "Well, well, well, what do we have here? Snow White. I wondered where you went to. We already got your Seven Dwarfs out front." The cop clicked off the flashlight and moved toward Didi, singing, " 'Hi ho. Hi ho. It's off to work we go,' " in a tuneless voice.

Didi backed away as the cop approached. She glanced around, searching for an escape route. A chain-link fence blocked off the alley behind her.

"So? What about it?" the cop asked, jerking a thumb toward the parking lot. "You wanna go with your little friends out there?"

Sounds of the arrested being loaded into patrol cars echoed back into the alley.

The cop in the alley moved close to Didi. "Or you wanna pay your fine right here? It can be arranged."

"A statutory rape charge can also be arranged," Didi shot back.

The cop coughed out a snort of laughter. "We drag you out of a room, one girl and a bunch of dopehead degenerates, and you're gonna cry statutory? Gotta do better than that, princess."

"I wasn't doing anything. Maybe you didn't notice? I had all my clothes on?"

"Fuck it, you don't wanna work with me on this, let's go."

Didi gave an exasperated gasp, hissed, "Shit," then followed the cop into the shadows at the end of the alley. As she walked, her skirt floated around her slender legs like wisps of smoke. I heard the scrape of his zipper being pulled down. With one hand, he fumbled inside his fly. With the other, he shoved Didi down until she kneeled in front of him. The matador skirt settled around her in a perfect circle, like a small, round cloth thrown on the grass for a picnic. His hand reached into the violet light above her head, threaded his fingers through her hair, and jerked her mouth toward him. His fingers stretched spastically, then clawed more deeply into Didi's hair.

The clang of the chain-link fence took on a staccato urgency and I looked away, looked back at the most handsome man I had ever known. He leaned forward so that I breathed in his smell of marijuana and beer, sharpened and made dangerous by lust. The rattling of the chain-link accelerated, then stopped.

Didi got to her feet and the skirt folded back around her like a closing umbrella. She pivoted and vomited on a pile of old roofing shingles. The cop pulled out a handkerchief and, with a surprising delicacy, wiped himself off. "Okay," he said, folding his handkerchief in half, then fourths, then neat, pocketable eighths. "Let's go." He motioned toward the parking lot with his chin.

Didi pivoted slowly. Her body was tense with rage. "You fuck. I blow you and you're still going to arrest me?"

"You are addressing an officer of the law."

"I am addressing a child molester with a dick the size of worm."

The cop sprang forward, bristling.

"Did I mention that? That I'm only fifteen?"

For a second, the muscle beneath the cop's flab made itself known and the saggy black uniform encased a hard and volatile creature. The cop's hand clenched spasmodically over the baton slapping his side.

"Yeah," Didi sneered. "Do it. That'll look good on the report."

Even from the second floor, I heard the angry snort of the cop's breath. My vision vibrated with an image of Didi's skull cracking open in the violet light.

The cop's held breath exploded out of him in one grandly, dismissive exhalation. "Get the fuck out of here." He gestured toward the dark end of the alley.

"No, *you* get the fuck out of here!"

The cop studied her a moment, started to say something, then laughed, shook his head, and walked away. "Have a good life, princess."

Didi waited a moment, then darted to the corner of the building, and peeked around. When the strobing light faded away, she left. A moment later, the Mustang throbbed to life and gravel spattered as Didi spun the car around and drove off.

The guitarist took his hand from my mouth, vaulted over the railing, landed on the side of the motel with a crunch, and held his arms up to me. Without a second thought, I dropped into them. He took my hand and led me around behind the motel, where we watched and waited until all the cop cars left and the permanent residents of the Ace High motel came back out to stare at the empty lot and drink from stubby green Mickey's malt liquor bottles.

Chapter Eleven

"Where'd you park?" he asked.

"I came with"—he didn't know Didi, didn't know that the girl in the alley was my friend—"I got dropped off."

"Yeah, the guys I was hitching with just got arrested. Oh well, good night for a walk. I guess. Which way you live?"

I pointed west and we set off down Central Avenue. Pup y Taco was on the other side of the street. I thought about telling him I worked there, but didn't. Nothing I could think of to say seemed right after what we'd just seen. We passed the Winchester Ammunition Advisory Center, then the Leather Shoppe. The guitar slung over his shoulder slapping his back with each long stride was the only sound that broke the silence.

"Thank you."

"For what?"

"For not letting me get arrested."

In the parking lot of the Pussycat Video, a skinny man in a porkpie hat and a woman in cheap heels stood beside a battered old Chevy, pointing at something in the open trunk and yelling at each other. Both of them were drunk and both of them had spent too much time on the streets. As their curses reached us, the stranger took my hand, tugged me in close, and cradled my hand against his chest. We watched the couple as if they were part of a movie being shown just for us. When we'd passed them and their curses had faded in the distance, I asked, "Why is this the worst night of your life?"

"Huh?"

"You said that this was, possibly, the worst night of your life."

"I did? I'm a melodramatic motherfucker, aren't I?"

"No, really, tell me."

"Like I said, it's complicated. More complicated than calculus." He smiled to show he remembered me saying that. "This is an entire history class. Maybe a major. You have time for the history of a few cultures, a thousand-year exile, and some really fucked-up skeletons rattling around a really crowded closet?"

"Sure. Seriously, I can research anything. Just tell me what it is."

He stopped and pivoted on the sidewalk so that we were face-to-face. The De Anza Motor Lodge sign behind him was a gigantic neon arrow shooting into the dark sky. The words *De Anza* were written in gold. At the point of the arrow the portrait of a conquistador wearing a Moorish headdress shimmered within a halo of white.

"Yeah, okay. Maybe if I can make you understand, I can figure it out myself." He ducked his head as he slid the guitar off his shoulder and held it out to me. "This looks like a guitar, right?"

I nodded.

"It's a fucking monkey on my back." The conquistador on the sign above his head was in profile, staring off into the sky. He stopped and threw his hands up in defeat. "Forget it. You're a good American girl. You were born yesterday like all good American girls. You believe that anyone can be anything they want. But in my world. In flamenco it's . . ." He searched for words but couldn't find the right ones. "Forget it. Let's just say that flamenco isn't like ordinary music."

"No," I said, desperate that he not give up on me. The words burbled out before I could stop long enough to figure out what cool, flirty thing Didi would have said. "It's not ordinary music. Anyone can hear that. Ordinary music is just that, it's ordinary. It's disposable, it's trivial, it's optional. What you were playing is . . ." I tried to think of a way to bottle up all the emotion his playing had let flow but couldn't. "It's essential."

He blinked. "Wow. Are you into the scene down here?"

"What scene?"

"Never mind. The less you know about it, the better. So you don't know anything about flamenco?"

"If that's what you were playing, tonight was the first time I heard it and knew what it was." Then I remembered. "But the Gipsy Kings? They play flamenco, right?"

He waved the question away. "Flamenco for tourists. Not *el puro,* not the real thing. The real thing, it's like, it's like . . ." His fingers twitched, clawing the air as he plucked chords from a guitar that wasn't there, trying to find a way to express what he couldn't express. Then, to himself, "Fuck. Maybe they're right. Maybe you do have to be born to it. It has to be in your blood." He caught himself and laughed. "You have no idea what I'm talking about, do you?"

"Not really."

He grabbed me in a hug and, laughing, swayed back and forth. "I love that!" he yelled. "I love that you could give a fuck about what kind of blood is running in my veins. Blood, I'm so fucking sick of everyone being so concerned about my blood. It's like I'm surrounded by vampires, everyone fighting over my blood."

I had to know what he was so upset about. I had to know so I could help him. So I could become indispensable. I tried to figure out what all the blood talk was about and thought of paternity suits, wills. "Is there an inheritance?" I asked.

"God, you are so cute. I should just marry you tonight and leave all this shit behind."

"So it's not an inheritance?"

"Oh, it's an inheritance all right. Just nothing so simple as money. It's all about whether I have the right pedigree to play flamenco or not."

"That's ridiculous. What does pedigree matter? It's music, not a dog show." This was like being with Didi, protecting her from anyone who didn't appreciate her genius.

"You're so American. I love that you are so American."

I didn't know what he meant. He tried to explain. "Okay, it's like the blues. Everyone knows that the only people who can play the real blues are black and they're from the Mississippi Delta, right?"

"You know, they have all these amazing tests now that they've used to find out stuff like whether Native Americans came over the Bering Strait from Asia. You can get a blood test that will pretty much tell who your ancestors were, ethnic-wise, right back to Adam and Eve." It was the wrong thing to say.

"Fuck that. I am never taking a fucking blood test. Tonight, this night, I am through caring about my blood. Here's where my talent is." He held up his fingers. "If anyone needs a blood test to decide if I'm good or not, fuck them."

I scrambled to assure him that I didn't need proof. "You're good. Your music is the best music I've ever heard."

"The best?" he kidded, then stopped and studied my face.

I wanted to tell him that his music was a drug, a door, a path, an element like air and water, essential to life, but all I said was, "Yes. The best."

My answer was lost in the rumble of a car coming up behind us. A lowrider car drove by, sapphire blue and smooth as a shark. The thump of the bass pulsing from an open window bumped against me like a wave. The car was barely moving as the guy in the front passenger seat leaned a muscled arm inked with smeary blue tattoos out the window and growled, *"Qué ruka tan caliente!"*

The guitarist laughed and yelled back at them in Spanish.

The lowrider at the window stuck his fist out and the guitarist tapped it. "Big ups to you, bro!" the lowrider said. They cruised on, showering us with silver sparks whenever the car scraped bottom.

"What did they say?"

He pulled me into the sheltered entrance to an abandoned store whose windows were covered with paper with a FOR LEASE sign on the door.

"They said you're a hot babe."

"Me?"

"You know that. You know you're hot." He pushed me into a dark corner and put his hands on either side of my neck. I thought he was going to kiss me, but he didn't. "You're not fifteen, are you? Because I know your friend isn't. Are you a wild girl too?"

So he knew that the girl in the alley was my friend. I should have said no, I wasn't a wild girl. But that night, with him, I wanted it to be true. I wanted to be anything he wanted me to be. In a voice tough and flirty like the one Didi used to tease boys, I answered, "I'm legal."

"Good." He grabbed my hand again and pulled me back onto Central, where we strolled like a couple from the fifties out on a date.

I cut quick glances to the side just to see how cool his guitar looked slung across his back. To check out the way his dark hair flicked over the top of his shirt and how he kept his free hand shoved into the pocket of his jeans so that his left shoulder hunched up as if there were a cold wind pushing at him that only he could feel. I tried to figure out how old he was. One second he seemed my age, a boy just out of high school. The next, he looked old in a way that precluded his ever having been young, like one of the kids at school who went to the Al-Anon meetings they held at lunch in the counselor's office.

He dropped my hand and drifted ahead. The current that had been charging through me went dead as the distance between us grew.

I thought about Didi. But it wasn't to worry if she'd gotten home okay. All I thought about was what she would do in my place. How would she intrigue and entrance him? I ran up and took his arm. Then I pretended that I was the one who wanted to run ahead, that he was the one who had to keep up, and I tugged him to speed up his pace. "You've got to see this!" I hurried us past the Town House Restaurant and the tiny diner across the street where the Toddle House had been.

At the next cross street, I stopped, held my arm out toward the crumbling building ahead of us, and announced, "The Aztec Motel." The Aztec was Didi's favorite spot on her favorite stretch of Route 66. The old motel tried for a Pueblo style with flat roofs on the rows of one-room units and a ladder on top of the first-floor roof of the two-story office. But the structures were just the armature for the baffling, schizophrenic jumble of junk that the owners had felt inspired to scatter about the premises. Didi had taken me on the "Aztec Motel pilgrimage" many times. She especially loved what she called the Gin Garden, a collection of old green liquor bottles planted around discarded tires.

I hurried ahead like a kid eager to be the first on the playground, like Didi every single time she'd ever dragged me to the Aztec.

"I like to start back here at the Gin Garden," I said, channeling Didi's enthusiasm and affection for the kitsch that had always seemed much more trash than treasure to me. Arrayed along the base of the stucco wall at the back of the motel were dozens, hundreds, of old tires, each one holding a bouquet of fake flowers and empty, green liquor bottles.

"Next, we move on to the Aztec Motel Zoo." I led him around to the other side of the wall where dozens of teddy bears peered down from an ancient cottonwood. Other trees held collections of other stuffed species. I left him staring up at hundreds of small, furry faces.

"Check this out," I called from the side of the motel. The pink stucco was covered with talavera tiles in blue and white, an odd assortment of oil paintings, a gold velvet headboard, and doors. Not doors leading into rooms. Just doors. Old brown doors covered in zigzagging patterns of tile and staked to the side of the motel. An actual garden with rosebushes and irises guarded by Saint Francis also hosted a melted fountain that cradled a plastic Minnie Mouse and a child's wading pool filled with old gazing balls and more green bottles.

"This is where the really great stuff is," I said. "The full-on schizophrenia." That was what Didi called it. I raced off and gestured for him to join me beneath a yellow steel overhang that shaded the front of the motel office. Lined up on the overhang were dozens of Tonka trucks. Beside them a white ceramic kitty with a pink tongue peered down. The wall beside the overhang was covered with ads for Indian-brand motorcycles going back to 1914. Pottery, vases, statues, figures of the Buddha, many Madonnas, Saints Joseph and Francis, all three wise men, a Christmas wreath, scenes from a Mexican village in tile, a small windmill, Daffy Duck, Sylvester, they were all up there, all presided over by a mannequin in a blue dress.

"I call her the Virgin of Route Sixty-six," I said, repeating Didi's name for the mannequin.

He stared at the incomprehensible jumble. "This is great. This is so great! I've driven by this place hundreds of times and never really noticed how incredible it is. I love it. I love the kind of total insanity that makes a person do all this. Not caring that the sun is gonna beat hell out of the oil paintings and street trash is gonna walk off with half the shit and most people are gonna walk by and think you're psychotic. I love it. I love that you love it. This"—he whirled around, his arm out to take in the entire mess—"this makes me understand why you get flamenco."

A light of such pure happiness flooded me, I worried I would start glowing. I had shown him the right thing. It didn't matter that it was Didi's thing. It only mattered that it was right.

"This place is *so* flamenco. If you understand it, you understand flamenco."

I nodded even though I had no idea on earth what the connection was between a garden of gin bottles and flamenco.

"I love that whoever created all this knows that they're never going to get rich or famous. They're not going to get anything. They're doing it because they have to. Just like—" He held his hands out and mimed a strum that flared all the fingers of his right hand, then ended in a gesture that threw away all the beauty he had just created.

I didn't want him to even pretend to throw it away. I snatched it back. "Your playing is unbelievable."

"In the world I come from 'unbelievable' is barely good enough."

"The 'world you come from'?"

He draped his hands over my shoulders and studied my face. "Are you sure you want to know about the world I come from?"

"I do," I said and it was true. The truest words I'd ever spoken. My tone was too solemn, though, like a bride answering the question, "Do you take this man to be your lawfully wedded husband."

"*Yo también,*" he said. "I do too."

I didn't know what he meant, what it was about his world he wanted to know, but I fastened powerfully on the absence, the hole that I could fill. Details. This is what I was good at. This is what I could offer him. Whatever it took, I would find and bring that knowledge to him.

"*Yo también,*" he repeated, his mouth so close to mine that I felt the words on my lips. Again, I was certain he was going to kiss me, but he spun away abruptly.

"Come on. It's my turn now to show you something." He led me down a street, away from the flashing neon along Central Avenue. There were no lights on anywhere in the quiet neighborhood. All the houses were dark. It was only then that I realized how late it was. That the rest of the world was asleep. I should have wondered about Didi then, if she was safe at home. But I didn't. My mind was completely filled with following this stranger wherever he led.

"Look." He stopped and tilted his face up. The full moon, which had been dazzling silver, was darkening to a color that reminded me of a blood orange.

"A lunar eclipse," I whispered as the moon vanished entirely and the street fell into total darkness. We had met on the night of a lunar eclipse.

He grabbed my hand and tugged me along. "Come on. The stars will really be amazing now."

We emerged on Lomas Boulevard where streetlights cast a dim glow onto the deserted road. When we passed Our Lady of Fatima, he crossed himself and kissed his thumb. To me, it was an act as exotic as if he'd knelt down before a cow in the streets of Calcutta. He glanced up and down the empty street, then set off west. "I think it's up here."

"What?"

"The secret park? You ever been there?"

I shook my head no.

"Good. I want to be the first to show it to you."

We turned, then turned again, and once more the streets grew dark and silent. In the middle of a block, he led me off the street entirely, off the sidewalk, and onto a path that ran between the houses themselves. It was so well hidden I would never have noticed it. The narrow passage slithered dangerously close to the windows of houses on either side where sleepers dreamed. I thought of the gun Mom used to keep in her nightstand in case of "home invasion" and worried for one second about a nervous homeowner shooting us. In the next second, I realized that this night I was immune. I had walked through the gold curtains and emerged into a world where I could prowl the night streets and capture the attention of a man who might have descended from conquistadors or angels.

As we stole along the narrow path, a cloud of fragrance like a tropical rainstorm enveloped us. Any other time, I would have identified it as the exhaust from a dryer blowing out the smell of fabric softener, but on that night it was a tropical rainstorm.

The path abruptly opened into exactly what he had promised, a secret park. Hidden behind the houses of this ordinary suburban block was gloriously open space where cottonwoods soared into the night. We left the choke of houses behind and walked into the middle of the park. Only three of the dark houses that ringed the park still had lights on. Without the moon, we hid in a night that was as dark as nights get and stared at the lives illuminated in the lighted rooms more intently than museumgoers studying dioramas. In one display an old man stood in his open patio door, T-shirt tucked into white boxers, and smoked a cigarette. In another a young mother in a shortie nightgown walked a crying infant. A woman in her fifties sat in a living room completely dark except for the flickering light from the television she watched.

I was outside all those rooms. All the rooms where ordinary life was happening.

He took my hand, sat us down at a concrete picnic table, bent over his guitar, and played more of the music that poured directly into the hole in my brain. An odd luminescence played across his skin as he sang a song in Spanish that made all the vowels sing their names. They sang the *a*. The *e*. The *i*. The *o*. The *u*. And sometimes they sang the *y*. Daddy had been right, I would fall in love with the first boy who gave me vowels.

"Hey, the giant's swing." He laid the guitar on top of a picnic table and ran to the tallest, oldest cottonwood in the park. Hanging from it on long, thick ropes was a swing. Not a cheap metal swing suspended from clattering chains either, but a big, old-fashioned swing someone had made from a plank of oak. It was a giant's swing.

He jumped onto the swing with an explosive, balletic grace and, standing on the seat, rode it into the air. He soared up, then swept back down, his dark hair rising around his face like black wings. Up again, he rose high enough that he could reach out, grab a handful of leaves, rip them loose, and toss them into the air. I tilted my face up to receive the rain of greenery that showered down. I caught a leaf. It was a perfect heart. I tucked it under the waistband of my skirt.

"Come." For a second, two, he opened his arms to me and balanced on the swing with no hands, then grabbed one rope with both hands and jumped off the seat, hanging by his arms, smiling a pirate smile. He was Errol Flynn swinging on the rigging across the deck of a ship he was about to plunder. His feet touched the earth; he sat down and patted the empty swing next to him. "Come on, *ruka tan caliente,* plenty of room."

I ambled over, hiding my nervousness behind a slow saunter.

When I was near enough, he clasped my hips and dragged me toward him.

I could either fall face-first onto him or step over the sides of the seat. I stepped over the sides of the seat and sat down, straddling him. He leaned far back, stretching the ropes in his hands as he went, tugging me toward him until my chest rested against his, my face hovering above. A pocket of warmth rose up carrying the scent of beer and sweat, shaving cream and soap.

His arms were cables beside my head, straining to hold us both. I felt their intricate machinery work, pulleys lifting his head until his lips pressed against mine. His breath had the dense, smoky scent of marijuana, illicit and sweet. His tongue was delicate, a calligrapher's brush on my lips writing words there I had never spoken, thoughts I'd never thought that became in that instant the only words I ever again wanted to speak, the only thoughts I ever again wanted to think.

Any lingering suspicions that I might be a lesbian vanished entirely.

I leaned forward, avid for his taste. The instant I pursued, the muscles of his arms bunched as he strained hard, pulling back against the ropes. His legs surged beneath me and we were launched, soaring together toward the black velvet sky. My hair streamed over my shoulders, onto his face, as the wind rushed through it. The stars, brighter in the eclipse-darkened sky than they had ever been, spattered dopplered light across his face as we flew heavenward.

At the top of the swing's arc, we paused, then dropped back to earth. The direction of the pendulum reversed and it was my turn to look into the sky as we sailed up into the night. As I streaked upward, his body pressed down on mine. Above the lofted twirl of his hair, the bright stars blurred. My eye was drawn to the North Star, the one my father had shown me so that I could always find my way home. But like all the other stars, it had become a silver smear across the night sky rather than a fixed point.

He hauled back on the ropes, pumping his legs beneath us so that the swing rose as high above the earth as the long ropes would allow.

We swung back the other way. High at the top of the next arc, he let go and wrapped his arms around me. "Take the wheel, Lucille."

"No!" I shrieked, struggling to hang on as the swing wobbled beneath us. He laughed, heedless and wild. I barely managed to keep my hands clamped on the ropes as we plummeted down. Willfully oblivious to the danger that I would lose my grip while we were thirty feet in the air, he kissed my neck, drew me close. His lips, his tongue whispered a warmth into my ear that made me forget to breathe.

"Don't let go."

As the swing rocked his weight onto me, he grew hard, a surging that, though I had never felt it before, still seemed both familiar yet thrilling beyond anything I had ever dreamed.

Gradually, the swing lost altitude, ticking through a shorter and shorter arc until we sat swaying slightly, me, drained, gulping for breath, still clinging to the ropes to hold us upright, him, kissing my neck, sliding the strap of the camisole off my shoulder, covering my breast with his mouth. My arms drooped from the ropes and he held me tighter. His hand was under my skirt. Pushing my panties aside, he felt how wet I was and fumbled with his fly. He pushed into me, then stopped.

"You're a virgin?"

"I'm sorry."

"*You're* sorry? How can you be a virgin?"

"I don't want to be. It doesn't matter."

"Yeah, it does." He reached down and buttoned his fly. "Being a virgin is a big thing. A very big thing."

"Not to me."

He unhooked my legs from around his waist and stood us both up. "Well, to me it is."

"But I thought it was, like, some big male deal to, you know, deflower a virgin."

"You did, huh? Where are you getting your information? That friend of yours? The one in the parking lot?"

"Where are you going?"

"Taking you home."

I followed him out of the park. The perfumed air no longer smelled like a tropical rainstorm; it smelled like fabric softener from a dryer.

We walked in silence back to Lomas, then up the street to Carlisle where he stopped and looked around. "Which way you live?"

I pointed in a vague direction. "Off that way. But don't worry, you don't have to walk me home."

He didn't argue. "Okay, well, see you around."

With that, he strode off down Carlisle, toward the interstate. Car lights approached from a distance. He turned so that he was facing the lights, facing me, stuck his thumb out, and kept walking backward. The approaching car pulled over. It was a beat-up Toyota truck with a camper shell on the back covered with stickers from scenic wonders around the country. The driver yelled, "Where you headed, man?"

I ran closer so I could hear his answer. But all he said was, "Wherever you're going. I'm headed wherever you are."

"Throw your stuff in the back."

He opened the little door at the back of the camper and stowed his guitar there. When he pivoted around and found me standing on the sidewalk blocking his way, he seemed surprised. Neither one of us could think of anything to say. Actually, I wanted to say a thousand different things and every one of them was wrong. Mostly I wanted the night to start all over, to sit at his feet and listen to him play the guitar forever.

"Will I—" I started to ask the most wrong of all the wrong things: if I would see him again. He was already shaking his head no, telling me not to say the words.

He backed into the truck and slammed the door. Before he left, though, he rolled down the window and peered up at me. "You're trying to play out of your league, *chica*. It's going to get you in trouble." His voice softened and was kind as he added, "Just be who you are."

He turned away and the camper drove off. I watched until the taillights were specks of red that flashed when they turned onto the interstate, then disappeared.

Far overhead, the hidden moon slipped back into view, but the sun was already rising. Night was over.

Chapter Twelve

"Where the hell have you been?" Didi woke up when I was halfway through the window we'd "retrofitted" so we could come and go without encountering Catwoman. She blinked as if I were part of a dream she was having. "I thought you got arrested. What happened? Where did you go? Did you leave before the cops came? What time is it?" She grabbed the alarm clock on the floor beside her bed. "Shit, girl, it's five thirty in the a. of m. I've got to pee." Didi jumped out of bed and ran into the bathroom.

I plopped down on my bed. Everything in the Lair looked different. I'd wandered around for hours after he left, then tried not to wake Didi up when I finally got home. I was worried that one look at my face would tell her that I'd seen her and the cop last night. More than that, though, I wanted to keep last night, keep him, to myself. I wanted hours alone to remember every note he'd played and every word he'd spoken.

"Okay, details, details, details." Didi came back out, patting her washed face dry with a towel. A stretchy orange band held her hair off her wet face. She plopped down on her bed, grabbed a Pop Tart from the package sitting on the nightstand, and settled in as if she were taking a seat in a movie theater. The Pop Tart's white frosting was speckled with colored sprinkles like a kid's birthday cupcake. Didi liked sprinkles as they fit in with her philosophy of Eating Obstacles. A fanatical dieter, always just a lettuce leaf or two away from anorexia, Didi made herself eat things in segments as small as were feasible so that consumption of the edible item took as long as possible. She could make a taco last an hour, eating every shred of cheese, every nubbin of tomato individually. Sprinkles, of course, offered fantastic food-stretching opportunities.

Sitting cross-legged on her bed, plucking first the blue, then the red sprinkles off her Pop Tart, her hair skinned back, no makeup, Didi looked about eight years old. I thought she would seem different after what had happened last night, what I'd seen. But she looked exactly the same as always, exactly the way she had looked after dozens of other nights. The only thing different about last night was that no one famous was involved and I'd seen what usually only happened after I left. It didn't matter. Nothing mattered anymore except him.

"So? Tell," she prompted. "Where have you been until five-thirty in the morning, young lady? Huh?" She bounced her eyebrows lasciviously.

"Deeds, it wasn't like that." It wasn't like anything that had ever happened to Didi. She wouldn't understand.

"Like what?"

"Like that. All hubba-hubba, baby."

Tone. Like pygmies deep in the forest who can give a word a dozen different meanings just by the tone or pitch, Didi and I spoke a language of tones. One word, it didn't matter what the word was, everything depended on the tone in which we spoke it. From that we could deduce all the rest. She read my tone, put the Pop Tart down, and studied my face. In the silence that followed, I heard what sounded like game-show music but had to be whatever jazz album Mrs. Steinberg had just sold. It was interrupted by her computer making the scary ambulance noise her software used to alert her that one of her auctions was getting some play.

"Oh my God, you met someone." Instead of the mockery I would have expected, there was a whispered reverence. She did understand. I couldn't stop myself then, I nodded, and made a face, a grimace that encompassed the enormity of what had happened.

"Oh my God," she whispered again. "This is the real deal." Briskly, she brushed sprinkles off her hands as she got down to business. "All right, what's his name?"

Just Didi saying that pronoun, "his," was enough to make me feel as if she had invoked his presence, as if he were in the room with us. "I didn't . . . He didn't tell me."

Didi shrugged as if that were a small detail, an obstacle, like eating sprinkles in a color-coded sequence. "Okay, then, where does Mystery Man live?"

"I don't know."

"Phone number?"

"He didn't give it to me."

"No digits? Wow, this is going to take some serious reconnaissance. Recount your exact movements for me. You must have met him at the Ace High, right? Or did you leave as soon as we split up?"

I didn't like her questions. She was treating this like a groupie mission. But it wasn't. Next week, when Didi had forgotten about Julian Casablancas or whomever she was currently obsessed with, I would not have forgotten about him. Not next week or the week after or any of the weeks that would follow. "No, I met him there," I answered, adding lamely, "but we left. Before. The cops. Or whatever." I didn't want Didi to know I'd seen her. In the alley. With the cop.

She stared into my face again and I couldn't help myself. I remembered. Again, I saw the cop hauling her face to his crotch. I ducked her gaze. "Never mind. This isn't like a, you know, mission."

Tone. Tone never lied. Didi, insulted, bristled, "Well, then I can't help you."

She went to her computer and started writing an e-mail. I curled up with my back to her and replayed the entire night like a miser running her fingers through a chest filled with treasure. I saw the heart-shaped cottonwood leaves twirling down in the starlight, feathering across my face. I plotted the lines and curves of his face, noting that his nostrils were perfect teardrops. Thinking about him made something fizz beneath my bottom rib like a fuse sizzling that would soon detonate my heart. He was so enormous in my mind that I imagined I could look out the window and find him looming above the city bigger than Sandia Peak. I thought about the taillights disappearing in the distance as he headed off toward the interstate. I didn't know his name. He didn't know mine. Before last night, I could never have imagined someone like him in my life. Now I could not imagine living without him. I panicked. "Didi, please, you have to help me."

When she turned back around, she didn't look like a kid anymore. Early morning sun raked in the low window, settled on the hard planes of her face, and lighted what was behind the harshness: she knew I knew. "So you want him?"

Want him? Last night, it had seemed too much of a presumption to ask him his name. How could I say it? How could I say I wanted him?

"I want him."

"You really want him?"

"I really, really want him."

"This is the one?"

"This is the one."

"And you don't care what you have to do to get him?"

"I don't care what I have to do to get him." I answered automatically, but automatic wasn't good enough.

"You don't care what you have to do to get him, even if it's . . ."

For a sliver of a second, the defiance that I thought saturated Didi down to her bones disappeared. The image in her mind transferred itself to mine and I saw her kneeling in the perfect circle of her matador skirt spread on the black asphalt of the Ace High Motel parking lot. That image was a pact laid between us waiting for my acceptance. If I repeated her words, it would signal my agreement that nothing Didi did in the pursuit of her obsessions could be considered a humiliation. I thought of taillights disappearing and imagined that I would never see him again. That the rest of my life would be the way it had been before he laid my head against his guitar, before he swept me in a giant's swing up to the stars. I could not go back. I would do anything I had to not to go back to the life I would have without him.

"I don't care what I have to do," I said.

"Just for your information," Didi said, her eyes holding mine, "I'm not groupieing anymore. That part is over. I just wrote to all the Kumfort Gurlz, telling them I'm through. From now on it's going to be all about Didi. My music. My career."

"Good. That's good, Deeds. No more groupieing." *No more of what I'd seen last night.*

"Good?" she asked, offended. "It's great. It's way overdue. It's my turn. I've spent way too much of my life focusing on everyone but me. Madonna had a record contract by my age! Shit, this town sucks so bad. I am never going to get anything going unless I leave this hole. I have got to get out of here."

I figured that this would be the motif for a very long summer and was surprised when, just as suddenly as the black clouds had blown in, they lifted and Didi was all smiles again. She plopped back down on the bed, and even bounced slightly in a slumber party sort of way. "All right, this marks the official beginning of Operation Mystery Man. So? Details?"

I told her a chain of events but not how each link closed around the other. I gave her the prose version and kept the poetry for myself. I only slipped when she plucked up, by its stem, the cottonwood leaf that had fallen from my skirt.

"And what do we have here?" she asked.

I snatched it back but, before I could stop myself, burbled over. "It's from the most enormous tree you've ever seen. From this park that's hidden in the middle of this totally ordinary neighborhood."

"No! You have to take me to see it."

"If I could ever find it again. It was all dark and everything."

"Hey, Rae-rae, don't ever pursue a career in acting. You're the worst liar on earth. If you don't want me to see your precious park, just say so."

"It's not that." It was exactly that. I wished I had never mentioned the park. My park. Our park.

"Whatever. Anyway, what would you say his mental state was?"

Her cross-examination style reassured me. "He said last night was the worst night of his life."

"He give any reason why? Woman trouble? Money trouble?"

I knew it had to do with his music. With flamenco and having to be black to play the blues. But I didn't want to tell Didi that. I wanted to keep that for myself. "Not really."

"Okay, he played this amazing music for you. What was it? Classical? Jazz?" I shook my head no. "Don't tell me, not country? He's not some C and W asshole?"

"No."

"Well then, tell me. What kind of music does he play?"

"What does it matter?"

"We need to narrow the known world a little here. You do want me to find him, right?"

"Flamenco." As soon as I said the word, I regretted it. It felt like the one piece of treasure I should have hoarded. "He plays flamenco."

"Oh, that is too easy," Didi said. All she had to type in the search was *flamenco, guitarist,* and *New Mexico,* and a list of matches popped up. She brought up one after the other. I peeked over her shoulder as images flashed past of guitarists in puffy-sleeved shirts, guitarists in flat-brimmed hats, and guitarists in black suits with white shirts buttoned all the way up.

Suddenly the screen filled with his photo. It was the cover of his CD being sold on the site of a very obscure recording company. His head was bent over the neck of his guitar just as it had been the first time I'd seen him. Dark hair fell across his face, covering everything except his lips, his chin. I didn't need to see his entire face; I would have known him from his hands, the fingers long, the beds of the nails the tiniest bit blue against his brown skin. His hands seemed older than the rest of him. Not wrinkled or spotted but filled with knowledge the way very old people's faces are. They curled around the neck of the guitar, around the strings.

"Whoa," Didi said, impressed. "I hope this is Mystery Man."

I couldn't speak, just nodded.

"Major hottie." She ran a finger over his lips and spoke the name that appeared beneath the photo: "Tomás Montenegro." Didi's tongue expelled the first *T* as she pronounced his first name the correct way. She repeated it in her beautiful Spanish accent, giving it to me like a gift, "Tomás Montenegro." *Toe-mas Mon-tuh-nay-gro.*

Vowels. So many vowels. Toe-mas Mon-tuh-nay-gro. Toe-mas Mon-tuh-nay-gro. Toe-mas Mon-tuh-nay-gro. The syllables ricocheted around in my head with the same propulsive rhythm as his music, then settled into a whisper that played as ceaselessly as the prayers that cloistered nuns never stop saying.

The only other bits of information on the page were the name of his CD, *Santuario,* his birthday, August 23, and a number to call to order the CD. Didi immediately started punching the numbers into her cell. I grabbed the phone out of her hand. "What are you doing?"

She grabbed it back. "Don't spaz out. We'll probably just get a recording."

But as she dialed, the feel of his presence, of him watching me, mounted again until it was like spiders running up and down my neck. I was certain that the next sound I heard would be his voice. Didi held the phone out so I could listen to an automated message inform us that the number was no longer in service.

"Oh well." Didi shrugged, turning her attention back to the Pop Tart. "We'll really dive in after you sleep for a while."

The jangly excitement that had kept me hiking all over the city for the past few hours made me protest. "I won't be able to sleep. I'll never be able to sleep again."

Didi smiled indulgently, the wizened veteran amused by the new recruit's greenness. "That's what I thought after my first mission. Wow, we really are blood sisters now." She broke off a big chunk of Pop Tart and held it out in front of me until I folded my hands under my chin and stuck my tongue out. She placed the piece of Pop Tart on my tongue as if it were communion. Then, in a rare moment of unbridled consumption, she stuffed the rest into her mouth and chewed. We grinned at each other through a mouthful of tart mush. A few minutes might have passed after I swallowed, but I don't remember them. I only remember falling asleep with my mouth full of Pop Tart thinking that I'd never tasted anything so delicious in my life.

Chapter Thirteen

I woke to find Didi hard at work with her protractor and ruler. "I scoured the Internet," she said when she saw that my eyes were open. "But there is no other trace of Tomás Montenegro, flamenco guitarist, so we turn to the stars, right?"

Pausing only to consult various texts and mumble names of planets, houses, cusps, trines, triplicity, anaretic degrees and aspects, Didi drew circles surrounding smaller circles. These she filled with numbers followed by signs for degree, latitude, longitude, and all the houses of the zodiac. In the inner circle, she carefully drew lines in pink, brown, and green from one precisely marked point to another, all the while muttering things like "Sun position, eighteen degrees forty minutes of Scorpio." And "Mercury, twenty-nine degrees, forty-five minutes of Libra." At the top of the paper she'd written his name, Tomás Montenegro. I knew then how seriously she was taking my quest: she was throwing his chart.

As she finished mapping out Tomás's destiny, her jaw dropped. She turned to me. "This is the most fucking amazing thing I've ever seen in my entire life!"

I didn't usually listen to Didi's bulletins about the most fucking amazing things she'd ever seen in her entire life since she averaged roughly eighteen such sightings a day. But since this was Tomás, I jerked to attention. "What?"

"All the positions of his planets are exactly the same as Julie's." She meant Julian Casablancas of the Strokes. She shook her head in wonder as she studied Tomás's chart. "Wow, they're virtually identical."

"Tell me! Tell me!" I insisted, wide awake.

"Okay, okay. Let's see." She studied the arcs and transits. "Venus in Aries. Wow, that means he is an ardent and passionate lover." Didi wiggled her eyebrows at me. "I'm starting to see the attraction."

I shrugged, happy as always to participate in the fiction that I was a hot number. "What else? What else?" I wanted every clue Didi could extract from the stars or tea leaves or reading head bumps. I didn't care. All that mattered was the answer to the question, "How do I get him?"

"How do you get him?" Didi repeated as she drew her finger along the lines she had charted, the lines of his destiny that, I prayed, I would entangle with my own.

"Okay, here it is." Didi pointed to the mandala tangle in the inner circle. "His moon is in the tenth house, which means the guy has this constant struggle between security and doing the high-wire act that his talent demands." She looked up. "That's it. That is how you get him."

"What! What!? Quit being so vague! Tell me, tell me how I get him!"

"Chill, okay? Okay, you have to be both this total, total hot vamp and the big, plushy mama cooking up pots of posole or whatever. You know someone who will be sexy *and* totally take care of him."

I absorbed this information, soaking it right into my DNA, willing, anxious, no, ecstatic to change everything about myself to make it fit whatever template would be most likely to ensnare him.

"Oh God, look at his south node."

"What the fuck is a fucking south node?"

Didi's eyebrows jerked up at my language, at my forgetting our roles: she was the bad girl, I was the goody-goody sidekick. But already, in that very moment, I had begun turning myself inside out, reversing all my polarities, waiting to become whatever, whoever, would make him mine. I tried again. "The south node?"

"Essentially that's whatever tendencies he developed in past lives. The north node is what he's gotta work on in this life. Since they're one hundred and eighty degrees apart, they totally control his relationships. His work houses and his love houses are inseparable. Can't have one without the other. His work is who he is and who he's gonna fall in love with."

"What does that mean? Should I learn to play guitar?"

"God, no. Guitar guys do not like guitar chicks. And don't say Courtney Love cuz she plays for shit."

"What then?"

Before Didi could answer, the phone rang. My first thought was *It's him. How did he find me?* But it was only Alejandro wondering when we were coming in to work.

Outside, I was surprised both by how bright the world was, sizzling in the sunshine of an early summer morning, and by how new it was. Every cottonwood tree we passed flaunted the green hearts that told the world my secret. His presence was so strong that it felt as if he were in the car with us. As we cruised down Central Avenue, I could barely glance at the Aztec, the De Anza, and just the barest peek at the Ace High as we pulled into the parking lot of the Puppy made me feel as if I were going to throw up. I felt his eyes on me as I got out of the car and walked across the lot.

Ever since my mother left, Alejandro had let us eat before we started work. Since I'd moved in with Didi, I was always starving because there was never any food at her house. He had my favorite, blue corn enchiladas with green chile, all ready and waiting for me. But I couldn't look at them. The jangly excitement that had seized hold of me the instant I set eyes on Tomás clamped around my throat so tightly that I couldn't even think about food.

"Not hungry?" Didi asked, teasing as she picked sesame seeds off the bun of her Mexi-burger and popped them one by one into her mouth. "You are so going to waste away." Didi, mistress of the weirdo diet, was jealous that I wouldn't have to resort to any of her old standbys—laxatives, a finger down the throat. "You are so lucky. Puking rips hell out of the old tooth enamel." She tapped her front teeth, which she'd had to bleach after they'd turned slightly gray from years of frolics with reverse peristalsis.

"It's gonna be all right, *mija*," Alejandro said softly when he caught me pushing the enchiladas away. He had been even nicer than usual to me since my mother left. But that day, hearing him talking to me as if I were his daughter made me miss Daddy so much that tears I pushed back stung my eyes. I knew I wouldn't have told Daddy about Tomás if he were still alive, but it would have been nice to think that I could have.

Didi, who usually got mad at me when I was sad, surprised me that day by putting her arm around my shoulders and whispering in my ear, "He knows."

I didn't have time to ask her who she meant, Daddy or Tomás, because the dinger started chiming madly and my breath caught. Against all logic, I was certain it was him. Of course, it was one of Didi's disgruntled fan/customers running back and forth over the hose that made the dinger ring.

"Take it away, ladies," Alejandro said as he shoved open the back door to leave.

Didi was actually eating her burger, so I slid back the order window, told the driver, a middle-aged guy in a Dodge Ram truck, that Didi was busy, and tried to take the order he barked at me: "Three Mexi-meals, cut the onions, hold the cheese on one, two diet D.P.s, a chocolate shake, two orders of tater tots, extra pico." But his order slid through my mind as if he hadn't spoken. All the synapses I'd formerly used to tend to details were now devoted to Tomás. I was making the truck guy repeat his order when a maid at the Ace High across the street opened one of the motel's glass doors to shake a rag out on the balcony and a gold curtain flashed in the sunlight. My heart stopped and all I could do was stare, certain that he was about to step onto the balcony.

Didi gently pried the pad out of my frozen hand and took over for me. Which is exactly what she was doing when a perfectly restored old Jaguar XKE pulled in. Logically, I knew it couldn't be Tomás, but that didn't stop me from peeking over Didi's shoulder just to make sure. I saw everything that Didi did: the driver was in his mid-twenties, okay but far from great-looking, and obviously rich. He had CDs of Marilyn Manson, Lou Reed, the New York Dolls, and the Strokes spread across the passenger seat. We also noticed a travel mug with a Brown University logo and some suspicious scars on the inside of his left arm that brought a distant memory to mind of one of Sheriff Zigal's drug lectures back in Houdek and the word *tracks*. I'm sure that Didi, who was always several steps ahead of me, had already put all the symptoms together and diagnosed a bohemian preppy with motive and means enough to finance a walk on the wild side.

Didi leaned out the window until she was nearly close enough to lick his ear and asked, "You like the Strokes?"

The driver picked up the CD, shrugged, and tossed it aside. "They're okay." He was one of those guys who acts like he's handsome even though he isn't. Everything about him was too long: his face, his nose, his teeth, his long neck with its long Adam's apple. He looked as if he'd been held over a flame and melted. That didn't stop him from staring at Didi and licking his lips in a cheesy way like some jerk watching a stripper circling a pole. None of that seemed to bother Didi. "Depends who you're talking about. Julie can be kind of a prick. Al's not bad. Fabrizio. Well, what can I say about Fabs?"

"You know Julie and Fabs?"

He shrugged. "I went to boarding school with them in Switzerland."

He kept staring at Didi like he was about to ask for a lap dance, running his tongue around his lips. He held a cell phone up. He asked Didi, "You want to talk to him?"

"No! You can get Julie Casablancas on the phone?"

"Come with me and find out."

As Didi looked at me, considering, he yelled out, "And bring a couple orders of taquitos to go!"

"I thought you were through with—"

Didi cut me off. "This isn't a mission. He's not famous." She smiled. "He just knows famous people." She handed me the order pad. "You've got Mystery Man now. Maybe it's time for me to see what's out there."

By the time Didi was out the door, the guy had cleared away the CDs so she could occupy the passenger seat.

"Didi!" I yelled and she stopped for a moment as she was getting in the Jag. Then I didn't know what to say. *Be careful?* Of what? Didi had negotiated much worse situations. She jumped into the car and was gone before I knew what I wanted to tell her.

She came home that night very late, giddy as a game-show contestant who's just picked the right curtain. She threw her arms around me. "I love you. God, I love you. I know you love Mystery Man best now, but I still love you best."

She was high. Extremely high. "What did that guy give you?"

" 'That guy'? His name is Paco."

That sounded affected to me since he was such a WASP.

"Oh, Rae-rae, you will love Paco and he will love you." Didi dragged out her big duffel with wheels, opened drawers, and stuffed whatever she scooped out into the bag.

"What are you doing? Are you going somewhere?"

"God, I sure the hell hope so." She laughed the way really stoned people laugh when they think they're in on a joke that the straight world will never get. She yanked open a drawer and shoveled bras and panties into the bag.

"Didi," I said sternly, "where are you going right now?"

"To camp!" she declared brightly as if that were the punch line to her special stoned-people joke. "A special camp in New York where I'll get merit badges in schmoozing, seeing, and being seen, and"—Didi had to pause for a full laugh attack—"using people on my way up!"

"Didi, really, where are you going?"

"New York. Can you believe it? Paco went to that same ritzy school in Switzerland as Julian Casablancas did! They smoked hash together! Or, well, actually, Paco's cousin did." Didi always had a fine disregard for degrees of separation. "But the important thing is Paco is way connected in the whole New York glam-revival scene and—best part!—he lovelove-loves my music."

"Your music?"

"The stuff I've been working on. I haven't written much down. It's mostly in my head. I told Paco my influences and he totally gets it. What? Did you think I was going to be a groupie my whole life?"

A horn honked outside. "Oops, Pock said if I wasn't back in five minutes, I would have to travel naked." Didi dragged the bag toward the door like a giant black dog on a leash.

I jumped up and grabbed her. "Didi, you're not going anywhere. You're stoned."

She let the leash drop. The bag fell to the floor and with it any hint that she might be high. She suddenly seemed more sober than I'd ever seen her. "I'm not leaving because I'm high. Rae, I got high so I could leave. I couldn't do this straight and I have to. I have to leave. School is out, baby. What could possibly, in a million years, happen to me that would be worse than spending the next three months sweating like a piece of old cheese in that grease trap?"

"But Didi, you don't know anything about this guy."

"Quit calling him 'this guy.' I didn't call Tomás 'this guy.' And I know everything I need to know about him. I know he's rich, I know he's connected, and I know"—she held up her pinkie and leaned in close to me—"I can wrap him around this. And that is a hell of a lot more than you know about Mystery Man, and tell me you wouldn't leave me for him in a heartbeat."

"Didi, I'm not leaving you. I'd never leave you."

She laughed as if the whole conversation had been a joke and I was stupid to have fallen for it. "Jeez, Rae, don't lez out on me. Here." She tossed me the keys to the Mustang. "Keep the battery charged."

"Didi, no. You haven't even told your mom. Didi, you can't just leave like this!"

But she was already out the door.

A few hours later, while I was debating whether to tell Mrs. Steinberg or just call highway patrol myself, Didi called on Paco's cell phone. She was singing, "'Would you get hip to this kindly tip?'"

I knew right off that I was supposed to sing back, "'Get your kicks on Route 66!' Deeds, you're taking Route 66!"

"As far as we can!"

"Are you okay?"

"Okay? This is how I want to live the rest of my life."

"I miss you."

"Can you hear me, because I can't hear you!"

"I said I miss you. I really miss you!" But the call had already ended in a crackle of static.

The next call came around two that morning. I was on Didi's computer, reading everything I could find on flamenco. She was singing, "'Cadillac, Cadillac. Long and dark, shiny and black,'" when I answered.

I sang back, "'Don't let 'em take me to the Cadillac Ranch!'"

"Ooo, girl knows her Boss."

"You're at the Cadillac Ranch?"

"At this very moment, Paco is spray-painting a giant white circle on top of all the graffiti so we can put the title of my first CD up there: DIDI'S CD. Isn't that perfect? A really good friend of Paco's does the cover art for the Strokes. Paco already called him and the guy is pumped to do my cover. Oh, he finished. I want to put the title up there while it's still wet so it'll run. Bye!"

I knew they'd detoured when she called a few days later and sang a question, "I'm going to—?"

"'Graceland! Graceland! Memphis, Tennessee!'" I sang back. "You got off of Route 66."

"Had to come and pay our respects to the King, right? But, God, Graceland is so small, you wouldn't believe it. And tacky? What's the point of being an icon if this is all you're going to do with it? Oh, Paco is waving for me. He's doing a series of me in front of Japanese tourists."

Didi forgot to turn the phone off and I heard Paco pretending that Didi was famous and they were on an important photo shoot. By the time the battery went dead the Japanese tourists were asking Didi for her autograph.

The next day, I visited every record store listed in the Yellow Pages: Borders, Music Mart, Hastings, Wherehouse. None of them carried

Tomás's CD, *Santuario*. There was only one shop left on my list, Onomatopoeia Records, an indie on Central. I didn't usually have the nerve to enter Onomatopoeia alone since the guys who worked there had a withering sense of superiority they used to shrivel anyone caught buying uncool music. With Didi, I was fine since she was cool enough for two people, but on my own it took an act of courage.

Inside the front door was a bulletin board blanketed with flyers for concerts and ads for henna tattooing, piercing, and a band seeking "Bass player into neo-funk." I pretended to be interested in an ad for "body modification" and wished Didi were with me as I sneaked peeks at the store, searching for a bin labeled FLAMENCO. I couldn't see one and tried to slip in unnoticed, but the clerk, a chunky guy with tattooed calves peeking out from beneath long homeboy shorts that held a wallet on a long chain, immediately lumbered over. "Need some help?" he asked, his attention on reordering the old vinyl records in the bin next to me.

I could not imagine saying *Santuario* out loud, much less uttering Tomás's name, so I shrugged and answered, "Just looking."

I guess the clerk didn't get many just browsers because he snorted and said, "Whatever," leaving me to search through all the bins that I thought might apply: Guitar. Instrumental. Latin.

I was about to give up when the clerk appeared beside me again. "Sarah McLachlan, Liz Phair, Indigo Girls, Lisa Loeb." He pointed down the aisle. "I've got them all quarantined over there in a special Lilith Fair section I just created."

"I'm not looking for them."

The clerk made a face at me to express both disbelief and disgust.

"I'm not," I protested. "I'm looking for *Santuario,* by—"

"Tomás Montenegro. Put out by the now-defunct Kokopelli label. They went belly-up before the release. No promotion. Underground hit among the dozen or so aficionados who managed to snag a copy before the IRS seized everything. Not my cup of tea but a very tasty product. I've got one copy over in . . ." He went to a bin labeled WORLD MUSIC and pulled out Tomás's CD.

Once I had it, I was glad that Didi wasn't around. She would have yanked it out of my hand and thrown it into the player in her car just as if it were any old CD. I rushed back to the Lair and didn't even take the wrapping off until I was ready. I wondered if he might have touched that very CD. Maybe he'd delivered it to the store personally. The moment was so private that I couldn't even bring myself to play it over the speakers. I clapped Mr. Steinberg's old headphones on and carefully placed the shimmering disc on the player. Every click and whir was magnified. My heart was racing by the time the sound of his fingers on guitar strings reached my ears. The instant it did, I was back at the Ace High, my head against his guitar as he fed rhythm and passion, mastery and excess directly into my brain.

Since listening to *Santuario* and daydreaming about Tomás took all my energy, I had none left over to find a better summer job than working at Puppy Taco. So when Alejandro, who'd opened a new location across town, offered me the manager spot, I took it. Unfortunately, the only interest I had in the Puppy Taco anymore was that it was across the street from the Ace High. All I did for entire days, long, hot days when the sun turned the stand into an oven, was stare at the motel and recall every second of The Night. I took out each moment I'd spent with Tomás as if it were a jewel on a black velvet tray and examined it from every angle. I replayed each word we'd exchanged, wringing a semiotician's range of meaning from every utterance. I felt his presence constantly. He was the invisible audience for which I played my life. I searched all the cars that pulled in, stupidly expecting to see his face. I lost my ability to juggle five orders at a time and calculate tax in my head. Alejandro assumed it was because Didi had left, and he didn't fire me. I was grateful for his patience and for my paycheck since it had been months since my mother had sent me anything from HeartLand HomeTown other than prayers and predictions of how badly I would suffer in the next life unless I accepted Jesus.

With Didi gone, I got homesick and even started to miss my mom a little. But it was Daddy I really missed. I wanted to talk to him, to tell him about Tomás even though I knew that, if he were still alive, I never would have breathed a word to him. Didi always said that you got through the tough times with distraction. Fortunately, for the first time in my life, I had a distraction powerful enough to wash everything, even missing Daddy and Didi, out of my mind. I bought some guitar strings and rubbed them until my fingers smelled like his; that scent alone was enough to block out any other thought for at least an hour.

But the best distraction ever invented was flamenco. I played Tomás's CD night and day. During the day, I listened to it on my player while I fried burgers or hauled tater tots out of hot grease. At night, I cranked it on Mr. Steinberg's old stereo while I surfed the Internet reading everything that popped up when I entered *flamenco*. I haunted the library, checked out the few books they had that mentioned flamenco, and ordered all the rest.

It took almost a week for Mrs. Steinberg to notice that her daughter was gone. She accosted me as I left for work, "Where Didi?" Her once-beautiful Natalie Wood face was puffy and perfectly outlined by a seam of gray at the base of her overpermed, dyed-black hair.

"She's gone to this sort of music camp?" I didn't know how much she understood or how much I could improvise, so I embellished with some feeble hand gestures somehow meant to convey *music* and *camp*. "To learn how to write songs and sing songs and do all the things that a rock star does." I tried to translate as much as I could into Spanish, but I doubted that *campo* meant "camp."

"With boy in Jaguar?" It took me a minute to realize what she'd said since she pronounced Jaguar the Spanish way, *hag-wahr.*

"Paco? Right. He's going to the camp too. He gave Didi a ride."

Mrs. Steinberg bunched her eyebrows together, increasing her resemblance to a Pekinese dog. Then she said something in Spanish that even I could understand: *"No se llama Didi. Se llama Rachel."* Mrs. Steinberg pronounced it the Jewish way, Rah-hel.

I repeated it in English, mostly so I could hear it myself and understand. "Didi's name is not Didi, it's Rachel?"

Mrs. Steinberg nodded vigorously, so pleased by our exchange that she ventured a bit more English. "Yes, father say Rachel but Rachel not good name of star. Not famous people's name. Didi good name of star. Since little little girl she only want to be star. You good friend. You be good friend, okay?"

I nodded. "Yes, okay."

Mrs. Steinberg's computer dinged loudly. She nodded and left.

The heat that summer broke records that had stood for a hundred years. The ravens, disoriented by thirst, came down from the mountains to seek out sprinklers. But the city started water rationing and soon no sprinklers were allowed. Lawns turned crispy and brown. Raven bodies appeared in the gutter. I felt insulated inside a bubble where heat waves, sound waves, and my obsession made the world around me wobbly and out of focus. Only the memories of the night I had met him and dreams of when I would meet him again remained Arctic sharp.

I passed the hours at work in a fog that lifted the second I stepped back into the Lair and worked feverishly on my strategy. Didi would have directed a frontal attack. We'd have tracked Tomás down and laid siege as if he were an ordinary groupie target. That was unthinkable. From the very beginning I wanted only one of two things: Either I wanted to worship him from afar and never speak to him again, leaving the memory of our night together the one, shining moment in my life. Or I wanted to own him. I wanted us to spend every second of the rest of our lives together, then be buried in the same coffin.

That meant that I would never see Tomás again, never allow him to see me, until I had transformed myself into the woman he could love.

I decided on a three-pronged attack. First was body modification. I had to completely change the way I looked. Fortunately, between the jangly excitement that kept my stomach sealed and the lack of edibles at Didi's house, weight loss took care of itself. The jittery excitement fueled marathon exercise sessions. I bought every workout video on the market and did them all, marveling at how my bread pudding of a body firmed up into a solid new consistency.

His work houses and his love houses are inseparable. Can't have one without the other. His work is who he is and who he's gonna fall in love with. I knew Didi was more right about that astrological projection than she could have ever dreamed. The path to his heart was through his work. In order to transform myself into the woman he would love forever, I had to learn everything I could about what he loved most, flamenco. Obviously that involved learning Spanish.

Third, I had to learn everything I could about Tomás.

Only after I had accomplished all three things would I even attempt to find him. Maybe most people, certainly Didi, would have moved the last element up. But like most people, Didi would have missed the point. I did not want to see Tomás, did not want him to see me again, until I was ready, until I had transformed myself into the person he would fall in love with. There would simply be no point in ever seeing him again if I wasn't that person.

I bought a set of Spanish-language tapes and managed to tear myself away from *Santuario* long enough to play them. The teacher would say, "*El libro,*" and I would imagine handing Tomás a book so dazzling it would change his life and make him swoon at my feet. I said, "*La pluma,*" and imagined saving Tomás's life with the click of a Bic.

I sought out Didi's mom for help with pronunciation. She was delighted that I was learning Spanish. As a teacher, speaking in her native language, Mrs. Steinberg was a different person, a surprisingly chatty person. She laughed in a good-natured way at my pronunciation, then chattered away at me in Spanish. I couldn't understand most of what she was saying. But since she was usually blasted, it didn't really matter. We were both blotto, really, she on frozen margaritas, me on Tomás. It was enough to build a friendship on. That and we both missed Didi.

Flamenco wasn't like anything I had ever studied before. Through Interlibrary Loan, I borrowed all of Carlos Saura's flamenco movies on videotape. Flamenco dance was a revelation. All the wild, inexplicable, irrational, undeniable emotions roiling inside me were there, splashed across the screen as vivid as a painting of my interior landscape. *Carmen* was my favorite. Platoons of dancers surged through it, stampeding ferociously across wooden floors, driven by flamenco's beat. It was like seeing my heart choreographed. I watched *Carmen* so many times that streaks began to appear where the tape became demagnetized.

Over and over, I listened to Antonio Gades, the ravishing dancer who played the director of the dance company staging a flamenco version of Bizet's opera, as he coached his student, the succulent Laura del Sol. "Your arm should rise smoothly and meaningfully. The hips must be detached from the waist. The breasts are like a bull's horns, warm yet soft. Heads up . . . a princely posture." I put Tomás in Antonio's place, molding my arms, my hips, my breasts into the perfect receptacle for his art. For him.

Everything I learned showed me how much I didn't know. All of flamenco was written in code, secret rhythms that could be read only by Gypsies and Spaniards. What I didn't learn in all my research was how a blond, blue-eyed Texan Czech living in Albuquerque, New Mexico, could ever break into this secret world. I perused the Yellow Pages under DANCE STUDIOS and found one that offered flamenco lessons. But when I called, the instructor had a Southern accent and two names just like me: she could never guide me into any world Tomás inhabited. I knew I would never get any farther in my quest in New Mexico. I was calculating how many years I'd need to put in at Puppy Taco to save enough to study in Spain when the Mustang died and I had to have it towed to a service station. While I waited for a new battery to be installed, I picked up a week-old copy of the *Albuquerque Journal*. Of course, Catwoman didn't have a subscription to the local paper. If she had, I might have already known that the answer to my prayer was in my own backyard. I found that answer in an article that read:

> In a sun-drenched studio in a gymnasium on the UNM campus an instructor's dark ringlets bounce tempestuously as she stamps her feet in front of two dozen students. No, she's not throwing a temper tantrum. Alma Hernandez-Luna is demonstrating flamenco footwork, or *zapateado*.
>
> "Bodies up, eyes forward," the energetic Albuquerque native commands, clapping her hands rhythmically. "Heel! Heel!" she commands. "Heel! Heel!" again, like some mantra. Finally, the magic words: "*Muy bien! Muy bien!* Olé! Olé!"
>
> Though Hernandez-Luna, 38, is the energetic director of the only university-level flamenco program in the world, she is quick to divert all credit to Carlota Anaya, who founded the program eighteen years ago. Though Anaya, contacted at her Santa Fe home, was unavailable for comment due to poor health, Hernandez-Luna maintains that "Doña Carlota is our goddess. She is the real thing. Born in Andalusia—some say seventy, some say eighty years ago, who knows? With someone of her vitality age is irrelevant. What is relevant is that both her parents were full-blooded Gypsies immersed in *el arte*, in the art and lifestyle of flamenco. Sadly, a lifetime of dancing has taken its toll and she was forced to retire and stop teaching ten years ago. But her true Gypsy spirit lives on here. In the program she established." The lithe and vibrant Hernandez-Luna stretches her arms out to encompass the studio filled with dancers stamping furiously.
>
> Although the program is widely known in the world of flamenco, enrolling students from all over the country and around the world, it has been a well-kept secret in its hometown. That is all about to change.
>
> "Doña Carlota's modesty has always prevented her from granting interviews and allowing us to do any sort of publicity. She has recently had a change of heart and has agreed to our christening the dance hall the Doña Carlota Anaya Flamenco Academy and doing more promotion outside of the flamenco community. So from now on, the rest of the world will know what we've always known, that the University of New Mexico has a world-class flamenco program and we owe it all to the amazing Doña Carlota Anaya."

When Didi came home a week later, she had crabs, borderline malnutrition, and a demo of her songs. I had a plan. "I'm going to study flamenco at the university."

"Oh yeah, right," she mumbled, struggling against exhaustion to remember. "Flamingo. Mystery Man. Cool." She dragged her eyelids up one last time and took me in. "You got buff. You look hot." Then her eyes dropped shut and she slept for three days straight.

Chapter Fourteen

Didi could barely rouse herself to chug down the smoothies I brought before plunging back into a state that resembled a coma. I was seriously worried. Worried that she was sick or that something traumatic had happened in New York. When she finally woke up, she wasn't sick, but that didn't stop me from treating her as if she were. I bought actual groceries and made scrambled eggs and toast that I put on a tray with a flower and brought to her in bed. I imagined the heinous things that might have happened in New York and kicked myself for ever letting her leave in the first place. Obviously, Paco had broken her heart. I tried, in very subtle ways, to bring him up by asking variations of the question, "So, how was New York?"

Didi didn't have much to say about New York. Not that it was good or bad. The most she would say was, "New York was useful and, for the moment, New York is over."

I thought that falling in love would have matured me, made me closer to Didi's equal. But switching from obsessing about famous people to obsessing about becoming one herself had changed Didi even more than meeting Tomás had changed me, so she was still quantum leaps ahead of me. While she lolled around in bed, getting her strength back, she plotted out how to merchandise the CD Paco had helped her make. It had great cover art. The title, *CD-DiDi,* was printed over a blurry close-up of her mouth. There was never a moment when she slipped the disc into the player for the first time, stepped back, and asked me what I thought. She was playing it when she walked back in the door and never stopped. Maybe it was just assumed that I'd think it was phenomenal, amazing. Maybe the CD was like Didi herself, and it didn't matter what anyone thought—she was going to be who she was going to be and do what she needed to do, whether you liked it or not, so why bother asking?

Was it good? I guess I would say that her songs, her voice, were, like Didi, an acquired taste. Who knew if her voice was good or bad? Did Courtney Love have a good voice? Did Bob Dylan? It didn't matter; the CD stood out, made an impact. It was Didi, it was unforgettable, and her life was now devoted to making it a success.

"Celebrity blurbs," she announced, grabbing a clipboard to make notes in bed. "I've got to get the CD to the ultimate killer celebs so they can give great quotes to use in the press release I send to radio stations." She started scribbling names furiously. The first on the list was Julian Casablancas.

Maybe because I was so in love, I just couldn't give up the idea that Didi had had her heart broken and was burying the pain. I was Didi's support person, that was my job, and I wasn't doing it. Which is why I asked, in as casual a way as possible, "What about Paco?"

She looked up from circling and underlining *Alanis Morissette* and gave me a blank stare as if she didn't recognize the name I'd just spoken.

"Paco?" I repeated. "What about him?"

"Oh, Paco." It took her a second to remember who I was talking about. "He's not a celebrity," she answered, thinking I was suggesting him for her blurb list. Her attention shifted to scribbling *Natalie Merchant!!*

I studied her face for signs of buried heartbreak. "Yeah, but I just thought—"

Didi slapped her pen down against the clipboard and peered up at me. "You just thought, for the one hundredth time, that you'd bring up Paco or New York, which is the same thing as bringing up Paco."

"Not the hundredth." Was it that many? "I'm just curious."

"You think I'm all hiding a deep, dark secret or something. Why do people always think there has to be some deep, dark, hidden secret? I got exactly what I could from New York and exactly what I could from Paco and now it's"—she swooped her hand across her face as if she were brushing away a bad smell—"next."

"Oh. Okay."

For a second, she teetered on the edge of being truly annoyed, then backed away. She sighed and said, "Thanks, Rae. Thanks for being the one person in the whole goddamn world who gives a shit."

"Deeds, Catwoman actually—"

"Catwoman is actually who she is. Catwoman gives exactly what she can."

"Didi, she really loves you. We talked a lot while you were gone."

"You talked to Catwoman?" She said it as if I'd betrayed her.

"She was helping me learn Spanish."

"Learning Spanish with Catwoman?" She winced at the impossibility of the concept, started to say something, stopped, and said instead, "You want to know my deep, dark secret?" She patted the edge of the bed and I sat down next to her.

I nodded. "Sure, Deeds. Of course. You know you can tell me anything. Everything."

Tears welled up in her eyes. She dropped her gaze. I scooted closer to her and took her hand. It was icy cold. I couldn't breathe. This was worse than I'd feared. Nothing cowed Didi Steinberg. Nothing made her cry. Whatever it was, I'd help her. It was my fault. Somehow I should have stopped her from leaving.

"Okay." Her voice trembled. "Okay, here's my deep, dark secret." I examined the veins above the icy hand I held, trying to warm it with mine. "My deep, dark secret is . . ."

As I was trying to think of one single adult I could call to ask for help when this turned out to be worse than even I could handle, Didi jerked her hand away, and snapped, "There is no deep, dark secret. A total lack of secrets is my secret. Okay? So, can we, please, just drop it?"

That was the last time we talked about New York. I assumed that it wasn't the crowning triumph she'd dreamed it might be, but whatever happened had only fueled her ambition and done a surprising thing: she returned open to the idea of going to the university with me. All she would say on the subject was, "Even Madonna did a few semesters."

I handled all the paperwork so she could register late. Naturally, the first course I enrolled in was Beginning Flamenco Dance. I was pleased that the instructor listed in the course catalog was going to be Alma Hernandez-Luna, the young and vibrant director of the program I'd read about in the paper. Then, since we both knew that the downfall of most great stars was corrupt or inept management, I signed on as a business major and added Intro to Financial Accounting to my course load so I could keep Didi's books when she was a star. Didi's schedule for the first three semesters included Movement for Actors, Voice for Actors, Speech and Diction, and Acting for the Camera. "Important for the videos," she explained.

"No music classes?" I asked. "Voice? Composition? Stuff like that?"

"Uh, how many *music* courses did Madonna ever take?"

"None?"

"Correctomundo."

I didn't remind her that Madonna had been a dance major. Dance, that was going to be my thing.

A week later, on the morning of our first day of classes, I was so nervous about going to the flamenco class I could barely breathe. "Is this better?" I asked Didi, holding a baby tee against my chest. "Or this?" I held up the camisole I'd worn when I'd met him. "Except, he's already seen me in it."

"Shit, you've got it bad. You actually think he's going to be there, don't you?" She shook her head hard as if it were an Etch A Sketch with a bad picture on it. "He's not going to be in a beginning flamingo dance class." She always said "flamingo" or "the big pink bird." Half the time, she was teasing me to keep me from being so intense. The other half, she just forgot. That was fine with me. Flamenco was the one part of Tomás I could possess and I wanted to keep it all to myself.

Didi studied me as I sorted through the pile of tops I was trying on and discarding, then trying on again. "Do you spend all day imagining he's watching you? In spite of the fact that he doesn't know your name or where you live, every time you step out of the house, do you think he'll be there? Every time the phone rings, do you think it's him?"

I didn't have to say anything. Just from the look on my face, she knew she was right.

"Wow. Okay, it's official. You're obsessed."

It was like hearing a doctor say you had measles when your body was covered with a red rash. The evidence was so obvious, there was no point in denying it.

"Don't worry. I was exactly the same with Julie. Back when I was into that. You probably feel like Mystery Man's here right now, invisibly watching and hearing everything you say."

I tugged off the camisole, letting it hide my face. I would never wash it. It had his smell on it mingled with mine. Together they made a new odor, sharp and feral. I didn't want to talk to her about Tomás, didn't want her to put him on the same level with any of her groupie conquests.

"Hey, aren't you supposed to wear a polka-dotted dress or something?"

"No, you're not supposed to wear a polka-dotted dress." My irritated tone objected to her mockery.

"Rae-rae, come on. Sit down. Let's make you beautiful." She dragged out the tackle box she used to hold her makeup, stair-stepped it open, and, holding up a lip brush, waited for me to sit. It had been a long time since we'd done makeovers on each other. She patted the bed and I plopped down.

"Do like this," she ordered, stretching her lips over her teeth. I mimicked the posture and Didi leaned forward, breathing coffee and Pop Tart breath into my face as she outlined my lips with a brush, then painted them the color of garnets.

"Sorry. I didn't think you were still so crushed out."

"Didi, I do know that he's not going to see me."

"That is so not the point, is it?"

She picked up her mascara wand and ordered, "Up."

I rolled my eyeballs heavenward so she could brush mascara on my bottom lashes.

"Keep looking up. I'm gonna put some white on the lower lid. Opens the eye up and makes the whites really pop."

Didi's ministrations calmed me. She spangled my cheeks with pink comet's tails glittering with crushed mother-of-pearl, my lips with the sparkle of a metallic bronze, and my eyes with glimmering lilac shadow. She burnished and glossed me until my face was a reflective surface, a mirror, in which Tomás Montenegro could see whatever he liked.

Didi stepped back and studied me, tilting her head from side to side, closing one eye then the other. She finally shrugged, said, "What can I say? I'm a genius," and handed me a mirror. In it I saw that Didi had transformed me into what I most desired to become: an offering.

Chapter Fifteen

The drive to campus was stiflingly hot. The once-regal 'Stang was a battered wreck, its AC a memory. Didi cracked the windows enough to let a little air stream in but not enough to mess with hair or makeup.

By the time we found a parking spot at the edge of campus on Central and Girard, we were late. We ran across the soccer fields outside Johnson Gym, hurrying to the student mall shaded by locust trees in giant planters, their dark, spiraling seedpods drying in the sun.

"Slow down!" Didi ordered as we reached the mall. "You're sweating. You're gonna ruin my cosmetic masterpiece."

We rushed by the student union building. Students sat outside at concrete tables sipping coffee and reading the college paper, the *Daily Lobo*. We were sweating by the time we passed Zimmerman Library. At the pond in front of the old library, a little boy in a yellow T-shirt shrieked. His mother scooped him up as a squad of ducks waddled menacingly toward him and the plastic bag of old bread he clutched in his chubby hand.

"Cut through Hitler and Eva Together Forever!" Didi yelled out her name for the fifty-foot-long, intersecting concrete tunnels that had been fobbed off on the university as art. No one liked the monolithic structure except the stoners who hid out inside the tunnels to sell dope and get high. We stopped at our traditional spot, right in the center where the two main tunnels met. The concrete was thick as a bunker. It was tomblike in the center; sound was deadened and the air was always damp. Didi sniffed. "Smells like we're too late." As usual, the tunnels reeked of pot.

"Okay." She pointed one index finger toward one of the four openings at the end of a tunnel and the other toward another opening. "You go to your flamenco class and I'll go check out"—she perused her schedule until she found her first class—"Acting for the Camera." She shook her hair back, flared her nostrils, then froze in a dramatic pose and said, "Mr. DeMille, I'm ready for my close-up." She unfroze. "We'll meet back here at burrito-thirty and grab some lunch at Frontier."

From somewhere outside the bunker, the sound of a guitar being played echoed in. As she turned to leave, I grabbed her arm. "Listen." Didi paused as the music wafted into the tunnel. "What if that's him?"

The playing was rough and amateurish. "Rae, if that's him, I'd say he's a pretty shitty guitarist. Don't worry, he's not here. That's some student practicing. Okay?"

I nodded.

"Rae-rae, you're not breathing."

"Deeds, I can't do it. I can't go out there."

"Then you'll never get him."

"Then I'll never get him."

"You mean you're not even going to try?"

"I can't. I just can't."

"Even knowing that he's not going to be in that class."

"It's not a logic thing."

"Whoa! Whoa! I'm the last person in the world who is going to insist something has to be logical. Logical shit is easy. It's the illogical shit that controls our lives."

"I can't. I can't do any of this. I'll just wait for you at Frontier." I started to walk out the opposite tunnel.

"Rae, come on. I'll go with you."

I stopped. I didn't really want Didi to go to the class with me, didn't want to share it with her. But I would never walk into the class by myself. "Just to walk in the door?"

"Sure. Walking in the door is always the hardest part. Then you're on your own, though, okay? The big pink bird thing is your perverted fantasy. I have enough of my own to keep track of. Deal?"

"Deal."

The Flamenco Academy was a recent addition to the back of Carlisle Gym, a two-story Pueblo-style adobe building painted a soft fawn. Didi pushed through the turquoise blue front door and I followed. The old gym looked like opening night of a Broadway musical. Dancers from tap, jazz, and African classes crowded the main hallway, changing into practice skirts, slugging down water, putting on makeup, and taping their gnarly, wrecked feet. The place smelled of decades of girl sweat and hair spray.

"Jazz hands! Jazz hands!" Didi whispered to me, waggling her fingers beside her head in a cheesy dance move. Although she was mocking the frenzy of activity, I could hear the thrill she was hiding behind the fake cynicism. Didi grabbed my course schedule out of my hand and read, "Studio 110. Instructor Alma Hernandez-Luna. Let's try that way."

Black wrought iron curled out the words THE DOÑA CARLOTA ANAYA FLAMENCO ACADEMY above a set of carved wooden doors so new they still smelled of varnish. Didi shoved them open and we found a larger-than-life-size oil portrait of a flamenco dancer staring down imperiously at us. She looked like a silent-movie star, a dark-eyed vamp from the twenties or thirties wearing a flat-crowned black hat with a veil of pom-poms ringing the crown, spit curl plastered to her cheek. I assumed this was the legendary founder of UNM's flamenco program, Doña Carlota. Even in the two dimensions of a portrait, she seemed ready to explode into motion. Back arched regally, her bosom heaved against the tight, scarlet fabric of her dress. A ruffled train cascaded off the back of the dress. The front of the dress was cut up high to reveal strong, muscled legs. Her ferocious gaze challenged my right to be there. I did not belong.

Dancers from the advanced classes, almost all Latina, rushed past us. Slender inkbrush ripples in their long, dark skirts, their long, dark hair; they belonged in a flamenco academy. As their skirts brushed against the polished floor, they strode forward with the single-minded devotion of novitiate nuns hurrying to chapel. As with Didi, if you'd taken a picture of any one of those girls, then looked at the negative of that photo, the exact reverse of all things flamenco, you would have seen my broad, pale Czech face, the evidence that, not terribly far back in my genetic lineup, there were generations of dozy, strawberry blond milkmaids, all pale as steam. I felt fraudulent. I was a support person. What the hell was I doing here even considering taking a dance class? I'd never taken a dance class in my life. All I wanted at that moment was to leave. I imagined the safety of an accounting class. Of being hidden in the last row, letting strings of numbers soothe the jittery anxiety scraping every nerve in my body. I would have left, but Didi was already heading down the long hall, searching for the right number.

She pushed through the chaos and I followed her to studio 110. "So, here you are." When I didn't move, Didi shook her head like an exasperated yet amused mother. "Rae, you have that scared-shitless look." She grabbed my arm and dragged me into the studio. "See? No Mystery Man."

I glanced quickly around the studio, found it completely populated by females, and started breathing again. The studio smelled new, untouched. High windows flooded the big room with morning sunlight that refracted off mirrors covering the walls. Brand-new wooden floors gleamed like a lake of honey. It was the most beautiful room I'd ever entered.

"Oh Jesus, look, ballet swans." Didi pointed a surreptitious finger at a clutch of girls in a far corner. Years of ballet training were obvious in the way they stood with their toes turned out like ducks. They had their hair skinned into ballet buns at the back of heads that wobbled atop freakishly elongated necks. The swans hooked pointed feet over the barre that ran the length of the room and folded themselves into the sort of stretches favored by Hindu yogis and serious dancers.

Didi nodded her chin toward another group of obviously experienced students and did jazz hands to identify their subtype. The jazz dancers performed scary head rolls, whipping their skulls around on rubberized necks. It all looked intimidatingly professional. I started to panic.

Didi shook her head. "I thought you said this was a beginner's class."

"It's supposed to be." The incipient panic broke into a full gallop and I started to turn. Didi grabbed me.

"Where are you going?"

"I can't stay."

"The hell you can't. No one runs my girl off. Especially not a bunch of binge-purge princesses like this pack here." With that, Didi jerked me down onto the floor where the good dancers were stretching. What they were really doing was checking one another out, sizing up the competition with sidelong glances, heads resting on kneecaps or upside down on the floor between straight legs. Then they pushed their stretches even further. Didi stressed every ligament in her body, attempting to reach farther and lower than any of them.

I flopped down next to her.

"This is a certified freak show." Didi's comment calmed me. It was like being back in the Mustang with her while she categorized all the different varieties of Whore-nut at Pueblo High School, putting each one in its place and all of them a safe distance away from us.

The door flew open and all the girls backed off the stretch competition as we waited for Alma Hernandez-Luna, the local-girl-made-good and current director of the flamenco program, to step through the door. Instead, an ancient birdlike woman crept in. Her hair, dyed an inky black, was plucked back into a tight braid at the top of her head that stretched her skin, tugging her eyes up until they had an Asian cast.

"Instant face-lift," Didi whispered to me.

It was hard to tell exactly how old the woman was from her face—over fifty, under a hundred—but her hands gave her away. Age-spotted, they were as twisted as a miniature bonsai tree.

"I didn't know that the university was hiring bag ladies." I touched a finger to my lips to silence Didi. She rolled her eyes.

The class buzzed with whispers that were all versions of "Where is Alma?"

The old woman tottered to the front of the class, squared her shoulders, and took several long moments to gather herself. Bit by bit, as if she were sucking energy up through the floor and out of the very air, the old lady stood up straighter and taller, until she looked as rooted and strong as a cottonwood down by the river.

"*Buenos días, señoritas.*" A trilling Castilian majesty whipped through her words. When all we did was look at one another, baffled, she repeated the greeting even more imperiously. "*Buenos días, señorítas.*"

Didi stared the woman right in the eye as she led the response. "*Buenos días, señora.*"

"*Bueno.* If you want to learn ballet, you must speak French, no? Well, if you want to learn flamenco, you must speak Spanish." Actually, what she said was, "Bueno effa jew wan to lairn flah-MEN-ko! Jew mus espick espanish."

Didi caught my gaze and rolled her eyes in reaction to the comical accent and I whispered to her, "You can leave."

"Are you kidding? A world-class freak show like this?"

A girl with the giraffe posture, bun at the back of her neck, duck-toed turnout, and bulimia-gray teeth of the Serious Dancer, subgroup Ballet Swan, asked testily, "I thought our teacher was supposed to be Alma Hernandez-Luna?"

At the girl's peevish tone, Didi, now highly amused, leaned toward me. "Wow, who put a toe shoe up *her* ass?"

The old woman stood even taller as she answered. "Señora Hernandez-Luna has much more important things to do than teach you burros."

The little ballerina's face screwed itself into furrows of further annoyance as the old lady trilled the *r*'s in *burros* until they rattled like machine-gun fire.

"Yeah, but—"

"But how can I teach?" the old woman snapped. "Is that what you want to know? How can I teach when I am old? How do I dare show myself when I am not young and tender? Because my face is wrinkled and I have here"—she held up an arm, which was surprisingly well muscled, powerful in fact; I had a second look at her legs and saw that the old woman had the calves of a soccer forward—"spots. Because my body is old, how can I not crawl into a corner and cut my wrists? Is that what you are asking?"

"Uh, no. I was only—"

"You are *only* an American girl whose *mamá neurótica* gave her her first tutu before she could walk. Who has studied jazz and modern and tap and African dancing and then, one day, she sees Joaquín Cortés with his shirt off and she thinks, Oh, jes, *flamenco*. So she decides she will put on the red dress and learn flamenco. Except that, *coño!* . . ."

Some of the Hispanic girls in the class flinched at the curse.

"Here is this old lady and she is not part of your flamenco fantasy. Well, *phhtt* on your fantasy." The old woman dismissed the little ballerina with a swirl of her fingers in front of her face in a gesture that was European, ancient. "How can such an old lady teach you?" She drew herself up, dropped her shoulders until her chest seemed to broaden to twice its size, and answered her own question. "Because I *am* flamenco."

"She 'jam' flamenco?" Didi asked, mocking the woman's accent. "Who *is* this whack job?"

I was embarrassed that Didi was there to see how ridiculous my flamenco fantasy really was. I knew her patience was wearing out because she stepped away from me and moved to the back of the class. I was certain that, any second, she'd wave bye-bye over her shoulder to me and the entire class and saunter out. I was glad to see her edging away.

Most of the class had started grumbling, all asking whispered versions of Didi's question. "Who is this whack job?"

"As a favor to Señora Hernandez-Luna, you, burros, shall be the first class I teach in ten years. Because it is a continuation of all that has come before, everything in flamenco begins with one word: 'and.' And so, we begin." She raised her gnarled hands, froze them in position until we were all silent, then, with great gravity pronounced, *"Y!"* and clapped. That was all. She just clapped. She clapped out a count of twelve with odd accents thrown in, sometimes coming down hard on the three, six, eight, and ten.

Sometimes the one, four, seven, and ten. With each change of beat she'd shout out *"Por alegrías! Por soleares! Por bulerías! Por tangos!"*

After several more minutes of the unexplained clapping, the testy ballerina and some of her friends walked out, which seemed to please our teacher enormously.

"Bueno, now that *las impostoras* are gone, we can begin. Those of you who remain must be able to hear the one essential of flamenco: rhythm, beat, *el compás. El compás* is everything. *Todo, todo, todo.* What is this?" she asked, raising her skirt, then stamping her feet so fast they blurred and all that emerged was a sound like a subway hurtling through a tunnel, like a hailstorm, like the Industrial Revolution hitched to a pair of human feet. As she stamped out a rhythm too complicated for any of us to follow, the flesh on her face, jowls, cheeks, even her forehead, bounced authoritatively, but she didn't break a sweat or get the least bit out of breath.

"This"—she pointed at the astonishing blur of her feet—"this is *nada*! *Mierda!"*

She brought her arms up, twining her hands like an odalisque dancing for the sultan. "All this is," she went on, hands and feet moving together, "is just to say something about this." She stopped dead and began to clap. "One, two, *three*! Four, five, *six*! Seven, *eight*! Nine, *ten*! *El compás!* Now you."

We tried to capture the beats, but they came in puzzling, unpredictable bursts.

"Come on, you American burros, you're already sixteen years behind. Little Spanish girls clap patty-cake *en compás. Vamos! Más fuerte!* Let me hear you! If you're gonna make a mistake, make a *loud* mistake! *Dígame!* Tell me something! *Dame la verdad!* Give me the truth!"

In response to our feeble clapping, she waved her arms. "Stop! Stop! I can't stand the sound of those sick kitten paws!" She mocked our attempt, patting her hands together with pathetic taps. In the mirror, I saw Didi grinning as if the teacher were making a joke. The old lady shot her a look fierce enough to make the grin fade. After that challenge, I was certain Didi would leave.

Following ten more minutes of clapping, a girl who'd come to the class hoping for a good cardio workout threw her hands up in disgust and walked out. Our teacher followed her exit with a series of eloquently mocking claps, chirps, and finger snaps before turning back to us and starting the odd beats that she'd called *el compás* again. The entire time, she counted, "One, two, *three!* Four, five, *six!* Seven, *eight!* Nine, *ten!*" Numbers. That was what I did. I grabbed hold of the digits and, as always, they hauled me to safety. It was incidental that I was clapping and stamping my feet instead of punching figures into a calculator. It all still tunneled directly into the odd pocket in my mind where numbers did curious dances that tranquilized my anxieties.

Figuring out this old lady's code of claps and snaps absorbed me to such an extent that I didn't have any mental energy left to be embarrassed about Didi witnessing such a ludicrous display. I was so intent upon duplicating the rhythms and counterrhythms this strange old woman was feeding us that I lost awareness of anything or anyone else in the class.

One by one, all the others gave up and dropped out until only one other pair of hands besides mine returned the teacher's rhythms. Doña Carlota stood directly in front of me and accelerated her clapping. I did the same, slapping the fingers of my right hand against my left palm until it reddened and stung. She indicated that I should continue the rhythm, then stepped back to the other remaining clapper. It was Didi.

Even more surprising, Didi was rapt with attention. Gone was her mocking detachment. She was immersed in a way I'd seen only when she was either on a groupie mission or working on her music. The teacher clapped. Didi wasn't able to copy it exactly as I had done. She came close to missing the basic beat structure completely. What she did, though, was return the rhythm with some topspin on it that was all her own. Perhaps the mockery wasn't gone entirely. It might have been embedded in the saucy smacks that Didi improvised on the spot. The two of them went back and forth, Doña Carlota backing up as they went, leading Didi forward until she stood next to me again at the front of the class.

It was Didi who finally ended the clap-off with a few comically exaggerated off-beat claps. A buzzer sounded, signaling the end of class.

"Esperad!" our teacher yelled at the students scrambling to escape. She strode to the chalkboard at the side of the room and, pronouncing as she went, wrote, *Sino.* "*Sino.* Fate. My people believe that each of us has our own *sino* that cannot be altered. If your *sino* is to dance flamenco, know this: you will never again set foot in my class unless you are properly attired." With a piece of chalk, she scraped out an address on the blackboard. "Go here. See Teresa. She will know what I require. Your assignment for next class is to begin reading Federico García Lorca. Not only was Lorca Spain's greatest poet, but he is the only writer anywhere

who has ever been able to put flamenco on paper. It is a miracle to be-hold."

We were again rushing for the door when she stopped us for a second time. "This will never happen again. Flamenco is an expression of respect for that which has survived. Out of respect that I have survived to my ad-vanced age, no one who wants to be my student will ever leave a class-room before me. And no one who wants to be my student will ever address me by anything other than my full name." She bore down so hard on the piece of chalk that it screeched as she printed out the legendary name I already expected to see: *Doña Carlota Anaya.*

"That is my married name." Then, with more screeching and great gravity, she chalked in an arrow and in front of *Anaya* and separated from it with *de,* she added her maiden name: *Montenegro.*

Chapter Sixteen

"Montenegro?!" I shouted the instant Didi and I were standing outside the old gym.

"Yeah, major affectation, don't you think? Very *High*-spanic to add your maiden name like you're from a royal house or something."

Cigarette smoke wafted over from the dancers gathered around a guitarist sitting in the shade of a tall spruce tree. They clapped along in a soft, patty-cake way and sang in warbling Spanish. Those who weren't playing, singing, or clapping were smoking cigarettes from a blue and white packet with the brand name, Ducado, printed on the front. They smelled harsh even from a distance. Didi's attention was strangely riveted on the group.

"Didi? Montenegro?" How could she have forgotten? "That's *his* last name."

"Oh, right," Didi muttered, distracted by her intense study of a regal beauty at the center of the group of smokers, a slender Latina dancer. We overheard the guitarist call out her name: "Liliana."

"Didi? Did you hear what I said?"

"Montenegro. Mystery Man's name. The old lady and Mystery Man, probably related. Not surprising, really. I mean, there can't be many flamenco professionals in the state." Didi didn't take her eyes off Liliana, who had started slowly twining her arms up, fanning out her fingers, in time with the music. Holding her thumbs and forefinger up to make a square, Didi held it over her eye like a director framing. "Liliana is the head flamenco bitch," she announced and made a sound like a camera clicking a photo.

Her intense interest worried me. "Uh, Deeds, you seem pretty into this whole big pink bird thing."

"Rae-rae, I'm only trying to help you. What am I good at? Costuming, right? I have to know how you're supposed to look. If you don't look the part, you don't hook the part, right?"

Hearing Didi talk in her usual way about fame and how to achieve it comforted me.

She concluded her study of Liliana, clapped her hands, and announced, "Let's go shopping."

In a small shopping center near campus, we found the shop Doña Carlota had told us to visit, La Rosa y la Espina.

"The Rose and the Thorn," Didi translated.

A bell above the door tinkled as we entered. The shop smelled of sandalwood and oranges and was filled with all things flamenco and Spanish—fringed shawls, long skirts, ivory combs, intricately painted fans, mantillas, rosaries carved from jade, pottery decorated with Moorish designs, silverwork filigreed like lace.

Didi beelined immediately to a rack of skirts and riffled through them.

A black skirt with several rows of ruffles and an inset of black polka dots swirling around it caught my eye. I plucked it off the rack. "What about this one?"

Didi removed the two-toned skirt from my hand, tilted her head to the side, and appraised it. "Uh-uh, I don't think so."

"I just thought—"

"What?"

"I would, you know, stand out. That he'd notice me in that skirt."

"Sweetie, we don't want him to notice you because you look like a barber pole. Here." She handed me a heavy black skirt with no ruffles, no polka dots, just a series of gores inset. It was the exact skirt Liliana had been wearing. "Buy that one," Didi ordered.

"May I hang that in the dressing room for you?" a friendly middle-aged Latina with a bad perm asked, taking the skirt from my hands. I figured she must be Teresa.

"And this," Didi said, finding the same skirt in her size and passing that to Teresa. To me she explained, "Just to keep you company." She zeroed in on a slinky wine-colored top, then added a stretchy black lace number and a couple of fringed shawls to the pile.

"And shoes?" Teresa asked, taking the clothes from us to hang in the dressing room.

"Shoes!" Didi answered. "Yes, of course, shoes! We're both eight and a half B." As Teresa left, Didi called out after her, "Bring lots."

Teresa returned with a stack of boxes that she separated into two piles: semipro and pro. Of course, the pros were a lot more expensive, but those were the ones I wanted. I couldn't appear in front of Tomás in anything less. When she removed the lids and folded back the crinkly tissue paper, the priccy smell of high-quality leather wafted out.

"This style is the Fandango," Teresa said, taking from its box a pair with a clever cutout at the base of the strap. She showed us other shoes, other styles, but before they were even in my hand or on my foot, I fell in love with the Fandangos—velvety black leather with a double strap across the front of the arch, medium heel. If I had never met Tomás, if I had never taken Doña Carlota's class, I would have laughed at the idea of paying more than two hundred of the dollars I'd earned sweating at Puppy Taco for a pair of shoes. But I had, I had met Tomás and he made the shoes sexy, exotic, and unbearably necessary. I turned the shoe over. On the bottom were dozens of tiny nails.

"*Claves,*" Teresa explained as I rubbed my thumb over the silver dots sprinkling the toes and heels like glitter. "Means nails. They make the sound," she added.

Didi and I wore the same shoe size, which had made borrowing easy over the years. Now she slid her feet into a pair of Gallardos and began tapping them on the tile floor. She caught my eye, winked at me, and asked Teresa casually, "Doña Carlota—she's not by any chance related to—"

There was no need to pump any further. Teresa was already primed. Shaking the fingers of her right hand beside her head as if she'd just burned them, she gushed forth. "Tomás? The *tocaor*? *Dios mío, qué hunk.*" Her gesture gave me a strange, dislocated feeling as if she could see the film that had been playing in my head nonstop since the night I walked through the gold curtains.

Needing no further prompting, Teresa continued, "The old lady? Doña Carlota, she adopted him from some distant relative back in *España,* no? Practically bred him from birth to inherit the crown or something." She leaned forward and added conspiratorially, "Just that I don't think her boy wants to be the little prince."

"Why?" I asked.

"Who knows? One of his *primos,* his cousin or something—you know how they are up north, everyone is everyone's *primo*—anyway, one of his *primos* told my aunt that he went to this wild party in Albuquerque and never came back. Just took off with some *güera.* Oops, no offense. Some

Anglo chick he met at the party and went off hitchhiking. He was supposed to be going home to Doña Carlota in Santa Fe, but he never showed up. No money. No car. Just gone. Been some stories about him playing at biker bars. The old lady's furious. She raised him to be the next Paco de Lucía, not play in biker bars. You've got to wonder what the *primo* told Boy Wonder. See how those fit."

As I stood, Didi asked me, "Didn't you say Mystery Man told you that that night was the worst night of his life?"

I shot Didi a look that said *Shut up*. I couldn't believe she would talk about Tomás in public like that. I wished I had never told her anything. I wished I were alone so I could pore over this new treasure, this revelation that he had been adopted into flamenco. This was what Tomás had been talking about. This was the blood problem.

But Teresa was already asking "You know Tomás? Shit! Please, don't tell the old lady I've been running my mouth. The shop would close if she stopped sending her students. Please."

"Don't worry," I said. "I don't know him. She was kidding."

Teresa looked dubiously at me. The doorbell tinkled. "I'm sorry," Teresa said, standing. "I'm the only one here today." She left to wait on the new customer, calling back to us, "Your things are all in the dressing room. Wear the shoes when you try the skirts so you get the length right. Just let me know if you need any more help."

"Oh my God," Didi hissed. "Mystery Man is a badass. I am definitely starting to see the appeal. So he dropped off the face of the earth after he met you? What is that all about?"

I shrugged, not wanting to talk anymore. Not in a public place where anyone could hear. But I couldn't silence the fear that rose up. "What if he never comes back?"

"That kind? The bad boy? They always come back."

I trusted Didi's wisdom about bad boys. More than that, I trusted a certainty I'd never had about anything before in my life that Tomás and I were destined to be together. It was my *sino,* my fate.

"Besides, he's in love with you and just doesn't know it yet."

"Didi! Don't jinx me." More than ever I wanted to be left all alone with this new cache of information we'd stumbled upon. I wanted to extract every fleck of golden knowledge. But Didi was enraptured with the flamenco shoes.

She pirouetted on her heel. "Aren't these amazing?"

She was right. The shoes had an amazing effect on me as well. They didn't just make me taller by a couple of inches, they forced my shoulders to fall back so that my head floated up higher. And, instead of making me wobbly the way heels usually did, those shoes utterly rooted me to the earth as if the tiny silver *claves* had nailed me there.

In the large fitting room, Didi announced, "Try-on party," like when we were at Le DAV, then tossed the wine-colored leotard my way. "That will be amazing with your coloring." She plucked out the skimpy black top for herself and we both slipped skirts on. They were heavy and slid into place with an authority all their own.

"God, you've wasted away," Didi said, watching the skirt settle onto my hipbones. "I've got to try the Mystery Man diet." It was true; Didi and I wore the same size now.

I went back out and found the skirt in a smaller size. When I returned, Didi was completely dressed with a silvery, fringed shawl thrown over her shoulders. Transfixed, she watched herself in the mirror as she twined her hands up, winding them through sinuous arabesques just as Liliana had, all to one of Doña Carlota's beats, which she rapped out with her feet.

"Didi? Deeds? What are you doing? You're not into this, are you? This 'flamingo'?"

She froze with her arms curved above her head, the fringe of the shawl trembling between us. "Why not?"

"Deeds, this is like a mission. My mission. You know? All the times I've helped you do the groundwork? Moral support? I helped you get in the door, then I disappeared, right? Because that was your thing. Deeds, this is my thing."

"But, Rae, can't you see how amazing this is for me?"

"For you? Why for you? You think it's a joke."

"Not really." She clapped her hands, almost duplicating a *compás*. "This is what has been missing in my work. These rhythms. Did you hear that shit? It is irresistible. I could read the damn phone book and it would be astonishing. I've discovered the missing ingredient. And the look." She held her arms out. "This is a gift from God. This"—she waved her hands at the skirt, the shawl—"this is a total persona. Flamenco is in my blood."

"Your blood? Didi, you're Filipino and Jewish."

"My mom is mostly Spanish. Her name is Ofelia, for God's sake." She pronounced it *Oh-fay-lee-yuh,* indisputably Spanish. "And, for all I know, Mort might have been Sephardic."

Doubt crinkled my face as I recalled the pale hipster Mr. Steinberg. Didi launched in. "Don't you see how perfectly it all fits? What a great persona this is?" She swooped her arms up and swung them around her head, making the fringe loft and soar, then hula wildly.

I didn't say anything. I didn't have to. As always, Didi read my mind. "Rae, flamenco is still your thing. You're going to actually do it, actually learn to dance. I'm just going to skim the surface. Lift the look and the beats. Why aren't you happy for me? You should be happy. You're one step closer to Mystery Man and I'm one step closer to immortality."

I shook my head. "God, you're such a bitch."

She threw the silver shawl around both our shoulders and dragged me close. "Yes, but I'm *your* bitch." Didi's laugh enclosed us in a conspiracy against the world. It was impossible not to laugh with her. She pirouetted, making us both spin around until the silver fringe danced and the silver nails tinkled like coins falling on the floor.

Chapter Seventeen

"*Y!* Warm up!" Doña Carlota clapped out a tempo for the guitarist to pick up as she marched to the center of the class and took command. Knowing that the old lady had raised Tomás, that they were distantly related, I studied her, searching to find him in her fierce profile, the determined set of her shoulders, the brisk cadence of her speech.

"Roll down!" she ordered, pressing a student's back forward until her body folded in half.

"Let the head relax! Relax the jaw! Let the weight of the head pull the spine down!"

Clapping all the while, she strode over to the student guitarist assigned to play for our class. Plump, pale, and uncertain, Will was the exact opposite of Tomás. Doña pronounced his name "Weel."

"*Por tangos,* Will!" Doña ordered the style she wanted. "*Dios mío,* Will, *por tangos!*" She clapped right next to his ear, louder and louder until the discombobulated player picked up the exact tempo she was dictating.

"*Plié!* Keep the quads released! And roll up! *Ocho! Siete! Seis! Cinco! Cuatro! Tres! Dos! Uno!* Cross the arms and let the weight of your torso pull you down! For flamenco, you have to be tight and loose. Cold and hot if you want to be able to do this."

I lifted my head from where it was hanging down between my legs and saw Doña Carlota do something out of the *The Exorcist,* pivoting her head until her chin swiveled behind her shoulder. I glanced over at Didi who bounced her eyebrows up to show that she was impressed as well.

"You must be loose, loose, loose! Keep stretching. Today you begin to learn what flamenco is. Loosen up those shoulders! Spread the scapula!

"Do you think flamenco is a dance? Is it polka dots and a rose between the teeth? Is it fans and mantillas? And roll up! *Ocho! Siete! Seis! Cinco! Cuatro! Tres! Dos! Uno!* No! That is not what flamenco is. It is a way of life. Until you understand that life none of you will be able to dance flamenco. Spread the scapula!"

Doña Carlota patrolled the rows of dancers and stopped behind me. Her twisted fingers were hot on my back as they pushed my shoulder blades apart, then tugged my shoulders down, making my chest expand and rise. I breathed and my lungs inflated with the deepest breath I'd ever taken.

She caught my eye and asked, "See? Better?"

I nodded idiotically, boinging my head up and down, a hula doll on a car dashboard. The corners of her lips lifted the tiniest bit before she moved on, speaking as she went, "And down! *Ocho! Siete! Seis! Cinco! Cuatro! Tres! Dos! Uno!* Will!"

The guitarist looked up at her, terrified.

"Más lente, hombre!"

He slowed down.

"Y los brazos!" She stiffened her arms into a taut circle, ordering, *"Fuerte! Fuerte!* Strong!" She patrolled the class, stiffening limbs as she went.

"No bellyache arms!" she barked at Blanca, correcting the sweet-faced Latina's tentative, retracted posture, arms held in as if she had a stomachache. I put extra starch into my posture and the old lady gave me an approving nod as she passed.

Doña Carlota strode to the front of the class. "You came here to learn flamenco. You are lucky. You will learn from the only teacher in this country who is *gitana por los cuatro costaos,* Gypsy on all four sides. Now stretch the whole body!" She reached up, then paused and pointed to baby-faced Blanca, whose leotard hugged the tender rolls of baby fat around her middle. "You, Chubby, reach those stumpy arms up!"

As one, the entire class sucked in an outraged breath. Blanca's pink face flamed crimson and her lower lip trembled.

Doña Carlota made a peeved face and waved her hand, swatting away the tears gathering in the girl's eyes. "Don't cry, Chubby, you just got your first, most important lesson in flamenco: tell the truth. If you can't hear the truth, you can't tell the truth. You Americans, you *gabachos,* you *payos,* you say this is cruel. You believe that the truth goes away just because you are too polite to speak it. That it is an insult to ever mention that someone is black or fat or crippled."

"So? What?" Didi spoke out, loud the way she always talked to teachers, like they were anyone on the street.

Doña Carlota stopped dead, her arms frozen in a stretch that made her look as if she were climbing an invisible ladder.

"You just insult them to their faces? That's *not* cruel?"

Doña Carlota shot Didi a glance that would have withered a redwood. "American girls." Everyone in the class tensed at the dismissive, acid tone of Doña Carlota's voice. "You know what makes you so strong, so sure?"

Didi gave a little half-shrug.

"You don't know how much you don't know. That is how you go through the world and never see what is in front of your face. And now you come in here and dare to tell me that my way, the Gypsy way, is wrong?"

"I wasn't exactly saying that," Didi said, not the least bit intimidated, though the rest of us were holding our breath, astonished to see such open conflict in a classroom.

"I am sick of it! All you American girls traipse through here and think that you can become *flamencas* by taking classes at a university! You think you can learn flamenco like history or geometry. You can't 'learn' flamenco. You must live flamenco."

"So why are you here if it can't be taught?" Didi asked. I felt as if the studio had become a plane flying through a storm that had belly flopped through the worst turbulence any of us had ever experienced.

Doña Carlota drew herself up until she was nothing but a steely armature. "What is your name?"

Didi looked around, the calm attendant on this very bumpy flight, and answered, "Ofelia." She rolled out the Spanish syllables of her mother's name.

"All right then, *Oh-fay-lee-yuh,* though you, especially you, don't deserve it, I will tell you a story. A story from the world you've never seen. The world where flamenco was born. You, all of you, keep stretching! I will give you the beginning of the story, but you will only hear more of the story when you have earned it."

We mimicked the ladder-climbing stretch, lifting our arms as high as they would go, miming Doña Carlota's movements perfectly. We did everything we could not to interrupt the strange spell that had fallen on the studio.

"When my oldest brother was a little boy, he fell and landed on his nose and squashed it flat. So we called him Mono, Monkey, because of his squashed-flat nose. Is this cruel, to call a little boy whose face has been smashed Monkey? If your spine is a little crooked, where I grew up you were called Joroba, Hunchback. If your face was a little round, your cheeks a little puffy, your lips a little small, you were El Guarrito, Piglet. If your voice was high and squeaky, you were El Capón. If you liked sex in the wrong place, you were called La Peste, the Stink. The name my mother gave me was Juana María, but no one ever called me by that name so she gave it to one of my five little sisters who came after me. Everyone called me Miracielos, Looks at the Sky. Most Miracielos are crazy or retarded."

We stretched, reaching out our arms, our torsos, to drag more of this story our way.

"Is that cruel? No. For a Gypsy, a *gitano,* a *calé,* the only insult is not giving someone a nickname because then they don't belong, and for a Gypsy, not to belong to the tribe is to stop existing. When I was a girl growing up on the Sacromonte, on the Sacred Mountain outside of Granada, the *gitano* way was to let the goats raise the children. We learned that knives were sharp by getting cut and fires hot by being burned. Our mothers did this because Gypsy children suffer so much in the *payo* world that we have to be stronger than *los payos.*

"My family lived in a cave. Yes, a cave in Sacromonte. Since there were no toilets, we all found abandoned caves to relieve ourselves in. Everyone joked that my brother Mono found his the hard way. He was two, old enough that he had stopped existing for my mother and would not start again until he was strong enough to do chores for her. As soon as he was able to step over the threshold at the door of the cave that was supposed to keep out most of the scorpions and some of the millipedes, he was off, exploring the dusty paths that ran through our anthill of a neighborhood.

"One day he toddled across what he thought was a pile of hay and fell down the chimney hole of an abandoned cave. Every year children died this way, either from the fall itself or from being trapped in an old cave where the earth has closed over the door opening. But my brother survived and screamed loud enough to bring help and that is why he liked his nickname, Mono, because it reminded everyone that he was tough enough to fall down and squash his face flat and still walk away. Besides, having a squashed nose did something to his voice. Made it different, special, so that eventually Mono became a singer. I liked being Miracielos because it told everyone, it told me, that I had my eye on something higher, something better. Chubby, you should like your nickname because in flamenco the biggest compliment you can give a dancer is to say she dances *con peso,* with weight.

"*Bien,* okay, you are wondering when I'm going to start teaching this." She ripped off a machine-gun blast of heel stamping. "No!" She abruptly stopped. "A baboon can learn this. I am here to teach you flamenco and you will learn more about flamenco just listening to me tell the story of my life than any *payo* teacher with a hundred heel-toe combinations will ever teach you. Now, you will start the right way, the proper way. You will start the way I started. The way all true flamenco starts: with *el cante.* I'm going to sing the first song I ever heard, the song my father sang. Will! *Por siguiriyas!"*

The guitarist nodded nervously to acknowledge the style Doña Carlota had called for, then studied her intently as she clapped out an intricate pattern to a beat slow as a dirge. He began to play a lovely melody ornamented with expressive frills and she shook her head violently. "No! No! No pretty *falsetas.* None of that *mierda.*"

Will stopped, his pink cheeks turning scarlet with embarrassment.

"Just this," she ordered him, pounding her feet. She led him through the pattern several times, listening as he tried to repeat the pattern, shaking her head and muttering, *"Qué feo,"* how ugly. "Listen to the stresses!"

Will played it several times as she shook her head and clucked. Finally, when he'd abandoned every bit of ornamentation and was banging at his instrument with all the strings dampened, she brightened. *"Sí, hombre! Eso es! Vamos ya!"*

She closed her eyes and clapped softly for one minute, two, hands held next to her ear as if she were listening for the ocean roaring inside a seashell. She swayed, her feet rooted not just to the floor but to the ground deep beneath it, and sucked energy from that dark place. Then an unearthly sound, deep and low, ripped from her throat. Just one word, *"Ay,"* that seemed not so much sung as exhumed from a world that was not Western, not modern, not the one I was standing in. Then she began:

> *We are the wretched* calés
> *poorer than larks in the sky:*

citizens and guards, alas,
deny us even our own shade.

Her song was more a cry, a scream set to complex harmonies I had never heard before. It reminded me of High Mass and Jewish chanting and a muezzin calling the faithful to prayer, but it was none of those things. It was Arabic, African, ancient, nothing so trivial as a song, a melody, and it cut straight into my soul. Dark emotions rose up from the dark place where this song originated and I felt them without thinking about Tomás, about Didi, about my mother, about my father. The sound became the leathery rustling of bat wings beating deep within me. They whirred, whisking the dust from all that was too painful to consider. For one excruciating second, I wanted her to stop more than I'd ever wanted anything on this earth. I would walk out of class and never think about flamenco or Tomás Montenegro again. I would pack away the grief and longing forever. I would take only accounting and math classes and have a safe life. That second was followed by all the rest in which, more than anything on this earth, I wanted the singing never to stop.

I glanced around, expecting the rest of the class, the ballet swans, the jazz princesses, to be as obliterated as I was. Mostly what I saw on the other faces was embarrassment at having emotion so raw and dark spilled forth in front of them. A few of the Latinas seemed to hear what I was hearing. But it was Didi whose face mirrored mine. The tears pooling in her eyes kept me from fearing that I was in the middle of a psychotic break.

Doña Carlota's *cante,* her song, resonated through the classroom long after she fell silent and Will stopped playing. She stared into each of our faces. The embarrassed dance princesses' eyes skittered away from hers. Didi though, Didi was another story. I watched her in the mirror. She studied Doña Carlota in the same omnivorous way she watched Madonna and Cher, the same way she read Sylvia Plath and studied Frida Kahlo's painting, the same way she absorbed anyone's work when the creator, the woman, had become bigger than the work. Didi knew a diva when she saw one and Doña Carlota was her first chance to study one up close.

When the old woman's dark gaze found mine, I stared back, asking for more information, more clues about what had happened.

"You," she said, pointing at me, "come to the front," then at Didi, "and bring your friend." She pushed a couple of the swans toward the back and installed us directly in front of her. "These are your spots. Those who can understand what flamenco has to say must be close enough to hear." She addressed the whole class. "That was *cante*. That was the last time I will sing to you in English. That was the song my father sang. Why aren't you stretching?" She stood on one foot and worked the other.

We all copied her, standing on one foot, then the other.

"STRETCH those metatarsals!"

She clapped another rhythm, which the guitarist tried to pick up, then turned to me and asked, "What *palo*, what style am I calling for?"

The weird number decoder chip in my brain translated the soft claps, the accented louder claps into the almost-Western four-beat count and put them together with what I recalled of the names she'd called out last class. "Tango?"

She dipped her head, acknowledging my answer. "*Increíble!* An American girl who can actually hear *el compás.*"

I bit my lip to keep from beaming with pleasure at the old lady's praise.

"Reach with the top of the head! Lengthen the body! Lengthen! My father didn't have a guitar for his *cante*. Like all the good Gypsy men on Sacromonte, he was a blacksmith and beat his rhythm out with his iron hammer, his *martinete*. Some believe that little children, infants, don't remember anything. I remember, I remember everything." She signaled and Will softened his playing.

"At night, in the old days before the factory came, I looked out onto our city of caves and I knew what hell was. Flames licked out of the earth as if the world were on fire. As if we Gypsies were the devils *los payos* believed we were and we could make dirt burn.

"They weren't the flames of hell, they were the *fraguas,* the forges where the blacksmiths beat metal all day and all night. They say that those born within the sound of the Gypsy hammers hear them all their lives. That is true. I tried to escape the constant pounding and failed. I was six when I tried the first time. I went all the way up the hill to the Alhambra, where for eight hundred years the Moors ruled Spain. I sat where jasmine blooms over the tombs of *los moros*. Where the stone walls have been carved into lace. Where *las sultanas* listened to the lutes of the eunuchs. Even there, I still heard the pounding. I hear it still. Everyone who wants to dance or sing or play flamenco guitar must hear it as well."

She clapped.

"One, two, *three*! Four, five, *six*! Seven, *eight*! Nine, *ten*! Eleven, *twelve*! *El compás.* I will clap it for you, loud, *con palmas secas.* One, two, *three*! Four, five, *six*! Seven, *eight*! Nine, *ten*! Eleven, *twelve*! *El compás,* the Gypsy clock. This was the time my mother set my heart to beat to before I was ever born. I never had a choice but to dance flamenco.

"Clap with me. Come on, clap. You will be terrible. Just do it. Don't think about it. Don't listen to your hands. Listen to the story."

I listened, of course, I listened. But what I heard wasn't her story, it was his. The story of the world he came from. The world I had to enter to win him. Watching Didi's face in the mirror, I saw that she was just as avid as I to enter this secret realm.

When we were all clapping, Doña Carlota started again. Sighing, she whispered, "*Granada, ah, mi Granada,* a city both sadder and more glorious than any other. The greatest poet of this century, Federico García Lorca, said that the hours are longer and sweeter in Granada than in any other Spanish town. And though I was the last person who loved Lorca to see the poet alive, I must disagree. The hours are longer and sweeter in Granada than in any other town anywhere on this earth.

"I knew the Granada of poets, but I did not live in it. At this time, the time I speak of, Sacromonte was not a show for tourists. It was a garbage dump on the edge of the city where we *gitanos* were tossed out with the rest of the trash. Eventually tourists, *aficionados,* from all over the world would come like pilgrims to see the real, the true Gypsy flamenco dancing. But they never saw the only true flamenco who ever lived in Sacromonte, the only one who didn't care about making a show for the tourists, my father, called El Chino because his eyes slanted like a Chinaman's."

Still beating out the rhythm with her feet, Doña Carlota stopped clapping and raised her arms, winding them upward in time to the beat. Without a word, the class followed her. At the top of the arc, she snaked her hands in languid circles above her head and we all copied her.

"My father was the smallest blacksmith on the mountain. But strong. Stronger than any two men. Just as with everything else, my father kept his muscles hidden. His hair was like a black ram's, a thousand tight curls. His skin was the color of old coffee, a color with sheens of purple and blue in it. He had a strong Gypsy nose, like me. Good for filtering the sand out of desert air. And his eyes. He had the eyes of a poet. When I pumped the double bellows hard enough, the flames leaped up and made the gold in his dark irises flicker to life.

"His *cante* was a tree, an ancient olive tree that has stood since the Romans ruled Spain. Since the Moors invaded. Since ships laden with gold from the New World sailed up the river Ebro. This old tree had roots that went farther into the earth than any other tree. Roots that went all the way to Hell and drew up the boiling water of the demons who torment us all. When my father sang, no one could pretend they had angel hearts because his songs made the demon blood boil in their veins."

She pointed at me and spanked her palms together. "You, clap louder. You are the only one here who is *en compás*. You are a natural. Get these burros back in time."

Blushing, I blocked out everyone else's faltering attempts—especially Didi's, since Didi, standing next to me, was way off—and clapped the beat Doña Carlota dictated. The blood rushed so loudly in my ears that it was hard to hear myself. *I was a natural!* I imagined Doña Carlota telling her nephew those very words, that a new student of hers was a natural. It didn't matter that Tomás had disappeared and wasn't speaking to his aunt. Somehow, he would know.

She started singing and writing on the board, translating the words as she went.

> *In my life I have known*
> *The sorrows of this world*
> *Others often have a look*
> *But not the knowing*

"The words of my father's *coplas,* his lyrics were not the silly words of folk songs about pretty girls with high combs and mantillas throwing a rose from her balcony. No, his *cante* came from him like a rusty nail pulled from an old board. His voice was what we called *la voz afillá.* Like sandpaper. A good *gitano* voice, *muy rajo,* very rough. But, more than rough, it was powerful and it was true. Do you know the worst thing you can say about someone in flamenco? *No me dice nada.* He didn't say anything to me. He didn't speak to me. No one ever said that about my father."

Didi studied herself in the mirror, watching the effect of each hand twirl.

It thrilled me to see Doña Carlota note Didi's self-absorption with a quirk of her eyebrow. Didi would not outshine me. Doña Carlota was on to her already.

"When my father sang, Gypsy men tore their clothes and Gypsy women scratched their faces because my father's voice reminded them that for more than a thousand years our people have had no home. His voice made them remember again that we were thrown out of India and forced to wander strange lands. Beaten, tortured, jailed, enslaved, and driven away. That even in Andalusia, where poets write poems about us and composers compose operas, even there, *la guardia civil* will throw a Gypsy man into jail for stealing a handful of grapes and let his wife and children starve. No place wants us. No place on this earth wants the Gypsy. When my father sang, the people heard their great-grandfathers in prison crying for their wives and children. They heard the whip that tore the flesh from his back. They heard the woman, all alone with no man to defend her, cry when the soldiers came to do what they will with her and her daughters."

She turned to the board and wrote CANTE JONDO.

"*Cante jondo.* Deep song. This is a song that must come from not only your broken heart, but the hearts of ancestors broken for a thousand years. The hungrier my father became, the louder the cries of his babies, the deeper his *cante* became."

Doña Carlota sang a lament so heartrending, the translation she wrote on the board was superfluous.

> *One judge cried: "Let them die."*
> *Another answered "Why?"*
> *Poor, pitiful Gypsies*
> *What is the harm they've done?*
>
> *All the world cries out to God for health and liberty;*
> *I cry out to God for death*
> *But he will not harken to my plea.*

As Doña Carlota sang, she began some footwork. I could not copy it and clap at the same time. Didi was the only one who followed her. Doña Carlota moved over in front of her and Didi mirrored her moves. They were sloppy, imprecise copies, but like everything Didi did, she executed them with confidence bordering on arrogance and her own reckless style.

"*Óle!*" Doña Carlota called out, accenting the *o*.

Didi blossomed under the praise and her arm-twining and foot-

stomping became more frenetic. She even started a deep, guttural hum-
ming moan to accompany Doña Carlota's singing. La Doña stamped to a
finish and Didi followed.

She barked a question in a rapid burst of Spanish. Didi shot back a
reply. As if she already knew what the answer would be, Doña started
nodding before Didi had finished.

"Bueno, mujer, bueno. You have something to say. You don't say it in
the proper form, but that will come. You have the fire. You are La Tempesta. And you"—she stuck her chin out at me—"you are *como un
metrónomo.* You will be La Metrónoma." She waved a finger at us. "The
two elements of flamenco. Fire"—she pointed at Didi—"and ice." Of
course, that was me. "The head and the heart. Together you are the perfect
dancer. Apart?" She gave an Old World shrug that dismissed both our
chances.

Chapter Eighteen

Pausing only to change shoes, I rushed out of class without waiting for Didi. Flamenco was my one bright and shining thing and Didi was snatching it away from me. The ducks quacked, demanding a handout as I stormed past the pond. I didn't pause at the Robert O. Anderson School of Management where my Intro to Financial Accounting class would start in five minutes.

Metronome? I was the Metronome and Didi was the Tempest?! Screw it. Screw her. She can keep her own fricking books. La Tempesta!

With no idea exactly where I was headed, my feet carried me across campus until I was staring down Lomas to the West Mesa, where the distant black cones of extinct volcanoes spiked the horizon. Didi's hangout. To the east were the Sandia Mountains. I headed toward them down Lomas Boulevard. The street was on fire. Pyracantha bushes flamed with orange berries, tall shafts of pampas grass were plumes of smoke in the diamond-sharp sunlight, chamisa blossoms blazed a molten yellow. I was back in the quiet neighborhood Tomás had taken me to before I realized that my destination was the jewel of a park hidden away like a harem beauty behind thick walls. I rushed down the street and found the narrow, unmarked path that snaked between two nondescript houses. Not until I was again within the park's secret expanse could I take a full breath.

The cottonwood with the giant's swing hanging from it anchored the park. As if it were an object of veneration I could not approach, I skirted around the place where Tomás had held me and found a spot at the park's edge. I sat on grass green and velvety from sprinklers as I recalled every detail of that night with Tomás. I stroked the grass as I remembered his hands on me, holding me as we swung up to the stars. The grass caressed me in return. It was soft, full, and green, unlike any other in the high desert city. It was fairy-tale grass.

I forgot Didi as I realized what should have been obvious to me from the beginning: I had walked into a fairy tale. Doña Carlota's story of Gypsies living in a world where the earth burned and everyone had names like Piglet and Monkey and Looks at the Sky, where a thousand years of a people's history were hidden in songs and dances, that story was a fairy tale. It was Tomás's fairy tale. It would have to become mine.

I had been sleeping and in this secret park Tomás awakened me with a kiss. I wondered where he was, what he was looking at at this very moment. I imagined him looking at me. I imagined myself dancing for him, passionate and devastating in my long, black skirt, dancing better than anyone had ever danced. Dancing so well that I won him.

I had to win him.

Though I had been the one sleeping, Tomás was the beauty of our fairy tale and the hero always won the beauty.

I would have to be the hero.

Every fairy tale had a trial where the hero had to prove himself. My trial was flamenco. That was the field upon which I would have to prove myself. Somewhere in Doña's story, somewhere in the very history of flamenco itself, were the clues that would tell me how to succeed, how to make my story twine around Tomás's so tightly that they would become one.

The sky behind the West Mesa, behind the volcanoes, turned into a dome of stained glass, violet, rose, and green, shifting to cobalt blue streaked with rose above the Sandia Mountains to the east. The air grew chilly, and damp seeped up from the ground beneath me. The colors left the sky as it darkened to navy blue.

Stars appeared in the night sky. I found the North Star that Daddy had shown me so that I would always be able to find my way home. I started to make a wish on it, but Daddy was gone and would be gone forever. All my other wishes clumped up in my chest with a weight that pushed the air from my lungs. The only name I could give to all I yearned for was Tomás.

"Rae! Rae-rae, are you here?"

Didi was at the entrance to the park. Even more than I didn't want her in my flamenco class, I didn't want her in my, in *our,* secret park.

"Rae! Rae?"

She couldn't see me. The second time she called my name, her voice broke and she sounded lost and scared. In the next second, she got mad at herself and, thinking no one was in the park or not caring if anyone was, she cursed herself, muttering, "Fuck it. Fuck it. Fuck it. Shit."

She was leaving when I called out from the darkness, "Didi. I'm over here."

"You bitch," she said, dropping onto the grass beside me. Her nose was running and I think I saw tears on her face, but she scrubbed them off, bending her head into the shoulder of her jean jacket before I could see for sure.

"I looked everywhere. Frontier. The duck pond. Puppy Taco. I even went to your old house and looked in the backyard. Couple of lesbians are living there now with a pack of rescue greyhounds. What would your mom think about that? It took me forfuckingever to remember about this park. Mystery Man's secret park that you wouldn't tell me about? Of course, this is where you'd be." Without stopping for a breath she asked, "Why did you run off?"

Tone, there it was again. As I've said, Didi and I could have done away with words altogether and just communicated everything we needed to tell each other, everything important, in the infinite vocabulary of tones and inflections we'd taught each other. We both heard in her question the admission that Didi knew exactly why I'd run off.

It was superfluous, but I said it anyway. "You're an asshole."

"Okay, I admit it. I'm an asshole. The big pink bird, that's your thing. I've horned in too much on it. I'll drop out." She tilted her head to look at me, but I kept staring straight ahead. At the far end of the park, the sprinklers came on, sending silver arcs of water over the velvety grass. In the silence that fell between us, she counted.

"Seventeen clicks," Didi said.

"What?"

"It takes seventeen clicks for the sprinkler to make one arc. Smells like the very end of summer, doesn't it? The grass when the water hits it?" She sucked in a deep inhalation. "It smells like watermelon."

I breathed in. The grass did smell like watermelon. We listened to the clicks, smelled the watermelon smell, and watched moonlight gleam on the rain of silver drops.

"Wow, reminds me of Lorca. Have you been reading your Lorca?

Doña Carlota is right. He is totally amazing. He has one, 'Ditty of First Desire.' Queer title. Probably a bad translation. But tell me this isn't killer. 'In the green morning / I wanted to be a heart. / A heart.'" Didi clapped the rhythm for a *bulerías* and repeated the words in time. "Then it goes on with how in the ripe evening he wanted to be a nightingale. A nightingale. The end will annihilate you. He tells his soul to turn orange-colored. To turn the color of love. Just that, just getting turned on to Lorca is totally transforming my work already."

I knew what Didi was doing. She was showing me why I should tell her it was okay for her to stay in the class. She was working me, but I could hear in her voice that she was also telling the truth.

I didn't say anything and she went on, her words tumbling out in a rush. "But the best, the absolute best, the most amazing thing you will ever read in your whole, entire life is his essay on *duende*."

"Do what?"

"*Duende.* Oh, Rae, this is the essential thing we have to understand. This is where real art, where anything good or true comes from. It's like inspiration or possession. But more. I can't even explain. It's the real deal. He said it burns the blood like powdered glass and rejects all the sweet geometry. 'Sweet geometry.' Do you not love that? So Lorca wrote that *duende* rejects all the sweet geometry we understand and it shatters styles. Isn't that amazing? It's not about perfection. True inspiration can be ugly and messy and radically *im*perfect! Sort of like us, huh?"

"Sort of like you," I corrected her. I was the geometry person being rejected.

She fell silent and we studied the houses that ringed the park. Light glowed in the windows and scenes of family life played out in each one. In one a father entered holding a white paper bag of takeout. A child of around eight, maybe a boy with long hair, maybe a sturdy little girl, reached out to grab the food away. The father pivoted from the child's grasp and the child ran around to grab from the other side. The father feinted again, then spun back, scooped the child into his arms, and swung her around. She was a girl.

I glanced over at Didi. The same hunger I felt was on her face.

"Fuck it," she said, dismissing the sadness with anger. "Fuck all this shit." She turned to me. "Rae, you are the one essential person in my life. I have to have you in my life. Nonnegotiable. If you want me out of flamenco, I'm out. No questions asked."

I didn't say anything because I no longer knew what to say. No longer knew what I really wanted.

"Rae, it's like I said, we want completely different things out of flamenco. You want love and I want to rule the world."

She was right. She wanted fame and I wanted Tomás. We could dance next to each other for the rest of our lives and our paths would never cross. I knew Didi like no one else in the world knew her. I knew what she had lost, I knew where all the holes in her heart were and just how big they were. I knew she cursed when she wanted to cry and railroaded through life the way she did because she was afraid if she took things any slower she'd fall off the tracks entirely. I knew all that, but I still couldn't share flamenco with her.

Didi jumped up, held her hands out to me, and dragged me to my feet. There was plenty of room on the giant's swing for both of us. I felt her hip pressed again mine work as she stretched her legs out then back, pumping the swing higher. Once we took off, she yelled, "Hang on!" and we both had to throw an arm around the other's waist to keep from falling off. As we gained altitude, she sang Doña Carlota's song:

> *In my life I have known*
> *The sorrows of this world*
> *Others often have a look*
> *But not the knowing*

"How do you sing like that?" I yelled as the wind whipped away the words sung in flamenco's ululating style.

"Melisma!" she yelled back. "I had to learn it for my bat mitzvah. Lots of warbly notes on one syllable. It's all a version of that urban yodeling thing Whitney Houston and them do. I'll teach you that if you'll teach me that compass shit."

I didn't answer and the swing went up, then fell back down three times. Finally, I said, "Screw it. Yeah. Okay. What's the point in resisting. You're the biggest brat in the world. You always get what you want."

"You say that like it's a bad thing." She used her standard line, then, grinning, put on a big push, hauling back on the rope she held in her right hand, forcing me to hang on for dear life to the rope in my left hand and to her waist with my right. When we were high enough that we suddenly seemed much closer to the stars than to the houses far below, houses where fathers brought home take-out treats and swung their daughters into the air, Didi screamed, "Fuck them! Fuck them all! Who needs normal life when you can fly above it! Fuck consensus reality! Right, Rae?"

She didn't want an answer and I didn't give one. Instead, we soared together into the night sky and, just as they had with Tomás, the higher we climbed, the faster we fell and the more the stars blurred into a silver smear.

Chapter Nineteen

Every time I set foot in Doña Carlota's studio, it was as if Tomás were waiting there for me. I bathed and perfumed as if I were meeting a lover. Every second of class, I felt his eyes on me. I believed that Doña Carlota was Tomás's envoy to me, sent to teach me about the art, the culture, the blood that had formed him. Every stamp of my foot nailed him to me. Every twine of my wrist wound him closer to me. She had been sent to tell me his story, to give me the information I needed to solve all the complications in his life. Once I learned enough, I knew I could make every equation in his life balance. I could do what no one else could for him and he would need me and love me. Didi would occasionally point out how long it had been since that night. I couldn't explain to her that it seemed I saw him or he saw me every day in class, that we were together, that everything I did was bringing us closer. It didn't make sense then. It wouldn't make sense later. It is impossible to explain obsession, to explain the irrational rationally.

The weeks passed and flamenco was hammered into me until my knees ached, my spine throbbed constantly, and my wrists felt as if they would twist off my arms. Pillows of blisters formed along the outside of my big toe, across the back of my heel, and on the balls of both feet. The nail of the right big toe turned black because I pounded on it the hardest. But every one of my toes felt as if they'd been run over. The muscles of my calves and thighs burned as they grew harder with each class, with each of the endless hours outside of class that I practiced.

Still, no more of her, of his, story was forthcoming. Doña Carlota had warned us, *You will only hear more of the story when you have earned it.* As the weeks passed without a single word from her that was not instruction, I began to fear that she would never consider us worthy to hear another word of the fairy tale that was hers and Tomás's life. Instead, she spent every second of every class hammering flamenco's diabolical rhythms into us, making our heels and toes into percussion instruments, our hands and arms into cobras curling out of a snake charmer's basket, and our hips into an ocean of waves that never stopped rolling.

Gradually, as I watched Doña Carlota and the more advanced dancers who practiced on the lawn outside the old gym, dancers like the mesmerizing Liliana, I came to realize that each stamp, clap, hand flick, hip bump, twirl, jump—no matter how apparently frenzied—hit one of the very precise beats of the *compás* clock.

Soon, I was hearing *el compás* everywhere—in a car's clacking transmission, in the hum and bump of a fan, in the pelting debris tossed around by a windstorm. Bit by bit, I began to see that flamenco was like haiku. Instead of seventeen syllables, though, the dancer, the singer, the guitarist, each member of flamenco's holy trinity, we all had a dozen beats, in however long or short a series we chose, within which to express what was in our hearts. Those beats were both the yoke that bound dancer, singer, and guitarist together and the instrument that transformed random movement into forward propulsion that could take them wherever they wanted to go. They were the one essential element in flamenco.

And Didi couldn't get them.

"God! I hate the fucking *compás*!" Didi burst out on a day when we left class and stepped into the glory of a New Mexico autumn that I'd somehow missed completely until that moment. The world, bathed in crystalline light, was a place so crisp and sharp, it was like being nearsighted your whole life, then putting on glasses and seeing clearly for the first time.

Doña Carlota had humiliated Didi that day. She'd stopped the entire class as we were trying to follow her through a routine and shouted, "Tempesta, you are *fuera de compás*!"

Didi had, once again, committed the greatest sin in flamenco; she was off the beat, out of *compás*.

"Can you count?"

Didi refused to answer and Doña Carlota asked her again, "Tempesta, I'm asking you can you count? Did you learn numbers or is that too boring for La Reina Oh-Fay-Lee-YUH! Is it?"

"Yes, of course, I learned to count."

"Good, she can count. So why don't you? Why don't you count? One, two, *three*! Four, five, *six*! Seven, *eight*! Nine, *ten*! Eleven, *twelve*! In Spain, we are doing this in our sleep."

Didi tried again but, although her heels cracked loud as a rifle shot and her arms were supple as silk and her expression was fierce as a Kabuki mask, she could not stay on the beat to save her life. That was when I truly trusted that Didi would never really invade my flamenco world. Knowing that she would never get it, I started in earnest that day to teach her *el compás*.

We took to walking everywhere *en compás*. I would call out the beats of the different *palos,* styles, to her in whatever scat improvisation I liked at the moment. "Tah-kah-tah-kah-*tah*! Tah-kah-tah-kah-*tah*! Pah-tah-*pah*! Pah-tah-*pah*! Tah-*pum*! Tah-*pum*! Tah-*pum*!"

Didi could stay *en compás* as long as I was hitting the beats hard for her, but the second I turned it over to her, she was lost. "I don't hear it," she moaned. "All this tah-kah tah-kah shit, it's an urban myth."

"How can you say you don't hear it? You can sing it. I've heard you."

"Shit, I can mimic anybody. But this?" She did a spazzed-out imitation of my footwork. "This is utterly insane. *Vámonos!* There's a chile cheeseburger at Frontier calling my name." She ran ahead. I followed, but found that even when I tried not to, my footsteps fell into *compás*.

I had almost given up, resigned myself to never hearing another word of the story that was Tomás's story, when, one Friday, Doña Carlota swept into class, clapping before she was even through the door. She walked in demonstrating the sequence she wanted us to learn. *"Golpe! Golpe! Tacón! Palmas secas!"*

My heart sank. There would be no more of her story that day.

"You, Metrónoma, you like the story the best, don't you?" With no warning I occupied the spot I hated most in all the world: the center of attention. The place where Didi bloomed so extravagantly made me writhe and shrivel. "I will let you be the one to decide if we hear more of it today." She clapped out a rhythm. *"Dígame!* Tell me something and I will continue."

Her request stunned me. *Tell her something?* I glanced at Didi, hoping for a clue. Didi mimed dancing. I turned back to Doña Carlota. What? What did she want me to dance? I echoed back the *alegrías* Doña was clapping, but my hands patting together felt wooden. The rest of my body was even stiffer. I couldn't move, much less dance. From the corner of my eye, I saw Didi urging me on by holding up her skirt and drawing my attention to the simple *paseo* she was executing. How ironic that it was a sequence I had drilled into her head. Holding on to the *compás* like a handicapped railing, I dragged myself from one beat to the next. Though I hit every pulse on the head, it was a stilted color-by-numbers affair until, gradually, I loosened up and began to flow.

"*Vamos ya!*" Blanca, the sweet-tempered girl, yelled out encouragement.

The praise both unnerved and inspired me. I ducked my head, but pretended that, instead of hiding my cheeks flaming with embarrassment, I was only looking down to gather my skirt. Recovering, I swirled the material in a brisk countertempo to the one I hammered into the wooden floor.

"*Todas!*" Doña Carlota ordered and the entire class picked up the *taconeo* I was executing. When we were all pulsing in time like one many-chambered heart to a beat that I set, Doña Carlota awarded me the equivalent of a blue ribbon: she nodded her head. I felt as if I might incinerate on the spot from an overheated combination of pleasure and embarrassment. The attention was a trophy that threatened to crush me.

I glanced over to see if Didi had noticed La Doña's approval, but she was absorbed in her own improvisation. Though she was wildly off the beat, a magical force streamed through Didi, animating every stamp of her heel, twining of her wrist, and fanning of her fingers. It was impossible not to stare at her; she embodied all that was savage and free in flamenco. She was so mesmerizing that I literally stumbled over my own feet.

Doña Carlota grimaced as if I had caused her actual physical pain and clapped her hands to stop the ensuing chaos. My wings had melted; it was a lesson I wouldn't forget soon.

She started us back on a simple beat with some simple marking steps, then, without any further preamble, began to tell the story. "My mother was fourteen when I was born. Fifteen when my sister was born. *Gemelos de gitanos,* Gypsy twins they call this in Spain. Is it any wonder that she, my mother, remained a child all her life? Charming and cruel, stupid and crafty, selfish and sacrificed? *Y doble.*"

She doubled the rhythm her feet were creating and we all kept up, stamping and listening twice as hard.

"Her name, Delicata, fit my mother perfectly. All little girls believe their mothers are pretty, but everyone said my mother was as beautiful as a saint. Even though she was *gitana por los cuatro costaos,* Gypsy on all four sides, still her skin was not typical *calé* skin, tough and brown as ox hide. She had the skin of an English lady, pale as milk. My mother stayed away from the sun like an owl. Next to her pale skin, her lips were pomegranates, with the same red in her cheeks. The long ruffled skirt she wore had once been that same pomegranate red, but it faded to an even prettier pink. Over this she wore a white apron that she had embroidered with red poppies. Her black shawl with the long fringe was crossed over her breasts, the ends tucked into her apron. She wore her hair, glossy and black as a leopard, in fat curls in front of her ears called *caracoles,* snails.

"Don't think about what your feet are doing! Just let them follow the rhythm! *Óle.*" She spoke the word softly, more in resignation than approval, and I allowed not just my feet but my heart to follow her rhythm, her words. I became the Gypsy with milk skin and pomegranate lips, the woman Tomás would fall in love with.

"Because I saw her with six babies after me, I knew how I had betrayed my mother. How we all had. With each new *chaboro,* that was our Gypsy word for baby, I saw her joy born again as well. While they were tiny, she loved nothing more than washing the babies' soft skin, oiling their tender bodies, sniffing the sweet-smelling spaces at the back of their necks. She even pointed out to me how their curdy shit did not stink. But, eventually, like me, all the new babies disappointed her. They refused to stay clean and sweet-smelling. Their downy hair matted and filled with lice. Fleas chewed scabs onto the chubby ankles. Their shit began to stink. Soon, the new babies weren't new. Soon they became as grimy as everything else in *la cueva* and it was as if, one day, my mother was no longer able to distinguish her newest child from the hole in the dirt that was our home."

Though what Doña Carlota told us seemed fantastic, it also rang truer than any words we'd heard spoken in any classroom we'd ever been in. The experience was embarrassing and mesmerizing. With each word, she drew us into a world we'd never imagined. With each *golpe,* she cracked away a bit more of the shell of Anglo reserve that kept us and our true stories hidden from one another.

"My mother was a prisoner in our cave. She had been the most beautiful, the best *bailaora,* the best dancer in a town of the most beautiful, the best *bailaoras* in the world, Sevilla. *Seh-vee-yah.*" Doña Carlota trilled and caressed the syllables.

"Then my father took her away and forbade her ever to dance again for strangers. She spent hours gazing out the opening of our cave, not speaking, not giving any sign that she knew her children were there. I would cook a pot of stew and bring her a bowl with a crust of bread to use as a *cuchara de pan,* but she would just let it sit in her lap.

"Sometimes, when my father was gone, I could creep up to her and, if I was quiet enough and her dreams deep enough, she would begin stroking my hair, easing the tangles out of it with her fingers, splitting the lice between her nails. As she smoothed my hair, braiding order into the wild strands, she would speak. Always about her home, about Sevilla."

It would be hard to say exactly how she did it, but with just a few minute adjustments in her carriage, her voice, Doña Carlota transformed herself into Delicata, her beautiful, spoiled mother. When she spoke, she spoke as Delicata.

" 'Granada is a gray town filled with gray people,' my mother would tell me. 'Don't you see how stocky and short and serious they are? The thumb of God has squashed them. In Sevilla, ah, Sevilla, people know how to laugh. They know how to dance. To sing. In my neighborhood, Triana, you can't turn a corner without hearing *cante.* Sevillanos have *chuso. Chuso y gracia.* Granadinos don't even know what humor and grace and charm are! Phoenicians, Greeks, Carthaginians, Romans, Moors, Christians, they all loved Sevilla. They all tried to conquer her. But she always belonged to us, her people.'

" 'To walk along the Río Guadalquivir where the galleons sailed in bringing the treasures of the New World. To gaze upon the Moors' shining Golden Tower. To stroll down the Alameda de Hércules and hear singing and laughter pouring out from every café and bar. This is to live. Everywhere there is laughter, gaiety, with enough to eat for everyone and more than enough for those with talent. Sevilla, my Sevilla. I would have been queen of Sevilla. They all said it, "Delicata, you will be queen of the *cafés cantantes!*" '

"At the mention of the singing cafés, I would nestle in more deeply between my mother's knees. This is what I wanted to hear about, the magic world of the *cafés cantantes.* But first she would always tell me about my grandmother.

" 'Your grandmother was the true queen. La Leona they called her, the Lioness, because she ruled the world of the *cafés cantantes* as surely as a lioness rules the jungle. Four performances a day, that is how often my mother and I danced with our *cuadro. Cuadro,* that is the proper term for a person's dance group, not this *zambra* nonsense these Granadino animals in their caves use. These stumpy, dreary—'

" 'Four performances a day?' I would prompt my mother, not wanting to lose her to the endless litany of grievances she had against Granadans, against Granada.

" 'Yes, and more,' she would answer. *'Los adinerados,* the rich ones with their cigars and whiskeys and walking sticks, would always select a few of their favorites to continue in *los cuartos,* the private rooms, after the regular performances. And my mother and I were favorites. Oh yes, they called for us, *los adinerados.* Many a time, we crossed the bridge to our Gypsy neighborhood, to Triana, with the sun high overhead, but we were back again at eight that evening.

" 'Back at the Café del Burrero, Café de Novedades, Café Filarmónico. Such beauty. You can't imagine such beauty, here in this miserable hole in the ground. The cafés were heaven. All of us dancers with our hair piled into gleaming *caracoles,* our waists tucked in by corsets, bustles rustling beneath the yards of fine silk and crinoline. The audience, always men, with their derbies and cigars. Some of the grand *señoritos,* the true patrons, with capes over their dark suits, white spats, and high-buttoned shoes.'

"My mother fell into a dream so deep as she spoke that I could smell the cigars, the polish on the gentlemen's shoes, the pomade on the dancers' hair.

" 'We performed on stages, proper stages raised high above the crowds. At our feet were rows of light, flames of gas, so that every move, every turn of an arm, every twist of a wrist, shone as if we dancers were made of gold. And the floor of the stages? Wood. No Gypsy had ever danced on wood until the cafés opened. For the first time, we could hear the rhythm pulsing through our bodies. That I loved. The sound of my feet stomping, pounding so fast that *los tocaores* could barely keep up on their guitars. Luckily, I was a young girl, not yet of marriageable age, so they let me get away with my wild *zapateado.* If one of the older dancers, my mother, any woman, tried to shake the dust from those wooden floors with footwork like mine, oh! Then they would start. 'Not feminine enough. Destroying *el arte*. Too masculine.' And the women would go back to their delicate *brazeo,* standing rooted on one spot, twining their arms with all the fire of ivy growing. Cows, stupid cows. *Los señoritos* might say they were true *aficionados,* that they only liked the old-style dancing. But who did they hire? Who did they want for their private par- ties? Who was the princess of the *cafés cantantes*? Yes, that is what they called me, La Princesa, and I would have been the queen, La Leona. I would have ruled over that world if only, if only—'

" 'What about the decorations?' I cut my mother off. Too many times all the wonderful stories had been derailed by 'if only.'

" 'Ah, the decorations.' She would sigh, close her eyes as if she were smelling the most delicious smell, and begin again, calm then as she re- membered the *cafés cantantes*. 'Always, the cafés were decorated in the most elegant style. Heavy curtains of ruby velvet hung at the sides of the stage. Giant mirrors in frames of gold made the big halls appear even larger. In front of the stage were rows of chairs. Each chair had a tray fastened to the back so that the customer would have a place for his *caña* of wine. Some of the cafés had little tables. Above all the spectators on the ground floor were boxes with armchairs, just like a theater. Up there, in the boxes, *los adinerados* didn't drink the little *caña* of wine for thirty- five centimos like the riffraff on the floor. No, they bought wine by the bottle, four and five bottles at a time. On the walls were posters that cele- brated all the beautiful places of Sevilla. La Giralda, the golden tower, Sevilla's cathedral, almost as large as St. Peter's in Rome. All the beauti- ful, beautiful places of Sevilla. All the beautiful places I will never see again because—'

" 'What dances did you perform?' I hurried to ask before my mother's dreamy mood sank beneath her sadness.

" 'On those wooden floors that were like dancing on a drum? All of them. All the dances that we *gitanos de Triana* had only danced for our- selves before, they all burst forth in the gaslight. *Tangos, tientos, bulerías, alegrías.* These were the easy ones, the light, happy ones for weddings and baptisms that the audiences liked right away. But we also brought out the slow, sad ones. *Los jondos* that we danced at funerals, *siguiriyas, soleás, peteneras,* these we danced too, but only the truest of the *aficiona- dos* liked them. Four performances a day and, with each one, the public begins to like *el baile* a little more until one day the singers are no longer the stars. It is the dancers the public come for.

" 'Even worse, the *tocaores,* the monkeys plucking away at their guitars, are starting to be noticed. One day, some player in some café plucks out a particularly sweet *falseta* and what happens? The audience applauds. Applauds a guitar player? That had never happened before and now all the guitarists want their moment in the gaslight. Ramón Montoya, Luis Molina, Habichuela el Viejo, Manolo de Huelva, Javier Molina. They all became soloists, each one trying to outplay the other. But the worst rivalry of all was between Paco Lucena and Paco el Águila. The first Paco played and the audience went wild. To show his disdain for his rival, the second Paco pulled a glove out of his pocket, put that on his hand, and played even better than the first! Well, First Paco can't let this stand, so he takes the *sock* off his foot, puts it on his left hand, and plays a solo!'

"My mother laughed at the memory, but the unusual sound of laughter echoing off the walls of the cave startled her. She remembered where she was and the cave became her prison again. My mother slapped my head and pushed me away, glaring as if I were her jailer, the one who had imprisoned her. I suppose I was, her first child, the one who had cost her her virginity. Because, really, what decent Gypsy man would have had my mother after my father kidnapped and raped her?"

Chapter Twenty

"Time to step up the program," Didi said, stuffing shoes and skirt into the bag she heaved onto her shoulder. Class had just ended and, as usual, we'd all waited until Doña Carlota had left. That day I wanted to stay in the studio for hours, savoring and committing to memory the new chapters of Tomás's family history. But, almost as if she were deliberately breaking the spell, Didi yanked me out of the classroom and dragged me down the hall toward the faculty lounge with its emphatic sign, NO STU-DENTS. *ESTUDIANTES PROHIBIDAS.* We waited until Señora Martinez, who taught castanets, punched the code into the keypad and entered. A second before the door closed on its automatic lock, Didi sprinted ahead and grabbed it.

"What the hell are you doing?" I hissed, refusing to enter the teachers' inner sanctum.

"I thought the whole idea of this flamingo thing was to get to Mystery Man."

"Shut up," I whispered, prickling with the sensation of being watched, heard not just by the unseen audience of one I had played my life to ever since that night at the Ace High but by the woman I'd made his proxy, Doña Carlota, who was probably still in the faculty lounge.

"Come on. The very least we can do is find the old lady, maybe tail her back to Santa Fe. View the boyhood home."

"No!" The thought, the remotest hint of intruding on Tomás's world to that extent before I was absolutely ready, appalled me.

"What?" Didi challenged. "You changed the mission without telling me? You seriously want to be a dancer now or something? Nice of you to let me know. Should I find someone else to do my books?" Didi held the door open for me. Terrified that if I didn't do something to end this dis-cussion, she would say his name out loud, I stepped through.

"Girls." Señora Martinez stopped us. "You know you're not supposed to be in here."

"Oh, sorry," Didi said as she fished her wallet out of the shoulder bag. "Doña Carlota left this in the studio and we wanted to catch her."

"*Ándale, pues!* She just left. Out the back way. *Ten prisa, chica!*"

Didi rushed through the dressing room to the back door and pushed it open. I peered around the edge of the door and caught a glimpse of Doña Carlota being helped into the backseat of a meticulously maintained old Buick by an elderly man. As he dipped his head, his silver hair glinted in the sun like a sheet of tinfoil. There was a timeless formality to his every gesture as if he'd been transported, not just from another continent, but from another time entirely. His face was oddly unplaceable. Not quite Hispanic, not quite Native American, not quite Anglo. His profile could have come off an ancient Roman coin. He slid behind the wheel in the front seat and drove away. Didi ordered, "Memorize the digits!"

We stepped outside and watched the Buick disappear.

"Whoa! A driver," Didi said. "Major diva action. Well, at least we know why the old lady ordered us to let her leave first."

"What do you mean?"

"She doesn't especially want anyone seeing that she's either too feeble or too prissy to drive."

"I don't know about that."

"Hey, don't get confused. It's the great-nephew or ward or whatever you're in love with. Not her. Shit, if we didn't have to park halfway to Gallup, we could follow her home." I was deeply grateful that there was no way Didi could engineer such detective work.

The usual Friday afternoon crowd was gathered on the front lawn outside the academy to listen to the guitarists practice their *falsetas*—the sweetly lyrical melodies sprinkled atop flamenco's driving rhythms—and smoke harsh cigarettes imported from Spain. The flamenco program's inner circle clustered around Liliana, the Christina Aguilera look-alike, whom Didi had correctly identified as the "head flamenco bitch." I recognized a few other standouts from the program: Liliana's chief henchbabe, Yolanda Gutierrez, a good but not great dancer; Adriana Ebersol, a ballet swan with a major eating disorder and a reputation for technical perfection served up with a side of soulless *güera* attitude; Paz Diaz, probably the best dancer but not most-likely-to-succeed because she had a rabbitty overbite and was stocky. Everyone paid a lot of lip service to how shape and size didn't matter in flamenco, that some of *el arte*'s greatest performers were old and fat. Yeah, right. No, flamenco wasn't as body-obsessed as ballet, but still, the stars all had the right look and that look was thin and dark.

"Could I bum one of those?" Didi asked a tall guy with broad shoulders and a ring of thorns tattooed around his biceps. His name was Jeff, a rock guy picking up a few flamenco chops. Good-looking in a rock 'n' roll way, tall, thin, long blond hair, the top part pulled back into a ponytail, he would have been perfect for Didi except that he was Liliana's boyfriend.

Jeff handed her a Ducado and she did that forties movie thing of letting him light it for her, leaning in close and looking up into his eyes. Didi and Jeff chatted in Spanish for a few minutes while she smoked. Liliana shot daggers at Didi when she made him laugh.

"Laters," he said to Didi, before sauntering over to Liliana.

"He seemed interested."

"Jeff?" She glanced over her shoulder and caught him staring after her. "Yeah, he'll be useful. He'll help us a lot more than the *pinche compás* ever will." She smoked the rest of the Ducado as if she were furious at the cigarette and wanted only to incinerate it. What she was furious at was (a) not being the center of attention and (b) Jeff walking away from her.

Will Thomas, the accompanist for our class, had taken up a spot by himself beneath a middling-size spruce off to one side and was playing a beautiful *falseta*. Some of the girls in our beginners class were scattered around the edge of the lawn watching Liliana and her group practice. Blanca, who'd encouraged me in class, sat by herself, reading.

"Come on," Didi said, heading toward Will. "Time to start our own cool group."

Will barely glanced up as Didi positioned herself in front of him and began working through some of the combinations Doña Carlota had been teaching us. Like most everyone else on the lawn, Will was smoking a Ducado, the official sign that he was applying for membership in the hardcore flamenco club.

I sat down and watched Will play, watched his hands on the strings. Of course, they made me think of Tomás's hands flowing like that across silver strands, coaxing beauty and passion from them. I thought of his hands on my face, my back, pulling me to him.

"You were really good in class today," Will said, barely looking up at me.

"Oh." I was surprised that he knew who I was. "Thanks."

"Who else do we need?" Didi whispered to me. "The Great White Hope?" she asked, nodding toward Jeff. "I couldn't agree more," she said before I could answer. "Take over here." Didi was already striding away before I stood and took her place, practicing the *bulerías* sequence the old lady had shown us last week.

"That's an amazing story she's been telling."

"Really." Will couldn't talk and play and his *compás* faltered a bit. Enough to throw me off. I clapped to get him back on the beat.

He listened, nodding, then lowered his head and started playing again, betraying his roots in classical music with lots of tremolos and arpeggios that seemed the absolute antithesis of flamenco. He finished a tricky run and glanced up at me. Only because he wore a look I'd seen on my own face once when I was thinking about Tomás and caught a glimpse of myself in a window did I realize: Will likes me. Then I heard all the tremolos and arpeggios for what they were: offerings. I checked to make sure Didi was occupied. She was executing a tricky maneuver, luring Jeff away from Liliana to play for her. I glanced around to make certain that no one else was within range of hearing before I asked as casually as I could manage, "Doesn't the old lady have an adopted child? Some kind of guitar prodigy?"

"Tomás?" Will pronounced the name with an ease so studied that it told everything about Will and Tomás and their places in the guitar hierarchy. Will was a roadie and Tomás was the star whose name had enough weight to be worth dropping.

It was nearly unbearable hearing his name spoken. I glanced around feeling nervous, exposed. As much as I wanted to hear more, I also wanted to run and hide. But Will seemed safe. It was impossible to imagine that he had any direct connection to Tomás. All I could manage to say was "Yeah."

Will shrugged, lowering his head as he moved down several frets. "Last I heard he had a gig playing at this flamenco club in Miami. This other dude, though, said he was teaching at Berklee. You know, the music college up in Boston."

"Does he come back much? Ever?"

"I doubt it. He's got this whole complicated thing with flamenco. I heard him interviewed somewhere."

"Where?"

Will shrugged. "Was it the radio? That guitar show that comes on Saturday afternoons? Or maybe it was something my professor was telling me. I don't remember exactly. It really wasn't anything he said. The interviewer asked Tomás when he was coming back to New Mexico and he answered, 'Next.' That was it, just cut him off. Then the guy asks when he's going to do another flamenco concert and he does the same thing. 'Next.' That's all. Hey, do that step again you were doing. I've got to figure out this accompanying thing. It's kicking my ass."

I went through all the combinations Doña Carlota had taught us, imagining Tomás as my ever-present, invisible audience. When we finished, Will asked me if I wanted to go across the street to the Frontier Restaurant to get something to drink. I looked around, saw Didi walking away with Jeff, and answered, "Why not?"

In the friendly, cavernous restaurant, we split one of Frontier's catcher mitt–size sweet rolls and watched the activity outside the window along that stretch of Central Avenue. Students bending like sherpas under backpacks, waiting to cross the street, blinking into the sun. Oddly speckled dogs tied with rope to the lamppost, waiting for their masters. A guy wearing cutoffs sliced down to the size of a thong, tanned to the color and consistency of shoe leather, frantically panhandling. A couple of senior citizens on recumbent bikes pedaling beneath high-flying orange safety flags. At the table next to us, a study group reviewed French subjunctive verbs.

Over the next few weeks, without anything being said, Will and I entered into a companionable relationship. He and Jeff became the guitarists for Didi's "cool new group." Blanca, the nice girl from our class, was our first recruit. Soon most of the other first-year girls were gathering under our spruce tree after class. We spent a lot of time outside that autumn, smoking Ducados and practicing beneath skies as bright as new pennies. Starting with Jeff, Didi entranced the male portion of the flamenco crowd so thoroughly that we were absorbed into Liliana's group without her permission. Liliana simply surrendered to Didi's inevitable encroachment with salvos of high-pitched compliments—"I lovelovelove that top!" "You've lost weight. God, you're a toothpick!" and, always, "Where *did* you get those shoes?"

The flamenco culture was made for Didi. Smoking and drinking were expected and many of its greatest stars had died of drug overdoses. So, though Didi still considered the tyranny of *el compás* to be a tedious nuisance designed for lesser mortals, she adopted every other facet of *el arte*. Overnight, she shed her Strokes T-shirts, removed all her fake piercings, let her spiky hair grow out until she could pull it back into a braid, lived in her long, dark practice skirt, and transformed herself into the *flamenca* she christened Ofelia. All that was missing were the spit curls and a rose between her teeth.

So, for different reasons, the Flamenco Academy became the center of the universe for both Didi and me. The only other class we paid much attention to was Spanish. Didi, already fluent, took it for the easy A. I struggled through it because I had to. It was the language of flamenco. As much as I could, I made Didi speak to me in Spanish. All other classes that first semester, we simply endured. We became part of the scene transforming the old gym into backstage at a Broadway musical. Our wardrobes became the dancer's grab bag of stretch and sweat everything, leggings with a short wrap skirt, yoga pants. We too were dancers doing their dancer things—changing into practice skirts, slugging down water, stretching, taping our feet. I aspired to have bulbous, inflamed bunions and an eating disorder that would turn my teeth gray.

I was worming my way into Tomás's world, learning to dress and act like its inhabitants. I still had a long way to go, though, before I would be ready to reenter his universe. I still had to learn flamenco and I still had to learn his story. And for that, I needed Doña Carlota.

Chapter Twenty-one

Doña Carlota clapped out a rhythm and ordered, "Name it!"

As usual, no one answered and too many gazes swiveled my way since I was the one who could always identify whatever *palo,* style, Doña Carlota clapped out. I stared down at my feet to avoid eye contact.

"Why do we go through this cruel charade?" Didi asked Amalia, a girl from the South Valley with the profile of an Aztec princess who threw a lot of hip-hop attitude into her dancing and was Didi's current favorite among her growing entourage. Amalia grinned because Didi gave "charade" a jokey French pronunciation.

"Metrónoma! Tell them!"

"Por soleares?" I answered hesitantly, pretending I didn't know. I did. Not just because I had a natural facility for hearing the rhythms, but because I spent every moment I could spare in the Lair listening to CDs with titles like *"Todos los Compases!"* and "Learn Flamenco Rhythms."

"In the style of?" she asked, pointing at me.

"In the style of *soleares,* songs of solitude, songs of loneliness."

Will winked at me. We were sort of regarded as a couple. He regarded us as a couple. Since Didi was either hanging out with Jeff or building her entourage, Will had filled the vacuum she left. In defiance of university rules, he was smoking a Ducado inside the studio. He plucked it from his lips and squeezed it into the gap between the strings and the wood on the neck of his guitar before he picked up Doña Carlota's rhythm and began playing. Without a word, she began the footwork. By that time most of the class was able to follow. The class was no longer a bunch of rank beginners and it showed in our outfits. Swanky pairs of shoes in purple and red now appeared among us and we'd all taken to wrapping our skirts in special ways just like the older girls. We wore jeans, gym shorts under the long skirts, then whirled the yardage around ourselves, tucking the ends into our waists in order to show off and air out our legs. Even Will with his Ducados was transforming himself. I tried not to think about how ridiculous he looked, a choirboy sucking on a cigarette trying to be a badass. Still, he was no more ridiculous than a Czech milkmaid attempting to become a flamenco temptress.

Doña Carlota noticed a couple of students in the last row, staring at their feet and trying to follow. She dragged them from their hiding places, brought them to the front, and made them stand behind me.

"Watch her feet," she told them, pointing to me. Then she pointed at Didi and added, "And watch her face." Clapping out the rhythm, she started again. My heart sank. Today would be another day when she wouldn't tell any more of the story.

"You girls, you have no idea how lucky you are. I had to learn to dance to the beat of an anvil. Yes, it's true. *Brazeo!*" She ordered us to bring our arms to life and they twined upward until we looked like a bed of kelp waving in the current. I wished fervently for the class to follow well enough that Doña Carlota would tell the story. For once, they did.

"*Cante jondo.*" Doña Carlota fondled the words, expelling them on a theatrical sigh. "Deep song, none was deeper than my father's. It came not just from his heart, but from the hearts of his ancestors for a thousand years. He beat the songs out on an anvil just as he beat out his specialty, fancy grillwork. My father's anvil was only a block of iron, but he could fashion anything on it. The fanciest designs, decorative grillwork that no one anywhere can do anymore. With him iron and hammer were like paper and scissors. Peacocks fanning their tails. Palm trees. A toreador swinging his cape."

While we concentrated on the story, letting our minds follow Doña Carlota's words, our bodies followed her feet, her hands.

"His customers, the rich señoras, said that El Chino had the blood of the Moors in his veins because it was those long-ago invaders from the desert who taught us how to turn metal and fire into palm trees and peacocks and, yes, cannonballs. It is said that Gypsy metalworkers forged the cannonballs that King Fernando fired upon the Moors to free Granada and reclaim her in the name of Saint James. For five centuries, the people of Granada had their horses shod, their pots mended, and the nails to build their homes forged on the *fraguas* of Sacromonte.

"And then one morning a shriek sounded through the sierra so loud that it made the chickens gabble and run into each other in a clucking fury of feathers and dust and all the blacksmiths put down their hammers to listen. What they heard was the sound of their children chewing their last mouthful of bread. Cima Metales had opened a factory in Granada. All day and all night, cyclones of fire whirled about this factory. Trains loaded with coal pulled up at one end and at the other out came an endless stream of pots, pans, metal plates, spoons, ladles, hinges, nails, and decorative grillwork in the shape of peacocks, palm trees, and toreadors.

"Suddenly all the housewives who used to walk up the mountain with their great-grandmother's miserable iron pots and pans to have our men patch the holes could now buy pots and pans from this factory so cheaply that it was not worth having new tin put on the bottoms of the old ones. Who cared that the factory pans were so thin the *tortillas de patatas* scorched and the flan turned to leather; suddenly these shiny pans were what all the housewives desired. It was such a joy to buy something new that they didn't care they would have to buy it again and again and again. At first, the Gypsy blacksmiths just laughed at this factory, my father the loudest.

"'Cheap things,' he said. 'Only for the poor people. The stupid. My customers, *los ricos,* know quality. They pay for the best and from El Chino they get the best.'

"And, for a while, for my father, this was true.

"But the smoke from this great factory, wrapping around the city like a beggar's blanket, bewitched everyone. Now they wanted only metal that had poured like lava from the great iron cauldrons, metal that did not show the marks of a *herrero*'s hammer. They wanted their hand to be the first to touch the shiny, new metal. Soon even my father's customers became infatuated with the idea of choosing something that was already made.

"One by one, *las fraguas* went out, the Gypsy earth stopped burning, and the face of Sacromonte went dark. For the first time, we were hearing a possibility mentioned that no self-respecting Gypsy man would have ever considered before: going to work for *los payos*. My father wouldn't allow such a possibility even mentioned in his home. He walked down into the city carrying samples on his back. Heavy grilles that would have broken a mule's back. These he carried down each morning and these he brought back each night.

"Like all Gypsies, my father had turned into gold every peseta he saved. As his children grew hungry, he exchanged the gold for bread for his family. At first my mother's necklace was sold. Then her bracelets. Finally only her earrings were left, and still my brothers and sisters and I kept eating like locusts. Delicata's *potaje,* the stew we ate every night, usually had tomatoes and garlic and whatever else my mother could scavenge, eggs, onions, beans, fish, chorizo, maybe a chunk of blood pudding. Each night it grew thinner and after El Chino and my brothers ate, there was less of it left for Delicata and my sisters and I, who, good Gypsy women that we were, always ate after our men. When the tomatoes, then the garlic disappeared, we knew we were lost. We children fanned out through the sierra, grubbing for prickly pear and acorns. Whatever we found was never enough to stop the rumbling of our stomachs at night, so we stole. We dug beets from gardens at night like raccoons and snatched grapes and oranges from the stalls in the market during the day.

"As a last resort, my father, who could make señoritas dance *sevillanas* across iron screens, was reduced to forging nails. It was beneath his dignity to take these miserable things into the city. He told my mother that she must join the other women who hiked down the mountain once a week to sell in the plaza the baskets they braided and the horseshoe nails their men forged.

"The walls of our cave were covered in whitewash. This coating of white over the rocks of the hill was what made it a house and not a hole. Even the millipedes that invaded when the rock showed through knew this. But the cave sweated off the whitewash like a whore sweats off powder. When my father gave my mother the order that she must sell his nails in the plaza, the walls were so nervous that they sweated away the last bit of white because my mother answered no.

"My father was momentarily too stunned to do anything, and she told him: 'I am the daughter of La Leona, who danced for King Alfonso himself. Every *café cantante* in Sevilla begged her to work on their stages. The name La Leona is known all up and down the Alameda de Hércules. And I would have been even more famous. Even now, after seven children, I am still the best *bailaora* on the Sacred Mountain. Every day the tourists squander thousands of pesetas to watch those cows in La Cagachina's *zambra* dance and you ask me to sell horseshoe nails in the Plaza de los Reyes Católicos?

" 'No,' she told him, 'I will dance. In one night I can earn more than I could make selling horseshoe nails for ten years!'

" 'And who will sing for you?' he demanded, sputtering in his rage.

"*Cante* is where El Chino always trapped her. The dance came from the singing and my father was the best on Sacromonte. Also the most feared for his violent temper and brute strength. He knew that no other *cantaor* would dare to sing for his wife.

"Because she was trapped, my mother had no choice but to spit in my father's eye. My father, in turn, had no choice then but to beat her. He beat her that day and the next and for many days after. At the end of a week, my mother groaned every time she breathed and we walked down the hill together and tried to sell nails in front of the statue of King Fernando and Queen Isabel in the Plaza of the Catholic Kings.

"My mother was right. We didn't make enough to stay alive and continued to live on acorns and cactus pads. Then one day, late in the fall, when we had all begun to wonder which one of us would die when winter came, my mother and I rose early and were on the trail into town while a sliver of moon still hung in the sky, then disappeared as the sky turned pink. Our breath froze in the early morning air. Frost sprinkled the tangled forests of cactus next to the path.

"At each cave, other women, wives and daughters of blacksmiths whose *fraguas* had grown cold, joined us. There was La Sordita—Little Deaf One—the wife of my father's uncle, a tiny sprite of a woman whose deaf ears stuck out like an elf's. My father's cousin, Palo Seco, who'd gotten her nickname, Dried Wood, because she was tall and thin and all the juice had dried out of her. I remember walking behind her, watching how her shoulder blades poked out the back of her blouse like the wings of a vulture. Last was my father's oldest sister, Little Burro—Burrita—a powerful, high-breasted woman who, alone among all the women, never had any bruises on her face because she had broken her husband's arm the last time they fought and promised him she would cut off his *janrelles* while he slept if he ever touched her again. By Little Burro's side was her daughter, Little Little Burro, Burriquita. I can't remember the names of all the daughters and cousins and nieces and the babies and small children who came with us, but, all together, we were more than a dozen strong.

"As we walked in the soft morning light, my empty belly growled thinking of the hot *churros y chocolate* that vendors sold in the marketplace. I forgot my hunger staring at my mother. She had on her pomegranate red skirt that had faded to a beautiful pink, a blouse trimmed in Badajoz lace, her shawl crossed in front of her breasts and pinned at her waist with a brooch carved from wood to replace the fancy one she'd had to sell. My mother bore herself like a queen. Next to her, the other women looked like mud hens beside a swan.

"With each step, we all jangled as loudly as the coins in a beggar's bowl. From our ears dangled linked hoops of tin. On our wrists were innumerable bracelets of the cheapest silver filigree since the gold had been sold. We wore skirts with tier upon tier of ruffles dotted in big polka dots of black on turquoise or yellow on red, whatever colors were the brightest we could find. The women and girls of marriageable age wore hairstyles fixed onto their heads with tallow. Maybe because her deaf ears stuck out so much, I remember La Sordita's hair the best. It was piled onto the top of her head like coils of dog droppings and greased with pork fat until it glistened.

"At the edge of the town, I watched my mother and her friends complete their transformation into the wild Gypsy band the townspeople expected us to be. My mother slung the newest baby, my brother Mateo, onto her hip, where he slumped like a bag of potatoes. Little Burro fluffed out the curls of black hair dangling onto her face from beneath the kerchief on her head and shifted the basket of nails she'd been carrying on her head onto a hip that she stuck out. Dried Wood and Little Deaf One did the same, sticking out what little they each had in the way of hips.

"'You know what los castellanos like to say,' Little Burro announced to the group in her foghorn voice. 'Everyone knows how to dance. Only we gitanas know how to walk.'

"Even the little girls imitated their mothers' special Gypsy way of walking, hips swaying like a baby rocking in a cradle. I cocked out my own little-girl hips, put the stack of baskets I was carrying onto one, and followed the women. I tried to make the hem of my dress twitch back and forth, the way theirs did, swishing figure eights around their knees. But I only succeeded in getting a stitch in my side.

"In Granada, we were a cloud of gaudy butterflies descending upon a hill of black ants. The town women all wore black. I saw how they shrank from us as we approached, stepping aside, pulling their children to them, staring. I saw how our women pretended not to notice. How their voices grew louder, the sway of their hips looser. How they spread out to take over even more of the narrow street. Little Burro's harsh laughter bounced off the tall buildings and echoed back down to slap the women in black who walked carefully, side by side, whispering to one another about us behind their black shawls.

"Then we entered my favorite street, Calle de los Geranios, Geranium Street. On every balcony, the owners set out pots of red, pink, and white geraniums. I lingered, staying behind while the women's party moved away and their blaring voices and rasping laughter came back to me in echoes that grew fainter and fainter, until the quiet of the street returned. Water dripped from the terra-cotta pots above my head, turning the cobbles under my feet into river rocks. Two canaries in a cage nailed to the wall outside a second-story window began to sing. The sun shone on their yellow feathers, but their eyes, like tiny, shriveled currants, reflected nothing. These people believed that canaries sang better if they couldn't see the world beyond their tiny cages, so they put the birds' eyes out. They must have been right, because nowhere on earth do canaries sing as beautifully as they do in Granada.

"Their song and the smell of that street were like a taste I hungered for but could never satisfy. All around me, the fragrance of geraniums scrubbed the air of the narrow street with a scent so pure I felt purified, as if all the dirt, the lice, the scabs had been washed away. I breathed in the clean, geranium air and the canaries' songs poured down on me from the balconies overhead like miniature waterfalls. I listened until all the other sounds in my head stopped and it was filled only with birdsong and geranium purity.

"In the next moment, I realized I could no longer hear even the echoes of the women. Panic overtook me as if the beating of my own heart had stopped. I ran after the others, unable to imagine that life could continue without my family, *mi tribu.*

"I caught up with them as they rounded the corner, then slowed down because they were approaching a certain *tienda de tabaco* run by a woman who hated us more than all the women of the town put together. She was there that day waiting, a big woman, gray hair yanked back in a bun, white apron tied over gray cardigan sweater, sweeping the street in front of her tobacco shop. As we drew closer, she held her arms out and blocked the area she had just cleaned.

"'Don't walk here! Don't bring your Gypsy dirt, the shit from the animals you sleep with, here!'

"We all sneered at her but moved away. All except Little Deaf One, who walked right up to the stout woman.

"'What do you think you are doing!' the woman screamed at her.

"Of course, Little Deaf One couldn't hear and kept trying to pass.

"The shop owner waved her hands furiously. You didn't need ears to understand what she meant. We all stopped and watched. Everyone on the street watched. People awakened in the apartments upstairs, opened their shutters, and screamed down, 'Go around, you stinking Gypsy bitch!'

"These are the words we had been waiting for. We lunged at the shopkeeper, screaming in our language, *'Achanta la mui! Achanta la mui!'*

"'*You* shut *your* mouths, you Gypsy whores!' someone who understood *Caló* shouted back at us.

"My mother pushed everyone aside and stood with her face so close to the shop owner's that her spittle sprayed the woman as she hissed at her, 'Whores? You call us whores? You, woman who stands in the doorway to make love!'

"The shop owner gasped and tried to slap my mother, but her hand caught only the wind. Ducking back, my mother hurled the worst Gypsy insult of all: *'Anda ya! Que te gusta beber mente para que se te ponga gorda la pepitilla!'*

"This time the gasp came from everyone on the street for, in perfect Spanish, my mother had accused the woman of drinking mint tea to fatten her clitoris. The woman swung her broom at my mother's head. Burriquita stepped forward, grabbed the broom handle, and twisted it out of the woman's hand with a flick of her thick wrist. Then Dried Wood, La Sordita, and my mother swarmed over the shopkeeper like a flock of blue jays pecking and screeching at the poor woman. In the uproar, only I noticed my mother slip into the store, take a sack of Silver Horse tobacco, and slide it beneath her skirt.

"Seeing that the townswomen were getting the worst of things, a cry went up: 'Call *la guardia*!'

"At this, we withdrew. The *guardia civil* were the worst torturers of Gypsies. Only last week Little Burro's husband had been arrested for hunting snails on the estate of a rich absentee landowner who lived in Madrid and both his thumbs had been broken. We backed down the street shouting curses and fixing *mal de ojo* on the shopkeeper until we turned the corner.

"Several blocks later my mother called a stop and pulled out the bag of Silver Horse. The women, who weren't allowed to smoke in front of their men, eagerly rolled up the tobacco in whatever scraps of newspaper they could find. By the time we were finished smoking our cigarettes, the story had changed: we weren't chased away, we'd left in triumph after we'd beaten *los payos* again with our quick wits and even quicker fingers. The proof was the cigarettes we smoked.

"This is the way Gypsies see the world. Always, always, always, we must be the ones who outsmart the *payo*. To celebrate, my mother started *las palmas*. Just a little *sordas*, a muffled handclap with the palm cupped, not the loud *secas*, dry, clacking on the flat palm.

"My mother clapped . . ." Doña Carlota waved at the class and they clapped with her.

"I clapped *contratiempo*." She slapped out a counterrhythm and pointed at me to pick it up.

"Then we started *los pitos*. Dried Wood was as good as her name, her fingers sounding like old sticks cracking as they clicked together."

Doña Carlota's twisted fingers snapping together rang out. She pointed at Didi, who was good at imitating the rifle crack of La Doña's *pitos*.

"Little Burro started the *jaleo*. *Vamos ya!*"

La Doña didn't have to repeat the exclamation a third time—the class immediately echoed Little Burro's *jaleo*.

"Little Deaf One, who could feel rhythm, was the first to raise the ruffles of her skirt and tap out an answering rhythm with her heels as she danced down the street.

"All the rest of us shouted encouragement at La Sordita. *'Vamos ya!'*

"La Burriquita was next to take her turn dancing. Then Palo Seco. Me. Then my mother. She went last because everyone knew she was the best. We were all *en compás* with her. The rhythm held us together so tightly that we became one person. One person with five pairs of dancing legs and five pairs of clapping, snapping hands."

In the mirror of Doña Carlota's studio I saw that my classmates and I, so mesmerized by the story that we were following Doña Carlota without thinking, had all become sassy Gypsy women. We swung our hips, happy to be ostracized by the straitlaced townswomen who were threatened by our wild ways. We were rebels. We were bad. Didi caught my eye, grinned, and shook her raised skirt at me playfully.

The class made a wild *jaleo*, yelling back every new cheer Doña Carlota taught us: *"Arza! Así se baila!"* When we were really moving, Doña Carlota pretended to fan her face as she called out, *"Agua! Agua!"*

We didn't need a translation to know that our teacher was calling for water because we were so hot. Doña Carlota calmed the pandemonium with little more than one circle of her arm. We clapped quiet *palmas sor-*

das as our feet automatically stayed *en compás* while we waited, expectant as good children in pajamas, teeth brushed, for the story to continue. La Doña did not disappoint.

"The sun and the peasants from the sierra were thronging in as we reached the center of the city. The air echoed with the clang of cattle bells, the braying of mules and donkeys loaded with casks of wine and oil, baskets of fruit and vegetables from the country. A customs official in his belted uniform stopped everyone who passed, poking their bundles, searching for contraband. We strode like queens through the Bibarrambla, where the last Moorish king had watched bullfights and jousts.

"From Bibarrambla, we wound our way to the cathedral, where the herb sellers hawked their wares: *flor de azafrán* for headaches and sadness; *manzanilla* for stomachaches and childbirth pains; *genciana* for men's disease; *azahar de naranjo* for bad temper; *alenjo* for lunacy; *siete azahares* for boils and earache.

"We passed the grand cathedral that the Catholic kings had built to try to outshine the Moorish rulers' Alhambra. I shivered from more than the cold as I ran past the gray, forbidding church. It looked too much like the tomb it was with Fernando and Isabel lying side by side inside, the queen's icy smile frozen for all eternity.

"All the women crossed themselves and touched their hair in honor of the sad story of Isabel's daughter, Juana la Loca. We *gitanas* loved Isabel's daughter, Juana the Crazy. Juana had been married to Philip the Fair, the most handsome man in the kingdom. Poor Juana had fallen madly in love with her prince. And how did he repay her passionate love? By betraying her with every woman who crossed his path. Worse, he mocked her in front of the whole court. He beat her. He made her cut off her beautiful hair. Yet in spite of his cruelty, when he died Juana went mad with grief. She rode through Spain in a gloomy carriage pulled by eight horses carrying his coffin, refusing in her insanity to bury him, hoping until her dying day that her faithless husband would come back to life. Come back to her.

"Is it any wonder that Gypsy women love Juana la Loca?" Doña Carlota stared right at me as if she knew that I was as crazed by love and beauty as poor, mad Juana had ever been.

"At the market we sat in the dust beside our baskets and our piles of nails for so long that we looked like beautiful flowers wilted in the sun that nobody wanted. We pretended we didn't notice the maids and the housewives passing us by, kicking more dust into our faces. When Mateo cried, my mother hiked up her blouse to nurse my new brother. As she stroked his clean, chubby cheek, the hairs on my cheek quivered, my body remembering when I was clean and sweet-smelling and she was gentle and affectionate to me too.

"After another hour of the Granadina housewives passing us by with their noses in the air, my mother swatted at me as if this was all my fault.

" 'Do you piss *horchata*?' she asked me. 'Do you shit *bolichones*?' I knew what that meant. I had to begin begging. I put my head down and wished I was back in la Calle de los Geranios. 'Then where is your food coming from today? Go, you lazy Gypsy bitch! Earn your keep!'

"She shoved me toward a woman in a tight brown skirt carrying a string basket filled with onions and peppers. I stuck my hand out, but the woman never even looked at me. Neither did the next shopper, a buxom maid with a metal scapular bouncing on her breasts. A grandmother with a black scarf tied tightly around her head also ignored my outstretched hand and the piteous look on my face. In fact, all the Granadans were so convincing in their pretense that they didn't see me that I had to touch myself to believe that I was really there.

"My mother waved for me to come to her. Her green eyes had turned pale as olives, a sure sign that she was furious. I had never seen her so angry, and in my fear, my ears stopped working. All the noise of the market stopped. Gone were the voices of our men trading horses and mules. Gone were the cries of the cheese vendor yelling about the creaminess of his manchego. Gone were the tinkling bells of the churro cart. I went to my mother. As soon as I was near enough, she grabbed the soft flesh on the inside of my arm and twisted until tears sprang into my eyes. I wiped them away. I had learned long ago that crying only made her pinch harder.

"She yanked me to her so that my ear was next to her beautiful mouth and hissed into it, 'If you can't earn your keep, we'll have to sell you to the *payos*, like Mariluna.'

"All us children lived in terror of the fate of Mariluna. She was the last of nine children born to a family on Sacromonte even poorer than my own. Her parents had sold her to the owner of the brick factory. We saw Mariluna at the market, trailing behind the family cook, her thin shoulders slumped under the weight of the baskets she carried in either hand, her head bent, her Gypsy defiance beaten out of her. We had heard that she slept on the floor of the kitchen and was fed scraps from the family's table. It was probably a better life than the one she had had with her family. But, in her family, everyone slept on the floor and shared scraps. With *los payos,* only Mariluna and the dogs slept on the floor and ate scraps.

"With the threat of Mariluna's fate ringing in my ears, my mother shoved me away. In panic, I ran up to the first person who crossed my path and jabbed my palm at a señora wearing a fancy navy blue drop-waist dress with stockings of finely spun white lisle cotton. A cloche hat shaded her ivory skin. Her maid, a stout, red-faced woman with stumpy bow legs, pushed me away.

"'*Para la niña,*' I whimpered, gesturing pathetically toward my baby brother. My mother had slumped into an equally pathetic lump in the dust. Even chubby-cheeked little Mateo managed to appear near death.

"'Don't bother *la señora tan linda, tan bonita,*' my mother yelled in Spanish, smiling wanly at the grand lady. In our own language, she hissed to me, 'Either you get money from this bitch or I will when I sell you to her.'

"I ran after the woman, harrying her like a dog nipping at the heels of a bull. My eyes were a baby fawn's, so sweet, so sad as I begged, 'My little brother, the baby, he's sick. My mother has no milk for him. We have not eaten in three days. *Un duro para la niña, señora.* It will bring you good luck. You and your children.' I sharpened my voice and hardened my eyes as I said 'your children.' These words reached behind the wall the woman put between herself and the dirty beggar.

"The grand lady's eyes flickered to my mother and I knew she was thinking of her own children and the curse I might place upon them. Her pace slowed. I put back on my pitiful beggar-girl smile, so that she would forget I had frightened her and would remember only that she was a kind and generous woman whom everyone admired for her saintly ways. I knew I had her, but then the maid pushed her lady forward and swatted hard at me.

"The maid was doing her job to swat at me, but she hit me harder than she needed to. Hard enough to freeze my eyes into beams of pure Gypsy menace as I snarled, 'Good luck to give. Very bad luck not to give. Who knows what might happen?'

"*La señora* dipped into her purse then and put three centimos on my palm. These coins were so light they could blow away like dried leaves and were worth barely more. This time I was not the fawn, sweet and sad;

this time in my eyes *la señora* saw the color of her children's flesh, dead and cold. I spit on her money. The bitch crossed herself and hurried away.

"I gave my mother the coins and she cursed me for letting the lady go with such a pittance. I believe that my mother might have found a buyer for me that day if a great clanking had not caught her attention. Everyone turned toward it. We had seen motorcars before, but only from a distance and certainly never in the market. The traders' horses, already on edge from having Mentholatum smeared on their rectums and fed coffee beans to give them a bolt of temporary spirit, reared and snorted and fought the traders, trying to run in terror from the clattering machine. A coop of clucking chickens burst free and the birds escaped, wings flapping wildly as windmills, straight into the path of what had scared them. Turnips, beets, heads of cabbage rolled out of the baskets shoppers dropped in their panic.

"In all the chaos, only one person remained calm: my mother. Anyone looking at her as she wedged her thumb into her baby's mouth to break his suction on her nipple would have thought she didn't have a care in the world. Only I noticed the centimos she'd taken from me roll down her faded pink skirt as she stood. This told me how scared my mother really was, for money meant more to her than air. Seeing how well she could hide her true feelings gave me the stupid hope that Delicata was hiding her true feelings of love for me. That when she slapped and cursed me, she was doing it out of love, to toughen me up for a world that hated my kind.

"I, on the other hand, could not hide my fear of this *automóvil*. Only the week before a little boy had been crushed with the touch of a tire. I'd seen the spot on Calle Ángel smeared with bits of his heart and guts. So, like the brainless chickens, in my fright I ran straight into the middle of the road.

"The machine stopped. It did not have a top. The driver stood up and pushed the goggles he wore back over his head. Two white circles stood out from the dirt on his face. His hair was the color of cinnamon. Underneath the dirt were freckles of the same color. He was *un sueco,* a Swede. This is what we called any of the tourists from the north who grew so heated that they turned the color of boiled tomatoes in weather we found chilly.

"'*Perdóneme, señorita.*' The *sueco* held out a hand covered by a glove of yellow leather and indicated the road. '*Con su permiso.*'

"Even for a *sueco* it was strange to speak so politely to a Gypsy. I looked around and saw the faces of the maids and their mistresses who had, only seconds before, pretended I did not exist. I saw the face of the elegant lady who had dismissed me with her dead leaf money. I knew they all expected me to ask him for money, so I stuck my hand out and asked:

"'Dame perras gordas.'

"At this, the voices in the market started again. 'Como una gitana.' Just like a Gypsy. They were surprised when el sueco got out of his automóvil. The man was a giant. He walked over to me.

"His guide, a small Spaniard with wax on his mustache, scrambled out of the car then and tried to pull his employer away. 'Señor,' he hissed at him, 'a los gitanos les pasa como a los perros; si no pegan pulgas, pegan pelo.' This was a very common saying that everyone knew so well no one had to repeat it except to a foreigner. 'Gypsies are like dogs: if they don't leave their fleas on you, they leave their hair.'

"The tall stranger stared at me and I saw myself with his eyes: a skinny girl with hair matted and dulled by dust, black dirt under her fingernails and in the creases of her hands, ground into her elbows, knees, bare feet, wearing a gray rag of a dress. Most shameful of all, just as the guide had warned, my legs were covered with fleabites, some of them infected, all of them scratched until they had bled and scabbed over.

"'What will you do to earn this?' he asked in a Spanish that sounded as if a machine were grinding out the harsh words. In his hand gleamed the coin I had asked for, perra gorda, named for the lion imprinted on it that looked like a fat dog.

"'I can dance,' I answered as I stared at the ground.

"The payo women clucked and hissed the condemnation, 'Sinvergüenza.' 'Shameless.'

"Yes, I thought, I am sinvergüenza and, grabbing the hem of my skirt, I began stamping the dust with my feet just as Delicata had taught me, just as I'd done at every baptism, wedding, and funeral I'd ever celebrated with my people, just as I'd done earlier that day leaving the street of geraniums. The difference was that, for the first time in my life, I was doing it for strangers and, even odder, no one was singing. I had never danced without singing. None of our people danced without singing. Cante was what made us dance. But my father had pounded his songs so thoroughly into my head that, in truth, I never lacked for a cantaor. So, with the memory of his hammering playing through my head, my heels pounded into the earth, reaching down to that place where black thoughts and blacker deeds form, even as my arms became willow branches in the breeze while my hands became geese flying to a cool and green land. I ignored everything—the women of the town pursing their lips into tight lines, the stones on the ground that hurt my bare feet. All I thought about was that, for as long as I danced, I held the line that separated dirty little Gypsy girls with lice in their hair from dogs.

"'*Anda! Anda!*' I was barely aware of Little Burro's shouts, of her claps picking up a counterrhythm. They only made me concentrate more on obeying the rhythm ticking in my head, my heart. Urged on by Little Burro's *palmas,* I finished *a matacaballos,* a speed to kill a horse. Only when I was holding my final pose, back arched, hand flung into the air, did I notice that the stones I thought I had been dancing across were pesetas.

"'Bravo! Bravo!' The giant blond stranger threw more coins. Then, although his guide tried to hold him back, he put ten more pesetas in my hand. The others in our band swarmed forward to snatch the centimos from the dirt. The *payo* women pretended to be disgusted even as their own palms itched for the feel of the *sueco*'s coins. Through the crowd, I saw my mother stand and walk away with my baby brother.

"I pushed through the Granadinas. A couple of the old women, the ones most toughened by hard work and bad weather, spit in my face. They pretended to do this to take off *mal de ojo,* but it would have worked just as well if they had spit on my feet. They really did it to show their contempt. I ran after my mother. As I passed the spot where we'd been sitting, I saw that she had left behind my father's basket of nails. I tried to pick it up, but it was too heavy for me to carry. My mother was almost out of sight.

"I ran to catch up with her and was out of breath when I drew close enough to yell, 'Mamá! Mamá! You left behind Papi's nails!'

"'I leave only trash,' my mother said as she pried the coins out of my hand. 'We are not nail sellers. We are dancers. And we don't need a singer.'"

Chapter Twenty-two

We are dancers.

I walked around with those words whirling through the fog in my head. I was barely passing any of my other classes and still I took even more time from them to practice. The blisters on my feet had turned to calluses and, beneath them, bone was thickening into genuine dancer's bunions. Will was my accompanist, my accomplice. He would play for as many hours as I wanted to dance. I stopped existing except in the mirror of a studio. Only in those mirrors could I occasionally glimpse the creature filled with passion and fury that I wanted to become. Had to become.

Around the same time, Didi got tired of Jeff, Ducado cigarettes, and Doña Carlota. She made an announcement: "I've wasted enough time. Cher was barely eighteen when Liberty Records signed her. She was on the charts by the time she was twenty. I have screwed around long enough." From that point forward, Didi's attendance at Doña Carlota's class became spottier and spottier. She was, she told me, "so over" flamenco. We barely saw each other. More nights than not, she wouldn't be home when I fell asleep. Didi told me that her work was evolving. "Spoken word," she said, was the new form her art was taking. For the first time in our friendship, I didn't know every detail of Didi's life. The only times we saw each other at the Lair, one of us was rushing off, so I wasn't around enough to hear any of the new stuff. This was fine with me. Since it meant I had flamenco all to myself, I was free to gorge on it.

Didi decided to debut her "spoken-word performance pieces" at Amateur Night at a coffee shop a few blocks east of the university on Central that catered to students in fleece vests and camou pants and professors in L.L. Bean khakis. She asked Will to play for her. Nothing fancy, nothing that would overwhelm her poetry, just a little background music.

The day before her first-ever public performance the weather turned from crisp fall to dead winter. The evening of the big event I drove while Didi sat beside me doing breathing exercises and vocalizations. She didn't say anything the whole way except "Hooo-hoooo. Haaa-haaa." The Skankmobile's heater had died and it was cold enough in the car that Didi's long exhalations froze. We found a parking spot right off Central just down from Nob Hill. I carried a box filled with Deeds's CDs. Will was waiting for us when we arrived. Without saying anything to him, Didi rushed to the ladies' room.

"How's she doing?" Will asked.

I shrugged. "I've never seen her so nervous."

I found a stool for Didi and put it onstage, then stacked and restacked her CDs into pyramids and ziggurats on a table next to the stage. Will dragged a chair onto the stage, bent his head down until his temple touched the neck of his guitar, and tuned up. People around us avoided eye contact, looking away as if we were doing something embarrassing that no one wanted to acknowledge. A chatting couple, seeing that we were setting up to play music, moved to a table farther away.

Didi came out of the ladies' room in an outfit calibrated to look as if she hadn't given it any thought. But I'd seen the hours she'd spent in front of the mirror, choosing the artfully battered hip-huggers and an embroidered bolero jacket she'd scored at Le DAV. Seeing it made me realize how long it had been since we'd gone thrift-shopping together.

Didi settled herself on the stool, turned to Will, and nodded. He began playing something cocktail loungish with lots of tremolos and jazzy inflections that seemed to beg for reminders to tip your waitress.

"Hi," Didi said.

The crowd glanced up and fell into an uncomfortable silence in which the hiss of the steam machine foaming cappuccinos sounded unnaturally loud. Everything about the setup was wrong. She was too close to the audience. She needed a microphone. Not to amplify her voice. Just for the psychic distance amplification provided.

"Hello, Albuquerque!" she yelled, a parody of every heavy metal concert, in every giant arena, she'd ever wormed her way into. Except that this was not a giant arena, and it was doubtful that any of the latte sippers had done much time at Guns N' Roses concerts. A few kindly souls smiled uncertainly. Didi's strategy was to take the place by storm. A punk poetry smack-down. She nodded at Will. He began churning furious chords while Didi yelled a couple of selections.

There was a lag of a second or two after she finished when even I wasn't sure if she was done. I didn't start clapping until Didi shot a murderous glance my way. The crowd joined me in a halfhearted round of applause that dwindled into an awkward silence. It was filled with the lethal sound of an audience choosing to babble about tests and boyfriends and diets rather than listen to the deepest outpourings of your soul.

Panic skittered across Didi's face as she realized she was dying. Almost as a nervous mannerism, she began patting her feet to the rhythms Doña Carlota had been pounding into us. I recognized the twelve-beat *compás* of an *alegrías* with accents on the three, six, eight, and ten, and a softer one on the twelve. With the same automatic response Doña Carlota had programmed into us, I picked up the beat. Will focused on me until he had decoded the style pattern I was clapping and started strumming in time, abandoning melody and simply hitting the beats with the driving percussive style Doña Carlota insisted upon.

Didi echoed what we were doing and her footwork grew louder. She clacked her heels harder and harder until she turned the wooden floor into a drum head resonating to her beat. The effect was instantaneous. The babbling in the audience grew softer as Didi's *golpes* and *tacones* grew louder. Soon the grinding and hissing stopped as the counter help paused to listen and the only sounds were our hands and feet. Didi added *brazeo,* her arms twining up, fingers fanning, out and then in, pulling attention into herself with each rotation. When she had every eye in the place focused on her, she started reciting:

> *I died of cholera*
> *My father threw the torch*
> *That turned the house*
> *Into a dervish of flame*

Somehow she fit the lyrics to the beat. The odd accents created a hypnotic rhythm that made unexpected words leap out in ways which lent them an originality that hadn't been there before.

> *"The contamination must be contained"*
> *He bellowed and hurled*
> *My breasts*
> *My lips*

My pimples
My bangs hiding my eyes
The new hair between my legs
Into the bonfire

Right in front of my eyes, I witnessed Didi change. Each gaze, each pair of eyes she managed to rivet, fed her with an energy that I seemed not just immune but actually allergic to. Didi was another story. The attention nourished a hunger she had had her whole life. She grew larger before our eyes. I clapped louder. I shouted out the *jaleo* we'd learned in class.

"*Vamos ya,*" I yelled. "*Así se baila. Toma! Que toma!*" They were all versions of "You go, girl." And Didi did. She recited in time to the beat until her voice took wing and she was singing in a style that was part rap, part *cante,* and all Didi.

"Save the innocents!"
He heaved in
L'eggs pantyhose
Tampax ultra-slims
Bonne Bell Boyz 'n' Berry gloss
Maybelline Great Lash
Summer's Eve Morning Rain douche
And all the CDs of the Strokes
Into the bonfire

"It had to be done."
He gathered my bones
Disinfected of flesh
And dressed them in
A pink tutu

She finished with a flurry of footwork ending in a dramatic pose, arms flung to the heavens, Will and I wringing out one final, monumental chord/clap that left no doubt in the audience's mind that it was time for massive applause. A few of the more highly caffeinated half-stood, half-crouched in a subdued, coffee shop version of a tentative standing ovation.

After milking the applause for all it was worth Didi spoke in the mock humble style of an acknowledged queen. Celebrity-ese was a native tongue she had been waiting her whole life to speak. It is a gentle language that can be spoken only from on high, down to fans. Based as it is on adulation, all it required was an elevation, and in that moment, arms thrown high, Didi became big enough to have little people.

"I call that one 'Quarantine,'" she said, looking down as if the revelation had come at a great price. "I wrote it after I visited my father in the hospital"—she paused, then went on reluctantly, as if the information were being dragged out of her—"for the last time.

"He was all, you know"—Didi's arms tented above her head—"covered in this oxygen thing. Tubes everywhere—" She stopped. There was silence, the pure silence that is a subtraction of all the normal sounds, even breathing.

"So, here's my father dying of cancer and all he wants to talk about, all he ever wanted to talk about since I betrayed him, and became a sexual being"—knowing snorts of laughter from a few women in the audience— "was that I was going to hell if I didn't watch out."

While Didi launched into another one, I thought about "Quarantined." Did it matter that Didi's father had treasured and approved of everything his beloved daughter had ever done? That it was my mother who predicted I was going to hell and threw all my contaminated goods away? Probably not. Probably all that mattered was that every woman listening mourned again for the father she'd lost at puberty and every person of either sex believed he or she had been privy to a dark personal revelation.

"In Sevilla, during Semana Santa, Holy Week, they have these songs? Called *saetas*?" Didi threw in a little upspeak as if this information was just occurring to her on the spot. "That means an arrow to the heart. They're sort of laments that the singer sings to Jesus or the Virgin Mary during these gigantic processions. So you have thousands of guys in black robes and hoods carrying these colossal floats that weigh tons and they stop while someone on a balcony sings their heart out. Anyway, I call this next one, 'Arrow Poem.'"

Another one I hadn't heard before.

"Because of the *saeta* thing. But also when you see it written down, the lines form an arrow." She shrugged as if to say that even she herself could not explain the random ways in which genius struck.

My kiss is summer
Your kiss is cut watermelon

Sprinklers click.
A shower every seventeen seconds.
Seventeen years.

Waiting for night.
Waiting for the moon.
Waiting for the breeze.
Waiting for owl screech.
Waiting for earth warmth.
Below.
I am waiting for heaven cool.
Above.
Waiting for your whisper.
Waiting for your touch.
Waiting for a breeze.
Waiting for a moon.
Waiting for night.
Waiting for him.

I was back in Tomás's secret park where the cut grass had smelled like watermelon. Where Didi had found me the day she came to say she was sorry she had taken my thing. Had she done it again? I felt embarrassed, exposed. But no one was paying any attention to me. I searched Didi's face for some acknowledgment that she had stolen the poem from my life. There was none. She was already on to the next one.

With each piece, the crowd leaned farther forward. Didi had started weak, but she finished invincible. All she'd had to do was figure out how to set her natural charisma to a flamenco beat and the coffee shop audience became hers just as surely as every lonely Sunday driver who'd pulled up at the Puppy Taco drive-through window had been hers.

"Thank you. Thank you," she said, putting her hands into prayer position and bowing her head until her lips touched her fingertips. "I'll be performing around town. Come on by and say hello. I'm Ofelia!"

This time, the entire place stood and clapped. I joined them. Didi *was* Ofelia. I clapped for her. I clapped for Ofelia.

Chapter Twenty-three

"*Y! Un! Doe! Tray!*" By the end of the semester, Doña Carlota was using flamenco shorthand to start us off. After an abbreviated countdown the class would run by itself. "Delicata's *paseo!*" She ordered and we all surged into the sequence of steps first choreographed by Doña Carlota's mother almost a century ago. Everyone in the class fell into the dream that she was putting her foot in history, following a path that led all the way back to the original tribes in India. But no one else dreamed as I did that the long trail of Doña Carlota's story would lead to a love nourished in secret. And no one else dreamed as Didi did that it would lead to immortality.

Didi's skirt whipped against my legs as we pivoted and turned sharply. Far from abandoning flamenco, after her coffee shop debut Didi saw that *el arte* was the key to success and she threw herself back into it with an obsessiveness that approached my own. She'd also restarted her affair with Jeff. Snatching him away yet again from Liliana had created a highly satisfying drama for the rivaling flamenco camps that had been established once Didi was acknowledged as a diva worthy of competing with Liliana for the title "head flamenco bitch."

Doña Carlota switched to an unfamiliar sequence and we all followed her through the new choreography like ducklings waddling after their mother. We knew that she would repeat the steps again and again through the class, that our feet would follow hers as mindlessly as the duck babies followed their mother, if only we surrendered our brains to her story. And though weeks had gone by without a new chapter, that day, with no preamble, she took up the tale once again.

"Since the day *el sueco* rained *duros* down upon me, my mother did nothing but work to create her own *cuadro*, what they called a *zambra* in

Sacromonte. She was *la capitana* of our group. She was the one who broke the astonishing news to the others: there would be no *cantaor.* 'We don't need a singer,' she insisted. All that *los suecos* care about is *el baile.*

"'But how,' the other women asked, 'will we dance without a song?'

"'Sing to yourself,' my mother ordered. 'We will all keep time. If you have to have a song, sing it yourself.'

"Late at night, after the women had worked all day carrying water from the distant well and cooking over smudgy fires of dried cactus, and after the men, who'd spent the day sleeping, left to drink at the *colmao,* we would meet. My mother and I taught Dried Wood, La Burra, La Burriquita, and La Sordita all her dances. My brother Mono played the guitar. The one problem was, of course, my father. He had forbidden my mother to ever dance again for strangers. But each time Dried Wood whispered to my mother in her scratchy voice, 'What about El Chino? He is going to find out. No one can keep a secret on Sacromonte,' all she would say was, 'Leave him to me.' Then she would go back to pounding the floor of the cave with the cane she used to beat out the rhythms she was harnessing us all to. Like this. *Y, uno, doe, tray. . .*"

The entire class, caught up in the story, believing that they were with Delicata on Sacromonte, moved to her beat.

"Next to my mother, Little Burro was the most committed to this new scheme. She had watched all of her daughters except the youngest, La Burriquita, grow up and marry men no better than her husband. La Burriquita was her last chance for one of her children to have a better life than she had had and her mother and her mother's mother all the way back to India. Little Burro was so desperate for something better that she took down the green and red polka-dotted material that hung in the door opening and with it made a real flamenco dress for La Burriquita.

"'Let me show you,' she said at our next practice. She lifted up the dress she was working on and we all sucked in our breath at its beauty, amazed that Little Burro's hands, strong enough to move her husband's *fragua* without any help, could stitch together a thing of such grace and femininity.

"'But this is the best part,' she said, smiling with pleasure at our amazement. She shook the dress out and a length of fabric unrolled across the packed dirt floor.

"I gaped at the dress's long train. *'Una bata de cola!'*

"*'Una bata de cola,'* my mother said, draping the long tail of fabric over her arm. 'With this and a *fenómeno'*—she meant my brother Mono. Though still a boy without a whisker on his face, he could play better than any of our men. 'We have two of the three things every *cuadra* needs. All we are lacking now is *un alcahuete.' Un alcahuete,* a procurer, was vital since he would bring the tourists to us. None of the women could ask their husbands because they would immediately tell my father, who had forbidden my mother ever to dance for another man.

"'We have no choice,' my mother said. 'We must talk to El Bala.'

"At the very mention of this name, Little Burro spit on the floor and crossed herself.

"'No,' Dried Wood said, her voice even more parched and raspy than usual because fear had dried the saliva in her mouth.

"El Bala, the Bullet. I don't know if he had always resembled a bullet or only looked like one after he went bald. But with no hair, his eyes sunk into his fat, greasy head, no neck, a body thick and stocky from the shoulders to the ankles, El Bala looked like a bullet. He worked as a collector for Juan 'Coronel' Fernández, the moneylender. A scar from the knife of a resistant borrower sliced El Bala's face, making one nostril and his top lip flap open so that his two top teeth and the inside of his nose were exposed. At the top of the long scar was one dead, white eye.

"'Who else then?' my mother demanded. No one spoke. The Bullet was the only man who spoke the language of *los suecos* and who would not immediately tell my father what my mother was planning. El Bala kept to himself. Even our men were so frightened of him that they kept their distance.

"'It is better not to catch the eye of the tiger,' the men said as they faded away at El Bala's approach.

"We found the Bullet loitering outside the *colmao* wearing a shiny black suit with tan shoes and a checked cap pulled down as low as it would go to hide his white eye. He agreed to be our *alcahuete* in exchange for half of everything we brought in. With no other choice my mother agreed, warning him that he'd better fetch enough paying customers to be worth all the money he would take from them.

"'You just be ready to waggle your *jojois* because I'll bring the tourists,' El Bala told my mother, using our word for rabbit, which means the same thing as your American word for pussy. It was a word I had heard often, but never spoken by an unmarried man in the presence of a woman. Gypsy men had gotten a knife in the liver for lesser offenses; still, my mother didn't object. It was the first deal she made with El Bala, but it wouldn't be the last.

"On the day of our first performance, my mother made me stand in the galvanized tin tub she used to mix sausage while she poured buckets of water over me.

"'Scrub harder,' she ordered as I rubbed the dirt that seemed tattooed into my skin with a slimy chunk of agave cactus. When we finished I was cleaner than I had been since I came from the womb. Over my head I slipped the dress my mother had made and was buried in the wonderful smell of sizing put in the brand-new fabric to make it stiff.

"Then, while my father slept, snoring loudly from a late night filled with too much *aguardiente*, my mother prepared herself. I did everything I could to keep the *chaboros* quiet. When she was ready, her hair shining with oil, her skin pink, she was a vision as beautiful as Christ's mother. Fear made her even more beautiful.

"'Let's go,' I said, pushing my mother out the door. We'd been lucky. My father hadn't woken.

"'No,' my mother said. 'He will find out where we are. If he is going to kill me, I want him to do it here. Not in front of the others.'

"I begged her to come with me, but she had made up her mind and woke my father. As she told him what we were going to do, my mother took off her new dress and handed it to me. She was naked when the first blow fell. It was usually deafening when my father beat my mother because her screams, then ours, would fill the cave. This time, she didn't say a word. That scared me and my brothers and sisters more than anything that could have happened. We watched speechless as the blacksmith's fists struck. He was as angry that she planned to dance without him, without a singer, as he was that she was going to dance at all. Her silence, her refusal to scream, to beg, drove my father to such frenzy that he bellowed out both his rage and hers.

"There was no thought that a neighbor would come to our rescue. Since Cima Metales had opened, the screams of wives being beaten had become as routine as the clang of hammers on anvils had once been. All *gitano* tribe business was taken care of on Sacromonte. All *gitano* family business was taken care of in the cave.

"We, her children, watched with the eyes of little beasts, each of us calculating how our lives would change with our mother dead. Tears ran down the cheeks of only the littlest ones. The rest of us were dry-eyed since we'd been on our own for so long already. My father would have beaten my mother to death if the most fearsome man on the mountain had not appeared at the door of our cave.

" 'What are you doing, you idiot?' El Bala asked, as if my father were making a silly mistake that would bring bad luck, like saying the word *lizard* or not touching iron to ward off the evil eye or owning a black dog. Startled, my father stopped and in that frozen moment, what we all noticed was my mother's body, not that there was blood trickling down it, but that it was naked and a man who was not our father was looking at it.

"El Bala stared at my mother as if she were made of gold, as if he could not believe that such a treasure could be found in a dirty cave filled with dirty children. My father turned on El Bala, eager to drive his fists into harder flesh. El Bala was quicker; his knife seemed to appear out of nowhere, plucked from the air. Its blue blade glinted in the flickering light cast by the *candiles*. Toledo steel. None of this hand-forged Gypsy shit for a professional like El Bala. Fear of that blade did not stop my father. Rather it was El Bala's ruined face—the sneer cut forever into his mouth, the blind eye, white and eternally weeping—that stilled my father's hand.

"I ran forward to give my mother her dress. Standing up as straight as only a true *flamenca* can, she pulled the dress over her head, careful to keep her blood off of it. Then we followed El Bala out of the cave.

"In the moonlight, I could see that both my mother's eyes had swollen and turned purple. She touched her teeth and smiled when she discovered none had been knocked out.

"At the doorway of Dried Wood's cave, El Bala inspected my mother. He took out his handkerchief, spit on it like a mother, and gently wiped a smear of blood from beneath her right nostril. 'Go in and wait.'

"Dried Wood had the nicest cave of any of us and one of the first on the whole mountain to have electricity. A bulb burned from the ceiling. The floors were covered with a checkerboard of white and green tiles. Around the edges of the kitchen was a border of vines and leaves. A dozen gleaming copper pans hung from pegs. A curtain of red and black polka dots with a ruffle at the top separated the main room from the bedrooms in the back. They had arranged two rows of three chairs each, leaving just enough room in front of the chairs for the dancers. They all stared at my mother. She looked much worse in the harsh overhead light.

"Dried Wood finally broke the silence. Pointing to my mother's swollen eyes, she joked, 'Chop up those plums. The sangria needs more fruit.' Everyone laughed then and crowded around my mother, repinning her hair, snagging loops of hair from either side of her face to cover her bruised eyes, giving her glasses of *aguardiente* to kill the pain.

"When they'd finished, we all sat on the straight-backed chairs borrowed for the evening, except for La Burriquita, who stood so as not to wrinkle the dress Little Burro had made for her with a *bata de cola* trailing behind. We lined ourselves up next to a rickety table where six borrowed copper cups and a pitcher of sangria waited for our first customers. We'd gone into town early that morning to beg and steal the fruit. The wine and *coñac* we had borrowed from the owner of the *colmao* with promises to repay him double after that night. The alcohol had kept the fruit we chopped up hours ago from spoiling immediately in the heat, but tiny bubbles of fermentation were now fizzing around the cubes of red-stained peach.

"As the bubbles released their evidence of rot, the group began to argue. With each hour that passed without any sign of El Bala, their words grew sharper.

"'I was crazy to believe in this ridiculous plan!' Dried Wood said.

"'Who comes to see flamenco in a *cueva* so far from Calle de Sacromonte?' Little Burro demanded. 'No one! El Bala is laughing at us.' Then she called El Bala a name that meant both cockmaster and master of the cock and, at just the moment when Little Burro had pulled out her knife and was threatening to go into Granada and cut off the cockmaster's *janrelles,* El Bala threw back the curtain at the door and gestured for the party he had in tow to enter.

"Over Dried Wood's threshold stepped three Englishwomen of the type who liked horses and dogs better than people, certainly much better than they liked men. They wore long khaki skirts and, under them, brown leather boots with thick soles that laced up to the knees as if they were going on safari. They each had a different cameo brooch pinned at the necks of the blouses they covered with cardigan sweaters. They squinted their eyes and turned their heads away as the smell of the cave hit them. One of them took out a handkerchief and held it over her nose. And Dried Wood's *cueva* was fragrant compared to ours.

"'Here are the suckers,' El Bala said to us in *Caló,* at the same time smiling like a gigolo and waving his arm elegantly toward the women, who smiled in return, lifting thin lips off of large, horse teeth. Little Burro's daughter Burriquita and I had to cover our mouths and lower our heads into our laps to hide our laughter. My mother eyed me sharply and I remembered my assigned role. I jumped up and showed the women to their chairs, then brought them each a glass of sangria.

"The fragrance of cinnamon and cloves hid the smell from the over-ripe fruit as I handed the glasses to the women. They responded with words that sounded as if they'd been spoken by horses. My mother started *palmas,* clapping softly, and everyone fell silent. My mother nodded at *las inglesas.* The women smiled back, holding up their copper cups in salute. My mother caught my eye and I jumped to refill the women's glasses. They waved their hands over the rims insisting they didn't want any more, then glanced at one another, laughed, and pulled their hands away, surrendering. Though that was the first time I saw this charade, it would not be the last, for surrender was what foreigners came to us for, what they sought in the caves of Sacromonte. They all came to us wanting to surrender. Surrender their white to our dark. Surrender their clean to our dirt. Surrender their tame to our wild.

"As I sat back down after refilling the glasses, Dried Wood added *pitos,* snapping her fingers. La Sordita clacked on the floor with her heels. I joined my mother in *palmas.* Because there was no singer, no *cante,* I came in on the wrong beat, and my mother shot me a dark glance. An instant later, though, the Englishwomen nestled their copper cups between their thighs and clapped their hands and my mother saw that she needn't have worried. The women clapped like El Maleta, the Suitcase, a half-wit with one arm longer than the other. They clapped like they were wearing mittens and listening to another beat. All of us glanced at one another because we had never heard such a thing; even a Gypsy baby could keep better time than these grinning *inglesas.* But my mother just kept smiling at the women and even held out her hands to them as if to compliment their talent and shouted '*Olé!*'

"Hearing my mother put the accent on the last syllable as if we were at a bullfight made us smile and look away because her *payo* pronunciation was a grave insult since it said the person was an outsider, and for us there was nothing worse.

"But *las inglesas,* their cheeks already turning red from the wine, didn't hear the insult. They saw only our smiles and shouted back, '*Olé!*'

"My mother, numbed by the *aguardiente,* took her pass first, shaking her skirt and stamping forward like a windup toy. She kept her head lowered to hide her bruised face. Her exuberant *zapateado* had nothing whatsoever to do with the mournful *soleares* Mono was playing. But we smiled even more when we saw that it didn't matter to the strangers.

" 'Brava! Brava!' the women shouted when my mother took her chair, huffing and puffing and fanning at her bosom as if she had truly exerted herself.

"Little Burro was up next. Her dance was tough and muscular, with lots of *palmadas,* slapping the side of her shoe, her thigh, and stomping the floor. She even sang a bit in her foghorn of a voice. It was a ridiculous charade of the real flamenco we did for ourselves, but, again, the Englishwomen loved it, clapping wildly. They no longer pretended to resist when I passed among them, refilling their glasses. Their cheeks were as red as a baby's with fever. They lolled against one another, whispering comments in one another's ears, laughing, and clapping in their mittened, half-witted way.

"My mother never stopped watching them, her gaze sharpening as theirs dulled. When she saw them leaning against one another, whispering secrets, she signaled to my brother and he strummed through a series of arpeggios and tremolos. He played the tricked-up, show-off fake flamenco that my father wouldn't allow at home but that these English ladies seemed to love.

"Then La Burriquita trotted out in her new dress. Eventually, La Burriquita ended up looking like her mother, like the driver of a mule team. But that night, she was magnificent in her new dress. Unfortunately, she had no idea how to dance with *una bata de cola.* Instead of making it her partner, La Burriquita fought with it as if it were a serpent that had swallowed all but her head and arms.

"Still my mother stood and clapped and yelled to make the tourists believe that this was the grand finale. Luckily, English people are so polite that they will see whatever someone wants them to see. So, it was true, those women really did see a grand finale and they stood, too, and clapped with my mother when La Burriquita held her arms up like a toreador dedicating a bull to his sweetheart.

"Then, before the English ladies knew what was happening, all the dancers disappeared and my mother was taking the copper cups from their hands and lifting the chairs out from under their bottoms. They turned then to leave, but their friendly guide, the poor fellow with his one eye gone dead, so polite, so courteous in spite of his gruesome face that they had taken pains not to stare at it, was blocking their way. Even more alarming, the friendly guide was no longer grinning and his sliced-up face no longer aroused their pity. It scared them.

"'Señor,' one of the ladies said in her horse Spanish when the Bullet didn't move away from the door to let them out. 'Por favor.'

"But El Bala still didn't move. The women stepped a bit closer to one another, the red draining rapidly from their cheeks as El Bala lifted his ragged lip up in a wolfish smile and presented them with a bill.

"'What is this?' the shortest one asked. She looked more like a bull-dog than a horse. 'We already paid you. One hundred and fifty pesetas. Back at the plaza.'

"'Yes, pesetas. But I said duros.'

"'Duros? What is a duro?'

"El Bala bowed his head and scrunched his shoulders to make himself and the total seem smaller. 'Perdóneme. We say duro, you say five pesetas.'

"The Englishwomen's eyes all popped open. 'This is mad. Seven hundred and fifty pesetas! You said it would be one hundred.'

"El Bala closed his eyes and shook his finger in front of his face. 'No. Duros, no pesetas.'

"'No, indeed not. We have paid what we agreed upon.'

"'Sí, sí, but if you will look here . . .' El Bala redirected their attention to the bill as if, because he had written them down, the numbers were truer on the paper. 'Por la cuadra. Por la sangría. Por el tocaor. The boy, truly a fenómeno, no? Then, is customary to buy everyone a drink.'

"'And this?' The bulldog woman stabbed a stubby finger at a figure.

"'For charity. Is for the sick, the old, the widow, the cripple, the—'

"'Yes, yes, yes. Back home in Derbyshire we're all quite active in the Parish Relief Society. But that's not the point. The point here is, we agreed upon one hundred and fifty pesetas. Not seven hundred and fifty.'

"'One hundred and fifty pesetas! In England you can have such an evening for one hundred and fifty pesetas?' El Bala turned back into the Bullet and stopped speaking. He refused to answer any more questions and he refused to move from the doorway. He gave the ladies enough time to remember that they had told no one at their hotel where they were going. They had wanted an adventure. They had wanted to be sponta-neous. They had wanted to surrender.

"They looked over at us expecting to find women who would be sympathetic to their plight. They saw for the first time exactly what we were: *gitana* wolves who fed on pale *payo* flesh.

"The one with the longest, saddest horse face finally snapped, 'Oh, just pay it. Let's get out of here. I can't stand this smell another second. It's all simply too, too authentic.'

"The instant El Bala had their money, he was all smiles and courtly manners again. He swept the curtain away from the door and stepped aside as if the women were marquesas and he their liveried footman.

"The next night, El Bala brought two Germans, heavy-boned men with gray shadows beneath their eyes, dull hair the color of toast cut too short on the sides.

"We were astounded to hear El Bala speak to them in their language as well, pulling aside the curtain and saying, *'Bitte, bitte.'* He pointed to me, La Burriquita, La Sordita, my mother, and said, *'Schonne, nein? Los damen son muy schonne?'*

"The Germans studied us like men used to driving hard bargains at brothels. Their faces were stolid, set against us. We didn't have to understand any German words to know that they did not find any of us pretty. This rejection made my mother mad enough that she danced with a fierceness that was like a train coming through the cave. My brother even had trouble keeping up with her on the guitar. She was so good that he yelled out *óle,* and Mono was just like our father; he never applauded anything that was not *flamenco puro.* On any stage in the world my mother's dance would have brought down the house. But those Germans just sat there like two rotten piles of wurst. Nothing, not a sound. You couldn't even hear them breathing.

"It was even worse for the others. The Germans didn't clap, didn't call out. All they did was drink. As I filled and refilled the copper cups, they gave me looks that made me aware again of the fleabites on my legs, of the way my shoulder blades stuck out like chicken wings against the back of my dress, of the black crescents of dirt beneath my fingernails.

"At last La Burriquita ended the performance with her grand finale, battling with the python of her *bata de cola.* Even though my mother screamed her *olés,* the Germans didn't twitch a muscle. Instead they called El Bala over, pressed money into his hand, and pointed to my mother.

"The Bullet threw the money back in their faces, drew his knife, and shouted in furious *Caló,* 'She is no whore some goatfucking German can point at.'

"That is how the Germans learned that flamenco was not an advertisement for Gypsy prostitutes. One of the men raised his hand to El Bala. Who knew why. Maybe he was going to shake hands. Maybe he was going to reach into his jacket for a gun to kill us all. Whichever, the Bullet's knife came down and when he pulled it away, the German's finger drooped like an elephant's trunk. It would never point again. El Bala had sliced the tendon in one *golpe.*

"That was the only night we didn't make any money. Night after night, El Bala brought the tourists. If we were tired, we danced. If we were sick, we danced. If we were sad, we danced. We learned how to get money from them all. We learned that the English would pay for smiles. The Spanish tourists from the north would pay for scowls. The Americans would shower us with pesetas for footwork at double, triple time, anything that was loud and made the sweat jump from our faces. Anything that looked like a lot of hard work. The Germans hardly paid for anything, but if I could make them laugh by waggling my bottom and pretending to be a *puta,* there might be a few *perras gordas* in it for me.

"For the other girls, our shows quickly became boring. They were always unpinning their skirts before the last note was played. I didn't understand it. For me all the rest of life on Sacromonte was boring. It was the hours we spent dancing that were exciting. When I danced, I dreamed I was my grandmother, that I was La Leona, queen of the *cafés cantantes.* I pretended that the tiled floor of the cave was the wooden stage of the Café del Burrero in Sevilla, where the happiest people in the happiest city on the face of the earth were happy all the time. Where there was always enough and more than enough for those with talent. Where a good dancer could rule over the city like a queen if she was talented. And I was. I was talented."

With that unequivocal declaration, Doña Carlota stamped to a finale and signaled the rest of us to stop. "Have you all been reading your Lorca?" she asked as we chugged water and wiped sweat from our faces, our necks.

"*Sí,* Doña Carlota!" we chimed back.

"*Bueno.* Today you will learn Lorca's *bulerías.*"

At the mention of Lorca's name, Didi edged closer to La Doña. She had become even more enamored of the charismatic poet as she read everything she could get her hands on about his life and, even more important, his death. She loved that Lorca was idolized in his own time, that his

flamboyant life and ambiguous sexuality enraged conservatives, that he
was martyred by fascists.

Doña Carlota clapped sharply; our break was over. She continued her
story: "One minute, it seemed, our *zambra* was new and frightening. The
next it was all any of us had ever known. I could no longer remember having a life that didn't revolve around dancing for *payos* who huffed and
puffed behind El Bala, climbing up the paths to Dried Wood's cave.

"But it wasn't one minute. Three snows had fallen on the Sierra
Nevada and three had melted since that first night. Three years. For the
first time I knew the year because in Dried Wood's cave there were two
miraculous things: electricity and a radio. I never had a lover I loved as
ardently as that radio. No sun ever lighted my life as brilliantly as the
glow from the tubes of that radio. If I'd ever been alone with it, I would
have wrapped my arms around it. The other girls called me La Catedral
because the first thing I did when I stepped over the threshold was to rush
in and kneel in front of Dried Wood's radio shaped like a cathedral. It was
there, on my knees, that I learned the year was 1934.

"'What useless information,' La Burriquita said, when I told her.

"'Find some music. A nice *cuplé*,' the others cried, begging to listen
to the syrupy ballads that were so popular. But I shushed them and
twisted the dial through spikes of static and a blurt of music that Little
Burro immediately identified. 'Leave it there! That's La Bella Dorita!' I
pushed on past the famous *cupletista* chirping about rosebuds and butterflies and love until the dial landed on Radio Union where an announcer in
a breathless, urgent voice told us:

*The army under Generalissimo Francisco Franco has suffered heavy
casualties in trying to put down the miners' strike in Asturias. Though
severely underarmed, the miners' skill with dynamite has inflicted a
humiliating defeat on the army. In the mountain passes they have
erected giant catapults to hurl the dynamite at the soldiers. In the
cities, dynamiters creep forward smoking cigars with which they light
the sticks grasped in their hands. Casualties have been high. Twelve
hundred miners have been killed.*

"'Who cares about some miners in Asturias?' La Burriquita whined.

"'You should,' I told her. 'If the soldiers can shoot miners, *payo* miners, what is to stop them from shooting girls, Gypsy girls?'"

" 'Go back to La Bella Dorita!'

" 'My father says the miners are *comunistas* and they want to turn us all into atheists like in Russia where there's no church."

" 'Pfft!' Burriquita spit on the floor. 'The priests! The nuns! Black crows! My father says we should kill them all. What have they ever done for us?'

" 'No! It's *los ricos* that we should kill and take their land.'

" 'Why? Who wants land? Land is just dirt. We already have plenty of dirt.'

"I put my ear against the rough cloth of the radio and tried to block out the sound of the women slapping and pecking at one another like chickens, but El Bala stuck his head in the door and yelled, 'They're coming! These are real *aficionados. Señoritos!*' *Señorito* was a magic word. Some *señoritos* were nothing more than spoiled playboys who pretended to love flamenco as an excuse to hold *juergas,* orgies of drinking and whoring. But the real *señoritos,* true connoisseurs of flamenco, were as rich in knowledge and reverence for *el arte* as they were in duros. We had heard stories of the real ones paying exorbitant amounts to experience flamenco, real flamenco, *flamenco puro.*

"El Bala pointed at my mother, then at me. 'You two, he heard about you two. He wants the authentic stuff. None of this tourist crap, okay?'

" 'Who is he, this *señorito?*' " my mother asked.

" 'Why do you care? How many *señoritos* do you know?'

" 'I know that this one is coming to see me dance.'

"Maybe my mother hadn't noticed that El Bala had also pointed at me.

" 'All right, if you must know . . .' He lifted his ruined lip in a jagged smile, pleased to announce his big catch. 'It is Federico García Lorca.'

"In Granada, the poet was as famous as his good friend, the bullfighter, Ignacio Mejías. We knew as much about him as we did La Bella Dorita.

" 'That *maricón!*' Dried Wood yelled.

" 'So what if he does like boys?' El Bala shot back. 'You're not pretty enough for him anyway. What are you worried about?'

" 'I hear things. Don't you know what they say about him in the market?'

" 'I don't pay attention to the gabbling of hens.'

" 'You should. They say his plays are filthy. He writes nothing but filth, this *maricón*. Worse, though, he speaks against the government, the church. He had to run away to Madrid because he was going to be arrested. No one can believe he came back to Granada. The *guardias* follow him everywhere. Men with notebooks watch him and write down the names of everyone he speaks to. If you bring him here they will write down our names!'

"'*Buen!* Go on then.' El Bala shooed her away. 'The others will be happy to take his *perras gordas.*'

"No one moved.

"'Good, then shut up!'

"We all fell silent and into that silence came the sound of footsteps. We jumped up, certain it was them, *los señoritos.* Instead my father walked in, followed by his uncle, an ancient guitar player named Antonio. Fear seized my mother at the sight of the two men until El Bala said, "I invited him. Tonight we need a real *cantaor.* A true singer of *cante jondo.* Tonight we need El Chino.'

"My father's chest swelled, but my mother was furious.

"'I refuse to dance if he sings,' she said.

"Before she could say anything more, though, El Bala yelled, 'They're coming!' and shoved us all into the other room.

"I pushed La Burriquita away and held a corner of the curtain aside to peek out at the party as they arrived. I knew the instant he stepped in that the man in the white suit was a poet. It wasn't just the way another man leapt across the threshold to sweep the curtain aside and allow him to enter first. Or the way the five others in the party stood back to give him his choice of seats. No, I knew he was a poet because of his eyes. Only a poet or the Madonna could have eyes so sad and kind and wise. His dark hair was brushed straight back from a high forehead. Eyebrows black as raven's wings soared above black eyes. A mole nestled beneath his right nostril as if one of the polka dots had escaped from the bow tie around his neck. Everyone knew that polka dots brought good luck. The poet would bring us good luck.

"Lorca sat down, crossed his legs, and looked around the cave with a half-smile on his lips as if each copper pot, each tile, each lump on the whitewashed cave wall pleased him immensely. He crossed one leg over the other, adjusted the crease of his trousers, twisted the cap off his pen, and wrote in a notebook he plucked from his pocket. While his head was bent, the others in his group caught one another's eyes and exchanged smiles as if they were sharing a special event. As he was writing, he suddenly turned his head so quickly that he caught me staring at him from behind the curtain. He smiled. Since most adult attention led to a swat or reprimand, I looked around to see if there were someone behind me that the pleasant expression might be intended for. There was no one—he was smiling at me. I smiled back.

"My father began his *temple,* the long, drawn-out *Ay* that rose and fell and rose again as he warmed up his throat. Tío Antonio strummed a rough *falseta.* He played the old way, entirely with his thumb, the nail thick as an old dog's. As my father began singing, the poet closed his eyes and nodded his head. His lips moved as if he were saying prayers or having a vision.

"El Bala ordered Dried Wood to go on. My mother crowded in beside me. As Dried Wood's feet beat against the floor, Lorca's eyes flew open. He studied Dried Wood, then turned to the woman beside him. She must have been his sister because she was his twin except with no bow tie and no mole. All Lorca did was arch one of his black eyebrows, and my mother and I both knew we were in trouble, these were not tourists. They knew what they were seeing. They knew what we knew: Dried Wood wasn't very good.

" '*Ozu,*' my mother cursed under her breath. She stepped out from behind the curtain and began *palmas,* clapping loudly, trying like a sheepdog to herd a wandering sheep back to the flock. Dried Wood responded with some footwork that was all pointless clacking and grimaces. My mother yelled out *Óle!* This was always the cue for the tourists to join in with some applause or, if they'd finished their sangrias, a few *olé*s of their own. But Lorca only shook his head, capped his pen, put his notebook into his pocket, and, with a nod to the others, stood up.

"Seeing Lorca's disgust, my mother stepped up, her heels drumming furiously, calling out to the guitarist, to the singer with clapping hands and stamping feet for a *bulerías.* Tío Antonio responded immediately. My father fell silent.

"Lorca paused while the women gathered their coats. He saw what I saw: that every molecule of my mother's being was *puro, flamenco puro.* Without taking his eyes from her, he motioned for the others to sit back down. He watched my mother like a schoolteacher listening to a pupil reciting her lesson. When she set up a tricky *contratiempo* with her arms, he nodded to indicate that she'd gotten the answer right and murmured, *'Sí, eso es.'* My mother glanced over at me. It was as if we, she and I, had spent the last two years surrounded by people who could barely hear, who only understood us if we screamed and waved our arms and acted out everything we wanted to say and, suddenly, we had met someone who could hear the faintest whisper.

"In her exuberance at meeting such an *aficionado,* my mother forgot herself. She must have imagined she was a girl again, shining in the gaslights on the stage of Café Filarmónico, for she danced with a liveliness I'd rarely seen before. I knew she could never keep up the tempo she was demanding from Tío Antonio. She should have called for my father to sing. But years of dancing for *payos,* for clods blind to her art, combined with her hatred for my father, erupted in a fever that boiled through my mother's blood so that she wouldn't, she couldn't, stop. Not to rest, not to allow my father to sing, nothing. Her hair, which had been oiled into fat rolls beside her ears, flew apart, swatting her red cheeks with greasy tendrils. Sweat streamed from her face. She sucked in air with wide-eyed gasps. Still she would not stop. Not until the coughing started. She ignored the first hacks, turning them inward into choked spasms. But eventually they exploded and my mother had to stop.

"Before the poet's sister could reach for her coat again, my mother, doubled over, had one hand plastered over her mouth, the other one she used to wave me on. She held up four fingers to signal to the guitarist to put his *cejilla,* his capo, on the fourth fret, and snapped her fingers in *pitos* loud as the crack of rifle shot to the *compás* of the style she wanted me to dance, a *fandango.* But I didn't want to dance *por fandangos,* a folk dance for Malagans wearing silly hats with ribbons and clacking away on giant castanets. I wanted to dance what the poet wanted to see and he wanted to see the real thing, *flamenco puro.* I pushed back the curtain and entered, clapping a different time from the one my mother was snapping.

" 'Keep it on the third,' I told Tío Antonio.

"He glanced over at my mother, La Capitana, to see if he should play the *soleá por bulerías* I was calling for or the *fandango* she had ordered. But she couldn't hear anything over the cannonade of her own coughing.

"I clapped out one *compás,* ordering *soleá por bulerías.* By the second *compás,* Tío had his *cejillo* back on the third fret and was following me. But I didn't make my mother's mistake. Lorca was a true *aficionado* and true *aficionados* know that *cante* comes before all else. I called for my father to sing. He was like me and did not allow his feelings to overtake him, as my mother had allowed hers to cloud her judgment. El Chino did not sing about faithless wives or the stab sharper than a knife of a woman's bitterness. No, he took the puny packet of his grief and added it to the burden our people had carried for a thousand years. Then it had weight, then it meant something. Then Lorca was enraptured. The poet uncapped his pen and wrote down the verses my father improvised on the spot. *Letras* with biting words about how *los payos* might try to enslave *gitanos* but who, really, were the slaves?

"Lorca loved the clever twist of his words that always turned *gitanos* into conquerors, rulers of a world where *payo* fools lived by the sweat of their brows and only *gitanos* were clever enough to live by their wits.

"In response to my father's verses, their message, their structure, my *taconeo* hammered out a celebration of our people. Lorca nodded his approval of my collaboration with El Chino. This was true flamenco and he knew true flamenco.

"Stepping backward and silencing my feet, I called my father back in. He was ready. He sang beautiful verses, tragic verses that told the tale of a simple blacksmith who journeyed to Sevilla to trade horses. Once there he was bewitched by a dancer from Triana whose *baile* was a tornado whirling about two precious stones, the emeralds that were her eyes. The tornado tore his heart from his chest. He sang about how he would die without his heart. How in claiming his heart, he'd had to steal the dancer too. It was sad to snatch *la bailaora* from Sevilla and lock her away in a cave, but how could a man live without his heart? Tell him, please, and he would do it. Tell him how he could set the dancer free and still go on. Tell him how a man could live without his heart?

"I didn't hear the words in my brain. I heard the tragedy of my parents' lives in my body and I danced it. Slow, *a medio tempo*. I lost track of everything and everyone around me, my mother, the poet, the fine ladies from Granada. Because I was only aware of my father's song and telling the sad story of his love for my mother, I was momentarily thrown off by the unevenness of the tiles on the floor. Then I realized that I was dancing over coins and not flimsy centimos or even pesetas, but duros! Heavy silver coins, some with the banished king's portrait on them, some celebrating the new government in Madrid, the Second Republic.

"In spite of the coins, though, I didn't make my mother's mistake. I didn't keep hammering my feet faster and faster like a cheap tin windup toy gone mad. I took a bold step back to signal what I wanted to the guitarist. Then I enfolded the wild calliope of movement, scooping it out of the air with my arms and drawing it all back in. In a split second, I froze the motion, holding it ticking inside of me.

"The poet's group pounded their hands together, but he silenced them, both his hands thrown out to stop every sound. Now he watched. Now he listened with his eyes, waiting to learn if I had anything to say. I had waited all my life for this. I opened my arms and released the motion, let it whirl me away until *I* was a tornado, until I had whirled every heart in that cave out of every chest and claimed them as my own."

Doña Carlota clapped her hands with a sharp crack like a hypnotist waking his subject from a trance. "That's all the time for today! Next class we talk about my friend, Federico García Lorca."

Chapter Twenty-four

Outside, Didi ran past. "Gotta blast," she yelled back at me. "Jeff's helping me put a new piece together." She stopped. "You wanna come? You've hardly heard any of my new stuff."

I shook my head no. All I wanted to do was stand in the sun and enjoy the spell Doña Carlota's story had cast over me.

"What? You're just going to hang here and pretend that you're the emerald-eyed dancer and the heart you steal belongs to Tomás Montenegro?"

"No." She was, of course, exactly right. That was precisely the fantasy I was looking forward to.

"Oh great," she said sarcastically. "Then that means you're actually planning to do something real about the Tomás obsession."

I pulled a foot out of the sandals I'd changed into and displayed my calluses, bunions, and blisters like they were merit badges. "And these aren't real enough?"

"Hey, girls who cut themselves get real scars."

"That is so ridiculous! That is a completely different thing al—" But before I could finish saying *altogether,* Didi left, waving her fingers at me over her shoulder as she went.

More to prove to myself than Didi that she was wrong, I moved without thinking. Thinking was a problem for me since it always led to nothing, to me daydreaming in the sunshine. So I didn't stop long enough to think, I simply made myself run to the faculty parking lot just in time to see Doña Carlota's driver pull up to the back of the academy, jump out of the Buick, and race around to open the back door for the old lady.

Because it was the last thing on earth I wanted to do, I called out, "Doña Carlota!"

It is possible that I hadn't called out loudly enough for her to hear me.

That I'd only called out loudly enough to say that I'd done it. That I had tried. But the handsome, silver-haired driver with the unplaceably ancient face did hear me. He stopped and looked my way. The thrill of recognition that I had always expected when looking into Doña Carlota's face hit me in the instant my eyes met this old man's. The eyes. It was like looking into Tomás's eyes. The ridiculous suspicion that he might be related to this old man was what alerted me to how dangerously overwrought I was. If the driver had not already been turning Doña Carlota's attention my way, I would have fled. But she was beckoning me to come to her and the driver was walking away to give us privacy, so I stepped forward.

"Metrónoma, yes, what is it?" Her tone, her expression, her bearing, all the eloquence a great dancer can bring to bear expressed how highly irregular and irritating my appearance was.

What would my lie be? A question about Lorca? About the *bulerías desplante*? Stopping her after class when she'd made it quite clear she didn't want to be stopped after class or any other time was bad enough. Now I had to compound the offense by asking an idiotic question. Nothing I could say would be any worse than the truth. So, because, it was the one word always at the center of my thoughts, I blurted out the name that was all questions rolled into one, "Tomás—"

"Tomás?" She cut me off, leaping at his name with the same ardor I spent my days hiding. "What have you heard? Do you know something? Has he been in contact with you? Someone you know? He's sent a message through you? He's done that before. Sent messages through unlikely sources. Where is he? Do you know where he is?"

"No, no, nothing like that. I don't really know him. I—"

"Ah, I see." The moment of excitement, hope, was gone, replaced by an Old World knowing that added my name to what was surely a very long list of breathless girls. "But you would *like* to know him, is that it?"

I shook my head no. This was my nightmare. I had tipped my hand. This was what I had decided from the very beginning never to do: I was a groupie. "I'm sorry. I didn't mean to bother you. Have a good weekend." I was babbling. I was an idiot. I backed away, twiddling my fingers in a silly wave, ducking my head to keep her from seeing how my cheeks now scorched with embarrassment.

"Wait. Come back. You just did the one thing you have to do in flamenco: you told me something. When you said my nephew's name, you showed me more about yourself than you've revealed this entire semester.

That, *that* is what flamenco is all about. And that is what you never do and what your friend does all the time. Show yourself. Tell me something. Tell me something true. *Dígame la verdad.*"

"Didi's not telling the truth. She hasn't even told you her real name."

"You think that matters? You think it matters that her truth is lies? I will tell you something." She waved me closer. "You could be a great dancer."

My heart clutched. These were astonishing words from a woman's whose most fulsome praise was usually *"No es feo."* It's not ugly.

"But . . ."

Of course there was a *but.*

". . . you never will be. Technically, you are *estupendosa.* But great?" She shook her head and muttered, *"Nunca, nunca."* Never, never. "Why? Why will you never be great? Because of her."

There was no point in even pretending that I didn't know who "her" was.

"Flamenco is *yo soy.*" The gravel of the parking lot crunched beneath the old lady's foot as she stamped the earth, taking, demanding her place on it with the essential Spanish declaration: I am. "Flamenco is *yo soy.* You are waiting for her permission to be. Why? Why do you stay in her shadow? She is too big a tree. You are barely a sapling. You will never have enough light because you will never have enough courage to grow past her and reach the sun."

She leaned in even closer, close enough that I smelled Maja soap, lavender, sweat, and, underneath, another odor I couldn't identify. It contained elements of the sweetish fragrance Daddy had about him toward the end, plus the spike of what I'd come to identify as an almost hormonal surge when Didi's ambition went into overdrive, all combined with the dusty scent of ancient books and rooms that have been closed for a long time. "I too once had a friend like Ofelia. From her I learned a secret, a secret that you must learn."

Suddenly, what she had to tell me seemed more important than anything, more important in that moment than even Tomás.

"She needs you more than you need her. Because of that, she will never release you. You will have to either live forever in her shadow or—" She made a swift, brutal hacking motion, an ax hacking down a tree.

How, I wanted to ask her, *does a small tree kill a big tree?*

But, as if she had literally slashed through some vital energy source, the gesture seemed to have exhausted Doña Carlota. Without the bristling nimbus of energy that always whirled around her, she shrank into herself, suddenly old and a bit confused. Mumbling, she turned away. Abruptly, her voice rose and she declaimed, "What had to be done, had to be done. Rosa, what other choice was there?"

"Excuse me? Doña Carlota, did you say something?"

But when she looked up again, her eyes were glazed. She hadn't been speaking to or even seeing me.

Her driver, sensing her disorientation, rushed forward. Murmuring soft words in Spanish, he led her toward the car. Before he closed the door, she turned to me and held a quivering hand out as if she were offering something unspeakably precious.

Or asking for it back.

Chapter Twenty-five

At Doña Carlota's next class, we found a note taped to the studio door saying we were to meet in the academy's main classroom. Once we'd settled in along with all of the other flamenco students, the director of the program, Alma Hernandez-Luna, swept in, brimming with an illegal amount of energy. "I have some good news and some bad news. The bad news for those of you in the beginning class is that Doña Carlota had a minor stroke yesterday and though the damage is not serious, she will not be able to finish what remains of the semester. I will be taking over her classes."

"What?" I gasped. She hadn't even gotten close to Tomás's part of the story.

Didi shrugged. "End of story time."

"The good news is that we have with us today the great *flamencologista,* Don Héctor Arribe y Puig. Don Héctor has come to this country to write the history of flamenco in the New World. Let's all welcome our distinguished guest, Don Héctor Arribe y Puig."

As Don Héctor took the podium, Didi turned to me and whispered, "Hercule Poirot."

She was right. Don Héctor was the very embodiment of Agatha Christie's hairnet-wearing detective. The professor was a diminutive man of a type that had either never existed in or had vanished long ago from the New World. A pince-nez would not have looked out of place clamped across the bridge of his thin nose with its quivering nostrils. More than that, though, Don Héctor Arribe y Puig was the embodiment of the compleat flamenco *aficionado* of the obsessive-compulsive type. There is no exact equivalent in our country to the true, the *puro,* flamenco *aficionado.* The comic book collector, the baseball trivia nut, the Civil War reenactor, the *Star Trek* fan, yes, the *aficionado* is all of those things but more. With flamenco's emphasis on *el puro,* its love of bloodlines, the mystical handing down of *el arte* through families, preferably Gypsy families, the die-hard *aficionado* also has something of the racetrack handicapper, the genealogy authority, and the slave-owning plantation owner about him as well.

Don Héctor started off by drawing a great tree on the blackboard. With much emphatic underlining, he labeled the roots, INDIA. Brushing chalk dust from his hands, he turned to his audience with a pugnacious tilt to his little chin like a backstreet brawler ready to take on all comers. He seemed deflated when we copied the tree into our notebooks without a question.

"The long debate over where *los gitanos* originated is over. A study at Hospital Puerta de Hierro, Madrid, Spain, examined the HLA class I and class II antigen distribution in a sample of seventy-five Spanish Gypsies and seventy-four Spanish non-Gypsies. They found that Gypsies have a statistically significantly higher frequency of these antigens, which proves that Spanish Gypsies are closer to Indian Caucasoid populations than to the Spanish non-Gypsy population."

He looked around, expecting a fierce reaction to what he obviously considered a bombshell revelation. All he saw were students either duti-fully scratching down what he'd just said or muffling yawns. I, however, was electrified. He was talking about the exact issues of blood and authen-ticity that haunted Tomás. This was the problem I could solve for him, the one that would win his love. I scribbled frantically as the professor continued.

"Gypsies migrated from or were cast out of India around the eleventh century. Records exist of their arrival in Spain as early as 1425. They named themselves Children of the Pharaoh, Egyptians, *los egipcianos,* a label that eventually became *los gitanos.* Many of the Gypsy chiefs called themselves *conde* or *duque de Egipto,* count or duke of Egypt, and trav-eled with their bands under forged letters of safe conduct, claiming to be pilgrims. They carried out this fabrication for so long that even the *gitanos* themselves forgot that they were not really Egyptian pilgrims, sons and daughters of the pharaohs.

"After the Reconquest of Spain in 1492, when the Moors were driven from the peninsula, an official persecution began against all non-Christian groups. The same year that America was discovered, Jews and Gypsies became hunted people. They were either expelled or forced to hide their identities. The Jews became *conversos,* practicing their religion in secret, or they fled. Gypsies had nowhere to flee.

"For three centuries, Gypsies were subject to laws and prejudice designed to eliminate them from Spain. Settlements were broken up; Gypsies were required to marry non-Gypsies. They were denied their language and rituals as well as being excluded from public office and from craft membership. In 1560 Spanish legislation forbade *gitanos* from traveling in groups of more than two. Gypsy dress and clothing were banned. Around this same time there were nearly a million Gypsy slaves in Eastern Europe, and Holy Mother Church owned two hundred thousand of them.

"Not surprisingly, Gypsies were driven into a permanently submerged underclass from which they are still emerging today. Just as hardship, however, nurtured the blues music of your persecuted African Americans, in my country it led directly to the creation of flamenco song, dance, and guitar.

"During the twentieth century in Spain, General Franco continued the persecution of Gypsies, as did the Nazis, who enacted laws twice as strict against Gypsies as against Jews. By 1933 Hitler was already sterilizing Gypsies in Germany. Eventually, a third of all Gypsies living in Europe, nearly one million people, were annihilated. A proportion as great or greater than the number of Jews murdered, yet not one single Gypsy was called as a witness at the Nuremburg Trials. Not one single Gypsy was ever compensated."

Don Héctor summarized the story of flamenco's beginnings among the outcasts of Andalusia: Jews, Moors, and Gypsies. He followed the trunk of his great tree to limbs forking out to ever smaller branches to, finally, the farthest extension, the one that bore the golden fruit that we were all feasting upon, flamenco in Nuevo México.

"According to my sources, flamenco truly took root in New Mexico in a club outside of Tesuque, a town on the edge of Santa Fe. The name of this club was, appropriately enough, El Nido, The Nest. Here, for a handful of *aficionados,* the godfather of New Mexico flamenco, Vicente Romero, danced. He danced his famous twenty-minute *escobilla,* the machine-gun footwork that would eventually kill him when, overweight and trying to keep up with a young Pepe Greco, Romero died onstage at the Joyce Theater in New York."

Didi turned to me, her eyes popping at this fabulously dramatic bit of New Mexican flamenco history.

"But Romero left behind several talented guitar-playing brothers and also inspired two dancers of seminal importance. The first, of Chippewa/ Puerto Rican heritage, María Benítez, would go on to become one of the most acclaimed dancers in America. The second is your own Señora Alma Hernandez-Luna."

At this the tiny professor bowed his head and extended his arm to Alma and the entire audience burst into spontaneous applause for our beloved homegirl.

"But the real reason I have journeyed to your state, to your *Tierra del Encanto,* the actual focus of the book I will be writing, is—" The professor turned back to the blackboard and drew one final branch. Beside this last branch he chalked in the name *Doña Carlota Montenegro de Anaya, bailaora.*

Didi's eyes popped open and she hissed in my ear, "Yes!"

I waved my hand to silence her, terrified that I might miss a single word.

"Not only was Doña Carlota the first to bring *flamenco puro* to New Mexico, she gave *el arte* its first academic home in the New World. Doña Carlota has established a dynasty of New Mexican dancers who are, even now, forcing flamenco to evolve in directions both unexpected and, for many traditionalists, unwelcome. But we shall save that controversy for another time. For now, let us examine the reasons why flamenco took root here in your majestic state as it did nowhere else in America, or the world, for that matter. Why was *el arte* embraced by Hispano residents in a way that no other Latino population in the New World has? The reason is contained in their very preference for the designation 'Hispano.' Not Latino, not Chicano, Hispano. Though it is not a popular contention in this country, some would say that something in the blood of your Hispanos, those descended from Spanish settlers, responds to flamenco. They hear, in its ancient rhythms, songs of home.

"Let us leave, for now, the fascinating question of why New Mexico, and turn to the other great gift that Doña Carlota has given us."

He picked up the chalk again and next to Doña Carlota's branch, drew one leaf. Beside it, he wrote *Tomás Montenegro de Anaya, tocaor.*

The sight of his name written by another's hand had as powerful an effect upon me as if the phantasm I constantly dreamed of had stepped into the classroom.

I didn't realize until a loud buzzer startled me that I had stopped breathing. Most of the class vanished before the buzzer even finished sounding. Didi jumped up, then waited for me so we could join the stampede. Instead, bereft, I pointed frantically at the lone leaf trembling at the end of Doña Carlota's branch. "He didn't get to—"

Didi pulled me to my feet before I could finish. "Not a problem. We'll just grab the old queen before he escapes and pepper him with questions."

"No, no, don't say anything, okay?" I hurried to wipe away such a possibility. After my humiliating experience with Doña Carlota I was actually relieved that the old lady wouldn't be coming back to class. I couldn't risk word getting back to her through the professor of my interest.

"Come on," Didi coaxed. "It'll be great reconnaissance. He knows a lot more than he's telling. We can take him to Cervantes and get him to spill the beans."

Cervantes was a gloomy cocktail lounge frequented by a midafternoon crowd of high-level defense contractors who hung around Sandia Labs and used the bar to cheat on their wives with their secretaries. Didi liked it for intelligence-gathering because of the air of betrayed trust that hung over the place. I grabbed her arm as she started toward the professor. "No. Seriously. I don't want you to talk to him. Or anyone. It's too early for direct contact."

" 'Direct contact'? Rae, can you hear yourself? We're going to talk to some castanet-sniffer who's writing about his great-aunt. How much more indirect can you get? And 'too early'? Dude, it's been"—she held up fingers as she ticked off the months—"May—"

"Not all of May."

She bent the finger in half. "Whatever. June. July. August. September. October. November."

I swatted her hand down to stop the count. "I know how long it's been."

"You know I'm absolutely the last person in the world to object to obsession, but even for me, this is getting a little strange. I mean, you met the guy once."

"Which is once more than you ever met most of the guys you groupied."

"Am I doing that now? Am I groupieing now? That was always a means to an end. You know that. It was a way to get to the life I'm supposed to have. This thing, what you're doing, it's a way to completely avoid having a life."

"I can't believe this. I cannot believe that you, Poster Girl for Fantasy, have the nerve to tell me shit like that."

I tried to walk away, but Didi planted herself in front of me and wouldn't let me pass. "Rae, I'm doing it. I'm putting myself out there. I'm going for it. What are you going for?"

"Like I really have to tell you."

"I know what you *think* you're going for. You *think* you're going for love, but you've got that right in front of you."

"Yeah, right." I gave a dry snort of fake laughter to dismiss her ridiculous claim.

"Okay, what about Will?"

"Will? What *about* Will?"

"He's insanely in love with you."

"What?"

"Please, please, please, don't be the only person who doesn't know." She studied my face. "God, you don't. Oh well, I guess you look in a mirror, you expect to see yourself."

"What is that supposed to mean?"

"Will, he's you. Hopeless, one-sided love sublimated into flamenco. Sound familiar?"

"As a psychiatrist, Didi, you make a really good poet. Move. I'm going home."

"Look, you're right, I shouldn't criticize anyone for living in a fantasy, but at some point you've got to intersect with reality a tiny bit. At least on our missions, the whole idea was to meet the band, right? If you've seriously got a thing for this guy, let's go to Doña Carlota and find out where he is. Huh? That's a start, right?"

"She doesn't know where he is. I asked."

"Okay, very good. I'm impressed. I'm not sure I believe you, but I'm impressed."

"Didi, I have to be ready, that's all. That's all it comes down to. I'm not avoiding life or any of that other horseshit. I will see him again. I know I will. But what is the point of seeing him again while I'm still—"

I flapped my hands at myself to indicate my total inadequacy and Didi filled in the blank, "You?" Her voice was soft and concerned again. "Okay, Rae, what do they say in AA? I can't enable you anymore."

"*You* enable *me*? You're kidding, right? You have got to be kidding. You, Miss Never Met a Controlled Substance I Didn't Like? Enable me? *Me?* The person who got you through high school? What? Has the quality of my service gone down now that I've found a genuine interest in life?"

"Flamenco or Mystery Man, Rae? Because they're two sides of the same obsession and flamenco isn't any better than Mystery Man. Flamenco is obsessive-compulsive disorder set to a great beat. You can dance to it, but, Rae, you cannot have a life to it."

"I am through with this conversation," I said, and for the first time ever, I walked away from Didi.

That weekend, I allowed Will to relieve me of my virginity. A part of me realized Didi was right. I'd left the realm of the rational. I thought Will might be a first step back. A first step away from Tomás. He wasn't. Fully clothed, with one kiss, Tomás had transported me to the stars. Naked in bed, with Will laboring between my legs, I had never felt more leaden and earthbound in my life.

There was a smear of blood on the sheet when it was over. Will held me tenderly as I cried. It was nice to be comforted even if it was for the wrong thing. Will thought I was weeping for my virginity. My tears were for the knowledge that had just been made certain that I would never be happy with anyone except Tomás Montenegro.

Chapter Twenty-six

At the height of the Ottoman Empire's glory, Topkapi, the sultan's harem, housed nearly five hundred odalisques. The most desirable women in the world—Berber, Nubian, Turkish, Albanian, Caucasian, Greek, Chinese, Egyptian, Hindu—they were all brought to Topkapi. Imprisoned behind the harem's eighteen-foot-high walls, they were guarded around the clock by eunuchs.

The sole purpose of the captive women's lives, and the lives of the slaves who attended them, was to give their master, the sultan, pleasure. Slaves in ten kitchens cooked for the pampered females, making their bodies sleek and desirable with extra fat. Three slaves washed and depilated each girl, removing every hair on her body: nostrils, ears, vulvas, anuses. They painted her hands and feet with henna. The captives were instructed in how to whiten their skin with almond and jasmine paste, to darken their lashes with Chinese ink, line their eyelids with kohl, stain their mouths with berries. Mistresses of the seductive arts spent years working with each new girl, teaching the Ninety-nine Means of Giving Pleasure. She learned how to excite and satisfy the jaded appetites of a sultan who had deflowered a thousand virgins. But in order to be one of the fortunate few who managed to achieve the purpose of her existence and spend a night with the sultan, a girl first had to catch the eye of the Shadow of Allah on Earth.

For this, the girl had to learn to dance.

As blind musicians played—no whole man was ever allowed inside the thick doors—the girls were taught how to make their bodies into undulations of desire. How to attract and arouse with the sinuous sweep of an arm, the roll of a belly, the swing of a pelvis, how to tap out an irresistible code of enticement with tinkling finger cymbals. Then, if each movement was choreographed and executed with a sensuousness so seamless that the odalisque's body became a fluid ripple of erotic titillation, then, and only then, might she be chosen out of the five hundred to give the sultan one night of pleasure.

During the years I toiled to learn flamenco, no one ever said cigarettes were a required part of the course, but Didi and I smoked as many Ducados as we could afford. None of our instructors in choreography, improv, *bulerías, alegrías, pitos, brazeo, taconeo,* no one in any of our classes ever mentioned alcohol, but Didi and I became experts on *manzanilla,* Cruzcampo beer, Centenario brandy, and all the other Spanish liquors so beloved by true *flamencos.* Not a single teacher ever told me that flamenco was a seductive art, but, after Will, I took a succession of lovers. I was never a heartbreaker like Didi, who left broken marriages and suicide notes in her wake. I tended to choose men likely to be as dispassionate as I. I was generous and adventurous in bed since that, too, was part of my unwritten curriculum. Not often—twice—my lovers wanted more. A commitment, a future, something more intimate than my practiced writhing and moaning. It wasn't hard to extricate myself without feelings being hurt. I simply told them the truth: I was already in love, but my passion was unreturned, impossible. They nodded and didn't press. Almost everyone in the program suspected I was in love with Didi. I didn't mind that they believed my impossible love was for her. Better that than anyone ever suspecting the truth.

What my instructors in Doña Carlota's Flamenco Academy did explicitly teach was the *compás por alegrías, por bulerías, por soleares, por tangos, por fandangos,* and at least half a dozen other *palos,* each with a unique feeling based on variations in key, rhythm, and pace, making a *Fandango de Málaga* completely different from a *Fandango de Murcia.* I learned that the insiders' insiders not only put the accent on the first syllable in *óle,* but pronounced it with a nasal twang like singers from Valencia. I learned that all true flamenco legends lived in poverty, ending their days selling violets on the Calle de Serpientes in Sevilla or dying young, preferably of cirrhosis or a flamboyant overdose.

I learned that in flamenco, the more you learned, the more you realized how much you didn't know. How much you would never know. I learned that in flamenco, Spanish rules: Spanish language, Spanish heritage, Spanish blood. I learned that Hispanic is better than Anglo. That Spanish is better than either, but Andalusian is a royal flush, and in the flamenco hierarchy Gypsy trumps everything. That, ultimately, the best anyone of any other ethnic extraction could hope for was to be an amusing novelty. I learned that I had started studying a dozen years too late ever to be really good. I learned that if I practiced *el arte* a lifetime, I would never be Gypsy, I would never be Andalusian, I would never even be Hispanic.

Still, I hadn't entered the harem to become the best belly dancer. All I wanted was to attract the sultan's attention. The higher up the flamenco food chain I went, the more I heard Tomás's name. It was always whispered with reverence. He was the heir apparent to the crown of King of New Mexico Flamenco and he had disappeared. Vanished. So, even if I'd wanted to, Tomás wouldn't have been easy to track down. Rumors flew, though. He had been spotted at the National Guitar Fingerpicking Championship, where he'd wowed the crowd of ten thousand, then disappeared before the judges could award him first place. That the Soka Gakkai Min-On Concert Association had organized a tour for him of a dozen Japanese cities and his fans in Tokyo had demolished the hall where he'd appeared. Every few months someone whispered that he was in rehab. The rumor that cropped up most often, though, was that Tomás had come home. Not to Doña Carlota's home, but to some mountain hideout in the north of the state. There was one other rumor, that he had OD'd.

I never believed the last one. I was certain that the moment Tomás Montenegro left this earth, I would know it. I would look into the sky and both Ursas, Major and Minor, would be gone, heart-shaped leaves would stop appearing on cottonwoods, and my own heart would settle back into its former dull rhythm and never beat again in time to *el compás*.

When Alma strode in and took over Doña Carlota's class, Didi and I started to learn flamenco the American way. Alma picked up a piece of chalk and wrote on the board the names of all the things Doña Carlota had already taught our bodies while our brains were busy listening to her story. Knowing that the high-chested stance we had absorbed from Doña Carlota was called *la postura* did not make us stand up any taller. That all the magical stuff we'd been doing with our feet was called *taconeo* did not improve how we meshed it with our *brazeo,* arm work. Though I did like knowing that the word for the way we fanned our fingers, *floreo,* was related to the word for flower, that didn't make my fingers unfurl into any more beautiful blossoms.

After the beginning class, I moved on to intermediate, technique and repertory. I took specialized classes: *bulerías, tangos, alegrías, alegrías por bulerías*. I studied with singers and guitarists, learning the intricate code a dancer used to signal when she was ready to begin, *entrada;* when she would mark time, *marcaje,* while the singer sang; when she wanted to solo with some fancy footwork, *taconeo;* and how to call for any of these changes, *llamada.*

For me every dance class I attended, every Carlos Saura videotape I watched and rewatched until I could dance each step in perfect time with Cristina Hoyos, every Paco de Lucía CD I listened to, every Donn Pohren book I read, every García Lorca poem I memorized, took me one step closer to entering flamenco's most blessed state: *enterao.* To be *enterao* was to be in the know, a true, initiated member of the flamenco community, someone worthy of admission to Tomás's world.

It is possible, probably likely, that I would have gotten over my obsession with Tomás if I'd never set foot in the Flamenco Academy. I would have been a straight business major. I'd have taken tennis for my PE requirement. Maybe a semester or two of German with the thought that it might somehow help me on some hypothetical trip back to the Old Country to find my roots. I would have dated nice guys who drove Hondas and Toyotas, cars with good service records. Guys who never in a million years would have led me around the city on the darkest night of the year into a hidden park. Who would never have been able to joke with lowriders or hold me while we flew to the stars.

The memory of that night would have faded because, outside of flamenco's hothouse world, I might never have heard Tomás's name again and my infatuation would not have flowered into such a dark blossom. But Didi had said it best: "Flamenco is obsessive-compulsive disorder set to a great beat." Everything about *el arte* fed my fixation. It fattened my infatuation until it metastasized into a full-blown mania. Until my every thought was metered out according to its ancient rhythm. Until my heart did beat to *el compás.* Until flamenco and Tomás Montenegro had become interchangeable.

Didi was remaking herself for the unseen audiences of thousands, millions, who would one day idolize her. I was remaking myself for an audience of one. Flamenco was always a means to an end for both of us.

Chapter Twenty-seven

By our junior year, Didi had acquired what she'd always dreamed of having, an entourage. Not friends, but a coven of ambisexterous hangers-on who fawned on her in the way she liked being fawned on. When they went out—all the chattering boys and heavy-lidded girls—they wore whatever uniform Didi specified. One night she would declare that they were wearing shawls thrown over the right shoulder in the style she had affected. Another night they'd all have on denim jackets embroidered on the back with La Virgen de Guadalupe that they'd picked up on a trip to Juárez. The next night the boys would do themselves up like homegirls with platform sneakers and velvet running suits, the girls like homeboys with giant droopy shorts, wallets on heavy chains, forearms covered in prison tattoos they drew themselves, smearing ink from a ballpoint in authentic designs cribbed from a master's thesis on the topic.

Me? I became one of the novitiates I'd seen the first day I walked into the Flamenco Academy. A flamenco nun, my long skirt whispering against the floor as I went from class to studio to rehearsal hall to the small stages where I performed student pieces with student groups. Who had time for trips to Juárez?

Of course, Didi charted a much different course. From coffeehouses, bakeries, and bars, Didi graduated to winning every poetry slam she entered. Who else *danced* their poems to a flamenco beat? And if the beat was off, who at a poetry slam would ever know? Or care? A regional house published two chapbooks of Didi's poetry and helped arrange a one-woman show to promote it. The show was Courtney Love meets Carmen Amaya by way of Sylvia Plath. There was even talk of a short LA/NY run. But that never materialized. The main venue for Didi's flamenco poetry became the rarefied world of spoken-word performances.

She was in demand at small colleges, women's studies festivals, and celebrations of Latina writers.

Everywhere she appeared, Didi left droves of devotional fans in her wake, all clamoring for more. They bought up her slender volumes by the dozens, had Didi write intimate messages in them, and gave them to sisters, mothers, lovers. The regional press that published her work was already talking about a boxed set. Didi acquired a rising star literary agent who was negotiating with several New York houses to reprint the slender volumes.

Instead of reveling in the acclaim, however, Didi became even more driven. The adulation only reminded her of how far she still had to go, how short she was falling of true stardom. When the dance critic from the *Albuquerque Journal* wrote a mash note of a review of her one-woman show, Didi leaped for joy, whirling around the Lair until the space heater rattled, then suddenly stopped dead and demanded, "What the fuck is the *dance* critic doing reviewing me? I should be on either the book page or theater page. That is so like Albuquerque not to take my work seriously. They're trying to turn me into a freaking dance monkey. Yeah, make the little Latina into your pet exotic. It's just another way not to take us seriously." *Us.* Didi had used her ability to reshape reality into whatever form she believed it should take to fully transform herself into a Latina. No one in her entourage, least of all me, would have ever mentioned Didi Steinberg, the little girl who wanted AC/DC to play at her bat mitzvah.

Didi's growing fame made her a target of controversy in the Flamenco Academy. For the purists, Didi was a travesty, a fraud who couldn't stay *en compás* if her life depended on it. Didi came to classes when she wanted. She worked when she wanted. She showed flashes of brilliance between long stretches of thudding incompetence. As Doña Carlota had told me the last time I'd seen her, the great goal of flamenco is to show yourself, and that was always something Didi excelled at. An exhibitionist by nature, she was a transparent conduit of emotion. Joy, rage, sorrow—they flashed through her bold as neon. She always kept up her end of the flamenco conversation. There were heated debates among insiders, though, about whether what she did could even be considered flamenco. There was no argument, however, about the fact that audiences, especially nonflamenco audiences, loved her. For them Didi was a star. For them Didi was their introduction to and embodiment of flamenco. They came to our student performances especially for her. It was a source of extreme irritation that the one standing ovation of the evening would always be for Didi.

It drove the purists mad to see how thoroughly charisma trumped technique. Watching her beaming in the hot lights, her devotees throwing long-stemmed red roses at her feet, her dark hair dyed even darker, a *mantón* of slinky black lace tied around her shoulders, no one could deny that Didi was the perfect amalgamation of every Spanish, Gypsy, Jewish flamenco fantasy. She so *looked* the part. Was it any wonder she *hooked* the part? Was it any wonder that newspapers around the state, tired of writing the same story about the Flamenco Academy, fastened on this new hybrid, the flamenco poet Ofelia? Of course not. Stories about her appeared in successively larger publications: *Daily Lobo, Santa Fe Reporter, Albuquerque Tribune, Albuquerque Journal, Santa Fe New Mexican.* AP picked up the last one and it ran all over the country. In short order, Didi became the public face of the Flamenco Academy.

What bothered the purists most, though, was that Didi really didn't care about flamenco. She would never form her own little *cuadro* and steal dancing gigs from the regulars at El Mesón or El Farol in Santa Fe. She had not the tiniest desire to open a studio and teach housewives to dance *sevillanas*. She didn't dream of being invited to the Olympics of flamenco, the Sevilla Biennale. No, flamenco was merely set dressing for a much larger show. Didi was simply passing through Flamencolandia on her way to true stardom, collecting souvenirs to lend authenticity to her flamenco poet persona.

Though her appearances around the Flamenco Academy became increasingly rare as her career blossomed, the one event Didi always made time for was the International Flamenco Festival. The festival was an annual miracle that Alma Hernandez-Luna managed to bring forth each summer at UNM. Over the previous sixteen Junes, every major international, which is to say, Spanish, star had made an appearance.

Years of catering to rock gods and their entourages made Didi a much sought-after volunteer during the festival. As always, I was her second-in-command. Together, we would pick up the Spanish superstars at the airport, fetch the endless *cafés cortos* they required, and keep up a steady supply of Ducados, Ace bandages, cold packs, heating pads, Advil, marijuana, speed, and Tampax. In the classes our visitors taught, we would translate, take attendance, and maintain studios at the sweat lodge temperatures the AC-phobic Old Worlders demanded, usually over the protests of their gasping American students.

When they were not teaching or performing, we drove the Spaniards to the little villages in the northern part of the state so they could be astounded by how much the landscape resembled parts of Andalusia and astonished by hearing the blue-eyed, blond-haired descendants of the conquistadors who'd battled up the Camino Real and fizzled out in the Sangre de Cristos speak a Spanish that hadn't been uttered back in the Motherland since the seventeenth century. Didi always made the most of her time with our visitors by picking up the latest styles in Spanish divahood and establishing connections to be used at her convenience.

"Laying groundwork" was what she called it. That is what I had been doing as well in my own private way: laying groundwork. By our junior year I did not believe I was ready yet to actually see Tomás again, but I was ready to begin the search. I'd had a series of work-study jobs on campus to cover expenses. I didn't need much since I had been awarded several scholarships based on need and was still living in the Lair. But that year, I sought out a job in Zimmerman Library cataloging recent acquisitions. I was ready to make contact with Tomás and needed to have unlimited access and time for my research. Because news about *el arte* barely made it into print and never onto the Web, I not only had to read actual printed material in a library but had to be in a position where I could order obscure items of possible interest. I immediately insisted that the university subscribe to every flamenco magazine printed as well as acquire any publication with the remotest of flamenco connections.

Since all the magazines and newsletters were in Spanish, it was lucky I'd learned to read the language. Speaking was another story. I'd gone into my Spanish courses mute in the language and had emerged in much the same voiceless state. But I could understand virtually every word that was spoken to me and was downright excellent with the written word. Didi, on the other hand, who was completely fluent going in, stopped studying the language the first time she received a failing grade because she couldn't read or write a grammatical word and saw no reason to learn.

Consequently, I spent a good portion of my time on the job cataloging magazines and books from Spain. After I entered them into Zimmerman's collection, I would be the first borrower. Anything that didn't circulate, I would pore over before, after, or during work. After a few months, I knew as much about all the reigning deities of the flamenco world as Mith Myth had known about her gods and goddesses. What I didn't know anything more about was Tomás Montenegro. To my surprise, his name didn't appear in any of the flamenco publications. And then, on the day before winter break started, I found it. I found his name.

It wasn't in an official flamenco periodical, it was in *España Hoy,* Spain's answer to *People.* It featured a long article about Juan Diego Amaya, a distant relative of the legendary Carmen, and the biggest singing star of the past decade. Like all good Gypsies, Juan Diego went by a nickname, Albóndigas, Meatballs, shortened into the affectionate Guitos, in honor of the meatballs the famous singer had loved as a chubby child and continued to consume right into a corpulent adulthood. That the nickname was also a naughty reference to the famously homosexual singer's manhood was an added bonus. Guitos had been tapped to succeed the greatest flamenco star of the modern age, Camarón de la Isla, a Gypsy singer with an affection for heroin that some say, ultimately, proved fatal. His true fans dispute the claim, maintaining that their idol died of lung cancer. Tobacco or heroin, it all came down to the same thing: flamenco offered its stars a lot of ways to go. Meatballs seemed to be choosing the fork. He was the Pavarotti of the flamenco world in both girth and talent.

I already knew Guitos's work since it was a point of honor to idolize singers among those of us who considered ourselves hardcore *flamencos.* If you wanted to enter the sacred state of insider status, to be *enterao, el cante* was essential. We had learned from Doña Carlota that flamenco singing is not pretty, it's not melodic, it's not anything that Americans like to listen to, but it is the heart of *flamenco puro.* Dancing, guitar, percussion, it all starts with *cante.* In the real thing, dancers dance to inspire the singer, players play to accompany the singer.

I skimmed the article about Guitos hurriedly. It was near quitting time and I was anxious to clock out. I had a rare date to meet Didi and her latest conquest, Belinda Díaz-Reyes, for dinner. Didi no longer cared in the slightest what a person's sex was—her basis for selecting romantic partners was far more elemental: what they could do for "Ofelia." Didi had taken to speaking of herself in the third person as if Ofelia were a worthy charity she and everyone in her world were selflessly devoting themselves to. It seemed to work. Belinda was Chile's most famous poet, teaching for a semester at UNM. Poor Belinda had seen Didi perform and fallen madly in love. She was currently devoting herself to getting Didi published by the best press in Latin America. "It'll open up a whole new market for Ofelia," Didi had explained to me.

I was barely paying attention to the lengthy article, in which Guitos attributed his success to a Hindu swami he followed then swore he would never get hooked on the heroin that had destroyed the lives of so many of "his people," when my heart stopped. Before the letters even had a chance to settle into TOMÁS MONTENEGRO, my pulse was accelerating wildly. I snatched up the magazine and read.

When the singer was asked who his favorite guitarist is, Guitos answered in the voice roughened by life and lost love that his fans love so dearly. "I have been fortunate to be allowed to perform with the greatest talents the art has to offer. But at this moment, the guitarist I most admire is a young man from New Mexico, Tomás Montenegro. Though raised in New Mexico, Montenegro is Gypsy on all four sides. He has the blood of the pharaohs in his veins and you can hear it in every note he plays. I will never perform with another *tocaor.*"

This was a gift from heaven. All I had to do was make use of it while my courage still held. I stuffed the magazine into my waistband, sneaked it out of the library, and rushed over to the Flamenco Academy. Alma was just coming out of class. Sweat plastered her dark ringlets into curlicues around her flushed face. I stuck the magazine, open to the article about Guitos, into her hands. "We should get this singer for the festival." It was perfect. I had asked for Tomás without ever saying his name.

Months of transatlantic phone calls followed as Alma worked her way through the rings of agents and assistants surrounding the star, most of whom were, in the grand Gypsy tradition, members of the great singer's extended family. Also in the grand Gypsy tradition, messages were never delivered, calls never returned. Alma threatened several times to give up, that this prima donna was simply more work than he could possibly be worth. But I would always beg her to make just one more attempt.

"Rae, I didn't know you had such *afición,*" she said as I pled with her to keep trying.

Afición was an all-purpose term that expressed whether someone had the flamenco fire burning within them or not. Doña Carlota's typecasting had stuck: Didi was fire and I was ice. "There's a lot you don't know about me," I answered. "I'm a *ruka tan caliente.*"

Alma laughed at me calling myself a "hot babe." But she dialed Guitos again.

A month later, just as the first winds of spring were starting to blow dust in all the way from Tuba City, Alma gave me a final list of that year's lineup for the Flamenco Festival. The biggest name on the bill was Guitos. I searched for his name. It wasn't on the list.

"What about Guitos's accompanist?" I asked, tamping down my mounting panic.

Alma was disappointed, annoyed. "What? Rae, I killed myself to get your guy. Now all you can ask about is his *tocaor?*"

I tried again. "You got him! Alma, that is amazing!" As I thanked Alma, I had to admit that I was relieved Tomás wasn't coming. I still needed more information and I finally had a decent source. There is no closer relationship than that between *un cantaor* and his favorite *tocaor.* If I was ever going to learn enough about Tomás to be a part of his world, Guitos would be the one to teach me.

Chapter Twenty-eight

By the time the festival rolled around that summer, Didi was on the road, touring with a national troupe of slam poets. Meanwhile, I had pulled all the right strings so that I got the assignment to pick up Guitos at the airport even though Meatballs had specifically requested that he be met by "a young man, handsome and charming."

I arrived at the Sunport holding a sign that read: BIENVENIDO AL FAMOSO GUITOS!!! SUPER STAR Y REY SUPREMO DE LOS CANTAORES!!! Before she left, Didi had helped me make the sign welcoming the Famous Meatballs, Super Star and Supreme King of Singers. It manifested not just Didi's all-around genius for sucking up to the right people, but was also designed to deflect Meatballs's pique when he discovered he was not being met by the *"joven, guapo y encantando"* he had specifically requested. I was glad Didi wasn't around. Meatballs was my first live connection to Tomás and I wanted to be alone with him. I clutched a huge bouquet of red roses, the basic unit of currency in the economy of flamenco adulation, as I waited for the singer to emerge.

Far down the airport great hall a statue of an Indian warrior, his cape unfurling behind him, reaching out to catch an eagle, took flight above the tangle of passengers. Remembering the many past missions at the Sunport when we'd waited beneath the outstretched warrior to ambush sleep-dazed rock stars, I grew nostalgic and wished Didi were with me.

Meatballs was easy to spot. He appeared wearing an overcoat and a muffler. Among the tourists in their pastel cottons and spongy white tennis shoes, he looked like a bear coming out of hibernation. He had a bear-shaped body that sloped down from narrow shoulders and expanded to the great tub of his gut below with an immense, bear-size head above. His hair, though, done in a traditional old-school Gypsy style, was all Wolf Man. Thick, coarse, and black, it swept straight back from a hairline that started barely more than an inch above his thick, coarse, black eyebrows and involved muttonchops that all but covered his ears.

Even though the air-conditioning in the terminal was barely keeping the heat below body temperature, Meatballs acted as if he had been caught in a polar blast, tightening the muffler around his famous throat and buttoning up his overcoat. He saw my sign and glanced around for the young male escort he'd requested. When it became obvious that I was the entire welcoming committee, the singer graciously threw his arms open, lumbered over, and wrapped me in a damp embrace that smelled of Spanish hair pomade and old overcoat. Carried within the folds of that voluminous overcoat, wrapped into the threads of the muffler wound around his neck, embedded in his coarse, black hair, his dark, blue-sheened skin, coursing through his blood were the compass points of the Gypsy world. Tomás's world. The world of flamenco. He would be my guide. I embraced him back.

"Bienvenido a Nuevo Mexico!" I delivered the welcome I'd rehearsed. Today, I had no choice; I had to move from a reader and a writer of Spanish to a speaker.

The first words out of his mouth were, *"Mi compinche Tomás dijo."* From there on it was a list of all the places that "my buddy Tomás said" the singer had to visit while he was in New Mexico. His buddy Tomás said that he had to eat at Sadie's; ride the tram up the mountain; soak in the hot springs in the Jemez Mountains; eat some of Roque García's *carnitas* on the plaza in Santa Fe; take the High Road to Taos. The recommendations cascaded forth, all delivered in a hoarse whisper that made me recall what Doña Carlota had told us about *la voz afillá*, the raspy, genuine Gypsy voice of her blacksmith father singing in a cave in Granada: *"La voz afillá* is the sound a man makes when the world tries to choke him to death at birth and he sings anyway. That is the true Gypsy voice."

After we loaded Meatballs's five large suitcases in the university van, he asked me, "Happy Hocker Pawn Shop? *Tú le conoces?"*

I told him I was familiar with the Happy Hocker. The pawn shop was a favorite with our Gypsy visitors who were always either buying or selling gold.

As I got behind the wheel of the van I rehearsed the questions that would subtly lead to Tomás. Just as I was about to speak, Guitos announced that he wasn't going to talk anymore. Touching his throat, he explained he had to save *"la voz."* At the shop, though, he didn't bother saving his voice as he used an array of haggling techniques that combined equal parts charm, intimidation, flattery, lies, and threats to acquire a dozen saddles, then paid for them with a wad of cash that would have choked the horses that all the saddles were intended for.

Like all the visiting luminaries, Guitos was staying at the Sculpture Garden Bungalows. Built by the university on the edge of its golf course, the cottages were sprinkled amid a collection of sculptures constructed from old farm machinery spread across the grounds. I parked in front of the cabin that housed the office and a young man appeared with a luggage cart. Guitos peeled twenties off his wad and stuffed them into the fellow's pocket as he loaded up as many of the saddles as he could, then led us off to Guitos's bungalow. We passed fifteen-foot-high grasshoppers and some tree-size nail clippers before we reached our destination. A pair of eight-foot-high stone angels guarded the gate in front of the bungalow.

"Muchísimas gracias." Guitos shook my hand and turned his attention toward piloting the cart into his bungalow.

The mission was ending before it had even begun. I had learned nothing. The wall of renown that usually encased the famous singer was sealing him off in front of my eyes. From that moment forward, Guitos would be caught up in the festival, surrounded by fans, handlers, peppered with demands. I would have no further access and I had not spoken one word to him about Tomás. What I had done was confirm every accusation Didi had ever implied or hurled at me. If I let him step away, she would be right: all I wanted was the safety of a fantasy.

"Señor, perdóneme." I had to say it twice before he stopped and turned back to me with a surprised expression on his face, almost as if he were startled that I'd continued to exist once he'd withdrawn his attention.

I rushed forward and spoke. For the first time, my brain unloosed its hold on my tongue and Spanish, unrehearsed, ungrammatical Spanish as simple as the baby I was in that language, poured forth. *"Tomás? Tomás Montenegro? Tú le conoces?"* Forgetting about formal forms of address, I blundered ahead, asking if he knew Tomás.

That was all I needed to say. Singers, *cantaores,* the great ones, along with their idiosyncrasies and egomania, have a gift for divining emotion. They witch it like a dowser hunting water. Instead of a green bough, though, they hold their voice over listeners until it trembles and twitches at the deepest pools hidden in your most secret heart. Without ever hearing Meatballs sing a note, I knew he was a great singer because after listening to me say those few words, he waved the cart handler away, took my hand, and guided me into the bungalow. It was a study in good taste, New Mexico–style. A Seven Hills rug hung on the wall, a black San Ildefonso pot occupied the place of honor between two kachinas, a basket of fragrant piñon sat beside a horno-shaped fireplace in the corner. Guitos beckoned for me to sit beside him on the Carpintero-style bench with Zias carved into its back. When I was seated, he retook my hand and pronounced the verdict: *"Tú le amas. Tú le amas a Tomás."*

"You love him. You love Tomás." He wasn't asking; he was stating the fact he saw before him. There was no point in denying it or even in adding that I knew I was stupid. That I'd only met Tomás once. That he didn't even know my name. That I should be spending my money on therapy, not flamenco classes.

Meatballs pressed my hand to his cheek and whispered a few words of English. "Es hokay. I luf heem too."

And then we were girlfriends. The relief of finally being able to talk about the person who had occupied the greater part of my thoughts for three years was so great that I laughed along with Guitos as if we were dorm mates in frilly nighties.

La voz was forgotten completely as Meatballs spoke in tones that ranged from wonderstruck awe to lascivious hebephrenia as he cataloged Tomás's charms in a torrent of fevered Spanish. "Those eyes. Those lips. That—" He cupped his hands to indicate the Montenegro ass. *"Por Dios."* He crossed himself and kissed the back of his thumb at the memory. "But that, all that is nothing," he declared, dismissing Tomás's beauty. A second later, he called it back with a deep, rumbling laugh. "All right, it is something. All right, it's a hell of a lot. But you know when I really, truly fell in love with this guy? When he played for me. *Ay Santa María de Dios.* When he plays . . . when he plays. *Qué monstruo. Un fenómeno.* No other *tocaor* has played like this for me. After singing with him for only a few minutes, I could not believe what I was hearing. We were speaking. I would say something and his response would be wise or witty. Mocking even. So I tested him to see if he was really as good as he seemed. I sang strange offbeats I'd never tried with any other *tocaor* and, like a compass always pointing to true north, he held the rhythm even as he created a brilliant new *síncopa.*"

I stretched to remember the word for syncopation as Guitos pressed the tips of his fingers together, then shook the gathered fingers in front of his face as if pleading for words to express Tomás's gift. "This, all this"—he indicated his own hair, his face, his body—"it was gone. All that is there is"—he pounded his meaty hand into his chest, his heart, his soul—"*this. This* is what he sees. *This* is what he plays for. *This* is what he makes me show. He read my mind. He read my heart. With his guitar, he made me show everything. With Tomás, I could hide nothing. Every night with him I went to confession and the black blood, *la sangre negra,* poured out. Like no other *tocaor*—and, mind you, I have sung with the best, the greatest guitarists on earth—but Tomás. Ah, *mi Tomasito.* There is no player on earth like Tomás. I called him Angelito. Because he was. He was my little angel. He *is* my little angel."

"Yes," I whispered. "I thought I was insane. That I had fallen in love with him because he was a phantom I could never have."

"I know!" Guitos exploded, the perfect girlfriend. "I thought I had fallen in love with him just to torture myself because he is so hopelessly straight. But no. It is him. *Mi angelito.* He is air and rain and gold dust and all others are mud. *Nada. Nada. Nada.* He poisons you for any other man."

"I know! My best friend always tells me that I am just using him to keep the world away."

"No! Tomás *is* the world."

"Sometimes I think I haven't wanted to know anything. To keep him the perfect, unattainable dream."

He shook his great head. "No. When you know him, he is even more out of reach. No one on this earth will have him, because he does not have himself."

"Why do you say that?"

Guitos slapped both his hands over his mouth. "No. I've said too much. He opened his heart to me. To me! The beauty told his secrets to the beast. It is all I will ever have of him. This much I will keep." He squeezed the enormous fists he made of his hands tightly in front of his heart to symbolize the eternal lock he would keep on Tomás's secrets, secrets he thought I intended to pry out of him.

"Of course, of course. No, don't worry. I know nothing about him. It's ridiculous, isn't it? I'm obsessed with, I love"—it felt so good to say it out loud, that I said it again—"I love a man I met once, three years ago, a man who doesn't even know my name." I giggled, giddy with the relief of pulling all my secrets out of the closet. "I am not a mentally healthy person."

Guitos didn't laugh. "Mental health? Pffft." He flicked his fingers, waving away the pathetic American cliché. He leaned in close so that I was engulfed again by the smell he carried from an older world and he whispered in his husky voice, "*Embrujados*. Bewitched. We have both been bewitched."

Yes, we had stepped into the same fairy tale and been bewitched. That is why, when he said, "Tell me, tell me about meeting Tomás," I told him the truth as it had really happened. "I met Tomás on a night when the earth ate the moon. His nails were phosphorescent fairies flitting through the darkness, plucking enchanted sounds from the strings of a guitar. A neon rainbow splashed across his face and I escaped the police by flying out of a window and into his arms."

The more fantastical my telling, the closer it approached the absolute truth of that night. Guitos nodded as I spoke, leaning closer and closer until the long whiskers of his sideburns stroked my cheek. He was the *tocaor* now, drawing the truth from me, the *cantaor*.

"He led me down a street where conquistadors ruled coffee shops and whiskey grew in a garden of green bottles. A secret park appeared in the middle of a sleeping neighborhood. He played *falsetas* so beautiful that the leaves on the trees turned into hearts and rained down on me. And, on a giant's swing, we sailed so high that the stars blurred into streaks of silver next to our heads."

Guitos looked as if he'd been struck. He dropped his head into his hands. His great shoulders heaved and tears ran in rivulets down the tendons of his wrists.

"Guitos, please . . ." I put my arm around his shoulders. He flinched and shrugged away from my touch. I backed off.

He raised his head and brusquely squeegeed the wetness from his face. "I want to be alone."

"I'm sorry. I shouldn't have talked about this."

"What you say or don't say to me doesn't matter. What is meant to be, will be." His tone was cold, dismissive.

"I've offended you. I didn't mean to—"

He shifted to turn away from me. We weren't best girlfriends anymore, we weren't friends or even acquaintances of any sort. "As I said, your intentions are irrelevant. May I be left alone? I have a performance to prepare for."

I muttered more apologies. Guitos didn't respond. Confused, embarrassed, I stumbled out of the room and found my way back to Popejoy Hall, where Alma Hernandez-Luna tried to control the chaos. I buried my humiliation by throwing myself into preparations for that evening's concert, the first of five that would be staged over the course of the festival. Alma was directing four different *cuadros,* troupes, each one needing its own set of lighting cues, props, acoustics, and costumes. I was dispatched to deliver a guitarist from Málaga to the nearest nail salon for a new set of acrylics. It was a relief to be away from the festival for a while. My encounter with Guitos had left me feeling as if I'd met, and then lost, Tomás all over again.

When I returned, I was grateful to be put to work ironing costumes. As I smoothed over wrinkles in acres of fabric, I watched Alma through a haze of steam as she smoothed over the inflamed egos of a dozen divas. She had to navigate through a minefield of the thousand and one slights that flamenco performers are apt to interpret as walkout-worthy signs of disrespect. Watching the temper tantrums and hissy fits calmed me the way flamenco always calmed me; volcanic emotions were made manifest and released.

The first crack in Alma's legendary composure came an hour before the curtain was to go up, when she was called away to speak to her star performer, Guitos, on the phone. She returned to the backstage area screaming my name. The usually unflappable Alma was utterly flapped.

With a hiss of steam, I tipped the iron up as she rushed over, shaking her head and muttering *"cantaores,"* as if the inexplicable eccentricities of these mercurial creatures were a personal curse upon her. "Guitos wants you, and only you, to come to the bungalow."

"Me? Are you sure?"

"Very sure. He was quite emphatic that he wanted you and no one else. Was he drinking when you left?"

"No. He hadn't touched a drop." One of the major duties of the flamenco celebrity wrangler was to keep our visitors sober until concert time. After that, all bets were off.

"Well, whatever is wrong with him, he believes you're the only one who can help. He's wailing about a pain that only you will understand.

I couldn't follow the whole drama. Just have him here on time and on stage."

I made the short drive to the guest bungalows and found Guitos's door ajar. The smell of leather from the saddles stacked beside the bed greeted me as I slipped inside. It blended with the fragrance of sandalwood incense.

"Hello?"

When there was no answer, I followed the sound of chanting into the bedroom. Guitos was kneeling in front of an altar he had assembled on the desk in the corner. Coils of smoke rose from the sandalwood incense burning in front of a photo of a dark-eyed Hindu man with a bindi dotted on his forehead. The mini-bar had been savaged and an Elvis-size assortment of prescription bottles lay scattered across the bed. None of this seemed to have slowed the big man down very much. He rang a silver bell and prayed incoherently to his guru. The only words I could pick out were *"Mi Tomasito, mi ángel, mi alma."*

"Guitos?"

He swiveled around and directed his rambling lament to me. Sobs wracking his giant body, he heaved himself up, then crumpled onto the bed. Pill bottles and empty miniatures bounced as his bulk hit the mattress.

I closed the door. Guitos, still sobbing, his head buried in the pillows, patted a spot on the bed and I sat down. After several moments of wailing, he hoisted himself up into a sodden clump, wiped his hand across his wet face, and regained some control.

"This is not what I thought would happen when I came here. I dreamed that I would find the key to Tomás's heart here. And I have. But I see now that I will never be the one to turn it." He heaved a giant sigh and composed himself a bit further. *"Mi angelito* guided me to you. Tomás and I have shared great love in past lives. Of this I am certain—we shall be united again after death, in *pitraloka.*" He turned to his guru and bowed his head in the direction of the photo. "But for now, in this current incarnation, *mi angelito* is meant to be with . . ." He paused and then, with a shuddering sigh, as if the word were his last breath of life said, ". . . you."

I couldn't speak.

"The moment you said you met him on the night that the earth ate the moon, I knew that I was not destined to be with him. Not in this life. You met *mi amor* on the night when his life cracked in two, the night he soared into the heavens with a virgin paler than the hidden moon into the stars."

"He told you. About me?"

"You were part of the story. One of the signs. Part of the answer he was searching for."

"The answer to what?"

"To himself. His life. That night, the night he met you, he learned that he could no longer hide from what he'd suspected for a long time." He stared at me. The candlelight and smell of leather, his raspy *voz afillá,* the bluish tinge of his dark skin, they all blended together to evoke the cave on Sacromonte where Doña Carlota had lived and given her life to the Gypsy art, flamenco.

"Gypsies cheat, steal from, and lie to *payos.* To tell a *payo* the truth is to betray your people. You are a *payo.* The palest of the pale of *payos.* How can I tell you the only secret I would guard with my life, because it is Tomás's secret?"

"I don't tell secrets."

He snorted a bitter laugh. "Who ever admits that they will reveal your secret? Who ever says, 'Tell me, tell me, please, tell me and I promise I will betray you to the world'? I don't even know who you are. Why should it be you? Why should I tell you the secret that controls Tomás's life?"

It was easy to answer in the way he would understand. It was more than easy. All I had to do, for one moment, was to stop reining in my obsession and it ran away with me. "Because I care more about him than I do myself. Because for three years I have devoted my life to becoming who he would fall in love with. Because he is more essential to my happiness than life. Because I am sick with love for Tomás Montenegro and I will die if you do not give me the cure."

"When you fall in love with *un flamenco,* you fall in love with his art, with his people. In America you tell each other the lie, 'Oh, the color of a person's skin. It doesn't matter.' In flamenco, we don't tell that lie. Blood matters. To be the best, you must have the best blood, the blood of the pharaohs. You must be Gypsy. And don't say, 'Oh, what about Paco de Lucía?'"

He waved away the name of the world's most famous flamenco guitarist.

"Pffft. Paco is great. The greatest of the decade. But for *payos* only. In *el flamenco puro, puro, puro,* for those who are truly *enterao,* Paco *no dice nada,* he says nothing. Do you understand this? Do you understand how even such a one as Paco de Lucía will never be accepted, truly, truly accepted, because he is a *payo*?"

"Yes, I know. In my classes, I am invisible. I don't have *el arte* in my blood. I will never have it. I can study flamenco for the rest of my life and I won't have it. I don't care. I study for Tomás. No other reason."

Guitos nodded, considering. He dropped heavy lids over his eyes, turned from me, and bowed in the direction of his guru's photo. Several moments passed as he prayed silently. He opened his eyes, said one word, *"Sí,"* and began to tell me the story I'd fallen into on the night I dropped into Tomás Montenegro's arms.

"When Tomás appeared on the scene in Madrid seven years ago, speaking his beautiful Spanish with words from the seventeenth century, he was a very young man. He came with a minor reputation. Good enough to get work in the tourist clubs. Word spread quickly, though. First *los aficionados* went so that they could dismiss this latest pretender and acquire a new object for their finely attenuated mockery.

"But they did not come away laughing and soon Tomás was playing in the best flamenco clubs in the world, El Corral de la Morería, La Torre del Oro, Casa Patas. He was accompanying classes at the greatest flamenco studio of them all, Amor de Dios. He was heralded throughout the flamenco world. At last, a real, a true *flamenco* from the New World, come back to us like an echo from the conquistadors five centuries ago. An ocean, a continent was between him and the sources of *el arte,* yet in spite of his isolation, he played with *corazón gitano. Alma gitano. Pasión gitano.* How could this be? Those of us who've given our lives to *flamenco puro* knew it had to be a lie. That year I, along with Chi Chi, the queen of *el baile gitano* from Jerez de la Frontera and El Pulgar, the last, true *calé,* were on the selection committee to pick the best, the purest, the most flamenco of all flamenco artists to perform at the Sevilla Biennale. Everywhere we turned, someone was telling us about this *tocaor* we had to consider, this Tomás Montenegro.

"Eventually we surrendered. We had to learn who the upstart from the New World was. So, late on a Tuesday, the first day of the flamenco weekend, we arranged to meet this *fenómeno.* We had already decided that he was a fraud. We intended not only to disqualify him from consideration for the sacred biennale, but to ensure that he would never play again at any respectable club. The heart and soul of our art hung in the balance. For this reason, we set the meeting at Restaurante Sonrisa, a tourist spot where they slam a bowl of gazpacho in front of you and some abomination in a red dress clacks her castanets in the imitation flamenco that Franco foisted on us after the war. The choice of Restaurante Sonrisa was an insult to the pretender and the three of us were quite pleased with our little joke.

"The joke was on us when Tomás appeared and the first words from his mouth as he looked around at the Japanese businessmen and the dancer in a polka-dotted dress were, 'I know a spot that's not far from here and not for *guiris.*' Chi Chi, El Pulgar, and I were impressed not just that he knew the *Caló* word for outsiders, but that he led us to ¡A Jalar!, a dive popular with the Triana crowd, *calé* from Sevilla—a rough, working-class place, exactly the sort of place where Carmen Amaya herself might have danced barefoot as a child.

"Because I did not want to be recognized in the company of a fraud, I had taken care that night to wear a fedora that covered the top half of my face and a muffler that covered most of the bottom. In this way, I slipped unnoticed into ¡A Jalar!

"'Eh, *churumbel!*' the proprietor greeted Tomás, yelling to be heard above the racket. Even if the owner had not called him 'kid' in *Caló,* we, Chi Chi, El Pulgar, and I, would have known the owner was Gypsy by the gold chains glinting against the masses of black Gypsy hair, poking from the top of his lime-green silk shirt. He stared at us suspiciously, mumbled something in Tomás's ear. He brightened when Tomás whispered something back to him.

"'Ah, you are *calé,*' the owner said, grabbing my hairy Gypsy hand in his hairy Gypsy hand. 'Why didn't you say so?' So it was Tomás who had to vouch for us! Us, we three who were there to be his Torquemada at a flamenco Inquisition! I began to regard this *nuevo mexicano* in a very different light. Of course, he was physically sublime. But since I have always had a weakness in that regard, I ignored his beauty. Then I suddenly saw what was behind the beauty. All at once, the three of us saw it. The dark skin that had been kissed farewell by India a thousand years ago. The hair so black it crackled with blue as if lighted by the moon. The lashes, the lips, the whole enchantment. He could be my cousin if any of my family had possessed such beauty. Here before us was the answer to a prayer we had never dared utter.

"In the end our Inquisition came down to one question. 'Who are you?'

"'*Soy gitano a cuatro costaos,*' he answered. Gypsy on four sides.

"In spite of what our eyes were seeing, we had to have more proof. El Pulgar took a guitar off the whitewashed wall. A piece of crap, put there for decoration at the end of a hard life as a *cantina guitarra.* He tuned it and stuck it in Tomás's hands. Tomás didn't protest, didn't hurl the joke of an instrument back at El Pulgar. He strummed quietly for a few minutes. But soon, ¡A Jalar! had fallen silent. Everyone in the place was straining to hear the falling notes of his magical *soleá falseta.*

"'*Él tiene aire,*' Chi Chi whispered to me. But everyone in that room already knew that he had the air, the thing that cannot be taught.

"'*Tiene fuerza en el compás,*' El Pulgar exclaimed.

"But I no longer cared whether he had the right air or was strong in the *compás.* I ripped away the hat hiding my face and made the only response I could at having found my soul mate. *En voz medio,* at half voice, I sang.

"*Ay*
Rompe la oscuridad de la noche
Pero en realidad es nuestra pena
Rompiéndose dentro de nosotros

"*They say each morning the dawn breaks*
But really it is our own grief
Breaking within us . . .

"He played and I sang and the crowd went crazy as only a Gypsy crowd can. Men ripped the shirts from their chests, women dug their nails into their faces until they drew blood. The unuttered prayer was answered. El Pulgar called the owner over and bought *una caña* for every *calé* in the place. They would have kept us there all night if every string on that old guitar had not broken.

"In the end, the owner had to drag us away to a private room in the back and lock a heavy door on the chaos. There, in that back room, we three sat in stunned silence as Tomás spoke. I will tell you his story as he told it to us."

Guitos paused to get into character. Drawing himself up, he sang the briefest of *temples,* a short *Ay,* to warm *la voz.* When he next spoke, it was in Tomàs's voice. Not an impersonation, but a channeling of his inflections, his tone so perfect that goose bumps rippled across my arms.

" 'I was raised by my great-aunt Doña Carlota Montenegro and her husband Don Ernesto Anaya. They were ancient when they adopted me and of a world where awkward details are never revealed. The details of my birth were awkward. My great-aunt was a dancer born in a cave on Sacromonte. Her mother had been *una sensación en las cafés cantantes* in the golden days in Sevilla. Her father was one of *los cantaores* who beat out the very form itself on their forges in Sacromonte. Then came the cursed days of the Civil War. My great-aunt spoke out courageously against the fascists and was marked for death. By the grace of God and a few well-placed admirers, she escaped. Her family was not so lucky. All her immediate relatives, everyone she'd known growing up, were massacred by Franco's *guardia civil*.

" 'The tragedy killed something in my great-aunt and she forbade anyone to ever speak of it in her presence. All I know is that my mother was a distant relative, daughter of one of the few survivors of my great-aunt's family. All that is known about my father is that he was Gypsy as well. I was taken from my mother because, as with so many of my people, there were drugs. I was sent to America to avoid this scourge. Later, my great-aunt searched for my mother only to learn that she had died of an overdose shortly after I was taken from her. No trace of my father could be found.' "

Guitos shook himself, and, in his own voice, plaintive and insistent, asked, "Can you imagine the impact this history had? You can't. Not in America where pretending that birth makes no difference and anyone can be anything they choose is your national religion. But to us who know that blood is everything, Tomás's story was a meteor, *an asteroid,* smashing into our planet of flamenco. The purists rejoiced. A Gypsy boy raised on the other side of an ocean and he plays like the incarnation of Sabicas? Here, at last, proof of what we had always said: you cannot play *flamenco puro,* the real, the true flamenco, without Gypsy blood."

I nodded, astounded again at what an insular and rarefied community Tomás had grown up in. How explosions of a colossal magnitude within it never registered the slightest tick on any Richter scale in the outside world.

"He was the great Gypsy hope, no?" Guitos asked. "He would take the crown back from the *payo* who had worn it for so long. Tomás would reclaim flamenco guitar from Paco de Lucía. There was no question. Yes, he had *técnica* as good as any *payo* but better, far better; he was one of us, he had *gitano* soul. He played at the biennale. Not a main stage, a small venue, too early for the crowds to have come out. But he was *una sensación*. If Paco had been there, they would have torn the crown from his head and put it on Tomás's.

"And then followed the happiest time in my life. Tomás became my accompanist. My *cante* was never better. Each night I sang of my hopeless love and audiences, never suspecting it was for my *tocaor,* wept. Sevilla, Madrid, Barcelona. And then north. Ah, the farther north we went, the more they adored us. London, Edinburgh, Copenhagen, Oslo. The more *represivo* the society, the more they worshipped us. *Santa María de Dios! Los japoneses! Demente! Totalmente demente!* They could teach us *gitanos* how to lose control. In Sapporo, security had to disarm a young woman who was stabbing herself in the chest with a knife!

"It was heaven. But I was the one who destroyed it. An excess of love was the culprit. I made love to him with my voice every night on a different stage and every night he left me and made love with his body to one of the women who threw themselves at him." Guitos beat his chest like a penitent sinner.

"Love finds its own way. Every city, we were interviewed. Again and again, I heard Tomás tell his story. Each time he was asked what he knew about his mother, his father, the silence deepened. In the world outside of Spain, Tomás had only to answer 'drugs' and no further questions would be asked. In Spain, however, the only answer Tomás had to give was *'la Guerra Civil.'* In our country, a veil of secrecy so profound has been drawn around the Civil War that where that fratricidal conflict is concerned, there are few good questions and no good answers. So, we learn from birth simply not to ask.

"But I asked. I asked because *gitanos,* who won't say anything to a *payo* except a lie and rarely even tell one another the truth, will tell me the truth. I asked because the old-timers think I am the great Antonio Mairena come back to earth and will talk to me of matters they wouldn't discuss with their confessors. I asked because I wanted to give Tomás my heart and he would never take it. All he might ever accept from me was knowledge. I will tell you how this tragedy befell me.

"We were in Frankfurt, where I have a tremendous following. The tour was coming to an end and I was frantic to find a way to keep Tomás in my life. I had almost succeeded in talking him into coming home with me to Málaga to record a new album when Tomás received word from New Mexico that Ernesto Anaya, the man who had raised him as a son, was gravely ill. Tomás talked all the time about Ernesto. Love flowed with every word when he told me about the small village in the north of the state where Ernesto had been born, where Tomás had spent the only happy days of his childhood. On the other hand, Tomás never spoke about his great-aunt. Never. So complete was his silence that it spoke volumes about a pain he would not approach. He broke that silence when his great-aunt, worried most about disturbing the tour, waited until the last possible moment to tell him how sick his great-uncle was. Tomás cursed his great-aunt then for that and for all the secrets she had kept from him.

"He packed to leave immediately and I, desperate for any way to bind him to me, made a promise. I promised to discover the names of his mother and father. I knew the heads of every Gypsy dynasty who had lived or had relatives who had lived on Sacromonte during the time his great-aunt had grown up there. One of them would know. I promised Tomás that, while he was back in New Mexico, I would go to Granada and would find an answer. Tomás was ecstatic. We were never closer. At Frankfurt Airport, in spite of the shadow that Ernesto's poor health cast over Tomás, joy at the prospect of learning who his parents were haloed him as we said our good-byes.

"I rushed to Granada, but not the Granada of Lorca, not the Granada Fernando and Isabel took back from the Moors. No, I did not visit the Granada of hidden patios where fountains splash and bougainvillea twines. I went to my friends on Sacromonte and was sent to a retirement home in an immigrant neighborhood on the far edge of Granada. The neighborhood was filled with Tunisians and Algerians in cheap polyester sweaters, Basques who'd come in the sixties and never left, Latin Americans who spent all their money calling home. The retirement home sitting between two highways, around the corner from a brake-manufacturing plant, could have been anywhere. A concrete building with no more charm than a warehouse, it smelled of piss and boiled potatoes. The relatives who'd sent me to that place where they'd packed away their *viejos* had called ahead. But, even if they hadn't been warned, the old-timers would have been ready for me. They had read the articles about this newcomer, this *fenómeno de Nuevo Mexico* who claimed Gypsy blood. They'd seen the photograph of the phenomenon's great-aunt. It was the one Tomás carried with him only because it was one of the few he had of Don Ernesto, who stood beside his great-aunt, grinning beneath a huge mustache like Zapata. In the photo that the old-timers shoved into my face and stabbed at with tobacco-stained fingers, Doña Carlota is pale as steam. In the articles Tomás explained that his great-aunt's mother, Delicata, was just as light-skinned. *Los viejos* talked. Oh, they talked. And I wished I'd never asked.

"I went home, had a tall drink and a long bath, but couldn't wash away their smells, their sadness, or my deep regret that I had ever met them. When Tomás called that night, I put on a bright voice and said, '*Lástima.* Too bad. They wouldn't talk. I learned nothing. Gypsies, you know how they are.'

"I will never forget what he answered. 'Guitos, for a lifetime you have told the truth in song. You have no training telling lies and you do it extraordinarily badly. All that we have, you and I, all that we will ever have, is honesty. *Dame la verdad.*'

"Give me the truth. That is what we always told each other before we went onstage. That was our pledge that we would never sing or play a note that was false. One note of falseness and the only link I had to *mi corazón* would be destroyed.

"'*Dame la verdad,*' he repeated and I told him what the toothless old men had told me: 'Your great-aunt never lived in Sacromonte. Yes, there was *una bailaora* named Delicata married to El Chino, *un herrero,* but she was dark, dark as a Moor. *Muy morena.* Dark, dark, dark. She had several daughters. The oldest was a girl named Rosa. All of Rosa's children were also dark, dark as the darkest Gypsy.'

"Tomás didn't speak for a long time. I listened to the galaxies of space between us crackle and hum. Then, 'Guitos, I'm going to disappear for a while. Figure this out. I'll call you when I can.' He thanked me and hung up before I could say another word."

I tried to grasp the heresy Guitos had just spoken. "Doña Carlota never lived on Sacromonte?" Even me, the *payo,* even I was having trouble turning loose of the one tiny claim to legitimacy in the flamenco world that Doña Carlota had given me: I had been taught by *una gitana por cuatro costaos.* I couldn't imagine the implications for Tomás. If what Guitos was saying was true, Tomás would have almost as little right to belong to flamenco's inner circle as I. But it couldn't be true. "How could Doña Carlota have fooled everyone for so long?"

Guitos clucked his tongue sympathetically. "Oh, *pobrecita,* if every *flamenco* who claimed *gitano* blood they didn't have were banished from *el arte,* you wouldn't hear a castanet clack or a *clave* tap from one Semana Santa to the next. They all claim to have a Gypsy grandmother tucked away somewhere. No, Doña Carlota knew she would never be discovered for many reasons." Guitos ticked them off: "She was on the other side of an ocean. Still, even now, we *gitanos* are not a people interested in keeping the record straight. We don't report things to 'the authorities.' We keep to ourselves. Besides, most of the ones who would have said anything are dead, no? Nearly a million people died in the Spanish Civil War. Who, aside from the handful of old-timers I spoke to, could say that the ancestors she claimed had not been among those who were killed? Doña Carlota could have claimed she was queen of the Gypsies and no one in Spain would have cared. Who was she? Some broken-down dance teacher on the wrong side of the water. No one cared about her, a nobody. But"—Guitos poked up one, cautionary finger—"but Tomás, Tomás was another story entirely. We Gypsies are only too happy to share failure, but success? Success like that Tomás was on the verge of? That, *that,* we will fight over."

Guitos spread his palms and gave a desolate shrug. "When I told him that his great-aunt had never lived on Sacromonte, he wasn't surprised. He'd suspected for a long time that she was a fraud. But if you are a fish, how do you question water? Not only was her story all he'd ever known of his own, but it was the basis for his own place on the earth. Still, he had suspected. That night there was a lunar eclipse. So after I told him, after I destroyed his world, I watched the moon disappear and hoped it had vanished wherever *mi angelito* was so we might be together in that one, last thing."

"And that was the night . . ."

"He met you."

"That's why he'd said it was the worst night of his life."

Guitos sagged. "Me, I brought that sadness to him. After that, he was changed. He returned a few times but refused to play in front of any audience that might be *enterao.* No more insiders. He would play with me on tours to Japan, Finland, Australia. Anywhere but Spain or North America.

If he began to receive too much attention, too much acclaim, he would disappear. Again and again he returned to the place he considered home, to the little village in northern New Mexico where he'd spent the only happy times of his childhood with his beloved Tío Ernesto."

"What village is that?"

"He never told me."

My cell phone rang. I knew it was Alma and quickly turned it off. But the spell had been broken.

Guitos turned from me. "I've said too much." A second later, his phone rang. He glanced at the name, swore, *"Caray!"* and answered. I could hear Alma cursing Guitos even before he lifted the phone to his ear. My name was mentioned several times as well. We were walking out the door and heading for Popejoy Hall before she'd finished excoriating both of us.

Guitos's performance that night was a master class on the meaning of the elusive term *duende*. The spirit moved through him, but every one of us in the hall shivered. *Black sounds*—that's how Lorca, quoting the great singer Manuel Torre, defined *duende*. "Whatever has black sounds has *duende*." From the moment he stepped onstage, Guitos filled the hall with black sounds.

His voice was a tortured rumble that contained the essence of Andalusia and embodied flamenco's heritage from the Moors' mosques, the Jews' synagogues, through every country the Gypsies wandered across, right back to the motherland in India. Guitos drew in a deep breath, diving far into himself, then exploded to the surface with his eyes and fists clenched, singing in a full-throated wail. He sang to the stars that had betrayed his dreams and turned his love to dust. Sweat ran down his dark face, pouring into the muffler tied around his neck as he reached even further into himself for notes so laden with despair that not a single person in the hall needed a translator.

As Guitos sat in the blazing light and wept for the love the earth eating the moon had stolen from him, I envied him. I envied that he was a part of Tomás's world, a true flamenco. I envied every second they'd spent together. Then he opened his fists, his eyes, he found me gazing up at him from the first row, and sang every second of my one night with Tomás. He sang the heavens opening as we swung together into the stars. Then, he sang with such clairvoyant precision the moment when the stars went dark and Tomás left me, a bubble of sorrow rose in my chest. If I were truly *una flamenca,* if I truly belonged in Tomás's world, I would have wept openly.

As I knew he would be, Guitos was swept away after the performance, and I didn't see him again until the end of the festival when I drove him to the airport. This time, the van was filled with other performers. Though I ached for him to give me a few more crumbs of information, Guitos spent the entire ride cajoling every visiting Spaniard into carrying some of his loot back for him so that he wouldn't have to pay duty on the saddles he intended to sell to Gypsy horse-trader friends.

I hoped to snatch a moment alone with Guitos, but the chattering crowd of muscled dancers and rumpled guitarists fluttered about him like egrets circling a bull. By the time they had all been herded into the airport and were heading toward the International Departures terminal, I had given up. We were within sight of the statue of the caped Indian warrior when Guitos broke from the group and hurried back to me. His muffler was wrapped tightly around his neck and he was whispering again. His Spanish was hushed and rapid. I leaned close and he asked, "You will always keep his secret, no?"

"*Sí. Siempre.*"

"Guitos!" A thin male dancer waved frantically for the singer to hurry.

"*Bueno,* I have to leave. One last question: If I send him back to you, will you be ready?"

I nodded without knowing what I was agreeing to. It didn't matter. Guitos knew I would have agreed to anything.

"Then God have mercy on us both." He wrapped me in *un abrazo fuerte,* then left, rushing past the warrior forever reaching out to catch an eagle.

Chapter Twenty-nine

Didi barely came home for most of the summer before our senior year. Mrs. Steinberg had abruptly stopped drinking and, through her Internet connections and extended family back in Manila, had found a new life. She never talked to me about it directly, so I had to gather clues from peeking at her computer screen and eavesdropping on phone conversations. From what I could piece together, she had become an onsite screener of potential husbands for the daughters of friends and relatives back in the Philippines. This involved lots of high-pitched, hectic conversations in which vital information was exchanged; then Catwoman would leave for days at a time. When she returned, more conversations followed that centered on descriptions of cars, houses, quality of lawn care, overall impressions of neighborhoods. If that was all satisfactory, face-to-face interviews with the prospective suitor would be arranged. It seemed that Mrs. Steinberg was the perfect person to investigate exactly how an unknown American man might treat a mail-order bride.

With both Didi and Catwoman gone most of the time, the Lair revealed itself for what it was: a converted garage furnished by two high school girls. Being there made me lonely. I felt as if I were living in a monument to our friendship, a friendship that existed mostly now in memory. It was time to move on. I found a garage apartment on the alley behind the Frontier Restaurant. It was cramped and drafty, but it was across the street from the university, and I could walk to the academy in five minutes.

Everything shifted once I left. Maybe it was leaving the hideout where I'd holed up after Daddy died and my mother decamped. Maybe it was just not having Didi around. With Didi, I was the solid one, the one with her feet on the ground. It was like standing next to a flaming red billboard. I could be wearing chartreuse and still look fairly ordinary. Without the three-ring circus of flaming red distractions that Didi always provided, the chartreuse began to stand out. I started seeing a therapist at the Student Health Center.

Her name was Leslie. She was a nice woman in her late forties with a placid manner and thin, pale hands. When she asked why I'd come, I told her I was depressed, lonely. My best friend had moved away, and I hadn't really made any new friends. Not any close ones. I didn't seem able to make a relationship work. I had no interest in dating. Leslie assumed I was gay. I actually laughed and told her I wished it were that easy. We talked about my mother running off to HomeTown and how it made me feel. I talked about how much I missed Daddy. Leslie was sympathetic and nice in a professional way. That changed when I mentioned Tomás. I'd been seeing Leslie for more than two months before I let it drop that I'd spent the last three and a half years of my life transforming myself into someone a man I'd met once would fall in love with. The way Leslie hunched forward ever so slightly and tried too hard to act casual, nonjudgmental, made me realize how polite her interest had been up until that point. Even though I held back the full story, she asked if I wouldn't like to start coming in twice a week, then prescribed a new medication that had just been released.

I Googled the pills and found out they were for obsessive-compulsive disorder. When I arrived for my next appointment, Leslie hurriedly put away a book she'd been reading. It had a plain cover, the typical binding for journal collections. I memorized the call number and looked it up later when I went to work at Zimmerman Library. It was the *Journal of Psychoanalytic Psychology*. The volume she'd been reading contained an entire issue devoted to erotomania. A medical dictionary told me that the official definition of erotomania was "the false but persistent belief that one is loved by a person (often a famous or prominent person), or the pathologically obsessive pursuit of a disinterested object of love." When I Googled erotomania, the word *stalking* came up frequently. I started taking the new pills. Other than nausea and sleepiness, though, they didn't seem to have much effect. Leslie told me I had to take them for three weeks before they would start working.

For my senior thesis, I'd chosen the topic "Flamenco: The Eroticism of Concealed Passion" and read every obscure book, article, monograph, and thesis ever published about flamenco. In my few remaining hours, I blotted out consciousness by rehearsing the *soleá por bulerías* that Didi and I were going to present for our senior project. Why Didi cared about getting a degree, I wasn't sure. But she did care, and I was happy to take care of this last detail. It kept me occupied, distracted. No dancers had ever performed a duet to fulfill the final requirement for a degree from the UNM Dance Department in flamenco arts. But it was generally accepted that Didi was an exception to all the rules. Even Alma and the rest of the purists acknowledged that Didi was our star, the one who opened up like a hibiscus, vivid and showy, under the glare of the spotlight. I, on the other hand, had shown, time and again, that the spotlight was a place where I tended to wilt. I suspect that we received special permission to perform together in the same way they would have granted a blind student permission to have her guide dog with her.

Since Didi only stopped in long enough to do her laundry before she hit the road again, I had to create a dance that was like a banquet in which I cooked all the food and she came in at the end to sprinkle on the parsley. My job was to make it appear as if the parsley was the essential ingredient. So I gave Didi all the splashier bits, the *zapateado,* the linked turns of the *vuelta quebrada* that would transform her hair into a waterfall flowing from her upturned head as she twisted around the stem of her waist. Meanwhile I would be keeping her coloring within the lines, pounding out the time so strongly that she could stay in *compás* and work the magic onstage that only she could perform.

On a day in late autumn when the light was so sharp it hurt my eyes, I stepped out of the old library and noticed that summer and most of fall had passed. I had a few minutes before my appointment with Leslie, so I ambled over to the duck pond to sit in the sunlight. The ducks were waddling toward me for a handout when my cell phone rang. It didn't ring often and I had to hunt for it in the bottom of my bag. It was Guitos calling from Madrid. His message was brief. "I talked to Tomás. He is going back to New Mexico. He wants to restart his career. He wants to tour again. I convinced him he needs a dancer and that the finest in the country are at the university. That is where he will go to find his dancer. This is all I can do. The rest is up to you."

Overhead, a hot-air balloon in the shape of a gigantic pink elephant wobbled drunkenly across the blue, blue sky. I waved at the tipsy elephant. The pilot pulled on the burner to roar a greeting down on me.

I canceled my standing appointment with Leslie. There was no longer time to spare for anything, not eating, not sleeping, certainly not therapy.

All I had time for was dancing. Tomás needed a dancer. I had to be that dancer. I didn't know when he would return, but I would be ready. I all but moved into studio 110. The blond wood of the floor became a Sahara I had to cross one *golpe* at a time to reach the oasis I saw in the silver mirror. The image there of a dancer who would bewitch Tomás proved to be a mirage that receded the closer I came. The only solution was even more hours of practice. I dispensed with everything that didn't make me a better dancer. Leslie's pills took the edge off my drive so I stopped taking them and came fully awake again. An electric charge that the pills had defused sizzled through me once more and fired my dancing. A vividness that had slipped out of my life reentered it, leaving me prone to fits of wild exultation and despairing crying jags. All the calluses and bunions on my feet broke out in fresh blisters that wept pink fluid when I danced. I bandaged them, tugged my shoes back on, and kept dancing. I had to be ready.

A week before Christmas, Didi returned. She had a gig at the KiMo Theatre for a show on Christmas Eve where she was opening for Bijou, a singer-songwriter who'd come up the hard way, sleeping in cars and getting electroshock before she'd risen to fame during the bygone heyday of Lilith Fair. Of course, Didi stayed with me in the little house behind Frontier Restaurant. It was like the time after she'd returned from New York. She collapsed into bed, slept around the clock, and I brought her smoothies. When she woke up, she bubbled over with stories from her new life. It was as though everything she'd done, every adventure, every romantic conquest, every professional triumph had all been achieved for me, just so that she would have stories for us to share. All she wanted to do was spend time with me. We went to the academy, and I showed her the duet I'd been working on. She watched as I danced with a beatific look on her face like she'd just fallen in love with me. When I finished all she said was, "Rae, it's really lonely out there without you." She didn't even want to try the sham part I'd cooked up for her. All she wanted to do was take me out and buy me the best meal I'd eaten in months along with more margaritas than even Catwoman could have put away. We talked about everything that night. Everything except Tomás.

The next day Didi had to start doing radio interviews and talk to reporters for Local Girl Made Good features to promote the show, but she dragged me along. We hung out together in a way we hadn't done since high school. I remembered how much sheer fun Didi could be. How she could make you feel like the most important person in the world when she turned her attention on you. I knew that Didi could lie about everything, but no one can lie about time and she spent every second with me. I stopped practicing. Maybe Tomás would come, maybe he wouldn't. The possibility began to seem remote. I believe, if we'd had another day together, Didi would have told me that I was insane. And, who knows? I might have laughed and agreed. But we didn't have another day because, on Christmas Eve, Bijou herself arrived. Singer-Songwriter was already half in love with Flamenco Poet, and fell all the way the moment they met in person. Bijou whisked Didi away to the suite her label had booked. Didi put me on the guest list for the show Christmas Eve and begged me to come. I told her I'd try to make it, but I didn't. The instant Didi left, I was seized by panic, realizing how much practice time I'd lost. While Didi was onstage, I was back in studio 110.

The next day I was home only because it was Christmas and the academy was locked and I couldn't find a janitor anywhere to let me in. That Christmas morning, I was sitting in the kitchen of the tiny apartment on the alley, my chair pulled up close to the space heater that was failing to take the chill from the dry, winter air, drinking a mug of Earl Grey tea, smoking a Ducado, and trying to wake up enough to absorb a text about flamenco's murky psychological underpinnings that I wanted to incorporate into my thesis when Didi sauntered in. She was still wearing her gig clothes, a cross between a toreador's suit of lights, shimmering with thick crusts of sequins, and a biker jacket worn with a pair of ultra low-rider jeans.

"Wow, I didn't expect to see you for a few days."

She had an odd, distracted look on her face as if she were adding numbers in her head.

I instantly went on red alert, assuming that something horrible had happened. "Didi? Are you okay? Was the show okay? I'm sorry I didn't go. I got—"

She held up her hand. "I have information for you, and I don't know whether I should even tell you or not."

My heart slammed. "What? Is it about my mom? What happened? Is she okay?"

"No, no, nothing like that." She reached into the depths of her floppy, woven bag and fished out a sheet of yellow paper folded in fourths, held it out, said, "Merry Christmas. I guess," and handed it to me. "Alma gave it to me last night. She got the call yesterday and had just finished making the flyer. She's only going to post them in a few places. Faculty lounge. The conservatory. Very selective."

I stared at her, searching for clues as I opened it. It was a call for auditions for dancers. Notices like this went up every week, a student production needing bodies, someone starting a company. Too often, it meant performing for free in a parish hall or school lunchroom. This was the level I was at, the level Didi had long ago left far behind. I would have seen a notice like that one the instant it was posted. Ever since Guitos's phone call, I had combed every possible newspaper and bulletin board and turned over every leaf on every grapevine I knew of, searching for information about Tomás's return.

And then I saw it, his name, at the bottom of the flyer. Shock froze every detail of that moment in my memory: The flyer, plain black type on goldenrod paper. The scent of bergamot from the tea, ancient and exotic. The leggy geranium on the rounded, adobe windowsill. The spider making a web in the corner of the casement window. The harsh sunlight streaming in the window turning the steam from my tea into a dazzling cloud above the mug. Each word of the last paragraph I read was burned into my memory:

> *The eroticism of flamenco is the eroticism of concealed passion, never of revelation or consummation. In a simple summary, the dancers are enacting a narrative about the pleasures and pains of human separateness, and of being alive.*

When time began to move again, I glanced at the flyer, my heart lurched, then froze. I gasped for breath that wouldn't come.

"Jesus, I guess I don't have to ask if you're still interested in Mystery Man. Breathe, *hermana*. Here, have a sip." She pushed the mug of tea into my hands, which had gone cold. I took a drink. She pulled a crocheted throw off the couch and wrapped it around my shoulders. "Wow, if this is what happens when his name comes up, it's no wonder you stopped talking about him."

I managed a laugh, a feat that only Didi Steinberg could have helped me to accomplish at that moment. "I'm really glad you're here."

She tucked the throw around me more tightly. "Rae, this is a total cakewalk. You do realize that, don't you?"

I didn't and she knew I didn't. I cared too much, and that was deadly.

"Rae-rae, sweetie, you really have nothing to worry about. No one can touch your technique. Your choreography is flawless. You are a machine with the fucking *compás*. You are Metrónoma."

"He can buy a metronome."

"Okay, maybe, possibly, *perhaps,* you could put yourself out there a little more. But, Rae, that's the easy part."

"For you."

"You too, Rae. Getting the spotlight is all a matter of a few tricks. I'll show you everything you need to know."

Overwhelmed, I shook my head at the impossibility.

"Don't stress. Rae, take it, take your shot. Girls always wait for the world to give them things. To see what sweet, smart, obedient girls they are, then paste a star on their foreheads. It doesn't work that way. The things you really want in life, you have to take. Do you really want this or not?"

She didn't wait for my answer, just barged on to ask what I planned to dance.

"Well, of course, I don't know what *palo* he's going to call for. So, I've been working up routines, rough ones, for all of them. I even have some ideas for a *siguiriyas.*" I mentioned that style hesitantly. Since it was the most *jondo,* the deepest, saddest, most intense of all the *palos,* it was almost never danced.

"Oh, brilliant. A light and lively funeral piece. Rae, come on, in a million years he's not going to go for that. The secret to winning anything is to play the game on your field. You've got to control this deal or it's going to get away from you. So decide right now what you want to dance and we'll work on that. Period. End of discussion."

"What? I just go in and tell him what I want to dance?"

"Absolutely. Oh my God, Rae, the duet, that is what you have to do. It's the most beautiful thing I've ever seen in my life."

"Uh, Deeds, it's a duet. He's not hiring two dancers."

"Duet, right. My part is a joke. It'll take, what? Five minutes to remove it and, honest to God, Rae, you nail that the way you did the other day and no one will be able to touch you. Pick up the other end, there." She was already moving the table out of the way. I helped her haul it and the few other pieces of furniture in the apartment to the alley. We pulled up the rug and started reworking the duet.

She was right. It took barely five minutes to turn the duet into the solo it always was. When we'd finished, I started going over all the *cambios* again so I'd know exactly where the changes were.

Shaking her head, Didi stopped me. "Rae, you don't need any more perfection. Perfection is your problem. Do it half as good. Do it sloppy. Do it like this." She gave an extremely rough approximation of the last sequence. It was only a brief passage, but it perfectly illustrated the differences between us. Her timing and technique were for shit, but there was a superhighway leading directly from her heart to her face, hands, and feet. When I danced, my emotions took a donkey path. Didi tried to share her charisma secrets with me, but attempting to artificially inject the magic that came to her naturally was an arduous exercise in reverse engineering.

The next day, Bijou appeared and whisked Didi away. The last thing she said to me was, "Stop working. If you spend the rest of the time smoking opium, you'll be in better shape than if you practice obsessively." Then she left and I spent the rest of that week practicing obsessively. Each time I danced the solo, I improved. Still, I couldn't help thinking how much more alive it would be if Didi were doing it. Tomás would choose her in a second. Thank God, she had no interest in playing second banana to another *fenómeno*.

Bijou left, and Didi reappeared with a contract to open for the singer's next tour. That evening, I took her over to the academy where we found a janitor to let us into studio 110, and she helped me some more with the solo. A couple of hours into the rehearsal, a loud booming sound jolted me out of a concentration so deep that, for a moment, all I could say was, "Are we under attack?"

Didi dragged me outside where golden fountains of fireworks were exploding in the dark sky. "Happy New Year," she said. "Here's to dreams coming true." Didi held up the panther bracelet I'd shoplifted for her on our last day of high school, and I fished out the cross she'd shoplifted for me.

"To dreams coming true," I agreed. We clinked the cross and the panthers together as silver sparks rained down above our heads.

Chapter Thirty

Of course, I couldn't sleep the night before the audition. I watched the snow that began falling around three, heavy, wet flakes that dampened sound and soil. That morning dawned gray as cement. The few luminarias left over from Christmas had been turned into sacks of wet sand by the damp snow. Didi insisted that we trudge over to the academy far too early. The janitor who had become my friend let us into studio 110, where the audition was to be held. Once inside, Didi forbade me from practicing so much as one *tacón*.

"Remind me again," I said, "why we're here this early? Is it so I can get even more nervous than I already am?"

"To get a sense of the room, pilgrim," she snapped, studying every corner of a space where I'd practically lived the past three and a half years.

"Whew, cold." Rubbing her upper arms, she strode over to the thermostat and adjusted it until the heat clicked on.

"Didi, I have a pretty good 'sense' of this room."

"As a classroom, yeah. But has it ever been the place where you're gonna get or lose the biggest dream in your life?"

I stood in the glare of the fluorescent lights, imagining Tomás sitting in the metal folding chair the accompanist usually occupied, and I went cold. The glib answer I was going to give froze somewhere beneath my sternum.

"See what I mean?" She glanced up at the fluorescent lights. "Oh, those have got to go. The mood we're trying for is not State Bureaucrat with a Hangover. Be right back." The instant she left, the studio seemed to grow large as an airplane hangar. I envisioned myself attempting to fill it with motion and, more impossibly, emotion, and grew cold even as heat blasted over me.

Didi came back, holding a roll of duct tape and a Sharpie. She flipped off the bank of glaring lights, taped the switches down, and wrote, DON'T TOUCH. UNM CUSTODIAL DEPT. across the silver tape. Gray morning light, overcast and moody, filtered in through the high windows. "Better?" I nodded. "Infinitely."

She gave the studio one last check, then announced, "Let's get out of here."

Outside, we holed up in the cross-shaped concrete bunker where we could spy on whoever entered the gym. We slouched in the shadows and smoked, trying to stay warm. I had enough time to read all the graffiti chalked on the wall behind Didi: STONER CHICKS UNITE. THE PEOPLE SMOKE POT. WWW.HEMPCOALITION.ORG. WE NEED WEED!

"Wow," Didi said, crushing a butt beneath her heel. "This is a historic moment. Hard to believe, but this will be the first time I actually get to see Mystery Man in person."

"What are you saying?" My tone warned Didi not to make any further comment. Not to open that particular can of worms at that particular moment.

"Nothing, it's just that"—I stared hard at her. She shook her head— "Nothing at all. You are here to kick butt, and I'm here to take names. Speaking of which, wow, looks like your boyfriend is a heavy hitter." I peeked around the edge of the bunker. Besides Alma and most of the dance and music faculty, every great dancer who had gone through the program appeared. Didi ticked the girls off as they hurried in, frozen breath trailing behind them. She handicapped each one: "Yolanda. No chance. Worse moves than Vanilla Ice. Adriana. Oh, Driana, doll, you've packed on a few elle bees. Blanca, sorry, babe, you're not going to chew your way into Tomás Montenegro's heart with those big ole bucky beaver teeth."

I laughed, loving Didi for trying to lighten my grim, fatalistic mood. And then she said the one name I least wanted to hear.

"Liliana Montoya."

"Liliana Montoya is here!" I pushed Didi aside in time to see the former queen of the Flamenco Academy hurry into the gym. Then I sank back against the cold concrete. "Shit, that's it."

"Why? Just because she dances in María Benítez's company?"

"Uh, yes, being chosen for, arguably, the most prestigious flamenco troupe in the country might do for starters."

"Liliana is certifiable. The woman is a psychotic break waiting to happen."

"I thought that was a prerequisite in flamenco. Didi, I can't beat Liliana Montoya."

"Cyndi Rae Hrncir," she said, putting on a thick Texas accent. "You do everything she does except compete. Story of your life in a nutshell."

Odd how when you're poised, ready to jump off one cliff, jumping off another one doesn't seem that bad. That is probably why I said, "Story of us, too." There it was, our relationship in a nutshell, the noncompeting sidekick and the action heroine. The air inside the bunker, deadened by half a foot of concrete, seemed to grow even stiller as I waited for her response. But her eyes flicked away toward a figure rounding the soft corner of the old gym, and what she did say was, "It's go time. He's here."

A violent stroke wrenched my heart. I peeked around the edge of the bunker. Illuminated by the flat light of a distant winter sun, the world of snow and shadows outside the bunker was the black and white of an old movie. Tomás sauntered into the frame with the casual assurance of an actor hitting his mark. He wore a rumpled, black-velvet jacket, collar turned up, a muffler wound around his neck. His hair was black, the smoke from his cigarette, white. The shadows etching his eyes, nose, mouth, all black. His guitar case, black. He stopped at the front door, drew deeply on his cigarette, flicked the butt, still smoking, into a clump of snow, and went in.

"Breathe," Didi ordered me.

I tried, but all the shallow inhalations seemed to accomplish was to jerk my shoulders up to my ears. I felt heavy as stone, leaden with an odd sense of finality and dread. "We should go in," I said, sounding as numb as I felt.

"Jeez, Rae, what is it? Lighten up."

Everything bright and shiny had leaked out of me.

"Hey, it's just an audition. Besides, the slut is going to love you. He'd be lucky to carry your bunion pads."

I snorted a thin, humorless attempt at a laugh, made my feet carry me out of the bunker, and stepped into Tomás's black-and-white movie.

Inside the gym, the halls were empty until Didi opened the carved wooden doors of Doña Carlota's Flamenco Academy. The sight of the old lady's imperious portrait almost undid me. More than ever she seemed to be scrutinizing and finding me severely lacking. Half a dozen girls sat on the floor outside the door to studio 110. Though I strained to hear the sound of Tomás's guitar, the hallway was entirely silent. Blanca waved and gave me a cheery greeting. I started to sit down next to her, but Didi yanked me back. "You're not planning on waiting out here, are you?"

She gestured for me to follow her into the nearest bathroom, shut the door, shoved a metal trash can in front of it, and dug a small bottle of Frangelico from her purse. "Here, drink." When I didn't take the bottle, she shoved it in my face. "Drink. You look all shocky and Goth. Worse, you look like you're ready to surrender."

I took a slug of the hazelnut liqueur, grateful for the spot of warmth it thawed in my solar plexus.

"Now, here's the plan."

I took another swallow, comforted as much by her tone, which was the tone she used to use when taking charge of a mission, as I was by the alcohol.

Didi unwrapped the muffler from around my neck, slid the duffel bag off my shoulder, plopped it down on the floor, unzipped it, and extracted my carefully selected outfit: the black top of stretchy lace that Didi had loaned me, my new gored skirt in the only other color acceptable to the true *flamenco,* wine-red, and a new pair of Menkes, also wine-red and done up with a vampy cutout on the sides and seven-centimeter heels. Didi had meticulously hammered three extra rows of tiny, silver *claves* into the toes to give me the secret advantage of louder *golpes.*

"We hang here until it's time. We don't loiter in the hall sucking up loser anxiety vibes. We go last, okay?"

"We?" I asked.

"We what?"

"You said 'we' go last. *I'm* going last. It's a solo."

"That's what I meant. What else would I mean?"

I sucked up my courage. "Didi, I can take it from here. In fact, I would probably be less nervous if you'd leave now."

She blinked several times and picked her woven bag up off the bathroom floor where she'd dropped it. "Sure. No, that's fine."

I had hurt her feelings. Guilt stabbed me. She had completely thrown herself into helping me for the past week. All she'd cared about was getting me to open up and be great. What was my problem?

She started to leave, but someone pounded on the blocked door. Didi yelled, "Janitor! Come back later!"

"Don't leave. I need you. For shit like that."

"The details." She grinned. "We all need someone to take care of the details."

I nodded. She helped me get dressed, taking my discarded clothes, packing them away, and handing over my outfit. When she passed me the new shoes, I balked. "Shoes too?" No one ever put their shoes on until they got into the studio.

"How many chances do you get to make a first impression?" It was one of her showbiz mantras.

"One."

"And if you're gonna hook the part, you gotta . . ."

"Look the part."

With that, Didi plucked an eyeliner from her bag and held it up.

"Thanks," I said, waving it away. I'd been doing and redoing my hair and makeup since four in the morning. "I'm good."

" 'Good,' that's exactly the problem. Come on, no one in flamenco ever went wrong with too much liner." I let her pencil dark circles on my lids, then smudge them until my eyes popped like a silent-movie heroine's.

"Fullness, fullness." Didi waved her hands around my head, indicating that I should bend over so my hair would fluff up. With my head between my legs, Didi directed hot air from the hand dryer toward the spots where the damp air had flattened my hair. When I straightened back up, my hair was twice as thick, there was color in my cheeks, and my eyes looked like Lillian Gish selling violets on a street corner. Confidence ebbed back. I was in the hands of the master. Didi spritzed the air in front of me with a little Must de Cartier, then made me walk forward so that the perfume settled on me in an atomized cloud. She picked a few bits of coat fuzz off my top, then pronounced, "Let's go nail an audition."

By the time we reached the hall, the only one left waiting outside the door was Liliana. Like Didi, she understood the importance of going last. She glanced at me, then looked away as if I hadn't registered, which, I'm certain, in her world, I hadn't. Didi, however, registered in a big way. Like a lioness defending her territory, Liliana stood and began doing the sorts of impossible stretches that only professionals could manage.

Didi leaned over and whispered, "I'm intimidated, aren't you?" Her cocky smile said she wasn't, but I was. Liliana *was* a professional. María Benítez had picked her out of all the dancers in the world. This was pointless. The past four years of my life were pointless. I wondered what the hell I thought I was doing.

The door of the studio opened, Blanca scampered out, and the door shut again. Blanca, the only dance major I knew who wasn't obsessed, anorexic, and cutthroat, made me wish for a moment that I could trade it all in and be exactly like her: goofy, cheerful, nice, normal. Instead, I was doubly obsessed. Blanca caught my eye and slapped her hands against her chubby cheeks, her mouth open wide like the *Home Alone* kid and whispered, "Oh. My. God. He is the hottest guy in this or any other galaxy. I mean, *en fuego* to the max."

I blinked twice as if I had no idea whom she was referring to, afraid she was going to utter his name aloud.

She bounced her eyebrows lasciviously. "I think I'm gonna go back and audition a few more times just for some more of that eye candy."

The door opened again, and Alma poked her head out. "Liliana, you next?"

Liliana stared at Didi, clearly revealing who she thought her competition was, then she bent over to massage her foot and answered, "No, I got a little cramp. It'll be fine in a minute." She waved toward Didi. "She can go first."

"Me?" Didi laughed. "Did you think I was auditioning? No, my girl, Rae, is the star today. You are just her warm-up act."

Liliana was not amused by Didi's trash talk.

"If you were smart you'd go on before her, because anyone who follows her is going to look like shit. But if you want her to go first, that's fine too. Rae?" She gestured toward the door, directing me to enter.

I panicked. I believed in Didi's directive never to be a warm-up, to always go last.

Before I had time to stress even further, Didi glanced down at my feet and pretended to stop me even though I hadn't moved. "Shit, Rae, you wore the wrong shoes. I told you the heel is about to come off those."

"They look brand-new to me," Liliana said.

"Funny how deceptive looks can be. No, there's no way she can dance in those. Don't worry, though, Lil, we're parked close. It'll only take a few minutes to run out and get the ones I told you to wear. Give you enough time to work out your cramp *and* get your audition over with."

Didi pulled me away before Liliana could protest. As we left, Didi twiddled her fingers in a fake-friendly wave and over her shoulder chirped, *"Mierda!"* the flamenco version of "Break a leg."

We retreated to the bathroom to sip Frangelico and wait Liliana out. "Okay," Didi said, checking her watch. "They'll give Liliana what? Eight minutes, max. Then she'll hang and flirt with Tomás for, what? Three, four minutes, until Alma kicks her out. Twelve minutes at the outside. Here." She passed me the bottle. "And quit looking so grim. I've got your back."

Didi had my back. I smiled and tipped the bottle up.

Twelve minutes later, we were back in the hallway when Alma opened the door for Liliana to leave. The star backed out, babbling, "Tomás, I can't tell you what an honor it was to work with an artist of your caliber. Even this briefly. I actually didn't really get a chance to warm up and, you know, like I said, I had that cramp in my foot. Anyway, you have my card. I'm available at any time for a callback. Any time at all."

Didi and I exchanged glances. *Groveling? The great Liliana Montoya was groveling?* My dry mouth went drier.

Alma pushed the door open farther. "Thank you, Liliana. Someone will let you know."

On Liliana's face was a dazzled expression. Tomás had dazzled a flamenco queen. I was a flamenco commoner. Did I even have the right to be dazzled? I wondered. I stiffened my spine and answered, *Hell, yes. I'd earned the right with every blister and callus on my feet.*

Alma looked at us. "Ah, the Bobbsey Twins. Ofelia, we haven't seen much of you lately. Who's going first?"

"I'm just a member of Rae's entourage." Didi waved her hand in front of her face and stepped away from the door.

In that instant, I caught sight of him. His dark head was bent over the guitar, his ear nuzzled against the neck of his instrument as he tuned it. He glanced up at the sound of scuffling at the door and, for the first time in nearly four years, looked at me. In that second of delusion, I believed that Tomás had spent every day of the past few years yearning for me just as deeply as I had yearned for him. I smiled. He returned my smile with the polite, distant smile he'd give any stranger. Of course he didn't remember me. How could I have ever thought otherwise? Leslie was right. I was an erotomaniac. I had stalked Tomás for four years. My mother was crazy, had been crazy my whole life, and so was I. *That* was what was in *my* blood.

"*Pásele,* Rae," Alma said, waving impatiently for me to enter.

Inside, sitting behind Tomás, was most of the dance faculty along with the entire guitar wing of the music faculty, all gathered as if auditing a master class. All waiting. Waiting with Tomás. What did blisters and calluses mean? They were bumps on my skin, minor modifications to an exterior. Nothing had changed the interior since I'd been too frightened to walk into my first flamenco class. I was born Cyndi Rae Hrncir and would die Cyndi Rae Hrncir. I would have left then, but my legs had turned to lumber. Didi jabbed a knuckle into my spine, but I still couldn't move until I grabbed her hand and pulled her in with me. Alma shrugged, waved us both inside, then closed the door.

The light filtering through the high windows inside the studio was blue and spectral. A trickle of sweat like melted ice ran down from my armpit.

Tomás stood. Holding the guitar in his left hand, he came forward with his right outstretched. Alma made the introductions.

"This is Ofelia."

She took his hand. *"Muy encantado conocer a un tocaor tan dotado."*

"You speak Spanish."

"Not as well as my friend," Didi said, smiling in my direction.

He looked at me and Alma supplied the name. "This is Rae Hrncir."

Never had I hated the soulless grind of Slavic consonants that was my name more than I did at that moment. Then, for one instant, as Tomás took my hand, he looked from me to Didi and a dim recognition flickered across his eyes. He remembered. He shook my hand, staring at me like a man trying to identify a distant sound. His hand was warm against my cold one. In the next instant, he decided he was imagining things and dropped my hand. He waved a questioning finger from me to Didi. "Both of you are auditioning?"

"No," Didi answered. "I'm just here for moral support."

"Bueno. Friends. That's cute. I like that." He held his hand out, palm up, inviting us with a gesture formal and very European to step into the open area encircled by folding chairs. There was no chair for Didi. She stepped off to one side.

He sat down, settled his guitar, and looked at me. "What do you want me to play?"

He had spoken to me. Everything I'd studied for three and a half years was for this moment. To know the language, the flamenco code, well enough that I could utter the password that would allow me to enter his world. I opened my mouth. My vocal cords were dry and tense. I croaked out, *"Soleá por bulerías."* I had spoken to him.

"Bien, soleá por bulerías." He nodded at Alma, who was *cantaora.* Yes, she sang, and, yes, *el cante* is the wellspring of flamenco. But not that day. That day Alma's singing was inconsequential. It was all about his playing and my dancing. Tomás plucked out notes that rippled through the studio, his guitar a paddle pulling water in concentric swirls that drew us all toward him. He played the warm-up chords a guitarist always plays for new dancers as a way to synchronize style and tempo. But even with those throwaway chords, it was clear why some of the best guitar teachers in the country had chosen to sit in on an audition.

Behind me, Didi began doing *palmas,* softly clapping muted *sordas,* picking up the beat. I tried to force the sway of the familiar twelve counts into my body, but my nerves were logjammed.

"Something like that?" he asked me.

"Sí. Perfecto," I answered.

"Okay, then." He gave me a practiced smile. *"De principio. Y . . ."*

Where the warm-up chords had been a paddle rippling notes, Tomás's *soleá* was a deluge. His left hand made the timeless journey from the A chord to B-flat and back while the long nails of his right hand plucked a torrent of notes that flooded the large studio with waves of precisely one dozen beats each. His ring finger struck *golpes* on the guitar, a surge on the three, the six, the eight, the ten, pulling against the rhythm I knew and loved. I usually found the six-beats-up and six-beats-back sway of a *bulerías* as easy as rocking in a hammock. Not that day. He played the *entrada* once, twice, three times. Each time his eyes locked on me, the dancer, the one who was supposed to conduct that performance.

Didi marked time, clapping, then stamping the heels of her boots. She was keeping time just as I had for her so often in the past. When I didn't enter the second time Tomás played the *entrada,* Didi's stamping grew louder, urged me forward more insistently. Still I didn't move. The waves of notes kept coming. Any other time, I would have exulted in having an ocean of music to dance in. But that day, the *golpes* seemed dangerous, a riptide that would pull me under. I couldn't find a safe place to dive in. The waves broke and receded, leaving me standing on the shore, terrified of drowning.

I tried to remember Doña Carlota's story, to lose myself in the tale of the Gypsy girl dancing in the caves, but all I could recall was Guitos telling me that there had never been a pale girl like that on Sacromonte.

When Tomás played the *entrada* for the fourth time and I still did not move, Didi began doing the solo I'd choreographed. At first, she was inconspicuous, standing on the sidelines, performing in a subdued way, just to encourage me. But the faculty, who knew her so well, interpreted her modest hesitancy, her reluctance to embrace the spotlight as a joke, a clever comment on her renowned divahood. So, with a few laughs, a smattering of applause, the spotlight turned decisively toward Didi. And she flowered. I'd never *not* known this about Didi: she was a slave to attention.

Clapping, she picked up the tempo. Her months on the road, years of experience in front of audiences, had turned her natural charisma into a force of nature. It was impossible *not* to stare at her. Tomás stared. He looked away from me to her. Then, thumping out the *golpes* like a shepherd herding a scattered flock, he corralled Didi back onto the beat. He played for her. She danced for him. Her *brazeo,* her *taconeo* even flashier than usual, she took center stage beside me. Tomás smiled, pleased by the routine he assumed we were acting out, the shy wallflower being coaxed out of her shell.

I forced myself to move forward, to show some signs of life and retake the dance that was supposed to be mine. I picked up the tempo, energy returning to my legs with each stamp of my foot, and moved forward until Didi and I were dancing side by side. I caught her eye and nodded to signal to her that I could take over. But Didi and Tomás had formed the closed circuit that is essential between guitarist and dancer. He was doing for her what good accompanists do for dancers, supplying strong, steady rhythm and covering up when she made a mistake. Didi was so intent upon Tomás and he upon her that they both looked straight through me. With the stunned feel of an accident victim having trouble believing the catastrophe happening right in front of her, I wobbled out of beat and backed away.

After marking time long enough to gather myself, I moved forward more strongly. Attempting to take the lead, I reached out my arms, the universal signal for a *llamada,* my warning to Tomás that I was going to come in on the twelve. At the same instant, Didi surged back and brought her hands down on the ten, a clear call for a *desplante* that would come in on the one. Tomás flicked his eyes from Didi to me, trying to interpret the conflicting signals. He could only take direction from one of us.

Tomás had exactly the amount of time it takes to lift one finger to decide which one of us to follow. He hit a *golpe* on the one Didi had called for with a metallic clarity that rang like a bell signaling the end of a round. I was the fighter who went to the corner. I was out. Completely *fuera de compás,* more off the beat than I'd been on my first day in Doña's class, I stumbled along, dancing as if I were wearing casts on both feet.

While Didi performed the sweeping *desplante* I'd choreographed, I withdrew. As I executed simple marking steps, Didi hiked up her skirt, calling for what she loved the best, an *escobilla.* As Didi initiated the driving footwork that characterizes an *escobilla,* Tomás accelerated his playing to keep pace. Didi hammered the floor, her feet stirring the dust left by years of students.

Didi's frantic footwork had the hollow echo of a porn star, hydroponic breasts being trampolined by some gym stallion. Tomás urged her on with a hectic cascade of notes as they both struggled toward a theatrical climax. It came in a machine-gun burst, Didi jackhammering her feet, Tomás fanning triplets so furiously his hand blurred, a frenzy of motion that built higher and higher like a wedding cake with ever-more-elaborate garlands of sweet icing piped on over a tasteless base. Didi signaled and Tomás magically managed to crash down on a final chord exactly as Didi stamped to a resounding finale. The elite audience applauded. Didi had gotten it, the money shot.

Didi stood panting, her sweat and hard breathing the only part of the performance that was real. Everyone except Alma and Tomás, however, leaped to their feet applauding wildly. Alma looked at me and shook her head, her expression a combination of disdain for the praise being heaped on Didi and disappointment with me.

Didi reached out and hauled me into the winner's circle."Don't forget Rae. This is really her show." Her calculated graciousness was as transparent as an opera diva thanking her dresser and just as easily dismissed as the group continued their hosannas. Contained within their congratulations was a foregone conclusion: Tomás would select Didi. She had saved us, saved me, saved the academy; that was what was on everybody's face. I had frozen and, in the space of one *compás,* I'd lost what I wanted most.

As Tomás laid his guitar down on the chair and came toward us, I saw the years, decades, stretch ahead of me. I saw that they would be spent living and reliving the moment when I had trembled on the shore, when I had not dived in and Didi had. Years that would stretch into decades when I'd struggle to find a way to believe that my blood sister had not betrayed me. If Tomás carried away the slightest impression of me, it would be as one of the worst dancers he'd ever played for. I saw that those years would commence the second he reached our circle and told Didi that, of course, she had been selected, she was the one. She would be his partner.

His great-aunt's warning came back to me: *Flamenco is yo soy. You are waiting for her permission to be. Why? Why do you stay in her shadow? She is too big a tree. You are barely a sapling. You will never have enough light because you will never have enough courage to grow past her and reach the sun.*

The question I couldn't ask Doña Carlota came back: *How does a small tree kill a big tree?*

Before Tomás could reach Didi's charmed circle, I stepped out of it and stopped him. I felt as if I were at the top of a roller coaster with no memory of how I'd gotten there.

"I would like to dance." My voice was a croak.

"You just did."

"Not really. Not . . . I'd like another chance."

Tomás glanced over my shoulder at the group waiting for him in the winner's circle, then back at me.

"Please," I whispered. "I know you're not going to pick me, but I'd like another chance. I'm really not a bad dancer."

He leaned in close to me, his lips brushing the hair around my ear, and whispered in a kind voice, "I don't think you're a bad dancer. But, maybe, a good dancer who is having a bad day."

"All I want is the chance to redeem myself. Nothing more."

He nodded and, walking back to the chair, asked over his shoulder, "What do you want to dance?"

By this time, Didi and the others had turned and were staring at us so that they all heard when a voice that was not my voice, answered, *"Por siguiriyas."*

"Did she ask for a *siguiriyas?*" someone behind me whispered, unbelieving.

I barely believed myself that I'd requested the darkest, the deepest, the most *jondo* of all the *palos, siguiriyas,* the song of lamentation, the song of mourning. It was as if a grade school piano student had announced her intention of playing Rachmaninoff. It was presumptuous and absurd, yet in that moment of losing a dream I'd named to no one except the best friend who'd just stolen it from me, the song of death was the right one to ask for.

Tomás shook his head. "No. *Siguiriyas* is to be sung, not danced. *Siguiriyas* is not for this." He waved at the metal folding chairs, the faces, avid, ready to judge. "*Siguiriyas* is not for today. Not for you." He reached for his case.

I started clapping, *palmas secas,* claps that rang out like rifle shots. One, two, *three*! Four, five, *six*! Seven, *eight*! Nine, *ten*! Eleven, *twelve*! I kept on, slamming my palms together on the eight where the *siguiriyas* count began. The rapping was a call, a command. Coded within it was not only the unique rhythm of the style I was demanding, but the message that I knew the password. That I had a right to ask for it. Tomás stopped closing the latches on his guitar case.

I clapped even louder, chanting out the rhythm, starting on the eight, "*bomp,* bom, *bomp,* bom, *bomp,* bom, bom, *bomp,* bom bom *bomp*." I hit a counterrhythm with my foot and clucked my tongue loud as my nail-studded heel hit the wooden floor. I used every syllable of the secret language I'd spent all those years learning and I asked for this, for one last dance before I slid forever from Tomás Montenegro's awareness.

Too late, years too late, I fought to reach the sun.

Tomás turned and stared at me for a long moment before he heaved a sigh of resignation, pulled his guitar out of its case, nestled it on his lap, then slowly raised his hands and began clapping the beat back to me. He was annoyed. I didn't care. If I was going to disappear forever from his thoughts, at least I would mark my passing with a wrinkle or two of irritation.

Tomás curled his hands and body around his guitar and strummed. This time his playing was dry, unadorned. He wasn't trying, I knew that. His body was angled away, as close as he could get to turning his back on me. In a world where communication had to be immediate, electric, this was the ultimate insult; he was shutting off the current. He'd already dismissed me. It didn't matter. Dismissal fit this *palo,* this moment. Where his *bulerías* had been an ocean, the parched desolation of *siguiriyas* required a desert. He played a *falseta* of Diego del Gastor, the master of old-school flamenco's from *el arte*'s ancient heart in Jerez de la Frontera.

I stood, keeping the rhythm with a soft, muffled *palmas sordas*. Then I walked toward him.

He glanced up, merely a perfunctory check asking if the tempo, the style, were right. The barest of professional courtesies. *Nada más.* I nodded. He settled himself. I breathed in, breathed out. Tomás started the *entrada,* playing the six-beat *compás* of the *siguiriyas.* Where other guitarists would have rushed in to ornament the silence with flourishes, tremolos, *picado,* where every note would have been frilled and filigreed, Tomás allowed the time I needed to descend to flamenco's most profound depth.

My hands twined in languid *floreos* that fanned the fingers out and around the pivot of my wrist. I lifted my arms as slowly as mist rising off a dark lake, and just that, just raising my arms above my head, filled one, two, three *compases.*

Tomás's elemental playing was a broad and infinite avenue to any destination I chose. On the last note of the *entrada,* I stepped forward, putting my foot down on the boulevard of his *toque.* What lay before me was not the typical dancer's challenge. This could not be a technical exercise. In choosing to dance *por siguiriyas,* I had chosen flamenco's essential challenge: *Dame la verdad.* Give me the truth, say something true. The one true thing I had to say at that instant was good-bye. The time that had started one night when the moon vanished was about to end and my fate now was to bid it farewell. My every movement was heavy with that inevitability in a way that made me understand at last what it was to dance *con peso,* with weight. Every *compás,* every *falseta,* every note I'd danced while trying to create a musical bridge to Tomás crushed down on me.

I did a twelve-count *llamada,* my loaded feet pounding the earth, pouring out the rhythms I would never need again. I held nothing back. I threw out every *golpe-tacón-punta* combination I'd learned. I tossed them away in double, triple time. When I was done, I had nothing to lose. All I had was the solitary promise flamenco ever makes, the promise of eternity if you can create one moment ravishing enough.

I was infinitely lighter walking through my *paseo.* Flamenco had been a yoke I'd harnessed myself to. The instant I threw it off, my shoulders rose—"Lift! Lift! Lift!" My chest expanded, growing thick and deep and, seizing control, I started the *desplante* precisely on the eight count.

For the first time, Tomás looked up, ready to seriously follow, ready to seriously play. He sat up, read the declaration I was choreographing before him, composed his response and struck a B-flat chord that broke every heart in the room because no B-flat would ever be played with such cruel beauty again. In it was all anyone needed to know about flamenco. The chord was played in honor of that exact instant, an instant that he and I had created that was gone before it could be noticed.

Tomás stared straight into my eyes. He studied every curl of each finger I fanned upward, read what I wrote in those twining arabesques and translated them into languages I understood, though I'd never heard them before. He was a mirror that reflected my betrayal, anger, grief. Every pluck of the string was a pact made with the eternity of now, the only place where flamenco truly exists. He was an amplifier that let me hear for the first time what my own heart sounded like. There was no possibility of lying, of hiding: I hated Didi and I danced that. She had betrayed me and I danced that. I danced my stubborn stupidity in wanting Tomás and my grief that I would never have him. I was dancing it before I saw the loneliness it had all sprung from.

Tomás stroked an A minor that made the angels weep. The past three and a half years vanished, taking with them every longing I'd ever had. Each note Tomás played was only for this second, an instant that was gone as soon as he'd thought of it. He was a lens that magnified, clarified.

An odd bubble of exhilaration rose within me like the moment when my father had taken his hand away and I'd ridden a bike for the first time. Tomás played that as well, the fear, a clutch of panic, the certainty that I was going to die the second my father took his hand away. Then soaring. I danced the wobbling, tipsy giddiness of life and the soaring that is only possible because we're all precisely one inch of rubber away from falling forever.

My body danced the realization before it hit my brain: *This is what flamenco is, knowing you're alone, you're going to die, and dancing anyway.*

I touched my forehead, the realization overtaking me so powerfully that I fell out of *compás.* I glanced at Tomás, who responded instantaneously to that split second of vulnerability, playing those emotions with a tenderness that undid me even further. Seeing that I was lost, he took control and switched to A minor to signal a *silencio,* the section where the guitarist claimed center stage while the singer and dancer rested. Gratitude for his kindness, for rescuing me, poured out to him in the sweep of my arms.

He created an asylum for me by laying back on the driving rhythm and filling the *silencio* with melody. While I collected myself, I executed some simple marking steps until I was ready to call for the next sequence. He decanted strength into me with each *falseta* he strummed.

It saddened me to realize that I was leaving flamenco just when I finally understood it. I strode forward, decisively calling for the *escobilla*. If I'd thought about any of this in advance, I'd never have considered introducing an *escobilla* with its machine-gun footwork into the deepest, most *jondo*, of all the forms. But I hadn't thought, hadn't planned. I was stepping into each new second and letting whatever instant I found myself in dictate how it was to be expressed. This second demanded an *escobilla*.

Tomás switched effortlessly out of the melody and transformed his guitar back into a percussion instrument. His hand blurred on the strings, pouring out a flood of precise rhythm metered by rousing thumps of *golpe*. He was the best accompanist I'd ever heard, live or recorded. His beat was so strong, with accents as clear as stepping stones, a dancer would have to be deaf not to be able to follow its path.

I moved aside and let my feet follow the rhythm. Doña Carlota had always told us to aim for a spot one quarter inch below the floor. I aimed for hell and woke up every sleeping demon at its dark center. They swarmed up into my heels and I pounded out my fury and rage at Didi's betrayal. Maybe it wasn't justified. Maybe she'd genuinely been trying to help me. Maybe she'd had my back. I didn't care. I was pissed off and I danced that in my farewell dance.

I grimaced, not caring what my face did as long as my feet could do what they had to. As I hammered out my message of anger and wounded pride, I understood the arrogance in flamenco. It rose up in me, seeming to pass through every century of exile and ostracism endured by the outcast people who'd created it. I stood directly in front of Tomás and held my swaying skirt up so he could see my beautiful legs, my astonishing footwork. I wanted him to get a good look at everything he was passing up. The fool.

I was in command again and ordered yet another *escobilla*. I increased the tempo, not believing myself how fast my heels were striking. Tomás leaned forward, strumming faster to give me the propulsion I needed. Yet, as my feet slammed harder and faster, time slowed and I felt myself escaping the gravity of everything I'd ever known. Fog, mists, clouds fell away until I was out of any atmosphere I'd previously breathed.

I looked around and saw every detail of the room. I noticed that my teachers were clapping *palmas,* snapping *pitos* for me. They were shouting *jaleo,* praise and encouragement: *Óle! Así se baila! Eso es! Que toma! Que toma!*

In slow motion, I saw a bead of sweat roll down the side of Tomás's face, tracing the beautiful, dark curves of his hairline until he leaned forward and it trembled for a moment at the edge of his eyebrow before dropping onto his guitar. There was only one thing I wanted any longer: for Tomás to keep playing. I knew then why Vicente Romero had died onstage dancing one last *escobilla.* I knew why *cantaores* had drowned in their own blood singing one last *letra.*

These deaths no longer seemed tragic to me. I understood every one. I felt I was on the verge of piercing a veil, learning the unlearnable, knowing the unknowable, when Tomás began to stare at me. Not at a dancer he was trying to follow, at me. His gaze drew me back into the present. I stared back and found what I had to express contained within that second: desire.

In some distant corner of my mind, I was ashamed of the desire that I was revealing more nakedly than if I'd stripped off my clothes. My mother's face, pinched, silent, stoic, floated into my consciousness. I stamped my shame down until it turned to rose petals beneath my heels, filling the studio with their fragrance.

I finished with a thunderous closing that Tomás had to labor to keep pace with. When it was over, we stared at each other, panting. It wasn't that I knew then we would be true lovers; we already were.

How does a small tree kill a big tree?
You take the sun away from her.

Chapter Thirty-one

Tomás stood, took my hand, and we left without a word passing between us. After the volumes we'd just communicated there was no need. As we passed Didi shouted high-pitched congratulations, pretending that she'd intended my triumph from the start. I closed my ears to her. My heart had already been shut.

Tomás drove an old Ford truck that looked like a piece of turquoise, faded blue with streaks of rust running through it. The companionable chug of its engine was the only sound as we drove down Central Avenue. He passed several motels and didn't stop until we reached the Ace High, just as if he, too, had spent the last years working to return to this place. When he came back to the truck with a room key that bore the number 312, my heart soared. What else could I conclude but that he remembered? It was as if we'd agreed, all those years ago, to meet back here as soon as we could, to return the instant I had learned all the secret flamenco codes and signals, rituals and rhythms that would allow me to enter his world.

We stepped into room 312. Tomás closed the door. At the second our bodies joined, time, the time that had stopped when he left me standing on Carlisle Avenue all those years ago, started again. In the glass of the balcony doors, I saw our reflections. The dim light behind us shone on the drapes, turning the mustard color gold. They were half open, framing Tomás and me as if we were onstage at the moment the curtains parted and the second act began. His head was bent above mine, his dark hair swinging forward, his face buried in my hair. My arms were raised, embracing him. He kissed me. I closed my eyes, but the image of us together remained, growing brighter, more golden, in the dark on the other side of my eyelids.

His smell was exactly as it had been the first time, sweat and marijuana and oranges. He tugged down the zipper on my skirt and it slid to the floor, a black shadow that I stepped over without a thought. I raised my arms high and he pulled the stretch top over my head. I pushed his clothes away.

The feel of his naked skin against mine was such a relief that I couldn't remember how I had existed without it for any second of the past three years. It was both an immediate essential necessity and the most voluptuous luxury imaginable.

In the reflection on the balcony doors, he knelt, dark head bowed, his hands drawing me to him. My pale fingers were icicles melting into his black hair. I had been chosen. I was the one odalisque, the one girl out of the five hundred whose dance had won the sultan.

He stood. The intricate pull and bulk of his back muscles came alive against my palms as he bent to kiss me. I tasted myself on his lips. His flesh inside of me was a formality, the signature on a pact we'd made in this room all those years ago, the fulfillment of a contract we had already written in twelve beats. We fit together with an inevitability that made each touch, each kiss as familiar as it was thrilling. The night was of one continuous piece as we reenacted every note, every pulse, every advance, every retreat of the dance we had already choreographed.

When the room filled with murky predawn light, I watched as he slept. He lay on his right side, facing me. His lips, severe and disdainful when he was awake, puckered needful and plump as a baby's in sleep. The black scrolls of his hair fell to either side of a broad shoulder and tangled with the gold chain around his neck. The chain jumped in rhythm to his heart beating through the vein at his neck. Women generally know better than to fall in love with beauty, the thing that the whole world can see and covet. They know to find what is only there for them alone. I tried to pick out flaws, tiny snags in his beauty that could be mine alone to love. Perhaps his nose was a bit too long? The furrows between his eyes, might they not deepen unattractively as he aged? His teeth were tanned by coffee and cigarettes, they were not perfect American teeth. His lower lip was dimpled and darkened at the spot where he always held his cigarette. All these flaws did was to make his beauty more memorable.

Tomás woke, caught me staring, and kissed each lid. We made love one last, exhausted time; then he wrapped his arms and legs around me and laid his head on my shoulder like the famous photo of John and Yoko. I toyed with his dark curls and breathed in his smell. He spread his hand across my heart.

"You might be the palest woman I have ever known."

"I know. I'm an albino."

"You're beautiful. Rae. Rae. Ray of sunshine. X-ray. Can you see through me, X-ray? Pale, pale Rae." He studied his dark fingers curving around my breast, fascinated as a child making shadow animals against a wall. *"Güera, rubia, gabacha, gringa."* He crooned the words that meant "pale," that meant "other." "Vermeer would have painted you. Scarlet here." He traced a finger over my lips. "Lapis lazuli here." My eyes. "Cream and rose here." My cheek, throat, shoulder. He sighed and whispered, "I have to get back to the gym."

His words were so at odds with his touch that I couldn't reconcile the two. "Why?"

"A few more auditions."

"But yesterday? There was no one after me. I was the last."

"I know, you should have been. But you know the flamenco grapevine. Once word leaked out, Alma started getting calls from all over. *Una bailaora* from New York was supposed to have flown in last night. Another is driving down from Denver. There's a pretty good scene in Denver. You'd be surprised." He kissed my shoulder, sat up, and lighted a cigarette. The odor of Ducados, harsh and strangely Oriental, filled the room. He clasped the cigarette between his lips and, shutting one eye against a coil of smoke, pulled on his shirt.

"No. Don't."

Flipping his hair out from under the shirt collar, he froze.

"Don't see any other dancers. Pick me. Take me with you."

Motion started again. He buttoned his shirt. "X-ray, you are definitely in the running. I promise. Definitely. You are insanely *fuerza en compás*. Really, one of the strongest I've ever seen." He offered the cigarette to me. I took it, dug out one of Didi's joints, lighted it from the cigarette's glowing end, inhaled as deeply as I could, closed my mouth over Tomás's and exhaled.

Passing the Ducado and the blunt back and forth, we fortified ourselves with the illicit airs of flamenco. Tomás sagged back against the pillows, eyes closed, mouth gone slack. I lay beside him, unbuttoned his shirt, and trailed my fingers along his chest as I murmured in his ear,

"Take me, Tomás. I am what you need. You might find a better dancer than me, but you will never find a better canvas for painting your art." All those missions with Didi. All the flattery, the cajolery. These were Didi's weapons. I took them and armed myself. "Your tour is to introduce the greatest guitarist in the world to America. Not the greatest dancer."

I had clung to Guitos's secret. Hoarded and harbored the knowledge that Tomás was driven by the fear that the Gypsy heritage he'd built his reputation on was a lie. It was time to use the one advantage I had: his secret. "I will be the light that exalts your darkness. I will be the pretender who proves your legitimacy."

Tomás opened his eyes. Skepticism tautened his features. I had over-reached. I was certain he suspected I knew his secret and would now hate me for possessing that knowledge. *"Ozu!"* he expelled the Gypsy curse on a snort of laughter. "What kind of shit do they teach you girls at that university? Lah-jit-tuh-mah-say?" He mocked the word with an exaggerated homeboy pronunciation. "What kind of shit is that?"

"Stupid shit. Kind of shit that says Tiger Woods can't be the best in the world. Kind of shit that says he has to decide if he's black or Asian or white. Kind of shit that says everyone has to declare themselves and be whoever their grandfathers back to Adam were."

"Kind of shit that says a white girl can't dance flamenco."

"Kind of shit that says a white girl can't dance flamenco."

His grin, white in the dark room, was a goofy, stoned flag of surrender. I had done it. I had used his secret to turn us into allies. "Fuck it. When did I say I wanted to spend two days looking at dancers? I never told Alma that. Come here, *güera*." He tugged me on top of him, sucked a hit from the joint, and exhaled it into my mouth. Flamenco communion. We'd both taken it. We both surrendered, sinking into the voluptuous abandon that was the birthright of all those born into flamenco. And all who could learn how to decipher its code.

We didn't leave room 312 of the Ace High Motel. We stayed all day and made love. But Tomás never recalled that he had been there before. That he had met me before. Why should he? Why should he have remembered the girl he'd met once many years ago when I myself had now forgotten who she was?

Chapter Thirty-two

The curtains that had been gold were mustard-colored in the early morning light. A shaft of that light illuminated Tomás. Hunched over his guitar, playing softly, he looked like a young monk bent over his prayers in a medieval cathedral. His music rose fragrant as incense toward the heavens. He had made love to with the same pure intensity.

"Did I wake you?" He put the guitar aside and crept toward me in a jokey, panther-stalking-his-prey way that turned serious as he slid beneath the covers.

"We're good together," he said, later, holding me. He put two fingers lightly on my neck and two on the carotid artery on his own neck.

"What?" I asked, but he shushed me as he concentrated, his lips moving as he counted.

"Just like I thought. Our hearts beat in *compás*. The exact same *palo*. Gypsy *compás*." Just saying the word *Gypsy* was a struck nerve and he bounded out of bed, dragging me with him. "*Vamos ya!* We have to start rehearsing. We should have started a month ago. The tour is already completely booked. I have to call the promoter and give him your name for advertising." He clapped his hands like a director calling for a new scene to begin, for action to commence. "Okay, do we need to stop by your house? You have your shoes, a skirt? Do you need anything else?"

Didi might be there, in the small house on the alley. I didn't want to see her. If I saw Didi, she would convince me that she had not betrayed me. Had not tried to steal my chance with Tomás. She would say she had not seen my signal that I was ready to step back into the lead. That whatever she'd done had been for me. I imitated Didi's laugh, heedless, taunting, and answered, "Shoes, skirt. What else does a dancer need?"

"*Ándale pues.*" Let's go then.

It was late afternoon when we emerged into a sunless day knifed through by a north wind. The worn seats of his old truck creaked from the cold when we sat.

"Takes a minute to warm up," he said, turning the key in the ignition. I shivered in the cold. "Here." He took his jacket off, wrapped it around my shoulders, and buried his face in my hair. The sun, already slumping down onto the West Mesa, broke through the clouds and lasered slices of light onto Central Avenue. Each crummy business—the Winchester Ammunition Advisory Center, the Leather Shoppe, the Pussycat Video, the Aztec Motel—was gilded in the dazzling illumination of late afternoon.

"Wait until you see this place where I'm staying," he said as we sailed along I-25, high above a dusty plain that stretched out to our west all the way to Mount Taylor, a distant, snow-capped blue. "It's *mi primo*'s from up north. He lets me stay there whenever I'm in town." Though I'd driven I-25 dozens of times, that day was the first time I noticed that painted on the side of a cinder-block building was a woman in a flamenco pose, her hand tossed to the sky.

"What's your cousin do?" It was a stupid question that I asked mostly to show him that I knew what *primo* meant.

"Little of this, little of that. Family business, you know. The kind of business they have up north." He tipped his chin up, toward a north where family business was conducted that anyone who was *enterao* wouldn't be stupid enough to ask about. "He's not really my cousin," he added, turning away to indicate that the subject was closed. At least to a white girl who wouldn't understand the intricate gradations of northern New Mexican *primos*.

The sun isolated everything on the fields below in shimmering radiance: a cemetery, white crosses stippled into a barren field; a lot holding acres of repossessed cars inside high curls of concertina wire; a factory that made bandages; another that manufactured wooden pallets; a tow truck impaled on a thirty-foot pole; the dusty filigree of dirt bike trails looping over the knobby earth that sprouted little aside from rabbitbrush, Russian thistles, and old tires. Monolithic pylons marched across the landscape unspooling loops of silver power line. The light haloed Tomás sitting behind the wheel of a truck like a normal human being. I kept looking away, then back again, just for the shock of seeing him beside me.

Erotomania, I screamed in my mind at the therapist, Leslie. *Here he is. He's chosen me.* But Leslie slipped away. It was Didi I wanted to tell, the only person on earth who knew that I had climbed Mount Everest, won seven Olympic gold medals, and been awarded a Nobel Prize. No one else knew what I'd done to win, who I'd had to become.

We turned on Rio Bravo. *"Vive Como Un Rey."* Tomás read the message on a billboard urging us to live like a king, drink Budweiser.

He scraped open the ashtray, pulled out a partially smoked joint, lit it, and, holding it out to me, joked, *"Vive Como Una Reina."*

I laughed. Yes, I *would,* I would live like a queen.

We crossed the Rio Grande. It flowed beneath us, a broad swath of dull, aluminum-colored water bordered by cottonwoods grown to primeval size. On Rio Bravo, we turned off and made our way through a tangle of ever-smaller streets, lanes, and paths running along the river. We finished the joint and the day turned much jollier.

"Did you see that?" I asked, pointing to a row of a dozen identical navy blue T-shirts flapping on a line. They suddenly held a comic significance only Tomás and I understood and we laughed until Tomás ran off the dirt road. That made us laugh even more. As did a piñata in the shape of a pirate hanging forlornly from a big elm. As did a miniature horse nibbling a flake of alfalfa. The midget horse made me laugh until I was afraid I'd wet my pants. We stopped laughing long enough for me to point to an artfully spray-painted graffito swirling in hectic gang-style script across the side of a metal storage shed that carefully instructed all viewers, FUCK YUO.

The thought of some homeboy misspelling his rage against the machine then became the funniest thing either of us had ever seen. As we reached the house where Tomás was staying, he was pounding my back and I was trying to catch my breath. We stopped outside a high adobe wall and he punched a code in. A wrought-iron gate swung open.

On the other side was a compound with a massive adobe hacienda tucked into the shadows cast by several prodigious cottonwoods. The estate's walled isolation made me recall Tomás referring to the "family business," and the words *drug lord's palace* appeared like a crawl beneath the unkempt opulence of the property. That suspicion was confirmed when we went inside. The house seemed to have been decorated by a thirteen-year-old boy with an unlimited line of credit: plasma TV, round bed with black satin sheets, monster sound system. Walk-in closets were filled with every article of clothing that FUBU and Sean John had ever manufactured.

"Can you believe this shit?" Tomás asked, laughing. Next to him a pump kicked on, powering a six-foot-high acrylic sculpture that sent ten-drils of orange and magenta oil droplets shimmying up a wavy panel where lights and bubbles vibrated. "*Mis primos* from up north are pretty basic guys."

I knew he was talking about the village in northern New Mexico that Guitos had told me was Tomás's one true home. I wanted to ask about it, about his *primos* and their "family business," but I didn't. I was an alien trying to slip through customs with forged papers, trying to enter a country where I did not belong. I was not going to call attention to my outsider status by asking questions. Not about northern New Mexico, not about flamenco, not about *los primos,* not about anything.

Still, answers to my unasked questions were in the simple acts Tomás performed. When he built a fire, he had the practiced expertise of some-one who has risen on many cold mountain mornings in places where warmth came from wood. Piñon wood. The fragrance of piñon filled the house, warming it even more than the fire.

"*Una copita?*" he asked me, tipping his thumb and pinkie up. He pulled green bottles of Dos Equis lager for us out of the refrigerator. "You like posole?"

"With red chile?"

"*Claro.* I'm going to make the best posole for you that you've ever tasted. *Mi tío* Ernesto taught me how." He'd already soaked the dried hominy and put the fat kernels of corn on to boil in a cast-iron pot, adding garlic, Mexican oregano, onion, green chiles; then he browned a cut of beef I didn't recognize.

"You don't use pork shoulder?" I asked, showing off what I'd learned from Alejandro, who had told me that pork shoulder was essential for good posole.

"A lot of people do. I asked Tío Ernesto once why he didn't. He didn't have a reason, just that they always used beef in his village and it was al-ways good. So why change?" Tomás asked, showing me how to pour boiling water to soften dried red chiles, then scrape pulp from the leathery skins to make red chile.

The history of New Mexico, of Spaniards in the New World, went into the stew of dried hominy, chiles, and meat. Certainly, Tomás's history was there as he performed each step of the preparation with the devotion of an acolyte. Still, as he chopped an onion, I realized that this was the first human moment I'd had with him, the first moment with Tomás that wasn't part of a fairy tale. That he was a real human and that we were in the same room, breathing the same air.

While the posole simmered, Tomás began my true flamenco education. In my years at the Flamenco Academy, I'd studied a complicated equation, but as Tomás played, he showed me that I had only solved half of the problem. The equation had to be balanced with a guitarist and a singer before it could be proved. I thought I knew how to work with a guitarist. I didn't. I'd learned a basic vocabulary at the academy. That evening, Tomás began teaching me how to combine the simple words and phrases I knew into eloquent passages that would express what he wanted expressed about his playing. I had had my last *yo soy* moment during the audition. Tomás was not just the star, the featured performer; he was the entire reason for my being onstage. I was his interpreter. My job was to translate from the ear to the eye.

It was midnight before he put his guitar down and we fell upon the posole, devouring it with thick tortillas dripping with butter, washing it all down with Dos Equis lager. Tiny cups of the espresso Tomás brewed followed, so that we could stay up even later. It was near dawn before we went to bed and much later before we went to sleep.

That period before the first tour was a space out of time. Our hours in the house by the river were measured out in piñon fires. He played and I danced. I danced harder than I ever had before. As harsh as the great-aunt had been, the great-nephew was twice as tough. My life took shape around the spaces I occupied while dancing or making love with Tomás. Within both those areas, I found equal parts ecstasy and terror. These elements created a compound as unstable as nitroglycerin. I hardly dared breathe, fearing it would blow up, that he would choose someone else. I had been picked, but I never stopped auditioning.

Then a fax machine spit out a cloud of itineraries that floated onto the floor. Tomás picked up the sheets of paper from the promoter and began packing for the tour that would establish him in the United States. We left the house on the river where I had learned to translate into motion every note Tomás plucked. Walking toward the airport, dragging bags behind us like obedient dogs on leashes, Tomás and I fell out of step. Going on the road required him to put on psychic armor and as he strode ahead of me, it locked into place. We passed beneath the caped warrior reaching for the eagle and, for a moment, I wished Didi had been there to say good-bye.

Our first stop was Tulsa, Oklahoma. We played a medium-size hall at the university. That night, I understood what Tomás had trained me for. His was the name that caused people to open their wallets and pull out forty, fifty, a hundred dollars for a ticket. His was the face on the poster. The pressure was on him. My job was simply to provide a little movement, a change of pace. I was his foil. My paleness accentuated Tomás's dark ethnicity. My understated dancing never stole the spotlight from his passionate playing. My white-bread American background never upstaged his pedigree as the Gypsy ward of a flamenco legend, *gitano a cuatro costaos*. The last year my family had lived in Houdek, Daddy brought home a novelty Christmas gift, a plastic flower in a pot, wired with fiber optics that would light up to music, flashing different colors for every tune that was played. I was that flower in a pot. That was the bargain I'd made, and I did everything in my power to live up to it.

For one month we did nothing but perform, party, make love, and travel to the next gig, where it all started again. In spite of being in a different city almost every day, a surprising sameness overtook our lives. In each new venue, we'd be picked up at the airport by someone I came to think of as the Guitar Nerd. The Guitar Nerd, holding up Tomás's CD, met us as we stepped off the plane. He was frequently a college professor, often accompanied by his prize student.

All the Guitar Nerds were driven to prove themselves to Tomás. After a few warm-up compliments in which they'd proclaim Tomás to be the next Paco de Lucía or, if they were really reaching, far better than Paco, they'd work in references to their own flamenco backgrounds. The older ones would mention their time in "Moron" with "Diego." The younger ones would ask nerdophile questions about nail filing: "Always in the same direction!" Or the merits of Hannanbach bass strings mixed with La Bella trebles over, say, just going with Luthier Concert Silvers on all six. To really prove themselves as initiates in the flamenco world, they would casually pass Tomás a joint.

After the performance, there would be a reception given by the head of the music department or the guitar society or whatever group had sponsored our visit. We'd sip Spanish red and eat olives and almonds; sometimes the faculty wife would attempt gazpacho or get her countries mixed up entirely and do taquitos.

Then the magic word, *juerga,* would pass through the group. If there were enough initiates, the real party would start right there. If not, the *aficionados* would slip away to adjourn at a bar or someone's ratty apartment. There the focus would be on the true *juerga*'s nearly sacramental use of controlled substances. In short, everyone would get utterly baked. That was when I would have to be my most vigilant, for the flamenco minxes truly swarmed at *juergas*. Fortunately, I'd studied with the master and knew every trick in the groupie playbook.

We'd all take a brief break from the party for that evening's performance, where Tomás would astonish the locals by playing with both passion and precision no matter how wasted he'd been only moments before stepping onstage. I'd provide a bit of color and motion. Then, the instant we took our last bows, we would be swept back into the bacchanal we'd just left. The party would typically go on all night and not end until whoever risked being mocked as anal-retentive for wearing a watch would yell out that our flight was leaving in an hour. Then there would be a mad scramble to the airport and, with many *abrazos* and *besos,* we'd be poured onto the plane where Tomás would promptly pass out.

In each city there would be an interview. It might be on the local NPR station, or the arts editor from the local paper would meet us in a coffee shop. The interviewer would have already read all the clips about Tomás, the stories that always mentioned the phrase *gitano por cuatro costaos* to explain that his birth mother and father back in Spain were both pure Gypsy. He would already know that Doña Carlota, a famous flamenco dancer and herself *gitana por cuatro costaos,* had been asked by the doomed addict mother, her great-niece back in Spain, to adopt the child because the family knew he would be brought up in the old Gypsy way.

The interviewers asked Tomás for refinements on the theme of authenticity. Did he feel he would be able to play *flamenco puro* the way he did if he hadn't been brought up in the tradition? If he didn't have Gypsy blood in his veins? They asked how his great-aunt was doing. Was she still living in Santa Fe? Did he see her often? After each successive interview, Tomás grew quieter and more distant. I knew why. I knew his secret, but I had already used it, used it to become an ally in his deception. Bit by bit, though, rather than being an ally, I became the emblem of his deception, a pretender slipping into camp under the protection of a powerful insider who was herself a fraud. His detachment grew until I came to live for the moments when I was onstage with him, dancing, being the flower in the pot that only his guitar could bring to life. Only then was he really with me.

The tour had been arranged in a circle. The top of the circle, the halfway point, was Madison, Wisconsin, where black ice covered the streets and Tomás had to loosen the strings on his guitars so the cold that tightened them wouldn't harm the fretboards. When we reached the bottom of the loop, the southernmost and last stop of the tour, we stepped off a plane in Austin, Texas, into heat so tropically humid that Tomás filled his cases with sachets of drying agents. The first thing we were shown in Austin was the site of America's first mass murder, a tower on the university campus where Charles Whitman had killed seventeen people including himself. The second thing was Barton Springs. Coming from the desert, the sight of a lagoon, a minor inland sea, cutting cold and clean through the center of a city, was the most improbable extravagance I could imagine. I had to possess this luxury, to have such opulence in my life.

That night, we played to a full house at the Hogg Auditorium on the university campus. After the show, a local *aficionado* dragged us to a tapas bar owned by a Madrileño who went crazy for Tomás's playing and offered to let him play for as many nights as he wanted in exchange for a percentage of the bar. There was no room in the small club for a dancer. I could stay or go home to Albuquerque. I chose to stay and have a vacation from flamenco. I never went with Tomás to the club, never met anyone from the local flamenco scene.

We rented an apartment in Travis Heights, a leafy neighborhood dotted with birdhouses on tall poles that purple martins swooped around, eating mosquitoes. I bought a jade green tank suit and an old robin's egg blue Schwinn and every day, as Tomás slept off the night before or practiced for the night to come, I rode to Barton Springs. My route cut through the campus of the Texas School for the Deaf.

I would sweat on the ride over, salty drops trailing down to my elbows, then plunge into the hypothermic waters of the chilly springs and stay until the sky was dark and the pool darker. Until the only thing that could warm me up was Tomás's body. At first, he loved my coming home to him, still chilly from the polar waters, curlicues of wet hair dripping water onto my shoulders. But as the summer wore on, the heat bludgeoned us. He took to leaving the apartment earlier and earlier and staying out later and later. Of course, he was having an affair. Maybe several. It was not my place to ask. I was in his country on forged papers and could be asked to leave at any time. My only toehold, what helped me hang on, was knowing Tomás's secret, knowing that his documents were falsified as well.

The last time I rode to Barton Springs, I was so sunk in gloom that I was halfway around the playing field before I sensed an entirely soundless game of soccer being played beside me. The spectacle of teams of young men screaming silently at one another in sign language mesmerized me to such a degree that I failed to notice a gaping pothole in the road ahead. I hit it, sailed over the handlebars, and skidded to a landing that flayed the inside of my arms.

The soccer team surrounded me, speaking in voices filled with complex harmonics, bird shrieks, and mechanical sounds. The coach and the rest of the team packed me and the battered Schwinn into a pickup and drove me home.

The windows of the little house were open and as I approached with my silent crew I could hear Tomás talking on the phone. All the heat that had cooled between us was there with whomever he was speaking to. His Spanish was too rushed, too animated for me to understand, but his excitement was easy to translate. I waved good-bye to my rescuers and, cradling my arm, opened the door. The instant he saw me, Tomás switched to English, pretending to be bored as he said, "Okay, well, I gotta go."

Then he noticed my arm and rushed me into the bathroom. He washed the wound, patted on ointment, and bandaged it up. But the cut needed to be scrubbed to remove all the bits of gravel embedded in my flesh. Tomás couldn't bear to hurt me and I couldn't summon up the courage to clean the scrape myself. So, eventually, the scrape healed over the tiny specks of gravel that hadn't been cleaned away and they left gray smudges that grew into the new skin like shadows beneath the surface. It didn't matter; the only time anyone saw the underside of my arms was when I danced, and in flamenco, it was good to have shadows to reveal.

Chapter Thirty-three

We went home to the house on the river. Tomás stopped playing anything but *cante jondo*. His *toque* was drenched with loneliness, regret, abandonment, and betrayal. I assumed that the last, the betrayal, was his confession to me and I fell into a state of panicked rage. We talked about this in the only way we had ever talked about anything, through flamenco. Since we exchanged so few words, his every gesture took on heightened meaning. The entire time I'd known him, Tomás had always held his guitar the way the old-timers had, with the guitar resting on his right leg, pointing upward on a diagonal that allowed the left hand easy access to the fretboard. Around this time he adopted an even more torturous position that made the fretboard almost invisible, with his right leg crossed over the left, guitar hugged into the hip and tilted away from his body. He looked like Picasso's Old Guitarist draped around the guitar, his left hand crooked painfully into a position that strained the muscles and made the nerves go dead. He complained about the pain, the numbness. Then he would go back to practicing with his instrument tilted even farther away.

One morning, I stepped out onto the porch and was surprised to discover that somehow the season had changed from late summer to winter with no fall intervening. The Sandias had turned a steely blue and a light dusting of snow crowned them. Tomás's booker had organized another tour: San Diego, Phoenix, Chicago, Montreal. He had a big following in Montreal. All solo engagements. There was no mention of my going with him.

If there was a gap long enough between gigs, he flew home. What survived of our relationship existed in those sputtering installments. On the nights before he left again, I tried to inoculate him against other women. That winter, it always started with my pulling him close in the darkness, yanking his sweater off over his head so that in the dry air, static electricity crackled and flared and an aurora borealis flashed across his back, his arms. His hair would rise above his head, an unearthly frame for his ruinous beauty, the beauty that was both animating and obliterating my life. We made love in panicky, desperate sessions. I put up NO TRESPASSING signs on him with necklaces of hickeys and let him flay my neck, my cheeks, my breasts with his beard. We ground ourselves into each other, brutal at some moments, then tender. In the only arena I had left, I was competitive in bed. I intended that each swivel of my hips, each touch, each syncopation be better than that of any of the other women I knew he would sleep with. I gauged each erection, calculating whether another woman could inspire one harder, more enduring. His orgasms were how I kept score. Were the convulsions of passion strong enough to ward off interlopers? I clung to the promises made by the wet slap of our bodies.

I inhaled his odor, the smell of our animal selves, the fragrance we made together. Before he'd even left, the scent made me nostalgic for us. I kissed the furrows of his ribs, his flat stomach, my tongue running over the small hairs, letting my own hair tickle him, and moving downward toward the place where the smell was strongest.

Near dawn, I would creep out of bed and write long letters, inventories of desire cataloging everything we'd done, everything I still hoped to do. I packed these missives into his suitcase. I spent a fortune express-mailing them to hotels, concert halls, whatever address I had, wherever they would reach him before another woman did.

At dawn, I would drive him to the Sunport. We passed the bandage factory as the sky just started to turn pink with early morning light and we gazed upon the woman painted on the side of the building, raising her arms in a flamenco pose that came to look more and more like pleading.

Denial and fantasy. Longing and deprivation. Like a cactus that could survive on little more than the moisture in the air, I was made for the arid emptiness of the long-distance relationship. After years of sustaining a one-sided relationship, I was ideally adapted to subsist on Arrivals and Departures. I could live on airport moments alone. At the Departures gate, after he pressed fervid last-minute erections against me, I would will myself into hibernation until the next arrival. Then, as Tomás sauntered in carrying the Santos Hernández guitar he would never dream of abandoning to the faulty attention of baggage handlers, my life would stutter and start up again. I didn't question this contract since I'd written it myself. My consolation was that I was the one he came home to. Of the five hundred, the sultan had chosen me to wait in his chamber. He would leave, would visit others, but I had been installed in his personal quarters. I waited for him in a house by the river that wasn't mine and wasn't his, dancing to his CDs, waiting for him to return.

Each time he came back, his dark mood would have turned darker. He played nothing but *soleares,* the Gypsies' songs of desolation and exile. Because I knew the code so well, I could translate the rhythms he played. I knew the songs of suppression, of a spirit yearning to be free. I knew that he believed his *duende,* his crazed flamenco passion, was suffocating. I assumed that he believed the blanket of domesticity I had enshrouded him in was the villain. I finally found the courage to ask if he wanted me to leave.

All he said was, "I have to show you something." We drove to the Rosario Cemetery in Santa Fe and he led me to the Anaya family plot. Though I couldn't have said where it had gone, a year had disappeared since the audition. The weather was as cold and gray as it had been on the day when Tomás had entered and Didi had exited my life. A black wrought-iron fence and thick hedges of lilac bushes encircled the plot, securing the rest of seven generations of Anayas. I spotted headstones with dates on them that reached back three centuries. Though the branches of the tall lilac bushes were bare and snow mounded over their roots, I could imagine that stepping inside the lilac maze when they were green and blooming would have been like entering a seraglio, a prison where scent alone could hold you captive.

"The twins," Tomás said, pointing to two small graves, side by side, guarded over by a granite lamb. "Efren and Jacobo. They were my tío Ernesto's cousins. They died when he was six, back in the twenties. They were all out playing when a storm rolled in over the mountains. Efren and Jacobo took shelter under a cottonwood. There was no thunder. Barely even any clouds. The two little boys were waving at him to come, get under the tree with them, when the lightning struck. He said everyone laughs at him, but when the lightning struck, he saw every bone in the boys' bodies. He hated El Día de los Muertos. All those grinning skeletons, they reminded him of his cousins.

"Mi tío Ernesto." We stood next to his great-uncle's grave. "He introduced me to everyone in this plot. He told me that it didn't matter that my parents weren't Anayas; everyone buried here was my family. All the Anayas had come from ancestors who'd come from Spain. That made me an Anaya. And he made me Anaya. It didn't matter what blood I had running in my veins. We're all just bones in the end and my bones would end up here, next to his.

"He had that carved before he died." Tomás pointed to the headstone. In the middle of the stone was chiseled ERNESTO TIBURCITO ANAYA. On one side was Doña Carlota's name with the inscription BELOVED WIFE. On the other was Tomás's name with the inscription BELOVED SON.

His long hair fell forward, covering his face. I would never have known he was crying if a cold wind had not lofted the dark strands away. I put my arm around him. After all the ways we had touched, at that moment when he needed the animal comfort of another human the most, he turned from me and walked back to his car. We drove in silence to the inelegant south side of town, past an empty lot humped with mounds made by prairie dogs, now hibernating in their burrows. We turned onto a street where no grass grew. All the small, square houses had lawns of round rocks. A semi cab was parked on the street. Tomás stopped in front of a house that looked like all the others and handed me his keys.

"Take the truck. Do whatever you want with it. I've got to go north. Spend some time at the cabin." He didn't reveal to me the name of the village that Guitos had said was his true home, where his heart was.

"I'll drive you up there," I said, but meant, *Let me in. Give me a chance. Let me see the world I* should *have reshaped myself to fit.*

"No, thanks. My cousin Chucho lives here. He'll drive me."

"When will you be back?"

"I don't know, Rae. I need to think. Then I've got a tour coming up. They want me in Spain again. The biennale."

"Will you come back before you leave?"

"Rae, I—I don't know. Maybe. Don't expect me. Don't count on me. Okay? That would be best. Just don't count on me."

"That's all? That's all you're going to say?"

"Rae, we . . . I . . . I'm sorry. Stay at the river house for as long as you want. I'll send money. The bills are taken care of. I'm . . . I'll call, okay?" He grabbed his jacket and his guitar and backed quickly away from the truck, his boots crunching over the gravel on the front yard. I didn't see who opened the front door and let him in.

I drove home to the house on the river, knowing that Tomás would never return to it. I'd made a deal long ago to do anything it took to get him. I just forgot to specify for how long. The opiate that had been plugged into my brain the night I first heard Tomás play was ripped out. The withdrawal was, literally, physical. I felt the way I had after Daddy died: like I was perched on the edge of a cliff about to fall. Didi had pulled me back then. Now there was no one to rescue me.

At the end of the first week, I called HomeTown and told each succeeding person who answered and informed me that congregants weren't allowed to take unauthorized calls that I was going to kill myself if they didn't let me speak to my mother. I was lying, but it was the lie that occurred to me.

Finally, she was put on.

"Mom, it's me. Cyndi Rae."

"Cyndi Rae, what's wrong? Are you crying?"

"Yeah, Mom, I'm crying. Mom, could you come?"

"There? To Albuquerque? Cyndi Rae, I work, you know I work. We just got an order in from a boutique hotel to do all their quilts. It's the biggest account we've ever gotten. I'm Team Mom and half of my girls are down with the carpal tunnel. Even if no one takes off a minute from now till Easter, we'll barely get the order done. And I can't fly. You know I can't fly."

"I know, Mom."

"I would if I could. You know that. I'm your mother. I'd do anything for you. You know that, don't you?"

"Yeah, Mom." My tears stopped. "It's fine. I'll be fine."

"Well, okay, Cyndi Rae. I'm glad you're fine. They need me. The hotel specified mauve and cream. They won't accept the order if it's anything other than mauve and cream. I have to get back."

"Yeah, sure. Okay, Mom."

"I pray for you, Cyndi Rae. Every night."

"Thanks, Mom."

"Brother Ed needs the phone now, I'm going to have to go. Call me if you need anything else. I'll do anything I can for you. Just don't ask me to do things you know I can't."

"Okay, Mom. I won't. Bye, Mom."

I hung up and didn't let myself think, just drove Tomás's truck into town and went to see Mrs. Steinberg. I knocked on the front door. After a long time, I heard shuffling. My heart seized up. Didi was there. She was home and, from the heavy, slow tread, it sounded as if she might be sick. A muscular teenage boy wearing a sweatshirt with the sleeves torn off opened the door.

"Uh, hello. Is Mrs. Steinberg here?"

"She moved."

"She moved? Where?"

He shrugged. The heavy bulk of his shoulders rose and fell. "Dunno. Malta or something. My mom'll be home later. You can ask her."

"Manila?"

"Yeah, that's it, Manila. Hey, are you gay?"

"Gay?"

"Your name. Are you Gay?"

"Rae. I'm Rae."

"Oh, cool. This weird chick came over and left some shit for you. She paid us to hang on to it. Said you'd be coming by. But shit, that was like a year ago or something. We almost tossed it."

The footlocker was too heavy for me to carry. The guy helped me haul it out and lift it into the bed of the truck. Back at the house by the river, I had no one to help me unload the heavy trunk so I left it where it was and opened it there. The inside of the lid was covered with numbers printed so meticulously they looked like a pattern. Neatly packed inside were my best skirts and tops, my favorite shoes. Everything I'd left behind when I'd walked out with Tomás a year ago. There was a note from Didi on top.

One Month After That Goddamn Audition

Rae-rae, Hey-hey,

If you're reading this, it means there's still hope. It means you came to find me. I guess you found out that Catwoman finally did it. Finally moved back to Manila. So we're both orphans now, right? Don't stop reading! I know that last statement just pissed you off.

She was right and that made me even angrier.

I tried to find you until I realized you truly did not want to be found. I don't know what you think happened at the audition, but it wasn't

enough for you to disappear. Jesus, you won, right? Talk about a sore
winner. Hah!
Rae, you were astonishing at the audition. But, before you were
astonishing, you froze. Whatever I did, whatever you THINK I did, I
did to thaw you out. Obviously, he picked you, you're with him. I miss
you sosososo much. Fuck, Rae, he's not even my type. He's a BOY for
God's sake and I am so over boys! GRRLZ 4Ever 4Me.
I'm leaving too. Really no reason for me to hang around Bookay
anymore.
Let's face it, you are what I have in this life and I am what you have,
Didi
Call me. You have my new number.

The pattern on the lid of the footlocker was Didi's cell number written
thousands of times. Underneath my skirts and shoes was her old cassette
tape of AC/DC. I dug through the trunk, reaching back through the geo-
logical strata of our friendship while Didi's signature song played in my
mind, the one about dirty deeds done dirt cheap.

Everything Didi had rescued from the Lair was stored in ziplock bags
and marked as carefully as if it all had come from an archaeological dig:
A shard of the Temple of Dionysus we'd constructed together and she'd
covered with a mosaic of glass from broken liquor bottles. A copy of one
of her dad's *DownBeat* magazines. A Puppy Taco take-out menu.
"McKinley and the Tariff of 1890," the American history paper I'd written
for her. A black basaltic rock from the West Mesa.

Didi had cataloged every tick of our friendship. What I had assumed
was service she'd taken for granted had been noticed, appreciated. Snow
began to fall, sifting feathery flakes across the bags. The slippery pile of
ziplocks was as much as I could claim of a record of my time on earth. It
was the baby book my mother had jettisoned for Jesus. I swept the flakes
away, closed the lid, and, with more strength than I thought I had, dragged
the trunk inside.

The drug lord's palace was freezing. I paced for an hour, fighting the
desire to call her. I counted how many times she'd written her number on
the lid of the trunk nearly a year ago. When I reached three thousand, I dialed. My fingers were stiff with cold and nerves. Each number I punched
in, though, warmed me. She was right. I *had* frozen at the audition. And I

was frozen now. Didi would thaw me. Didi would help me out of the hole. It was only then, with her phone just starting to ring, with the hope of rescue forming, that I could admit how much I needed rescue. It would be all right now. Didi had my back. She answered my call as if she'd spent the past year sitting by the phone waiting for it.

"*Mi amor, mi amor, mi amor!* Why didn't you call sooner?"

I was overcome at the sound of her voice. My throat tightened against the sob of relief that rose from my chest. And then it hit me: the number she was responding to with such love was Tomás's.

"Are you there? What's wrong? Can you not talk? Is she in the room? Why are you calling from the river house? You said you were never going back there. *Mi amor,* what's—"

I clapped the receiver down before she could finish asking what was wrong. Asking her "*amor*" Tomás what was wrong.

Chapter Thirty-four

That week a cold front blew down from the Arctic and broke records that had stood for a century. I lay awake all night beneath mountains of covers and watched my breath freeze into a halo above the round bed. Some of the oldest cottonwoods froze so hard that they cracked open, the explosions as loud as thunder. One giant fell on the power lines, cutting out the heat and light. I used all the firewood.

When I went to bed the only thing I was sick with was betrayal and longing so intense my entire body ached as if I had the flu. And then I did have the flu. It was a relief to slide into physical pain strong enough to blot out thought, to have a real reason to hurt as much as I did. The most I could handle in the way of taking care of myself was to fill a glass with water, drink part of it, then stagger back to bed. Soon, I couldn't even manage that. Didn't want to manage that.

I wouldn't have actively done anything to cause myself to die, but I was no longer concerned about it happening on its own. Shortly after I stopped getting up for glasses of water, pulling the blankets up to cover myself became more than I could handle. The cold air felt good on my hot skin. Sleeping felt good. Dreaming felt good. The nights came and went. I lost track of them.

Then Tomás came back. He was banging on the door. Pounding and yelling. Didi was with him. I was sorry that they were too late, that I didn't have the strength anymore to wake up and unlock the door. Somehow he got in and carried me into the living room where he had built a fire, not of piñon, but of branches splintered from the frozen cottonwoods. They burned quickly, warming the house. He and Didi pushed the couch where I lay close to the fire and tacked up blankets around the couch like mosquito netting to keep out the drafts. Didi put a cup against my lips and filled my mouth with apple juice. Tomás placed a tea kettle on the fire and it puffed clouds of steam scented with the eucalyptus smell of Vicks into the Arctic-dry air. The steam filled the tent around the couch with tropical air that made me dream about Austin. About diving into icy spring water that turned into air thick and dense enough to swim through until the moment when it evaporated and I was falling. I tried to scream, but my throat had rusted shut.

Then Tomás was holding me. Everything had been explained. He loved me, and Didi was my friend. Everything was fine.

"Rae, wake up! Wake up, *mija,* you're having a bad dream! Come on, baby, open your eyes."

Why, I wondered, was Alma holding me? Why was Blanca standing by with a cup of juice? Why was Will poking wood into the fire?

"Where's Tomás and Didi?" My voice was a croak. It wasn't a dream. My throat had rusted shut.

Alma and Blanca looked at each other. Alma answered, "They're not here, *mija.* Nobody except Blanca and Will and me have been here. Didi called and told us to check on you."

Blanca stepped forward. "Here, drink this." She guided an accordion-pleated bendie straw into my mouth. I sipped apple juice, then closed my eyes and was asleep before the sweetness had left my mouth. When I woke again, I was back in the round bed. The sheets had been changed and the heat and lights were back on. The house was empty, but there was food in the refrigerator and a note that read: *When you feel up to it, come and see me about a job. Alma.*

Alma found a little apartment for me near Nob Hill and paid the first month's rent. She deducted the loan from the job she gave me organizing the festival coming up that summer, then enrolled me for enough independent studies classes that I was able to finish my degree. As soon as I was registered as a student, I started seeing Leslie again. I took the pills she prescribed, and the clenched thing within my brain loosened enough. Just enough.

When my strength returned, Alma started using me as a substitute. I turned out to be a good teacher. My orderly mind, my tendency to see things in black and white, all the qualities that prevented me from being a reliably extraordinary performer, made me good in the classroom. I liked teaching. It kept me occupied, kept me from thinking. Not thinking became my major goal after I dragged myself off of the round bed. I taught as many classes as Alma would let me. I volunteered to keep the festival's books and reconciled them every day. I did what I could to repay her kindness to me. To Blanca, to Will, to the others who had helped me. Long after my health returned, I felt wobbly around them. Wobbly and obligated. Obligated to pull myself together.

I took up marathon running. The route I returned to again and again circled from my apartment near Nob Hill to Highland High School, on to the Disabled Veterans Thrift Shop, then over to Route 66. From there I took a right and charged past the Pup y Taco, the Ace High, the De Anza Coffee Shop, the Aztec Motel. I always ended up heading west, toward the future.

Spring came and the cottonwoods filled the air with ghostly seed puffs, haloed filaments that floated on breezes too gentle to be felt. Cottonwood fluff piled up in the gutters like drifts of diaphanous snow. In early summer the buds unfurled into apple green leaves that spangled hearts across the sky.

I believe that if, even for one spring in all those years, the cottonwoods had failed to bloom, had not filled the air with their promises, the sky with their hearts, that I could have learned to stop loving Tomás Montenegro. But did they? They did not. I ran, accelerating at increasing speeds past all the landmarks. I just never got fast enough to escape any of them entirely. I made a full recovery from my illness, but not from Tomás. He turned out to be a disease that had just gone into remission. As soon as I was strong enough, he flared up with a new virulence. This time, though, I knew that if I didn't have him I would die. I needed another secret. And that is how I came to learn that flamenco was a giant tree with roots over a thousand years old, still sucking sustenance from India, Spain, Mexico, and New Mexico, and that my story was nothing but the tiniest heart-shaped leaf in a vast canopy.

Chapter Thirty-five

Doña Carlota almost seemed to expect my call. It was inevitable, probably, that I, the other spurned woman in Tomás's life, would eventually find my way to her. On the drive north to Santa Fe, as the earth lifted toward a sky opening onto infinity, I remained oblivious to the beauty beyond my window. My entire concentration was on what I wanted to say and how I would say it. Of course Doña Carlota knew about me and Tomás. About Tomás and Didi. Everyone on the flamenco grapevine knew. That embarrassed me, though not enough to turn back.

The cottonwoods in Santa Fe, a few weeks behind their sisters to the south, had piled drifts of fluff at the base of the coyote fence made of saplings lashed together that ringed the Anaya compound. The gate was unlocked. A Black Forest of untended spruce and pines surrounded the house, casting it into deep shadows rare in the sun-blasted city. Old snow surviving in the shade glittered dully. The vintage Buick used to drive Doña Carlota to class was parked beside the house. Where the houses nearby turned faces brightened with ristras of scarlet chiles and turquoise blue lintels to passersby, Doña Carlota's house was devoid of such public Land of Enchantment adornments. Unadorned, unkempt even, it turned in on itself, showing a blank facade to the outside world.

The front door was massive, made of dark wood and held together with black studs. I knocked and had ample time to study the figure of Saint James, patron saint of Spain, lance in hand atop a rearing stallion, guarding the house from his place tucked inside a *nicho* in the thick adobe wall. I was leaning in close to read what was painted on the tile behind the saint: SANTIAGO SEA CON NOSOTROS, Saint James be with us, when the door opened.

I recognized the elderly family retainer who had driven Doña Carlota. He found me examining the saint. He smiled, displaying a full set of very white teeth. In spite of the threadbare work khakis held up by suspenders and an old olive sweater frayed at the cuffs, the old man seemed as distinguished as he had when I'd caught a glimpse of him dressed in a suit and tie. He gave the saint a fond caress, then stuck his hand out to me and introduced himself. "Teófilo." His hand was warm, the palm rough with calluses. *"Pásele, pásele."* He waved me into the house.

I followed him down a dark hallway into a dark living room and took a seat on a mahogany chair big as throne. "I'll tell La Doña you're here." He disappeared into the back of the house. Masses of velvet red roses in various stages of decay were bunched in vases throughout the room. Their cloying aroma combined with the scent of piñon from decades of fires to create a fragrance that defined flamenco in New Mexico. *Retablos, máscaras, bultos, santos,* and every other conceivable piece of art that could have been lifted from a church in northern New Mexico gave the room the feel of a museum. Then I noticed the contents of the shelves lining the large room on three sides and saw that the true focus of enshrinement was Tomás.

Every moment of his young life in flamenco was documented. Handsome professional photos of him lined the shelves. The photos were all framed, all in black and white, and in every single one of them, he held a guitar. There was not one photo of a grin with front teeth missing, not one in a Cub Scout uniform. No pictures of friends, classmates, teachers. No First Communion. No mortarboard. There weren't even any photos of Doña Carlota or her husband, Ernesto, with Tomás. The only other thing with him in any of the photos was a guitar. From a solemn boy with a guitar, he grew, photo by photo, into a solemn young man with a guitar. The last one in the chronology was a photo that depicted Tomás in his midtwenties, the age when I met him, the age when he had walked out of Doña Carlota's life.

"She's not feeling up to coming out." I turned around. Teófilo was gesturing toward the back of the house. "You mind going back?" His voice was pleasant. I followed him down the dark hallway to a door at the end. He opened it and stepped aside as I entered. Doña Carlota's bedroom was something out of a Gustav Klimt painting, with dozens of photos in glittering gilt frames, acres of ornate fabric covering every inch, and her, pale, emaciated yet made up like Sarah Bernhardt about to take the stage. Resting on a chaise longue, her feet propped up with a dozen pillows arranged just so, Doña Carlota wore a quilted pink robe, streaked with dribbles of orange and purple medicine. She seemed old and frail, a sugar sculpture of a human that would dissolve in a light shower. The real shock, however, were her feet, if the gnarled stumps at the ends of her legs could even be called feet. They were as misshapen as I imagine the bound feet of Chinese women might have been. The toes were welded into one striated claw gone violet from lack of circulation.

"La Metrónoma." She held her hand up, and I didn't know whether to shake it or kiss it. She decided for me by grabbing the hand I extended and drawing me to her so that I could kiss her powdered cheek. Up close, I saw that her scalp was permanently tattooed blue from decades of dying her hair jet black and that she was painted not like Sarah Bernhardt, but like herself. Like the silent-movie-vamp self she had been half a century ago when the portrait that greeted everyone who entered the Flamenco Academy had been created.

"Did you meet my brother-in-law?" she asked.

Teófilo grinned.

"Yes, we met at the door." *Brother-in-law?* The brother of Ernesto, the man Tomás considered his father? I thought of Teófilo in the faculty parking lot behind the Flamenco Academy, opening the door of the old Buick. Her sitting in back, him in front like a chauffeur.

"Teófilo, could you bring me. . ." She pointed to a bottle of pills next to the bed and he fetched it.

"Is the pain bad?" he asked her in Spanish, shaking several capsules onto his callused palm.

She answered in Spanish. Her Castilian, all the vowels clacking as crisply as a good break in pool, was another language compared to Téofilo's softly lyrical New Mexican version. I recognized the pills. Daddy had taken them toward the end when the pain had become unbearable. One had always been enough to knock him out. She swallowed three.

"I'm gonna take off now," Teófilo said. "You need anything before I leave?"

She shook her head no.

"*Bueno,* I'll take the car then. Work on it at home."

He shook my hand with a courtly warmth that made me want to cling to him. The room seemed much chillier after he left. With an effort, Doña Carlota swallowed the pills, then gathered herself and said, "Alma tells me you were sick." So there it was. Cards on the table. She was acknowledging that she was plugged into the flamenco grapevine. That she knew everything. It was more humiliating than I'd expected it to be. "Are you well now?"

"Yes, how have you been?"

"Look at me. My feet are destroyed. I hope you wear good shoes. The feet, the feet take the punishment."

I nodded. "Yes, Menkes."

"A good shoe, but there are better."

"Oh? Which ones do you like?"

Just as I was feeling grateful to Doña Carlota for saving me with this gift of small talk, she cut it off and asked, "Have you heard from Tomás?"

His name was a punch in the gut. I searched her eyes. Were they glassy? Had the drugs taken effect? "No, I haven't heard from him for a while now."

"They chatter. Everyone in flamenco chatters. It reaches me even here. What we both care about is Tomás. He cut me out of his life. He won't speak to me. Tell me, why is he so unhappy with me?"

"I don't know."

"But you have ideas."

"I have ideas."

"Metrónoma, if you don't know why he is unhappy, you will never make him happy."

"We're not together anymore."

"I know. He's with your *gemela*."

"Didi? She's not my twin."

"You're closer than that. You're one coin. Two sides."

"That's not true either."

"At first I was surprised that he picked you. But as I thought about you and him together, it made sense. Didi? No, that will never work. You, he will come back to you."

"He will?"

"He needs to be worshipped, doesn't he? Didi, the same but worse. Two gods together?" She shook her finger in front of her face. "This only works in mythology. I know. Why did you come?"

"I came because—" All the lines I'd rehearsed in the car on the drive north vanished. I couldn't imagine why I had come. I certainly couldn't imagine asking the questions I'd planned to ask. "I came to visit. To see how you are."

"Metrónoma!" My spine stiffened at the snap of command in her voice. I expected to feel the grind of her knuckles in my back next, just as if we were back in class again. "You're not a timid little girl anymore. You were always so good with time. Now is the time for the truth. Tell me what you want. *Dame la verdad.*"

"I want to know why he is unhappy so that I can be the one to make him happy."

"Happiness comes from within."

Her statement was so out of character, such a blatant lie, that I laughed. "Now who's not telling the truth?"

She smiled. "I like you, Metrónoma. You are exactly what Tomás needs. Not this Didi-Ofelia person. Not La Tempesta. That will not end well. I would like to see you two together before I die."

"You can." The words rushed out of me. I knew what I needed from the old lady. I had used Tomás's secret, the one Guitos had told me once before to make him choose me. Now I had to use it again to win him back. To take him from Didi. But first I had to make Doña Carlota *dame la verdad.* I had to make her give me the truth. "There was only one Delicata who lived on Sacromonte and was married to El Chino the blacksmith. Only one who was *una bailaora.* But this Delicata had dark skin. Dark as a Moor. And all her children were dark, as dark as the darkest Gypsy."

For a moment, the air crackled with the electricity Doña Carlota had always been able to generate, and once again she was the fierce, intimidating lioness who had ruled the classroom. A second later that energy sagged and she slumped back onto her pillows. "Could you please massage my legs a bit? The blood has to be encouraged to move into my feet."

I felt another shift in energy. Perhaps it was the pain pills taking effect. Perhaps we really did slip into the foggy zone where fairy tale met flamenco and those bewitched by love must meet impossible challenges in their quest for love. As I knelt beside her, my sleeve brushed the dragon's claw of her foot. She winced in pain at even that touch. Gently, I rubbed the still-taut muscles and tendons of her calves until her feet pinked up from violet to lilac.

"Thank you," she whispered. I sat down. I had passed one test.

Bit by bit, she uncoiled as the pills held pain at bay. Still, it was a long time before she spoke again. When she did, her voice had a dreamy quality, as if she were asking herself the questions she had spent her life answering. "Is flamenco in the blood? The feet? The throat? The fingers? Or is it in the soul?"

She nodded toward her own ruined extremities, a small part of the price she had paid for admission. She didn't expect me to answer. She waited for the drugs to take full effect. When all the muscles in her face had gone slack and her breathing had settled into an even rhythm, she spoke. "Metrónoma, I have told you the story of one girl, a dancer, daughter of a Gypsy mother and a Gypsy father, themselves born of the blood of the pharaoh. Now I will tell you the story of another girl. It will be for you to decide what to do with the story. Perhaps it will lead you to love. Perhaps to knowledge. But what is flamenco except knowledge? Being in the know? *Enterao?*"

Her eyelids drifted shut and she suddenly seemed not just old and frail but, quite possibly, feeble as well. I waited several long moments before deciding to leave. The instant I started to stand, however, her eyes sprang open and she launched in as if there had been no interruption.

"Her name was Clementina, and if there is such a thing as blue blood, what ran through the little girl's veins was as dark as ink. Clementina was the daughter of a duke and a duchess born of two of the most venerable houses in the entire Spanish aristocracy. Her ancestors fought beside Isabel and Fernando at Granada to beat the Muslims back into Africa and complete the Reconquest of Spain in 1492. They rode with the conquistadors to conquer the Incan and Aztec empires. At one time, you could travel from Granada to Cádiz without ever leaving the family estates. King Alfonso the Thirteenth and Queen Victoria Eugenia held the infant Clementina over the baptismal font.

"Clementina grew up on an estate in the very shadows of Granada's Alhambra. The floors were laid with sixteenth-century tiles in strict accordance with the rules of heraldry as befits a member of the Andalusian aristocracy. The family patio was paved with Roman mosaics brought from the ruins of Italica four centuries before her birth. Galleries of Mudejar columns and arches. Rugs from the Alpujarras, Roman busts, plateresque railings, family portraits painted by Zuloaga, fans inscribed with personal dedications by Julio Romero de Torres himself.

"Clementina had everything a little princess needed except a queen, because her mother had died in childbirth. Her father adored his only child, a little girl who resembled her sainted mother more and more each day, and for this he guarded her. Perhaps, a bit too jealously. School, of course, was out of the question. Tía Rogelia, a maiden aunt with whiskers white as bean sprouts on her chin, taught Clementina to sew and embroider with stitches the width of a hair. She also taught her to read and write, which the duke considered superfluous. But mostly she taught the little girl to accept her *sino,* her fate, which was to guard her purity with her life until such time as she would be called upon to surrender it to the son of a suitably noble family whom the duke would select to be her husband.

"Clementina wondered exactly whom she was expected to guard her purity from, since the only time she was allowed to leave the family estate was on Sunday when she and her father and Tía Rogelia were driven in the duke's first automobile, a recently acquired Hispano-Suiza, to the cathedral to attend Mass with all the other leading families of Granada. Other than that, the girl was little more than a prisoner in her home. She grew up without a single friend.

"And then, one day, the lonely little girl's father employed a *herrero,* a blacksmith, a metalworker, to repair the extensive grillwork, the elaborate screens in front of the fireplaces, as well as retinning all the copper pans that had been handed down through the generations. The blacksmith, called El Chino for the tilt of his eyes, brought his daughter with him.

"But this was no ordinary metalworker, and his daughter was no ordinary little girl. They were *gitanos* from Sacromonte, *gitanos puros* who lived in the caves of the sacred mountain. The little girl, Rosa, had learned her *compás* by dancing to the beat of her father's hammer as he sang his great Gypsy *martinetes.*

"Oh, this girl, this Rosa. Dark, dark as a Moor. Her clothes were rags; her hair was a mat of knots alive with lice; her hands and feet were black from the cinders from her father's forge, from the dirt floor of the cave. The duke forbade Clementina from even speaking to Rosa, for everyone knew that Gypsies were thieves and cutthroats, that they stole babies and were in league with the devil. And the worst, the worst of all was their music, flamenco, the music of drunkards and prostitutes.

"Little Clementina was so lonely, she disobeyed her father and tried to speak with Rosa. Rosa, however, was as wild as a mountain goat and ran from her. So Clementina set a trap for the little girl in the patio and baited it with *mantecaditos.* Rosa, always starving, could actually sniff out the little cookies of almonds and olive oil and would gorge herself on the delicacies. Her hunger forced her to trust the young mistress of the house.

"Thus they became friends. Clementina, barely older than Rosa herself, took this creature under her wing. She bathed the wild Gypsy child, scrubbed her until the brown skin showed beneath the black. Washed her hair until the water ran clear and Rosa's black Gypsy hair glinted blue in the sun. She fed the Gypsy girl all manner of delights: candied chestnuts in syrup with brandy, perfectly grilled sardines, tender marinated octopus. Clementina went to her own closet and took out her pink silk party frock embroidered with rosebuds, a delicate gown of English lawn trimmed with Belgian lace, her black velvet slippers, a mantilla blessed by the pope, and gave them all to Rosa.

"Rosita, overwhelmed by such kindness, had only one thing to give her generous benefactor in return. In secret, the wild Gypsy girl began to share her art with the highborn aristocrat. From the first, Clementina loved flamenco, for the rhythms that Rosa clapped out were not strange to her. She had heard these rhythms echoing through the lonely house late at night behind the locked doors of her father's rooms. With these bewitching rhythms came other sounds she was forbidden to investigate, men's hoarse voices, the furious stamping of heels on the heraldic tiles, women's laughter. Clementina didn't know what happened behind the locked doors, but she knew it spoke to her lonely soul. When she danced with Rosa, her spirit was set free.

"'*Un fenómeno*' is what Rosa called Clementina, for she had never seen anyone learn her people's dance so quickly. For the first time in her life, Clementina was happy. Rosa was even happier. She had a friend, a friend who was desperate to hear everything about her life. So, as they danced, Rosa told her stories from Sacromonte. She told her about her mother, Delicata, how she would have reigned like a queen over Sevilla if her father had not stolen her away and imprisoned her in a cave. About the *cuadro,* La Sordita, Little Burro, Dried Wood, La Burriquita. About dancing for *los suecos* that El Bala brought to them. Rosa even told her friend she suspected that the fearsome El Bala was in love with Delicata because the pair spent a dangerous amount of time whispering to each other. Rosa's stories came alive more vividly in Clementina's mind than anything that had actually happened in her dull and confined life.

"For months the girls danced in secret until the inevitable day when the duke discovered them. He threw the nasty little Gypsy girl and her father out of the house and forbade Clementina to ever speak with her again or to ever dance another step of flamenco. The exalted gentleman told his daughter that he would kill her with his own hand before he would see her associate with such a tribe of degenerates.

"Clementina was desolate. She missed her friend and all the friends she had made in her imagination. Flamenco had opened the world to her and now she was in prison once again. Day and night, she roamed the grounds of the estate. When she was as far from her father's prying eyes and from his spy, Tía Rogelia, as she could get, she would take off her shoes and dance. Over pebbles, over acorns, over thorns, burrs, she danced until her feet bled. It didn't matter: once the spirit had captured her, she felt nothing.

"One day, Clementina returned to the house expecting her aunt to scold her for allowing the sun to burn her face. But she heard nothing from the old lady. Not when she returned. Not through the endless, silent evening. Not a word. Clementina was not surprised when she knocked at her aunt's door and heard no answer. She was even less surprised to find her aunt lying atop the matelasse cover, her hands folded in prayer on her chest, her mouth gaping open.

"All of Granada came to the funeral. Clementina looked around at the funeral Mass and there were all the fine young men from the best families. One of them would be her husband. Would it be Esteban, with a bow tie and pimples on his chin? Would it be Arturo, pear-shaped heir to an almond fortune? Would it be Juan Pablo, with his hair parted in the middle and flattened with too much hair oil? It could be any of them. It would all end the same, locked away in the rooms of his family's house until she was as old and shriveled and dead as Tía Rogelia. At that moment, Clementina envied her aunt because she had escaped. Only then did she weep. She wept so copiously for the utter pointlessness of her life that her sniffles turned to sobs. The assembled took Clementina's grief as testament to the young girl's devotion to her aunt. However, when the sobs turned to great heaving moans that caused *el arzobispo* to turn from the altar and shoot disapproving glances toward the source of the racket, Clementina's father took his daughter outside. When she was unable to collect herself, he summoned a taxi, telling his daughter that important business would keep him in Granada that night and, most likely, for several nights to come. Then he ordered the driver to take her to the family estate.

"As the driver, approached the iron gates of the estate, Clementina felt she would die, literally suffocate, if she were to hear the lock click shut behind her one more time.

"'Driver,' Clementina asked politely, 'could you, please, take me to Sacromonte?'

"The driver turned in his seat and looked at her. 'Sacromonte is not a place for a fine young lady such as yourself. Your father told me to take you home.'

"Ahead of them the old caretaker was wheeling the gate open. Her heart pounded so furiously that the rush of blood past her ears prevented her from hearing her own words as she ordered, 'Driver, the only location you will be paid to take me to is Sacromonte.' This time her voice was as strong and sure as the stamp of her heels against the heraldic tiles when she danced.

"'*Ozu!*' the driver uttered a Gypsy curse and turned around, leaving the old caretaker to gape in puzzlement as the taxi disappeared.

"The driver delivered Clementina to the foot of Sacromonte and she stepped into a world she already knew in her imagination. A world where the inhabitants lived, not in tiled rooms, but in caves. Where children ran naked. Where the bathroom business was done outside just like a dog. Sacromonte had smelled much better in her imagination. For a moment, Clementina's courage faltered. But she had only to think of Tía Rogelia dead without ever having lived to take her first step on the dusty path that wound through the human anthill. She asked for Rosa, daughter of the *herrero,* and was sent higher and higher up the hill.

"Night was falling and with each upward coil of the winding path, it grew darker and the caves became even more wretched. Flames from the blacksmiths' forges leapt out of from the cave openings as if the very earth itself were on fire. As if she were in hell. Though *gitanos* of every description bustled past her, Clementina did not recognize any of the characters she knew so well from Rosa's stories. Each time she stopped to ask for directions, the Gypsies would either shrug and pretend they couldn't understand her or they would send her in the opposite direction from the last person who'd offered help.

"At the top of the hill, Clementina gazed down on Granada. Off in the distance, the Alhambra shone like a great ship cruising through the night, a ship that the superstitious *gitanos* believed to be filled with the ghosts of the Moors who had died clinging to the beauty they had created. Everyone she stopped claimed they had never heard of anyone named Rosa. No, never in their entire lives had they known anyone with the most common girl's name in Spain. Clementina accepted that she would never find her friend. That she would be forced to return to her father's house. That she would die without ever having lived. She was walking back down when Rosa sprang out from behind a tangle of prickly pear cacti.

" 'It's true!' Rosa exclaimed as she embraced her friend. 'I didn't believe it when the first three told me that there was a *payo* looking for me.'

" 'But I didn't meet anyone who knew you.'

" 'Didn't you listen to any of my stories?' Rosa laughed. 'A *caló* never tells a *payo* anything. Certainly not anything that has to do with *el tribu.* Come on.'

"As she followed her friend through a warren of paths, the magic of that word, tribe, settled over Clementina like a spell that dissipated all her lonely years. As they approached Rosa's cave, the sound of an argument filtered out, so terrible that even the side of a mountain couldn't silence it. Though the angry words alarmed Clementina, Rosa didn't seem to notice. Hugging the shadows, she sneaked Clementina into the cave where her family lived.

"The cave, lighted by one *candil,* was almost as dark as the night outside. The girls slipped in unnoticed, though in truth Rosa's parents, Delicata and El Chino, screaming and trading blows, wouldn't have noticed if King Alfonso had walked in. For several seconds a few of the younger children stopped watching their parents and gaped at the little aristocrat hiding in the shadows. The next second, though, the impossible apparition of a *payo* was dismissed as a phantom, something that could not possibly exist in the stinking cave they inhabited, and the children turned their attention back to the fighters.

"Clementina feared she would pass out from the smell of goats and people, the heat of the cook fire, the forge, the shrieks of the mob of children crying for their parents to stop fighting. In spite of the stink and the heat and the noise, she was ecstatic. It was as if the characters from her favorite book had come to life in front of her eyes. She spotted Mono with his squashed nose. And El Chino was even fiercer than she'd imagined. But Delicata? Where was the dancing beauty with the flashing emerald eyes Rosa had spoken of? Delicata was the least delicate woman Clementina had ever seen. She was a dark troll of a woman with dull eyes the color of a dried cactus pad. Clementina could not imagine her enchanting anyone. While Clementina was still trying to identify the others, Rosa dragged her away. In a small room, dug into the mountain off to the side of the one large room the family lived in, Rosa tossed a long, red dress covered in white polka dots at her and told Clementina to put it on. Then Rosa made Clementina sit while she covered the girl's light brown hair with olive oil mixed with soot until it was as black and greasy as Rosa's own.

"'Why are you doing this?' Clementina demanded.

"'You want to dance flamenco, right?'

"'Of course.'

"'Then you must look like a *flamenca,* so sit still and let me finish. We've been called for a *juerga* tonight. The poet Lorca recommended us. He especially asked for my father to sing. Maybe when everyone is drunk enough, you can dance with us.'

"Clementina's heart soared at these words, and she sat still as a stone while Rosa covered her face and arms with the soot mixture until her pale skin was even darker than Rosa's. The fighting stopped and El Chino began warming his voice, tempering it with *aguardiente.* Hours later, when *la voz* was sufficiently 'broken,' when it sounded like a ruptured foghorn, Rosa's father yelled, *'Vamos ya!,'* the signal that the time had come.

"Rosa and Clementina hid until everyone was outside in the dark night. Then they followed her father down the twisting path. At several caves, El Chino roared out his bear's rasp, *'Vamos ya!'* The curtains hanging over the front openings would part and another of the characters from Rosa's fabulous stories would step out. A powerfully built mother-daughter pair with identical spit curls pasted onto their foreheads. *Little Burro and her daughter, La Burriquita!* A stick-thin widow with powder covering the dirt on her arms. *Dried Wood!* A sprite of a woman with deaf ears sticking out like an elf's. *La Sordita!* In this way they assembled their *cuadro* and headed into the city.

"'Stay with me in the back,' Rosa whispered to Clementina. 'And no one will even know you're with us.'

"Clementina did not need to be asked. She could not keep up with the pack in the dark. Again and again, she tripped on a root growing across the path or was stabbed by the thorns of the cactus that hung overhead while the rest of the group scampered ahead, nimble as mountain goats.

"Rosa's father passed around a bottle of *aguardiente* and with each switchback, the group grew more boisterous until, by the time they reached the bottom rung where caves had real doors and windows, where animals were penned outside instead of bedding down with the family, where some even had electric lights, neighbors were yelling at them to shut up or they would feel a knife in their livers. The only one who wasn't boisterous was Delicata. Not a sound came from her as she followed the group down the twisting path.

"They all grew quiet as they came to the bottom of the hill and passed the bottle around one more time for a little courage before they stepped into the world of *payos,* all those pale-skinned outsiders who existed to either exploit the *calé* or to be exploited by them. And then they set off.

"The road flattened and they were in the city. The cobbled streets were silent and shuttered. Moonlight shimmered on the whitewashed walls as brilliant as a veiled sun.

"Clementina crept along with them, stunned by this first taste of freedom that had turned so unexpectedly into a banquet, a feast she was having increasing difficulty digesting. With each step, Clementina grew more certain that her father's hard hand would reach out and trap her. Since he knew everyone in Granada, why was there any reason to think he wouldn't find out? She walked in silence behind the others, who were moving now soundless as cats, and tried to imagine what her punishment would be when her father discovered what she had done. Since simply being born a girl had condemned her to a life of virtual cloister, she decided that tonight's offense was certain to result in the real thing. In a narrow alley, filled with geraniums hanging from balconies, Clementina thought of spending the rest of her life behind the walls of a convent and stopped dead.

"'*Ándale!*' Rosa hissed back at her, but Clementina was frozen on the spot. Rosa, cursing her Gypsy curses, ran back and grabbed Clementina's hand and tried to drag her forward, but Clementina would not budge.

"'I have to go home,' she stammered.

"And Clementina would have, would have run all the way back to the safety of her gilded cage, except that, at that moment, El Chino began to sing. His voice made the hairs on the back of her neck stand on end as it pierced the darkness, echoing off walls and summoning ghosts of the Moors and Jews who had loved Granada more than any of her citizens before or since. The cruel Christians had taken from them the city they had created, and lost love is always the deepest. The voices of the Moorish dead were in El Chino's voice. Wailing, warbling, sobbing, they stabbed directly into Clementina's heart. Perhaps it was the revenge of the exiled Moors and Jews who decided that they would enslave this pretty young

Catholic girl. Who knows? But as powerful as the spell of the dance had been on Clementina, the magic of the *cante* was even stronger. In that instant, drunk on rapturous emotion and the fragrance of jasmine, a lifetime in the convent in exchange for having a sound that was the sound of all life pouring through her head seemed a fair trade.

"Though many of the words he sang, words from the language of Rosa's people, *Calé*, were strange to Clementina, she understood enough to realize that the song was about a husband who has been betrayed and his plan to kill the treacherous wife. Clementina saw fear on Rosa's face, fear for Delicata.

" 'Do you think he will?' Clementina asked.

" 'Kill my mother? No one in *el tribu* would blame him. She has been seen many times with El Bala when no male member of our family was present. Husbands have killed wives for less than that.'

" 'Shouldn't we do something? Call the *guardia civil*?'

"Rosa laughed a harsh laugh. 'What a *payo* you are. *La guardia* looks for reasons to torture *calós*. We can never give them any.' Rosa's eyes flickered upward until she found the Alhambra, floating radiantly through the night, and Clementina remembered her friend's Gypsy name, Miracielos, given for her habit of watching the sky, of finding the beauty that released her from the ugliness. Now it released her from fear. 'Whatever happens,' Rosa said, 'my mother's dance will live on in me. No man will steal me and trap me in a cave. I will go to Sevilla and dance in the *cafés cantantes*. The city will fall at my feet and I will wear the crown that should have been hers. Come on.' Rosa grabbed Clementina's hand and the two friends ran through the street, their heels clattering on the cobblestones, both ready to follow El Chino's *cante* no matter where it might lead.

"They entered a maze of narrow streets that led to a pair of tall, weather-beaten oak doors, locked tight. El Chino rapped out a complicated rhythm on the thick planks and, with a rusty creak, a lock turned and the doors swung open. Clementina had lived her whole life seeing plain doors open into courtyards of unsuspected splendor whose beauty was all the greater for being hidden. Yet the courtyard she stepped into that night rivaled the Alhambra itself. She had no time to wonder which of the great families might own it for the old crone who'd opened the door was impatiently waving them inside. Filigreed columns looked like pillars of lace with moonlight filtering through. The scent of jasmine, rosemary, and sandalwood hung like a cloud above fountains that pattered silver coins of water into basins decorated with Roman maidens trailing diaphanous gowns.

"The sounds—clapping, heels hammering on tile floors—that drifted into the courtyard once the great doors were closed were the joyous sounds she'd learned from Rosa. The whole *cuadro* came to life once the doors shut behind them. They picked up the distant beat of the *flamencos* who were already performing and followed it to its source. With Rosa clapping beside Clementina just as if they were on the patio back home, Clementina's fears melted away. Nothing bad could happen tonight. She clapped along with her friend as the whole group capered through the courtyard to a side entrance where they crowded together, walking up a flight of stairs to a room on the second floor. Clementina had never been as happy as she was at that moment. For the first time in her lonely life, she was part of a group laughing and making noise.

"The old woman opened the door at the top of the stairway. '*Pásele! Pásele!*' she hissed. Delicata was the first to enter. She stepped into the private room as regally as a queen. Her entrance was hailed by a roomful of drunken Spanish aristocrats, *señoritos*, who pounded on the tables and yelled for the replacement dancers to enter.

"'*Pásele! Pásele!*' The old woman ordered the girls into a room that consciously tried to duplicate the caves Rosa's people inhabited, right down to the odor of tobacco and unwashed bodies. The only light was from *candiles,* pots of oil with wicks in them. Their illumination flickered across the sweaty bodies of the exhausted dancers whom they had come to replace and threw shadows against the walls. As Clementina's eyes adjusted to the room, which was darker than the moonlit courtyard, she saw that other than the dancers and the serving girls passing among tables, clearing away and replacing empty bottles of *fino,* dumping ashtrays, the room was filled with men. A head bobbing up just above a table caught Clementina's eye. Its owner was a dwarf with a hunchback, holding a large serving platter containing small plates of ham, glasses of wine. As he passed, the revelers reached out and touched his hump for good luck.

"An especially drunk carouser noticed the new girls and yelled out to the dwarf, 'Those two look hungry! Bring those girls some fried eggs!' A rumble of low chuckles greeted the request. The dwarf ducked behind a screen, then reappeared in front of Clementina and Rosa. He held the platter low and it was now covered by a napkin. The little man stared up at the girls and jiggled the platter anxiously.

" 'I don't think he can talk,' Rosa said.

"The dwarf bobbed his head toward the napkin until the girls understood that they were to remove it. Clementina glanced at Rosa. Rosa nodded for her to do what he wanted. Afraid of attracting even more attention, Clementina lifted the napkin and everyone in the room, including Rosa, exploded in bellowing laughter. Clementina dropped the napkin and turned away immediately, but not before seeing the dwarf's testicles, swollen by disease to mammoth proportion, resting on the platter.

"Clementina bolted away, rushing to the darkest corner of the room. Rosa, still laughing, found and chided her, 'Clementina, what's wrong with you? Don't you have any *gracia*? It was just a *chiste*.'

"Not having any sense of humor, not getting a joke, was the worst thing you could accuse an Andalusian of. It was so bad that Clementina tried to hide the shock that had made her feel faint.

"'*Ay! Mira!*' Rosa grabbed Clementina's arm and pointed at a sad-eyed, slender man in a white suit like a *cubano*. 'It's him.'

" 'Who?'

" 'You know, García Lorca, the poet who loves my dancing. I told you about him. He came to see our *cuadro*.'

"As Clementina followed Rosa's finger pointing toward the poet, though, one familiar face after another began to pop out of the darkness at her. First, she saw Esteban, still wearing the bow tie he'd had on at Tía Rogelia's funeral. His frog eyes goggled as he watched the dancers. Then she spotted Arturo, pear-shaped heir to the almond fortune, whose face suddenly disappeared as he leaned over to vomit. At another table, Juan Pablo and his father, they of the matching over-oiled haircuts parted in the middle, clinked glasses and tossed back a bolt of *fino* that caused the boy to sputter and cough. The other fathers laughed as Juan Pablo Senior pounded his son on the back, refilled both their glasses, and held his high, yelling out a toast to Clementina's aunt above the clamor: '*A la vieja!*'

"Clementina was touched that, throughout the shadowy room, men held up their glasses and toasted her dead aunt. She'd always thought that the men of Granada either didn't like or simply didn't notice her aunt. It pleased her to discover that the old woman had actually been esteemed.

Her pleasure ended abruptly when other toasts followed. These were composed mostly of filthy words she didn't precisely understand. The brays of male laughter they incited made their meanings clear.

"'Did your aunt really die of a dry cunt?' Rosa asked, confirming Clementina's worst suspicions about what the men were saying.

"Clementina turned away. This fiesta was nothing like she'd dreamed it would be. The dancers moved among the revelers and a few shadowy figures near the back grabbed the women and dragged them toward a door that opened into another room that couples disappeared into.

"'Where are the dancers going?' Clementina asked.

"'Dancers? They're not dancers. They're just *palomas torcaces*.'

"'Wild pigeons?'

"Rosa laughed at her friend's ignorance. 'Whores! Those women are whores and they're going to do what whores do with men who have money. Don't you know anything?'

"Clementina was beginning to understand that she didn't know anything. She didn't know anything at all.

"'Miracielos!' Delicata's sharp voice cut through the uproar and Rosa rushed to her side. Clementina lifted the scarf up to hide even more of her face and joined Rosa at the front of the room in time to hear her mother say, 'Lorca is the one who asked for our *cuadro*. He specifically asked for you. He told all his friends about you. Tonight, I will go first and you will go last.'

"'Oh, Mama, thank you.' Rosa threw her arms around Delicata. To be the final dancer in a crowd of *aficionados* such as this was a great honor.

"Delicata pushed her daughter away. 'Don't thank me,' she snapped, then added, her voice softer, sadder, 'and don't blame me either. Not for doing what a Gypsy woman has to do to keep her family alive.'

"Clementina and Rosa didn't have time to wonder about Delicata's strange words, for Mono, Rosa's brother with the nose smashed in like a monkey, began to play. He bashed at the strings of his battered guitar, beating brutal rhythms. The poet was the most intent of the spectators. When someone behind him called out drunkenly, '*Baila! Baila!* Dance! Dance!' Lorca shot the man the most withering of glances and the room fell silent. Delicata took her place at the edge of the area that had been cleared for the dancers.

"El Chino broke the intense silence with a wail even more unearthly than the one he had unloosed while the troupe had walked through

Granada's dark street. More scream than song, the *cante* of Rosa's father evoked bewildering surges of despair and ecstasy in Clementina as he sang of his love for a woman that none could compare to except one and that one was on the wall of a church with the moon at her feet.

"Delicata raised her arm above her head and, in that gesture, transformed herself from a troll into a queen and left no doubt whom El Chino was singing about. Staring at the men with a defiance that bordered on disgust, she stamped her foot hard, sweeping her hand down with a decisive finality. She dropped her head and everyone in the room held their breath until, two, three *compases* later, she slowly lifted it again, her arms rising along with it. They twisted like flames above her head.

"Rosa clapped the beat that brought her mother's feet to life, stamping out an intricate counterrhythm. The poet's face stood out from the crowd as he encouraged Delicata with nods and mutters of '*Eso es! Eso es el flamenco puro!*' Delicata signaled for a *silencio,* a quiet place in the dance where El Chino's *cante* could take over.

"Delicata stepped back and pushed her daughter forward. Rosa executed simple *marcaje* that kept the beat while El Chino sang. Clementina waited for El Chino to settle into one of the songs that Rosa had taught her. But he didn't sing anything Clementina had heard before. She was puzzling over what manner of song he was singing when the door opened and a man strode in. Clementina knew instantly that it was El Bala. Just as Rosa had described, he looked like a bullet with his bald head and thick neck, all smooth except where a long scar puckered his face. Delicata and El Chino stared first at El Bala, then at each other, then together their gazes fell upon Rosa who, lost in the dance, didn't notice their sudden attention. Clementina thought her friend had never been more beautiful. Even doing the marking steps, she was exquisite.

"El Chino's song was so *jondo,* so filled with *sangre negra,* black blood, that even the *señoritos* were moved. Several had started to weep. So powerful were the emotions aroused by El Chino's voice and the words he was making up on the spot that Juan Pablo's father stood and ripped his shirt from his body. Possessed by the moment, El Chino sang on. He sang the story of his delirious love for a green-eyed dancer who stole his soul and forced him to steal her because, after all, how can a man live without his soul? He sang of how every man who saw his wife was as bewitched as he had been. He had hidden her from all except one, a killer who would put a bullet in the heart of his love. His woman loves the killer. Driven mad by jealousy and love, he put his hands around the neck of the only woman he would ever love. As his fingers tightened, her green eyes bulged, and his woman swore that it is not her that the killer loves but their daughter. The daughter is the one the killer wants.

"Heartbroken tears flowed from El Chino's eyes as he sang his lament. He has two choices. He can either give his daughter in marriage or kill her mother. How, he asks, can his children live without their mother? How can he live without the soul that mother stole from him?

"Clementina knew that she had understood the strange words correctly when a look of horror spread across her friend's face.

"El Chino's *cante* was the catalyst the playboys, already half-mad from days of drinking and debauchery, required to reach a state of near-hysterical group catharsis. The aristocrats keened and wept. The old men lamented that life was too short. The young that it was too long. Juan Pablo's father, driven into a frenzy, scratched his fingernails across his naked chest, drawing blood.

"In the clamor, Rosa, her face wet with tears, slipped back into the shadows and whispered to Clementina, 'They can't! They can't marry me off to El Bala. He's old. He's ugly. I will kill myself.'

"Clementina stopped her friend. 'Rosa, don't even say that. We'll run away.' She remembered all of Rosa's stories. 'We'll go to Sevilla, where there is laughter, gaiety, with enough to eat for everyone and more than enough for those with talent. Rosa, you will be queen of Sevilla like your grandmother La Leona. You will be queen of the *cafés cantantes*!'

"'How?' Rosa asked.

"El Bala guarded the door. There would be no escape. El Chino sang again and the men calmed themselves. Clementina felt that the whole world, since the world was run by men, wanted only to lock her away, her and Rosa and every other girl who would dance and sing. Cave or convent, mountain or mansion, it didn't matter how fine the rugs might be, how ancient the heraldic tiles, a prison was a prison. With the barbarous El Bala guarding the door, there seemed to be no hope. Clementina realized they were both condemned. Then, his white suit shining like the moon in the darkness, one faint beacon of hope presented itself: the poet.

"Clapping out a staccato answer to her husband's lament, Delicata stepped forward. The blood of her mother, La Leona, queen of the *cafés cantantes,* surged through her veins and when she danced, she became a whirlpool that sucked every man's attention into its fathomless well.

Thankfully, none was left for the two girls. In the dark, Clementina motioned for Rosa to follow her and they made their way to the table where a flickering *candil* lighted the face of the poet. Clementina knelt at his feet so that her features would not be caught in the illumination.

" 'What is it, *bailaora*?' the poet asked, his voice soft with kindness.

"Clementina poured Rosa's tale out and, in the telling, divulged a bit of her own as well. The poet was enraptured. 'I shall write an ode,' he exclaimed. 'Your stories, your *baile* capture all that is *flamenco puro.*'

"Clementina ducked her head even lower, scared that the poet's exclamations would call attention to her. When she lowered her head, she noticed to her alarm that the front of her borrowed dress was damp with sweat, darkened with soot. She touched her dripping face and found no soot on her finger when she looked at it. She had sweated her disguise away.

"Delicata finished and the thirsty crowd turned back to the wine. For a moment, the only sound was the clinking of bottles against the rims of glasses. Just then, a man stepped out of the back room. The wild pigeon he'd just finished with was hanging onto him. All the men hooted as he made a great show of buttoning his fly, tucking his shirt in, and pulling his suspenders up. '*Ándale, muchachos,* I warmed her up for you.' He lowered the dancer's blouse and kissed her nipple. The man was Clementina's father.

"The poet, recognizing the duke, tried to hide Clementina. But it was too late. Smears of soot, a scarf covering all but her eyes, the darkness, the surprise of the setting, none of it mattered. The duke recognized his daughter instantly. His gaze fixed on her. In his look was not only recognition of who Clementina was but of who she would be for the rest of her days: a disgrace, a scandal that would have to be hidden. Marriage to even the lowest of families, internment in even the meanest of convents would no longer be enough. Clementina could not imagine her fate, but death was not out of the question since any life she had ever known ended the second her father set eyes on her.

"A hammering at the door threw everyone else in the room into a panic, but the duke remained frozen. He did not even register the shouted words, 'Open up! *Guardia civil!*' Without waiting, the guards began pounding the door down.

"Though the *juerga* was a traditional right of the playboys of the aristocracy, none of them knew if their immunity would stand up in the perilous political climate that had reigned since Franco had come to power. The military and the Church had put him in power and the Church hated flamenco. All the dukes and barons scrambled for a safe exit. And though every Gypsy was terrified of the state police who made their lives such torment, the most frightened person that night, for his own very singular reasons, was the poet Lorca. *Candiles* were extinguished. The room fell into darkness. Panic ensued as the men stampeded toward the door, all of them ready with bribes to thrust into the guards' hands. Rosa screamed for her friend. Clementina ran to her side and, not knowing where else to turn, they followed the one spot of brightness they could distinguish, the luminescent white of the poet's suit.

"While all the others churned futilely, the door was broken down and the guards entered carrying lanterns. The light reflected off the black patent leather of their hats, turning the uptilted corners into horns. They entered and demanded, 'Where is the poet?'

"But the poet was gone. At that very moment he was helping Rosa and Clementina clamber out a window. He followed, climbing down the lattice that held up a bougainvillea and dropping into the alley below. The three of them set off running. Clementina kept turning back, expecting her father to appear behind her at any second. She fell behind and Rosa went back to hurry her along. Then they chased the waning moon of the poet's white suit. They ran until they caught him. They ran until all three were out of breath and far from the site of the *juerga*.

"The first thing Lorca did when he caught his breath was laugh. 'Franco, you idiot! What a terrible and tiny tyrant you must be to fear a poet. Well, girls, at least we all know what we're up against, eh? We'll go straight to my friend's house, where I'm staying. Those apes don't know where it is. I'll send word to my sister, my mother. We'll collect my papers, what money I have, and leave Granada tonight. My friends were right. I should never have returned. We'll escape to Madrid, to some place not yet controlled by that bloodthirsty, sanctimonious monster. Some place where Spaniards are still Spaniards and still love poetry more than blood and dance more than murder.'

"Clementina and Rosa suddenly felt as if their lives, which had seemed over only moments before, were just beginning. Lorca hurried ahead of them through the quiet streets, his heels ringing against the wet cobblestones. The girls were barely able to suppress giggles born of hysteria, fear, and joy. Rosa and Clementina caught up to Lorca, and the rest of the way he talked even faster than he walked. He talked about the evil that gripped his beloved Spain. About his country's demonic desire to kill what is best in herself. 'She's done it before,' he ranted. 'The Inquisition, driving out the Moors and Jews, persecuting the Gypsies, now this, this civil war. This is the most grievous act of cannibalism in all her bloody history.

"'Politics? I don't care about politics,' he railed. 'About Loyalists, Rebels. Republicans, Falangists. I hate all uniforms except *el traje de luces!*' The thought of the bullfighter's glittering suit of lights as a uniform made him laugh. 'Not much farther, señoritas, my friend's house is just around this corner. Then we are safe from those jackbooted—'

"Words and motion stopped dead when they turned the corner. Waiting along the street was a gauntlet of soldiers in dung-brown uniforms carrying rifles, standing in the murky light cast by a lone streetlamp. Rosa grabbed the poet and dragged him back into the shadows.

"'They didn't see you,' she whispered. 'We can sneak away. I have relatives in Sevilla. We'll walk. Don't worry about your papers, your money.'

"Lorca didn't answer. He merely pulled a Turkish cigarette from the case in his pocket, lit it, and held it in that way he had, pinched between thumb and forefinger, his palm cupping his chin as he inhaled the smoke. He looked like the hero in a movie, his hair black as ink, his face, hands, suit, all white, the stuff of clouds in the mist swirling through the narrow street. They stood hidden in the darkness and listened to the tramp of the soldiers' boots against the cobblestones, to the rattle of rifle barrels, the slap of a leather holster against a thigh. Lorca finished his cigarette and stared a long time at the butt before he tossed it away.

"'Papers?' he said. 'Money? No, these I don't worry about. I worry about honor, dignity, and art. Good luck, *muchachas*. I wish I had more than luck to give you. I wish I had more to give Spain.'

"'No,' Rosa whispered, but he had already stepped into the light. The soldiers seized him. The last they saw of the poet was the back of his white jacket before the sudden slam of a black car door, a moon being eclipsed by a dark cloud. They watched long after the car bore him away into the night."

Chapter Thirty-six

Doña Carlota fell silent then. If she'd been younger, stronger, I might have questioned her a bit about this account of the night Lorca died. Since he was one of the major saints in flamenco's pantheon, any student at the academy named for her could have told Doña Carlota what details were known about his death, that Lorca was hiding at his friend's house when he was arrested by Franco's Falangists on August 19 at three in the morning, handcuffed to a lame teacher, and taken by car to a holding camp for condemned prisoners. But I could see from her expression that she had told her truth: innocence and hope had disappeared from her life along with the white-suited poet.

I assumed the old woman regretted her candor and that her revelations were at an end. I stood to leave and her eyes, the white spotted brown like an old dog's, found me.

"Are you tired of my story, Metrónoma?"

"No, I thought you were through."

"I wish the story had ended that night, but it was just beginning. *Siéntate.* Sit, sit. This is the first and will be the last time I ever tell it all."

I sat back down. Doña Carlota, her bony shoulders hiking up to her ears, edged a bit higher into the chaise longue, settled in, and began again.

"When the sun rose after both the happiest and saddest night of Clementina's life, the girls were tramping along the high road to Sevilla. Rosa purposely bumped and jostled against the farmers coming into Granada to sell their produce. By the time they'd passed the vendors, Rosa's blouse was as heavy as a black marketer's with the apples, onions, carrots, and potatoes she'd filched from passing baskets. She even managed to pluck a small round of manchego cheese, which the girls devoured with the apples and vegetables. With food in her belly, the full horror of the previous night returned and tears commenced streaming down Clementina's cheeks.

"'Are you crying because you lost your father?' Rosa asked.

"Clementina nodded dumbly.

"'Are you crying because you have no money? No place to sleep? Because you might be killed by bandits on this mountain road? Because no decent man will ever marry you and we'll probably starve to death? Or are you crying just because your feet hurt?'

"Clementina's tears poured faster as she listened to this inventory of her miseries and realized how much worse off they were than she'd feared.

"Rosa slammed the back of her hand against Clementina's sternum so hard that the air caught in her chest and she could not get enough breath to continue crying. 'Well, look at me. Not only have all those things happened to me, but El Bala is going to hunt me down to drag me back to be his wife. Am I crying?'

"'You're made of much sturdier stuff than I am.'

"'Oh, you poor little rich girl. Your suffering is so much more refined than mine, is that it?'

"'No,' Clementina said with her mouth while her mind said yes.

"'Come on, we're lucky. All I have to do is imagine being trapped in a cave with El Bala and I want to burst into song. Think of lying in bed with one of those boys from last night on top of you. How about that one with the head shaped like an almond and all the pimples?'

"Clementina shuddered at the thought and her tears fell faster.

"'Do you like being sad?' Rosa asked her friend.

"'No.'

"'Then don't think sad thoughts.'

"'It's not that simple,' Clementina said, but her words were lost in the growl of a truck laboring past, hardly traveling faster than they were walking. It required little more than a hop for Rosa to jump onto the back of the flatbed. She laughed as the truck rumbled away and Clementina ran to catch it, then jump up beside her friend. The vast, fertile Granada *vega* stretched out all around them, rust and golden and green, all the way to the Sierra Nevada frosted with snow. When Rosa started singing, Clementina joined her with *palmas* and *pitos*. Even though it was a sad song *por soleares* about never having a home again and wandering as Gypsies have wandered for hundreds of years, Clementina's spirits soared.

"Every person they passed shouted greetings, for the road to Granada was the most sociable in Spain. It was clogged that day with goatherds, muleteers, washerwomen, horse-dealers, and hawkers of every description. A couple of the vendors heading into Granada even reversed their direction and walked swiftly enough to keep up with the lumbering truck so they could ask the girls how they could live without the needles or pans or bits of lace they were selling. Being with Rosa made Clementina bold, and she yelled back retorts so saucy that one merchant, a boy really, barely older than the girls, was inspired to fling a lady's souvenir fan painted with a view of the Alhambra into the back of the truck. He shouted honeyed *piropos* comparing Clementina to a rose, a dove, a lily until he was out of breath and stood by the side of the road watching as the truck carrying the two girls, giggling madly at his compliments and fanning themselves with the fan, disappeared from sight.

"Clementina and Rosa watched the Alhambra that had stood invincible over their childhoods grow smaller as one terrace after another slipped from view until only the top spire was visible, a shimmering rose patch above Granada. Clementina remembered her aunt's stories about Boabdil, the last Moorish ruler. In 1492, when he was driven out by the Catholic kings, he looked back at the paradise his people had created and he had lost and wept. His bitter tears at the thought of never again seeing his beloved Alhambra caused his mother to scorn him, saying, 'Weep like a woman for what you have not defended like a man.'

"'What do you think happened to Señor Lorca?' Clementina asked Rosa. When she received no answer, she looked over and found Rosa fast asleep against a bag of wheat. Clementina already knew what Rosa would answer: 'Do you want to be sad? No? Then don't think sad thoughts.' She lay back next to her friend, let the sun pour over her, and repeated those words until the rumble and sway of the truck rocked her to sleep.

"A horrible scything sound followed by sudden stillness woke the girls. Rosa ordered Clementina to hop with her off the back of the broken-down truck and hide before the driver could discover the stowaways. Cursing loudly, the driver turned the engine over again. It sputtered and caught. Unfortunately, the girls couldn't scramble from their hiding place fast enough to catch the truck and it rumbled off without them. Looking around, they found themselves in a forbidding landscape of lunar starkness. Pinnacle upon pinnacle rose up on all sides. Sheer precipices careened down from the rocky road. Stunted pine tress, moss-covered boulders, and an occasional white house perched like a watchtower in the distance were all that broke the landscape. A solitary vulture carved lazy, black Vs across a nearly white sky.

" 'Have we landed on the moon?' Rosa asked.

"They might as well have for all the idea Clementina had of where they could be. She wondered whether it might not have been better to die quickly back in Granada rather than slowly of thirst out there in such a desolate wasteland. 'We're certainly not on the road to Sevilla.'

" 'That's good,' Rosa said in a chirpy voice that made Clementina wonder if the heat had overtaken her friend.

" 'It's good that we are in the middle of nowhere with no idea which way Sevilla is?'

" '*Claro!* Where would I go if I ran away from Granada?'

" 'To Sevilla, of course. To dance in the *cafés cantantes* and rule over the city of charm like an empress.'

" '*Claro.* So, the first place El Bala is going to search is the road to Sevilla, *verdad*? Your father has probably alerted every *guardia* already, and they'll be watching the main roads. So this is perfect.' Rosa gazed around at the desolation and smiled. 'Yes, this is just where we want to be.' She found a bit of shade cast by a rock outcropping and plopped herself down in it with a satisfied sigh as if pleased with how events had worked out. Clementina stood beside the sun-blasted road, baffled by Rosa's insouciance.

" 'You better get out of the sun, *paya.*'

"Clementina started to join her friend when the low-throated rumble of a truck laboring up the winding hill stopped her and she ran back into the middle of the road, ready to flag the driver down.

" 'Someone's coming!' Clementina's joyous shout was cut short when Rosa abruptly yanked her off the road and shoved her behind the rocks. A second later Clementina saw that the canvas covering the back of the truck was painted with red stripes at the top and bottom, with a yellow stripe in the middle where a black eagle with a red beak perched clutching the arrows and the yoke of Fernando and Isabel. She saw that the army truck was filled with soldiers wearing the same dung-colored uniforms as the ones who had taken the poet Lorca away.

" 'They might have given us water,' Clementina said wistfully as the truck disappeared in the vast beige wasteland of rock and dust.

" 'The only thing men in uniforms give Gypsies is misery. Come on up here where there's a breeze.' Rosa clambered up the tallest rock, untucked her blouse, and lifted it out.

"Clementina perched next to her friend. 'Tell me about the *cafés cantantes,*' Clementina said.

"An updraft blew along the ridge. It filled the girls' untucked blouses like wind in a sail and Rosa told Clementina again all the stories about the life they would have when they reigned as princesses of *el baile* in Sevilla.

"Hours later the screech of a wooden oxcart wheel axle interrupted Rosa's stories. A farmer drove a two-wheeled cart up the mountain. He was a stoutly built fellow in worn, brown corduroy pants, an ancient cap perched jauntily on his head, bald except for a few silvery strands.

"Rosa stepped into the road weeping tears she summoned on the spot and sobbing sobs so piteous that they drowned out the shrieking of the cart. 'Señor, señor, *por favor.*' She held out a trembling hand and begged for him to stop, something the farmer, exhausted from a long day's tramp and hungry for the supper waiting for him, was not inclined to do.

"'We're lost! My poor sister and I are lost! Our parents are dead. We're going to our aunt in Sevilla. We have nothing. We're lost.'

"With a gusty sigh of resignation, the farmer stopped and gestured for them to help themselves to his water barrel tied to the back of the cart.

"'You don't look like sisters,' he observed as pale Clementina sipped delicately out of the dipper and dark Rosa all but dunked her head, drinking directly from the barrel like a horse.

"Rosa laughed and shrugged. The farmer turned out to be a garrulous sort who accepted Rosa's little subterfuge as a fine example of *gracia,* Andalusian wit. He was happy to join them in the shade where he passed around sausage and a flask of *aguardiente.*

"'To kill the worms,' he said, raising the aniseed brandy. Before the flask had gone around twice, the sun was slipping from the cloudless sky, coloring the bleak landscape with browns, hazels, reds, blues, and purples, and turning the distant olive groves bluish green. Far to the east, the delicately tapering peaks of the Sierra Nevada glowed pink in the fading light of day.

"Muttering about Long Steps, the most feared bandit ever to maraud the Sierra Nevada, the farmer heaved himself to his feet. He warned the girls that they shouldn't stay out unprotected and offered to let them sleep in his barn, less than an hour's walk away.

" 'Why should we tramp another hour to sleep where your ox shits?' Rosa asked.

"The farmer roared with laughter. More *gracia*. 'Take your chances with the bandits then.' He whacked his ox until the creature moved and the wooden axle screeched.

" 'We have nothing to steal!' Rosa shouted after him.

" 'Then Long Steps will steal *you*!' the farmer yelled back.

" 'Only if he can find us!' Rosa hurled back, already stealing away from the road. Beyond a stand of pines, dwarfed and twisted by the ceaseless wind, she found a perch at the very edge of the precipice. Clementina's stomach lurched and panic clutched at her throat as she peered into the chasm below. Rosa, on the other hand, was as comfortable as a mountain goat bedding down for the night. Rosa, who'd never slept alone in her life, snuggled up to her friend like a puppy settling in with its litter mates. Clementina, who'd never slept a night with another human beside her since her mother died, was comforted by Rosa's presence.

" 'Guess what?' Rosa asked Clementina. 'I've picked a stage name. In Sevilla, I will be known as La Leona, the Lioness. Just like my grandmother. Clementina, you have to change your name so your father won't find you. What's it going to be?'

"While Clementina pondered what her new name would be, Rosa fell asleep.

"Night fell with a stunning velocity. In the darkness Clementina became terrified of falling into the void below and was certain she wouldn't sleep a wink on the rocky earth. But as the pricks of light that were the farmhouses below blended with the stars blazing overhead, it seemed as if she were swimming through a dark sea with diamonds floating and glinting all around and Clementina relaxed. Whether it was the farmer's *aguardiente* or the unaccustomed solace of a warm body, Clementina joined Rosa in a sleep lighted by dreams of the golden radiance of the gas lamps of the *cafés cantantes*.

"In the dream, she learned what her stage name would be and awoke eager to tell Rosa, but when she opened her eyes, the only creature she beheld was a lone eagle riding high above a pink dawn.

" 'Rosa. Rosa? Rosa!' Her shouts grew louder when a search turned up nothing but a few lizards that skittered away, twitching their tails in the dust.

"The only evidence that Rosa had ever been there was the fan flung to them by the smitten young man on the road to Sevilla. Clementina found it crumpled behind a rock, near a dark spot still damp from where Rosa had relieved herself. The impression of a man's boot heel was pressed into the small circle of mud. Long Steps. Rosa had been stolen by bandits. Tears flooded Clementina's eyes. She opened Rosa's fan. Each time she waved it in front of her hot face, it dried one tear and two more poured out. Soon all her tears had spilled and she regretted every single one because a thirst worse than any she had ever known burned in her throat. Shriveling like a chile drying in the early morning sun, Clementina was so thirsty that she forgot Rosa, she forgot her hunger, she forgot everything except water.

"When Clementina heard the rattle of an approaching vehicle, she didn't care who it belonged to. If it was Franco's soldiers, at least she'd have a quick death instead of dying of thirst. A car like her father's, an Hispano-Suiza, approached in a cloud of dust. Unlike her father's, however, this once-luxurious automobile was now an ancient rattletrap. She dragged herself into the middle of the road and the car stopped. *Espectáculos Vedrines,* the name of a famous variety show that toured the country, was written on the side. The man driving barely slowed down long enough for one door to fly open and a woman with dark red lipstick, her hair covered by a snood, to gesture to Clementina. 'Come on! Come on! Get in or he will leave you here!'

"Clementina jumped in the back and wedged herself between trunks, hatboxes, and a guitar.

"'Hurry, Gustavo!' the woman yelled at the driver.

"'Elena, you're the one who told me to stop!' Gustavo ground the car's gears in his haste.

"'Yes, well, you're the one who couldn't keep up with the rest of the company and now we're lost in this godforsaken place!'

"'I? I was the one? Was it I who made the tire on this pile of junk blow out? Was it I who lost the ration coupons so we couldn't buy petrol? I know it was I who had to steal enough petrol to get us here! And we are not lost! Where else would this road go if not to Sevilla?'

"Clementina noticed that the handsome couple, though they yelled everything they said to each other, seemed to enjoy the yelling. At least they were going to Sevilla.

"'And again, I ask you, was it I who insisted we stop for this, this,

this—' The man waved his hand in Clementina's direction but could not decide exactly what to call her.

" 'And I suppose you were just going to leave her by the side of the road?'

" 'Why not? You're too softhearted. If it was up to you this car would be filled with skinny dogs and'—he glanced at Clementina in the rearview mirror—'skinny girls. Maybe she lives on a nearby farm.'

" 'Look at her. A farmer's daughter? You must be insane.'

" '*I'm* insane? Who's standing in the middle of the road in the middle of nowhere?'

"Elena whispered to Gustavo. 'Maybe she is a little . . .' She tapped her temple.

" 'I'm not crazy,' Clementina felt obliged to tell them. The couple blinked at each other as if surprised she could speak even though they had not given her a chance to do so.

" 'Good!' Gustavo boomed. 'Then maybe you can tell us if we are in rebel or Nationalist territory! We have to know which flag to put up so we won't be killed!'

" 'I don't know, but a truck filled with soldiers passed by yesterday.'

" 'Did you hear that?' Elena yelled at Gustavo.

" 'I heard! Of course I heard! Do you think I'm deaf? An army truck, yes. But which army? The rebels? The loyalists? The Falangists? Which one?'

" 'I don't know.'

" 'She doesn't know!' Elena shouted at Gustavo before asking Clementina. 'The flag? What did the flag look like?'

" 'It had stripes.'

" 'Stripes!' Gustavo bellowed. 'They all have stripes! Elena, show her the flags!'

" 'But Gustavo, is it safe?'

" 'Is it safe to drive around flying the wrong flag? We can't make a mistake! Show her!'

"Elena opened the glove box, dumped maps and documents onto her lap, then felt around until she dislodged a partition covering a secret compartment, and retrieved a handful of scarf-size flags. 'Which one was on the truck?' She showed Clementina a flag with red, yellow, and purple stripes and another with just red and yellow stripes. There were several others, but Clementina ignored them as she plucked out one with red stripes at the top and bottom and a yellow one in the middle where a black eagle with a red beak perched clutching the arrows and the yoke of Fernando and Isabel.

"'Falangists!' Gustavo yelled. 'They're the worst of them all! Get that flag up!'

"Elena leaned out of the window, the wind tore off her snood, and with her black, curly hair streaming behind, she tied the Falangist flag to the car antenna. When she'd finished, she packed the other flags back into their hiding place, shut the glove box, and turned to Clementina. 'So what are you doing out here in the middle of nowhere waiting to get run down or shot by soldiers?'

"'I was on my way to Sevilla with my friend, Rosa, and the bandits stole her. Her father back in Sacromonte promised her to El Bala and she was going to have to live the rest of her life in a cave with an ugly old man so we ran away.'

"'Your "friend," eh?' Elena caught Gustavo's eye and winked at him. 'So Rosa was stolen by the bandits. I had a "friend" once myself whose parents wanted her to marry a rich old man, but my "friend" was stolen too.' Elena nuzzled up next to Gustavo and nibbled his ear as she crooned in it, 'Stolen by a handsome *bandido*. Don't worry, Rosa, your "friend's" secret is safe with us.'

"'Do you have any water?' Clementina was too thirsty to care that Elena thought she was lying.

"Elena handed her a jug of water that she drank dry.

"Then Gustavo asked, 'Have you eaten today?'

"Clementina shook her head no, and Elena produced from a basket at her feet a yellow pear and she began to cut up. The smell of the perfectly ripe pear and the sight of juice dripping from Elena's knife made Clementina's mouth water.

"'Do you like pear?' This time Gustavo was the one who winked at Elena as he added, 'Rosa?'

"All her life, Clementina had been taught to bow her head as if she had just taken Communion and accept her *sino*. Her father and Tía Rogelia had believed that her fate would arrive in the form of a young man from a venerable family. When Gustavo called Clementina by her vanished friend's name, she realized what her true fate was. Elena reached around and handed Clementina a slice of pear with a kind and understanding smile. Clementina bowed her head and accepted the pear as politely as she had always accepted her fate.

"'And what do you intend to do in Sevilla?' Gustavo asked.

"'I will find work as a flamenco dancer at a *café cantante*.'

"Gustavo studied her in the rearview mirror. 'A *café cantante*?'

"'Yes, maybe the Kursaal or Café Silverio. Or any of the cafés on the Alameda de Hércules.'

"'The Kursaal? Café Silverio?' After each name, Elena burst out with an eruption of laughter louder than the last.

"The well-brought-up Clementina simply blinked several times at Elena's rudeness, causing Elena to explain kindly, 'Oh, *niña*, the last *café cantante* in Sevilla closed more than ten years ago.'

"'That's not possible. I was going to be La Leona, the Lioness, like my grandmother.' Somehow, the shock of learning that Rosa's dream world had vanished made it seem all right to claim it as her own.

"Elena turned in her seat, holding a piece of pear in her hand. 'You had a grandmother who danced in *los cafés cantantes*?'

"The juicy slice of pear glistened in the morning sunlight, slanting into the big car. Clementina nodded yes and Elena handed over the bit of fruit. Clementina told La Leona's story and was rewarded with a slice of pear. The tale of El Chino and Delicata won her an even bigger slice. The first time Clementina told the story of Rosa's life as her own, she was driven to it by hunger. But in the telling Rosa's life became much more real to Clementina than the lonely, uneventful one she had led, so real that it truly did seem to be her own. Clementina didn't think that she had stolen her friend's name, her history, her life. She intended only to borrow them for a while. It would be much safer to be Rosa than Clementina. There were so many Rosas. Who would notice one more? A Clementina? Yes, a Clementina would be noticed and, eventually, her father would come. But a Rosa, *una gitana*? Even Rosa's own family would not search for her since that would mean going to the enemies of the Gypsy people, the police, *la guardia civil*. No, no one would be looking for Rosa.

"Especially not now. Now that the country was at war with itself. Gustavo turned on the car radio and they listened to the warbly voice of Generalissimo Franco on Radio Zaragoza. He called Manuel Azaña, the president of the Republic, 'a monster who seems more the absurd invention of a doubly insane Frankenstein than the fruit of the love of a woman. Azaña,' Franco insisted, 'must be caged up so that brain specialists can study perhaps the most interesting case of mental degeneration in history.'

"Elena and Gustavo burst out laughing. When Clementina asked if this meant they were on the side of Franco's Nationalists, they laughed even harder.

" 'Side?' Gustavo asked. 'This damn war has more sides than you can count. The Carlists, the Falangists, the Communists, the Church, the aristocracy, the unions, the laborers, the miners. Everyone has a side. Now even the Germans who are flying Franco's troops from Morocco in their Junkers and the Italians who aren't doing anything except seducing our women have a side in this war. The only ones who don't have a side in this unholy mess are us, the entertainers.'

" 'Oh yes, we do!' Elena disagreed, then asked Clementina, 'You know which side is our side, Rosita?'

"Clementina shrugged.

" 'The side that claps for us. The side that pays us. The side that puts bread in our mouths. That is our side. That is the only side entertainers ever have.'

" 'Shut up, you. Listen to this.' Gustavo tuned in Radio Sevilla and the high-pitched voice of General Queipo de Llano came in very clearly. 'We must kill the enemies of the Spanish nation, like the animals they are. We must kill the Reds. Kill the leftists. Kill the Republicans. Kill the Masons. Kill all those who would bring down Holy Mother Church and Spain herself.'

" 'Find some music!' Elena cried out and was not happy until Gustavo tuned in La Bella Dorita chirping her syrupy songs about roses and butterflies. She asked Clementina to pass her the basket sitting atop the suitcases in the backseat. It was filled with costumes in the process of being either repaired or constructed. Clementina volunteered to help. Elena was so impressed with the precision of her needlework while mending a tear in the crotch of Gustavo's clown costume that she declared, 'We have found a new wardrobe mistress!' and dumped the entire basket on Clementina's lap. Clementina was delighted with her new title and stitched away happily as the barren landscape slid past her window.

"She woke that night with her head resting on the nest of ripped costumes as the Hispano-Suiza came to a halt in the alley behind the Teatro

Olimpio. Seventy years later, long after Clementina had forgotten everything she had to do to survive for all the years of the war when the starving country chewed itself to bits like a mad dog, Clementina would remember one thing about her first moment in the fabled city of Sevilla: the smell, an ineradicable combination of cement dust, death, and perfume.

"She would learn later that the smell of death hung over all of Sevilla and that it came from the *plaza de toros* where thousands of 'Reds' had been executed, labor leaders, teachers, leftists, students, anyone who opposed the Church or spoke out against the landowners. A few of the condemned were allowed to escape the massacre in the plaza so they could tell how Moorish soldiers, men dark as *café solo*, were encouraged to rape the victims before executions. It was August in the south of Spain and the mass graves could not be dug fast enough. The stench of the corpses mixed with the smell of cement dust from the Santa Marina and San Roque churches blown up by the Republicans. The odor of burning rubber from the trucks set on fire by the Nationalists and cordite from the rifles that fired sporadically through the day added to the stink that choked all of Sevilla.

"But the smell of perfume could be detected for only a few blocks around the Teatro Olimpia because just a few streets away the Perfumería Tena had been blown up, allowing the fragrances of jasmine, sandalwood, tea rose, musk, lily of the valley, lavender to pour out over the stink. Their sweetness tricked the nostrils into opening so that each inhalation was a fresh horror.

"Barely awake, frightened by the smell of death, Clementina clung to Elena and rushed with her into the safety of the theater. Elena and Gustavo were not surprised when Clementina confessed that she knew no one in Sevilla and had nowhere to go. And, also, Clementina added, she was starving.

"'You want to eat?' Gustavo demanded, adding in an aside to Elena, 'She wants to eat!'

"'Rosita,' Elena yelled, 'we all want to eat!'

"Gustavo tossed her a costume. 'You're a dancer, right? Okay, dance. Señor Vedrine pays after the show. Then we eat.'

"Clementina nodded dumbly.

"Elena explained, 'Okay, you're dancing *La Pulga*. Anyone with a nice pair of legs can dance *La Pulga.* Just watch me.' In the hubbub back-stage, with girls penciling their eyes in black and rouging their cheeks, with a plate-spinner rattling his china, with five poodles in bow ties and jackets yapping, Elena taught her *La Pulga,* a dance routine about a girl with a pesky flea in her clothes.

"That night, Espectáculos Vedrines put on a show for Generalissimo Franco's troops. Clementina, now officially Rosa, did not dance in golden gaslight for an elegant crowd that revered flamenco and would crown *una bailaora* queen simply for the quality of her exquisite *brazeo.* No, Rosa was but one of many acts in a traveling variety show, each one coarser than the last.

"Just before Elena shoved Clementina onstage, she hissed at her, 'Remember, Señor Vedrine only pays if the audience claps!'

"Clementina swatted at herself as Elena had shown her and danced faster and faster to the accelerating music. The theater 'liberated' by the Nationalists was filled with troops wearing the blue uniforms of the Italian army, the gray-green of the German. Their officers wore peaked caps and sat in the front row next to General Gonzalo Queipo de Llano, who was surrounded by the leaders of the Army of Africa and officers of the Spanish Legionnaires. Behind them were soldiers wearing the red berets of the Carlists, the dark blue shirts with yellow arrows of the Falangists. Germans with blond hair and big, square heads sat next to Italians with the soulful eyes of poets. Standing in the very back, allowed to enter yet not to sit, were Franco's Moorish soldiers. Black as ink, they wore red fezzes on their heads and had dusty puttees wrapping their legs. All the men were different, yet to Clementina they were all the same. In her fear, their gaping mouths seemed to meld into one voracious maw poised to gobble her down.

"They watched with a hungry insatiability. But they didn't clap.

"She danced more furiously, her footwork better that night than even Rosa's had ever been. Yet not one man clapped. Perhaps they couldn't see how her heels hammered like pistons? She raised her skirt the tiniest bit and a sprinkling of applause broke out. Offstage, Gustavo prompted her to raise her skirt higher. She did and the applause grew. Only Clementina could hear the growling of her stomach, but it told her what she had to do next. She had to do what Clementina could never have done. Only Rosa could do what was necessary to survive. She raised her skirt higher and the men clapped louder.

"Señor Vedrine, owner of several companies touring the country in his Espectáculos, resplendent that night in black evening cape, mustache waxed to fine points, dropped a few centimos into 'Rosa's' hand. What he gave her was exactly enough to stay alive for one more day and to arrive back at Teatro Olimpia the next night hungry enough to do again whatever was necessary. He welcomed the newest addition to his company with these words, 'More clapping, more centimos. Tomorrow, look a little harder for that flea.'

" 'Rosa' didn't begin her search for the flea in earnest the next night. No, she had to get much, much hungrier before she even removed her shawl. But when she did, oh the applause. Better still, Señor Vedrine parceled out a few extra centimos as a reward. Enough to buy a tomato to eat with her bread. The next night, off came her shoes and she earned enough applause to buy a small piece of cheese. So it went until 'Rosa' stood beneath the blinding lights wearing nothing but her corset, pink stockings, and a false Gypsy's false smile plastered on her face.

"For this Señor Vedrine gave her a little more, but never enough. Never enough to fill her stomach. Perhaps, if Clementina had grown up like Rosa with an empty stomach growling her whole life, she would have been stronger. But she hadn't and she wasn't. So, when a German officer gestured for the pretty *chica,* light-skinned and delicate unlike her swarthy sisters, to join him at his table, a table piled with candied chestnuts in syrup with brandy, perfectly grilled sardines, tender marinated octopus, *mantecaditos!*—the little cookies of almonds and olive oil she had used to lure Rosa into friendship—was it any wonder she said yes?

"And that is how Clementina survived the war in which a million died. A million in a country of twenty-two million. She became the *puta* her father had cursed her for. She entertained in all the ways in which a half-starved young woman can entertain a man. She thought of all the men, German, Italian, Spanish, as *señoritos,* as the wealthy patrons who had always supported flamenco performers. She smiled at the German officers who told her how lucky she was to be a little Gypsy girl in Spain. Back in the Fatherland, they had been sterilizing people like her and putting them in concentration camps since 1932. She smiled when the Italians complimented her manners, saying she wasn't a pig like most Spaniards. She smiled when Spanish officers joked about making the *maricón* poet Lorca dig his own grave—'The only work that fairy did in his life!'—before they shot him in the back of the head.

"German bombs fell on Spain and anyone with enough influence or money left. Carmen Amaya, Sabicas, all gone to Paris, New York, Buenos Aires. In 1939, the Civil War ended. The Germans, the Italians, and the Moors left, but the memory of what they had done remained. Spaniards on the left and the right remembered the nineteen thousand Luftwaffe personnel who had rotated through the Condor Legions learning all they needed to know about bombing civilians in places like Guernica before they moved on to Poland, to Czechoslovakia, to France, to the rest of Europe. They remembered the tanks flying Italian flags that had bombarded their homes. They remembered what Franco had incited the Moors to do to their women. The foreigners left, but those who had danced and sang for them remained. And people remembered.

"Life after the Civil War ended was grimmer in many ways than it had been when guns were being fired. Franco tried not just to freeze time, but to turn back the hands of history. Spain became a prison camp secured by *la guardia civil* against dissent, against progress, against the outside world and the war sweeping the Continent, then the globe. While the rest of the world fought the Second World War—the war that Germany and Italy had rehearsed in Spain—the only blood Spain spilled was her own. Franco exacted a terrible revenge upon all who had opposed him. All who might oppose him still. Rumors that a person did not attend Mass regularly were enough for him to end up in front of a firing squad. Franco purged the country of 'Reds,' of anyone suspected of supporting the Republicans. Thousands starved in the years of poverty that followed.

"As the people grew hungrier, their memories grew sharper. They remembered the girl who'd searched for a flea, throwing her clothes off for Nazis, both on the stage and off. But no one dared say anything to Clementina. No one would castigate a girl who had entertained Franco's generals and all the foreign generals who had aided him. Not when Franco was still executing prisoners by the thousands. In Sevilla alone eighty citizens a day were killed. In the light of day, no one dared whisper a word to Clementina. But in the safety of a dark theater, when the curtains parted and 'Rosa' went onstage, the whistles that are a Spaniard's boo would shriek through the theater.

"Clementina knew that scores were being settled. A knife between the ribs in a dark alley, a piece of wire around the neck, a lead pipe to the back of the head, that was how the defeated, how ordinary Spaniards, retaliated against their conquerors. On moonless nights when even the wary slept, when even *la guardia* could not protect them, that was when revenge was exacted. Clementina, who had survived the war eating delicacies fed to her by Nazis, who had taken her clothes off for captains and done so much more for majors, who had lived when so many others had died, knew that her name was on the list of those scores waiting to be settled.

"Which is why on a night seven years after the war ended, when Clementina's feet hurt so badly she could barely drag herself home, she was not surprised that a heavily built man stepped out of the shadows and blocked her path. She had been expecting him or someone like him for a long time. It was right that it should happen there, in an alley, with only the faintest glimmer of moonlight shining on the cobblestones slick from the damp night air, an alley just like the one where she and Rosa last saw the poet Lorca. What did surprise her, though, was that the man knew her name, her real name.

" 'Clementina.'

"Then she realized that, of course, it would be someone sent by her father who would kill her.

" 'You don't recognize me, do you?' He tilted his head up so that moonlight found the scar on his face and turned it into a silver pucker running from his scalp, over his whitened eye, down to his chin.

" 'El Bala.'

" 'Well, I barely recognize you either. You look like you've aged twenty years. Wait until I tell Rosa.'

" 'Rosa? Rosa is alive?'

" 'Rosa is my wife. The mother of my three children with another on the way. The woman whose name, whose very blood, you have taken and dishonored.'

" 'Rosa is alive?'

" 'Only because I rescued her from the side of that mountain you had led her to.'

" '*You* stole her? Not Long Steps? You stole Rosa just like her father stole her mother?' The weight of memory, of longing for her friend, pressed down upon Clementina so heavily that she could not draw a breath. 'Is she happy? Does she still dance?'

" 'She is my wife.' Those four words were the walls that imprisoned

Clementina's friend. They described the prison she had been sentenced to by her own parents. 'I have come to collect what you owe us for stealing her name.'

" 'You are looking at everything I own in this world,' Clementina answered.

" 'Then I will have to kill you for the shame you have brought upon my family.' El Bala was used to speaking these words, then watching hard men turn into babies, crying, begging for their lives, soiling their pants. Clementina barely shrugged, and El Bala saw what the years of hunger and shame had taken from the little aristocrat: her fear of death. So he selected another weapon from his arsenal, blackmail. If regular sums were not sent to him, he would expose Clementina for the fraud she was.

" 'Send money to Rosa?' The flicker that had been Clementina's interest in staying alive flamed back to life. 'Where? How much?'

"El Bala had never had such an eager extortion victim. He named an outrageous sum and Clementina agreed so eagerly that he doubled it.

" 'It will take me a few months. Let's say six, no, three, at the most, to have the first payment. I assume you'll expose me if the first payment is not made. Then find me and kill me if I miss the second.'

" 'Uh, yes.'

" 'Good, good. Fine. Oh, this is wonderful. Rosa is alive.'

"El Bala stood alone in the dark alley for several moments after his wife's strange *payo* friend bounded off looking twenty years younger. Yet again he cursed his heart, his fate, for making him fall in love with Delicata. The daughter, Rosa, grown thin and silent, was nothing like her explosive, fiery mother and now, for the rest of his miserable life, he was trapped. A churro vendor pushing his cart to the plaza to sell his fritters to late-night revelers and early risers startled El Bala. He sheathed his knife and slipped into the shadows. It was a long trip back to Sacromonte.

"After that night, Clementina was reborn. She had a reason to live. To make money. Lots and lots of money to send Rosa. There was nothing but poverty, deprivation, and revenge in Spain. One of the companies of Espectáculos Vedrines was setting sail next week for a tour of Argentina and they needed a dancer. Just someone for the back row who could shake a ruffled skirt and do the tourist kind of flamenco that Franco had promoted since banishing the real thing. Clementina seduced the manager of the overseas companies and convinced him that since all the Nazis had fled to

Argentina anyway, the old Luftwaffe pilots and Panzer commandants would be delighted to see the girl who had searched her clothes for a flea while they were training in Spain. She got the job. They gave her an advance on her salary. Clementina intended to send it all to Rosa, but somehow, when she passed the shops that sold candied chestnuts in syrup with brandy, perfectly grilled sardines, tender marinated octopus, *mantecaditos!,* the money flew out of her hand. She boarded the ship for Argentina without having sent one centimo to Rosa.

"Though Clementina felt guilty about abandoning her friend, Argentina was a new country where it was almost possible to forget old memories, old obligations. The streets were broad and clean, there was plenty to eat, and no one had scores to settle with her. No whistles of derision greeted her when she appeared onstage. She danced with the company at the Teatro Maravillas and the Teatro Mayor right on the broad, tree-lined Avenida Mayor in the middle of town. When their engagement was finished, the company moved on, but Clementina stayed. A woman as strong as she was *en compás* never had problems finding work. She danced in the chorus with La Argentinita and even the great Carmen Amaya herself. Though a sturdy and reliable dancer, she was known as someone who kept to herself. It was rumored that she was a lesbian, though she didn't seem to have any more interest in women than she did in men.

"What did interest Clementina was forgetting. Unfortunately amnesia was expensive. Amnesia required dresses of silk, shoes of kid leather, sheets from Portugal. It required the finery of her girlhood. But mostly it required an absence of scent. Only when her body and hair had been scrubbed with the plainest of soaps to remove any possible fragrance, only when her tiny apartment was cleaned of every particle of matter that might rot, only when nothing remained to remind her of a bombed perfume factory, of corpses bloating in a bullring, of the things hunger could force a woman to do, only then could she forget who she'd had to become. Forgetting was essential. Forgetting took all her money so she had none left to send Rosa. Memories of her old friend, of all Clementina owed her, proved impossible to forget. Rosa came in her dreams, as sad and bedraggled as Delicata, to remind Clementina that she owed her her life.

"The years slid past, then the decades. In the beginning, when she was pretty and talented enough to have moved up from the back of the chorus line, she hadn't wanted to for fear of calling attention to herself. When, at last, in a foreign country far from her father, from El Bala, from the passions of the Civil War, she felt it was safe to step into the spotlight, it was too late. She had already ruined her feet. It was a point of honor with Clementina that, though she might be in the last row, there would always be puffs of dust rising from her spot and no one else's because she would be the one pounding dust a century old from the boards of the stage. Three decades of such stomping had taken their toll. When the pain became too great to ignore, she went to the best podiatrist in all of Buenos Aires. He gasped at her mangled toes and pronounced surgery the only answer.

"Clementina hobbled out on her battered feet. She had seen the results of foot surgery, big toes that stuck out at ninety-degree angles, feet that curled up like sultan's shoes. No, she would not allow anyone to cut her feet. Instead, she did what most of the dancers did: she found ways to deal with the pain. Some drank, some smoked herbs. Clementina did both, along with taking any of the medications that floated through the dressing rooms. Paregoric, opium tincture, beneficial for everything from teething babies to chronic diarrhea, became a favorite.

"The orange syrup did relieve Clementina of her pain. Unfortunately, it also relieved her of her timing and the iron discipline that had kept her alive when so many others had perished. The orange syrup unlocked doors that had been closed thirty years before and Clementina wept for all she had lost. When her tears dried, she took stock. It was 1966. She was almost fifty, though she could pass for ten, fifteen, twenty years younger. Her body was firm, slender. Her feet would last another year doing three shows a day. Longer if she only had to teach. She had no savings since she'd spent every peso she'd earned pampering the horror of her life into submission. Clementina had to find a husband. A rich one. Preferably one very close to dying.

"She joined the first troupe heading north. They danced up the continent to Mexico City. From there, they followed the Camino Real, the same route Clementina's distant ancestors had taken in their conquest of the New World. It led her to the Lensic Theater in Santa Fe, a once-majestic vaudeville palace, now, like her, on its last legs. Still, with the right lighting, she and the old place could be magnificent. The lighting was right the night that Ernesto Anaya sat in the audience. A lawyer who had grown wealthy accepting land as payment for his services, a widower whose wife had died before they could have children, he was the answer to her prayer. Ernesto. Ernesto Anaya."

Doña Carlota repeated her dead husband's name as if it were the chant that broke a spell. Her voice grew weaker and weaker until it was the barest of whispers. Then she fell silent.

"Doña Carlota?" The sun long set, the last of the piñon logs burned down to smoldering embers, a gloomy chill had entered the room. "Doña Carlota?"

The old woman shivered and tugged the shawl more tightly around her shoulders. She nodded toward the fireplace and I placed another log on the hearth. Next she nodded toward the bottle of pain pills. I shook a couple out and handed them to her with a glass of water. She winced when she swallowed as if even that effort hurt. The new log caught fire with a crackling that was overly loud in the silent room.

"Should I leave?"

She held up one finger and I sat back down. As she waited for the pills to take effect, I studied the filigreed crucifixes, portraits of suffering saints, and beatific madonnas hanging on the wall. It took me a moment to realize that the dry scratching I heard was not leaves scraping against a window in a far corner of the big house; it was the old lady whispering.

"Please," she said again, waving a skeletal finger toward the massive armoire. It took a few more languid waves before I understood that she wanted me to retrieve something from the ornate antique cabinet. She shook her head no until I retrieved a box carved of rosewood and inlaid with lapus lazuli. She beckoned for me to bring the box to her. With some effort, she removed a thin gold chain from around her neck and handed it to me. A small key was threaded onto the chain. She gestured and I used the key to open the box. All it held was a Certificado de Nacimiento, a birth certificate, from El Hospital Virgen de las Nieves in Granada dated twenty-nine years ago.

"Is this Tomás's?"

She nodded.

The *Nombre del Padre,* father's name, was left blank. In the space for *Nombre del Madre* a long name was carefully printed. Amid the *y*s and *de*s was the name ROSA.

Doña Carlota's eyes had drifted shut. I raised my voice to ask her,

"Was your friend Rosa Tomás's grandmother? Great-grandmother?" When she didn't answer, I raised my voice higher and asked the only important question, "Is Tomás *gitano*?"

She screwed her eyes shut more tightly like a dreamer clinging to a dream, resisting being awakened. Though her eyes didn't open, they relaxed. Doña Carlota sighed, nodded yes, then fell into a sleep heavy as death.

Chapter Thirty-seven

I never had any choice about what to do with the truth Doña Carlota gave me. Tomás was an addiction. I craved him at a cellular level. I was a junkie who'd been clean for months only because I didn't have money. The instant I had the means to procure my drug, I set about trying to make a connection. Doña Carlota's truth was my means. I now had what Tomás desired most: proof of his authenticity.

But I wanted more. I wanted Tomás's entire story. Names, dates, places. I called the old lady repeatedly. Each time Teófilo answered and said he would ask La Doña if she felt up to speaking on the phone. Sometimes he would return to inform me that she was under the weather and would return my call when she felt better. Other times, he would not come back at all. I drove up to Santa Fe twice and knocked on the door guarded by Santiago but no one answered. I wanted more, but I had enough, enough of the story to accomplish what needed accomplishing.

Up until the moment when Doña Carlota told me her secret, I had been dreading the high point of the New Mexico flamenco calendar, the Flamenco Festival Internacional. Instead of a celebration the festival that year would present only limitless humiliation. Everyone would know that I was the pathetic third leg of a triangle, the one who'd been abandoned by her lover, betrayed by her best friend. Armed with Doña Carlota's secret, I had reason to endure the festival. She had given me another chance with Tomás. But only if I learned enough to be able to make full use of what information I did have, and the festival was nothing if not a place to learn. I was bolstered further when Alma informed me that I had been selected as one of the few locals to teach at that year's festival. That honor would deflect some of the pity certain to rain down on me.

In the weeks leading up to the festival, I prepared myself as best I could. Once again I told Leslie that I would be too busy to keep our regular therapy appointment. She answered that with the festival coming up I needed to see her more, not less, or all the work we had done would be lost. I told her I would think about it. Instead, I stopped taking the pills she'd prescribed, stopped returning her calls, and threw myself into preparing for the classes I would be teaching.

A week before the festival started, the fires that had been raging out of control in southern Colorado started creeping farther south. The smell of scorched newspaper hung in the air. Four firefighters had already been killed and still the fires moved down. On the morning of the opening, the Archbishop of Santa Fe announced that he would say a novena to lead all the citizens of New Mexico in prayers for the rain needed to save our state. I prayed for the strength to face the flamenco community. Then, that night, armed with the power of my secret, the history that only I knew, I marched across campus toward Rodey Theater, where the Carmen Amaya documentary was to be shown. As I neared the theater, I slowed my pace. I dawdled in the shadows until everyone had entered and the lights dimmed. After the film started, I slipped in unnoticed and found a seat near the back.

Carmen Amaya in motion was the revelation and exultation I had expected. Then came the revelation I had not expected, the bomb that blew me out of the theater and into the grip of memory: Didi was coming home. I fled the theater and spent the rest of the night driving Route 66. I hurtled west to east. From the future to the past. From the moment that would define my future—when I learned Didi was returning—all the way back to the moment that had defined my past—that day in the oncologist's office when I'd first met her.

The new day was leaching the brilliance from the neon lights along Albuquerque's stretch of Route 66 when I realized I had figured nothing out. It was only a few hours until I taught my first class and I was already exhausted.

Chapter Thirty-eight

Before I even reached the Flamenco Academy a river of sound cascaded out, surging against my body. Classes were in full swing. A banner above the academy announced: 16TH FLAMENCO FESTIVAL INTERNACIONAL BIENVENIDO! TONIGHT! OFELIA AT THE KIMO! My eyes stung from lack of sleep and forest fire smoke. Fortunately, I didn't run into anyone I knew.

The entire gym had been taken over for the festival. Every room held a class already in session. Each one presented not just a different turn of the flamenco kaleidoscope but twists on my own personal history with *el arte* as well. The first open doorway framed a famous Gypsy guitarist playing a *bulerías* for an advanced class. He filled the hall with crystalline *falsetas,* melodies, that floated above a raw, driving rhythm. He finished and a student asked, "Did you start with a D minor chord?"

The guitarist shrugged and answered in Spanish, "If you say so."

The class laughed. Reading music, rehearsing, even knowing the names of the chords was antithetical to the renegade Gypsy spirit. I wanted to warn the laughing students that beneath that spontaneous, untutored surface lurked a *Titanic*-crushing iceberg of hard work.

A rain of silver notes poured from the next classroom, where a teacher demonstrated the maligned art of castanets. Clacking two pieces of wood together, she rained intricate rhythms down on her students that dissolved the snags of their stuttering mistakes.

The main studio, once a gym where past generations of Lobos shot basketballs and did jumping jacks, had been taken over by *los pequeñitos,* kids, being taught by sweet Blanca. A couple dozen little girls in puffy pastel dresses stamped their black patent leather Mary Janes on the academy's wooden floor. The loudest stompers, though, were the three little boys in the class.

Blanca caught sight of me and came over to the door, circling her hands and yelling behind her as she walked, "*Bueno, niños!* Let's practice our hands. Come on, let me see those snakes twining around."

"Rae, how are you doing?"

"Fine." Leslie had told me some old hippie saying about how nine times out of ten when someone says they're fine, it stands for Fucked-up, Insecure, Neurotic, and I can't remember what the *e* was supposed to mean. I was not the one in ten who actually was fine.

"Really?" She rubbed the side of my arm in a warm, comforting way that made tears come to my eyes. "I can't believe Alma did that. You know, invited . . . her."

She didn't say Didi's name. She didn't have to. It was all there in her face, all that I dreaded: sympathy, concern, pity. Of everything Didi had done, this might be the worst, making me an object of pity.

I stepped away and, struggling to inject a note of peppiness into my voice, said, "Hey, your class is starting to revolt."

The boys had turned their twining snakes into rattlers bent on striking the shrieking girls.

"*Ay! Muchachos!*" Blanca rushed to stop the boys' rattler attacks. She pressed the boys' fingers together so that they wouldn't fan out in a way that flamenco purists considered lethally feminine. She pushed their little chests out and instructed, "*Muy macho.*"

The little boys hardened their tender mouths, thrust out puny chests. I imagined Doña Carlota instructing Tomás, pushing his spindly chest out, resetting his heart so that it beat only to flamenco's pulse and, for just a second, flamenco did seem like something carried in the blood, a disease that no one can be responsible for. I wondered if it was irresponsible for me to step into a classroom and pass the infection on to another group of innocents.

I left and headed for the new addition, the Flamenco Academy itself. I shoved the doors open and there was Doña Carlota, staring down at me from the portrait that would be hanging at the entrance to the academy she had started long after I was gone and forgotten. So what if I knew her secrets? Some version of the truth? Queens always shared secrets with handmaidens because no one ever remembered the handmaidens. I lowered my eyes and I hurried on.

I was late. I entered the studio with the high ceilings and honey-dipped floors where my engagement with flamenco had started. I felt nearly as fraudulent as I had that very first day. The class was big: several dozen students. I heard accents from all over the country as well as one that sounded Germanic, maybe Swedish. All my students were female, teens to late fifties, a comfortable mix of young and old, slender and plump, hip and dowdy. I was grateful that Alma had given me a beginner class. I wasn't up to proving myself to a bunch of flamenco hotshots. In fact, I no longer felt up to flamenco at all.

I went around the room. The students introduced themselves and told why they were there taking their first flamenco class. They had the usual assortment of reasons: exercise, love the flamenco beat, want to try something different. I would never have admitted in my first class why I was there, that I was sick with love and thought flamenco held the cure.

I stamped my feet, warmed up with a few quick combinations. In the mirror I watched mouths fall open and friends turn to each other, to exchange expressions of amazement. I remembered then how astounding the rhythms that had become as automatic as breathing to me had been the first time I'd seen them demonstrated by Doña Carlota.

"I'm sure we'll be doing that by the end of the festival," a girl with multiple piercings said sarcastically, her tongue stud flashing as she opened her mouth to laugh.

"That and so much more," I joked back. I stopped and drew myself up into the tall, proud flamenco *postura*. "Let's warm up those feet." I demonstrated a basic heel-toe stamp. The class imitated it with a few tentative taps.

"No, no, no!" I silenced the weak stamping with a wave. "Not this." I mocked the puny taps with a few inaudible heel pats. "This!" I hammered the floor. Everything I had learned at the Flamenco Academy poured back into my head. I opened my mouth and knowledge ran out. "Aim for a place one inch *beneath* the floor. If you're going to make a mistake in flamenco, make a *loud* mistake! Make *your* mistake! *Y otra vez!* Try it again! *Tacón! Tacón!*" I pounded my heel, showing both the dance and the language it had to be taught in. *"Y punta!"* I shifted between the heel and toe. "Louder! Okay, twice with each foot! Louder!"

A clattering chaos echoed back to me.

"Now this!" I demonstrated the basic heel-toe combination. "Start with a *golpe*! *Golpe!* Stamp! Tap! Tap! Stamp! *Y UNO! Dos. Tres. UNO! Dos. Tres. UNO!*"

Behind me, the class stamped their feet. They felt the first intimations of what it was to turn your body into a machine that produced rhythm. All the students were staring at their feet as if their toes were on fire. I passed among them, tapping each woman under her chin, forcing her head up.

"*Cabeza! Arriba!* Keep those heads up! *Cuerpo!* Bodies up!"

The heads went up and we began again. Then, without their eyes telling their feet what to do, flamenco went where it was supposed to go, straight into the heart. The smiles of apology for all the mistakes their feet were making disappeared as the class tried to echo the beat I clapped out.

"*Y los brazos!*" I held my arms in a circle in front of me.

"*Fuerte! Fuerte!* Strong!" I patrolled the class, stiffening arms, making them stake out claims to the space around them. "No bellyache arms!" I ordered a student with the profile of an Aztec princess, just as Doña Carlota had when she'd corrected my own tentative, retracted arms. The student's arms rose, making perfect, sweet dimples appear at the back of her shoulders.

The class concentrated on their arms and the foot stamping became feeble and unfocused. I waved my arms. "Stop! Stop! I can't stand the sound of those sick kitten paws! Now, let me hear those feet!"

They picked up the volume and I spoke louder in order to be heard above the fumble-footed noise. "Flamenco is not the fox-trot! There is no box step in flamenco!" When all my students were gazing ahead, pounding out whatever beat they could manage, I announced, "*Al frente!*" pointed forward, and started walking, all the while keeping the beat with raised arms. The addition of bipedal locomotion threw the students into rictuses of concentration. They all looked as if they were adding long columns of numbers in their heads. It was exactly how I had looked my first class.

Wanting to keep this momentum going, I barked at them like a drill instructor. "Flamenco is all about showing what's inside of you! Telling the truth! The First Commandment of flamenco is, *Dame la verdad!* Who can tell us what that means?"

The Aztec princess shouted out, "Give me the truth!"

"*Bueno!* Give me the truth! Give it to me, ladies! Stamp! Come on!

Make some noise! You're not in Kansas anymore! This isn't Barbie World! Don't hide those unpleasant feelings! Use them! What makes you mad? Who in here is mad?"

I studied the students behind me in the mirror. Nobody responded.

"Nobody? Nobody is mad? How is this possible?" This both astonished and annoyed me to a degree far out of proportion to the instructional question I had posed. It suddenly seemed desperately urgent to wring the truth from this collection of novices. In the mirror, I caught the eye of a sun-spotted lady visiting from Tucson and demanded, "Anybody in here work for a big man who takes all the credit while you do all the work?" The lady lifted her head and started stamping her feet.

I scanned the rest of the group. "Any of you in here work three times as hard as your jerk of a boss and make one-third his salary?" Smiles of recognition played across several faces and the tempo picked up. "When you get that shitty little basket of flowers on Secretaries Day, do you want to shove it up his fat ass?" The smiles turned to grins. "Okay! You *are* mad. Dance that!"

I studied the rest of the students. Figuring out how to get them to admit their anger seemed like the most important thing I'd ever done in my life. I zoomed in on the girl with the tongue stud and asked, "When you turn on the television and realize your country is an oil oligarchy, does that make you mad?" Her many piercings caught the overhead light as she lifted her head and hammered the hardwood.

I caught a couple of helmet-haired students who'd said they were from Dallas exchanging eye rolls and asked them, "Are you sick and tired of liberals with their hackneyed, knee-jerk idiocies always blaming America for everything that's wrong in the world? Then pound the ground!"

I zeroed in on a clump of Latinas. "Does it annoy you that you paid good money for this class and now you've got some skinny gringa standing up here yelling at you? Are you totally sick of Anglos appropriating every scrap of your culture? Okay, show me you're pissed off!" They smiled good-naturedly even as their feet picked up volume.

I spotted a shy girl trying to avoid eye contact and asked, "Does anyone in here ever get sick of people always telling you to smile? To speak up? Speak out? Whatever? Do you think there is entirely too much speaking up and out? Do you wish people would just shut up and leave you alone?"

The girl kept her eyes on the ground, but I could hear her feet and feel the breeze from her whirling skirt as she joined in.

"Who in here is mad?" I asked, because there was still one person in the studio who was not giving the truth. The answer sprang from my feet, from my gut. It leapt from every muscle fiber in my body. My body was telling me the truth, delivering it in a thundering sermon that even I could not ignore.

"Who in here is mad?"

I smashed the floor with my answer: Me. I was mad. I had to dance it and see it in the mirror in front of me before I could accept its immensity. Rage leached out of my bones and poured into my feet. I thought of all the years I had wasted being a handmaiden and my foot came down like an anvil. My fury was not for Didi, Doña Carlota, Tomás, my mother. My fury was for me. For telling everyone else's story but my own.

I stamped harder. I stamped so hard a shimmer of light of the sort that announces a migraine haloed my sight. A radiant nimbus oscillated around my reflection in the mirror, making it hard for me to recognize the savage dancer there, striking sparks of fire with her blazing footwork, the intensity of her passion. I felt disembodied, possessed. Behind me, the class teetered to a halt, then froze watching me, jaws hanging open.

"*It burns the blood like powdered glass . . . it exhausts, rejects all the sweet geometry we understand . . . it shatters styles.*" I felt the whisper of Didi's breath against my ear just as I had when she'd quoted Lorca's definition of *duende* to me in the hidden park.

I was possessed and I was exhausted. I had forsaken sweet geometry. I stopped, planted myself on the earth, hurled my arms to the right, then the left. I shook off both demons and angels. I regained control of myself, and with my next word I erased all that had gone before and opened a blank page upon which to begin once more: "*Y!*" And.

I stopped. The class gathered behind me, ready to follow wherever I led, and I began again.

"*Fuerte! Brazos! Cuerpo! Arriba! Cabeza! Arriba!*" We stormed across the floor, each student staking an emphatic claim to every inch we advanced. For just a minute, two at the most, all the heels hit the beat exactly in time with mine and we became one tribe, a tribe of wild, clacking, frenzied girls making a sound louder and more beautiful than any sound they had ever dreamed of making on their own.

At the end of class, I rushed from the Flamenco Academy, still dripping with sweat. The one, true gospel of flamenco that I had just preached more to myself than to my students still thundered in my blood: *Fuerte! Cuerpo! Arriba! Cabeza! Arriba! Strong! Body! Up! Head! Up!* I paused in front of the looming portrait of Doña Carlota. Then I hoisted my head as high as it would go and settled it decisively upon my ramrod of a spine. I raised my middle digit and I shot Doña Carlota a big, fat bird.

Chapter Thirty-nine

I strode out of the Flamenco Academy, believing that my moment of *duende* had transformed me, that I was through with being a handmaiden. I would serve no one else but myself. I would obey no one else's desires but my own. When I confronted the banner outside the gym announcing Didi's performance at the KiMo that night, however, I was stunned to discover that I could no longer identify what I really wanted. My first thought was that, of course, I didn't want to see Didi. I never wanted to see or speak to her again. But, in the past, I had always made a point of seeing every performance during the festival. If I stayed away, wouldn't Didi still be controlling my life? In the end, I went. I went to prove to myself that I could. That I could sit in an audience and watch Didi. Just so long as I didn't have to speak to her. That was the bargain I struck with myself.

The scorched air was still hot that evening as I walked down Central Avenue toward the KiMo Theatre. It was as if the forest fire smoke had sealed the day's heat into the city, not allowing it to cool off as Albuquerque usually did once the sun went down. Lightning sliced through the sky above the West Mesa, a summer electrical storm of the sort that promised but almost never yielded rain.

The exterior of the theater with its thunderbirds and zias elaborately painted in shades of gold and blue glittered beneath the lights of a marquee that spelled out OFELIA. The KiMo was a twenties fantasy collision of art deco and pueblo style where residents once watched vaudeville, then the new talkies. The only tickets left for Didi's show were in the balcony, which is exactly where I wanted to be. I bought one and, for the second night in a row, was grateful to be late and entering a theater where the houselights had already been dimmed. The stairs leading up to the balcony were lined with panoramic murals. Each panel depicted one of the

mythical Seven Cities of Cíbola, the Cities of Gold that had lured the conquistadors ever farther north, all the way up to the Spaniards' last frontier
outposts on the Camino Real: the city they named after El Duque de Al-
burquerque; Santa Fe, the city of Holy Faith; Truchas; Peñasco; Taos.

In the balcony, air vents were disguised as Navajo rugs and chande-
liers as war drums and death canoes. Ceiling beams, textured to look like
logs, were painted with dance and hunt scenes. Rows of garlanded long-
horn steer skulls with amber eyes glowing eerily stared down at me. In
their dim light, I found my row and felt my way to a seat, stumbling over
a backpack.

"Sorry," a young woman, her hair a pre-Raphaelite cloud in the darkness, whispered to me, shoving the book-anchored pack out of my way as
I took the empty seat next to her. I recognized her from one of the classes
I had substitute taught. In the reflection of the stage lights her face
seemed as if it had been printed that very morning. A book almost finished but never opened. She'd never had a class with Didi. Might not have
ever seen the disdain in which Didi was held by those of the *flamenco
puro* school who considered the academy's biggest star a complete fraud.
To her, Didi was Ofelia and Ofelia was famous.

Onstage, hundreds of votive candles flickered in amber and red holders on and around an altar. Arrayed around the altar were dozens of vases
filled with roses from the pastel/sunset color group. Both the roses and the
candles were backdrops to the stool where Ofelia/Didi would sit. It was
draped with a black shawl, a genuine *mantón* from Madrid with a fringe
that shimmied in air currents no one else was sensitive enough to feel.

The house was packed with Didi's obsessive fans, most of whom
couldn't have cared less about flamenco and how pure or impure Didi
was. Virtually all were female, their faces frozen into expectant expressions of adoration that Nancy Reagan could have learned from. Then, before I even registered why, my heart lurched. It was him—Tomás—sitting
half a dozen rows ahead. I could tell, just from the tilt of his shoulders, the
dark curl of his hair. Of course he would be here. Then he turned. It was a
student. Someone who looked the way he had all those years ago when
I'd fallen in love with him at first sight. I pressed back into my seat, my
heart still pounding, scrambling to reclaim the righteous anger that had
steeled me earlier in the day. But when a team of five guitarists filed onstage, my breath clutched again. They were led by old-time *gitano* flamenco legend Diego Herredia. Will was among them. Tomás was not. I

exhaled. The crowd of hardcore *aficionados* pounded their palms together for Diego. Nearly eighty, he padded slowly to the straight-backed chair where his instrument waited. His double-knit pants, pulled up a little too high, cradled the low-slung lobes of his old-man's buttocks. He took his seat, pants hiking up still farther, exposing garters holding up black socks.

The four other guitarists followed his lead. Softly, though with great power, they began playing an *alegrías*. The low undercurrent of sophisticated chatter stopped cold as every member of the audience was connected into the rhythm machine that is flamenco. With five great guitarists playing, it was impossible to resist. Didi knew what she was doing. After this warm-up, she could have come out and recited "Little Jack Horner" and enthralled. Plus, Diego's old-time playing would sanctify the bleedings of her suburban girl heart with enough flamenco authenticity to placate the purists.

The guitars chimed and pealed with a silvery clarity, rhythms piling on top of one another, frilled and accented by the loveliest *falsetas* imaginable. And then Didi entered. In an instant, I saw that she had become who she'd been transforming herself into from long before the day we'd met. All the tiny homages and lifts from all the one-name goddesses were there, Madonna's overamped physicality, Cher's no-shit subversiveness, Marilyn's vulnerability: they had all come together in the persona she presented. Even her dancing had gelled. It was flamenco, but mixed with enough hip-hop, African, and belly dancing to be something else entirely. Something that couldn't be graded on flamenco's merciless scale were she was destined to fall short. She had shattered flamenco time, she was operating outside of *el compás* even as she made every flamenco fantasy work for her. She was Hispanic, Jewish, Gypsy. Mostly, though, she was what all the legends aspired to: she was life on the edge. She was the worst bad girl going. She would shoot heroin, drown in *aguardiente;* she would kill herself. And she would do it all to present her lucky audience with one moment of eternity. Out of time, off the beat, it didn't matter, she had the quality she'd had from the first moment I saw her in the oncologist's office: you couldn't take your eyes off of her. Even if she had ruined your life, stolen the one person you'd ever loved, chewed you up and spit you out, even then, you could not take your eyes off of her.

A long, susurrous "O!" sighed through the theater like a mammoth exhalation. Ofelia was in the house. She was magnificent in a long dress of red lace worthy of Bob Mackie that had the right heft for dancing, yet turned diaphanous when lighted from the back. Onto her short hair, she'd woven a hairdo of braids and spit curls with a black lace mantilla floating down from the high stake of a carved tortoise-shell comb driven into the crown of braids. She *was* the flamenco poet.

Diego watched Didi's every move. Clearly from the old school, he was there to serve Ofelia. Leading the others, he softened his playing until his thumbnail stroked a deep, rich major chord that became a buzz caressing the audience's collective frontal lobe, preparing them to hear the flamenco poet speak.

"Hello, New Mexico, *mi Tierra del Encanto,* land of my birth, land of my heart, land of my enchantment." She punctuated her greeting with a fiery *zapateado.* The footwork elicited a wave of applause and *óles.* She clapped a rhythm that the initiates in the crowd were delighted to pick up and turn into an *alegrías* that became a roar of applause. A deep cannonade of thunder from outside the theater interrupted the clapping. Didi raised her arms to silence the audience and we all heard the staccato patter of a heavy rain. Didi turned her palms up and grinned as if she had ordered the downpour to accompany her.

Then, snapping out a volley of *pitos* syncopated with the sound of the deluge, she wondered in a way that almost seemed idle, "What is the right poem for you tonight?" A great settling swept through the hall as audience members snuggled, satisfied, into their seats, the rain we had prayed for was falling, and Ofelia was searching for *exactly* the right piece for *exactly* this night for *exactly* us. Even I, who knew, forgot that her shows were as canned as Wayne Newton's, that she'd been making set lists for years, just like one of the bands she'd spent her teens groupieing.

In spite of my resolution not to allow Didi to dictate one more second of my life, I scooted forward to the edge of my seat, ready to leave if she performed any of the pieces that had come from our shared history. Nothing about fathers dying, young girls yearning. I wasn't ready for that, though I wasn't ready for what she eventually did read either.

"In flamenco the holiest of the many song forms is one called the *saeta,* the arrow. *Saetas* are sung during Holy Week in Sevilla to celebrate the passion of Christ."

I hated the way she pronounced Sevilla, Sah-BEE-ya. Hated hearing a girl who had once devoted her life to the Strokes, whose father was Mort Steinberg, Jewish hipster, speak so rapturously about the passion of Christ. I glanced down the aisle. It was clotted with the rapt figures of acolytes hunched forward, waiting like baby birds to be fed from the mouth of experience.

Reading the cues like the master accompanist he was, Diego matched Didi's tricked-up theatrics with a showy arpeggio, a gaudy gush of notes. He squinted up into the spotlights, his eyes watery, vulnerable.

"I call this poem 'Secret Park.'"

I had to leave, but Didi had already shot the arrow. It found its mark and staked me to my seat. As Didi read, my perception of her fractured into black spit curls, red lips, tent of black mantilla all melted away into the smell of summer and the hunger of waiting.

> *My kiss is summer*
> *Your kiss is cut watermelon*
> *Sprinklers click.*
> *A shower every seventeen seconds.*
> *Seventeen years.*

> *Waiting for night.*
> *Waiting for the moon.*
> *Waiting for the breeze.*
> *Waiting for owl screech.*
> *Waiting for earth warmth.*
>   *Below.*
> *I am waiting for heaven cool.*
>   *Above.*
> *Waiting for your whisper.*
> *Waiting for your touch.*
> *Waiting for a breeze.*
> *Waiting for a moon.*
> *Waiting for night.*
> *Waiting for her.*

Her? Did I really hear Didi whisper "Cyndi Rae" into the microphone, a lapping of syllables so gentle they were lost in the wild applause? Was she really searching the crowd trying to find me?

Onstage, Didi raised her arms like a charismatic Christian. A gleam caught the spotlight and I noticed the silver bracelet made of two panthers twining together that had been hidden beneath the sleeve of her dress. The sight of the blood-sister bracelet caught me off guard for just one moment. But one moment was all Didi ever needed.

"I dedicate that poem to my pale twin, the light I shadowed, the ray I darkened. I've come home to you, Rae-rae. Are you here? Is she here? You all know who I mean. Cyndi Rae Hrncir, is my blood sister here tonight?"

Why did it take me one frozen moment before I could believe that Didi would do the unbelievable? When had she ever done anything else? I lurched from my seat. The backpacks were boulders blocking my path. Not everyone in the theater knew our story. But everyone wasn't required, just the handful of students, of devotees, of fans who spotted me and started up a jungle telegram of *pitos,* fingers snapping as loud as the crack of a bullwhip. Loud enough to call Didi's attention to the balcony.

"She's here? You're here, my pale twin?" She visored her eyes with her hand, squinted up into the balcony, and implored. "Please, just for one moment, could we have the houselights?"

The lights came up. Didi followed the wave of heads turning in my direction and caught me as I stumbled into the aisle. She was already heading to the edge of the stage as I hurtled down the stairs, four centuries of New Mexican history whizzing past as I raced for escape. The unexpected downpour had turned the water-sheeted glass doors at the front of the theater into an aquarium. In the second I paused before shoving the doors open, a frantic rap of *claves* hammered my way.

The rain, smelling of ash, of doused fires, drenched me. I ran for the truck, plucking keys from my pocket even as I trampled past gutters rushing with muddy water. In my haste and agitation, I fumbled the rain-slicked keys and dropped them into a puddle half a block from the truck. I bent to fish them out and when I straightened up, Didi stood in front of me. Rain beaded up and rolled off her pancake makeup in streams. Mascara coursed down her face as if she'd been crying. Up close, without the stage lights, she was haggard and hollow-eyed. Her irises were a sapphire thread around the black fish egg of her dilated pupil.

"Rae-rae." She held her arms open to me and said my name as if it were a benediction that only she could offer. "You came! I knew you'd come! Oh, Rae, my Rae." Every sob and blubber outraged me. She lunged forward and draped herself on me. "Rae, I am so sorry. I fucked up. I am so sorry. I want to spend the rest of our lives making it up to you. Rae, I miss you so much. Nothing in my life is—"

"You're dripping on me." My voice was frozen acid, cold and caustic enough to momentarily dry her up.

She detached herself. "Rae, please, you're all I have. We're all each other has. It was you that I loved. You're the one I wanted. I'm sorry. I made a mistake."

Though I'd sworn I wouldn't, wouldn't ever speak to her again, the words flew out of my mouth. " 'Mistake'? A 'mistake' is using the wrong fork at dinner. Stealing your best friend's lover goes way beyond 'mistake.' "

"Rae. Please." Didi grabbed my arm and made me look at her. Beneath the makeup, she was destroyed. It had started long ago, but not being around her for more than a year forced me to really see Didi. Her teeth were decalcifying, turning the twilight gray that only decades of bulimia can bring on. I tried to focus on her teeth, but my gaze was drawn to her omnivorous eyes. "I am killing myself, I'm so eaten up with guilt at what I've done. Literally, I want to die. I'm sorry, Rae, I will do anything to show you how sorry I am."

"You think confession redeems everything. You think you can get up onstage and parade your destroyed life and the lives around you that you destroyed and be granted absolution on account of your 'honesty.' Fuck honesty, bitch. Try being a decent human being."

"Rae, we have to talk."

"Not in this lifetime. Could you, please, just get out of my life."

"Rae, it's *our* life. You have to know that. Rae, I never wanted him."

Him. Suddenly, I wasn't angry, wasn't hurt, wasn't jealous, I was just tired. Tired because that ridiculous three-letter pronoun had only one antecedent in my life. Tired because it still had the power to bleed me white, to make me stop and listen.

"It was you I wanted, Rae. It's always been you, my pale angel twin."

"Jesus, Didi, save the dark, tortured sexuality horseshit for your fans. I watched you invent that crap."

"Okay, okay, Rae." Stunned to hear me, her doormat, talking back, Didi cooed in a hostage negotiator voice. It pleased me that she recognized what an unstable compound, what a vial of nitroglycerin, I had become. For once, I was the high-strung one who had to be catered to.

"Just, just, do me a favor. Do one thing for me?" She waited to see if I would blow. I allowed her to continue. "Come to where I'm staying. You know the place on the golf course? Come tonight. I've got an early flight to D.C. tomorrow, big deal at the Kennedy Center with Joaquín Cortés and that whole—"

I squinted in irritation, astonished at the limitless depths of her narcissism, even now dropping names, expecting me to cheer her success. "I don't care," I said, amazed that I was telling the truth. My new, imperious manner worked miracles.

"You're right. You're right. Just come, okay? Please? You saved me, Rae. From the very first, from that day in the doctor's office, you were what pulled me through. I . . . I'm lost without you." A sob as theatrical as her statement caught in her throat and I shook my head in disgust. The handmaiden didn't live here anymore.

She switched off the dramatics and added dryly, "I know you don't owe me anything anymore, but—"

"'Anymore'? Didi, I *never* owed you anything."

"You have a right to feel that way."

"I have to leave."

"No!" She clawed at my sleeve as I opened the door of the truck. "You have to come, Rae, please. We have to talk. Please, oh God, please. I can't do this without you."

"Do what?" I let a homicidal level of irritation curdle my voice.

"Any of this. Rae, I'm not kidding. If you don't come tonight—" She stopped abruptly. When she next spoke, her voice was utterly scrubbed of emotion and she stated plain as if she were explaining gravity, "You have to come tonight."

I jerked my arm out of her grasp. "You will never tell me what I have to do again."

Didi stood in the red glow of my back-up lights, a smeared palette of red and black. Someone from the entourage ran up holding out a poncho and wrapped the little diva in it. It was clear from the acolyte's frantic gestures toward the theater that Didi's adoring public clamored for her. Didi remained immobile, the poncho draped over her like the Madonna playing out a pietà moment. Rain trickled down her sorrowing face, her arms held out in front as if the crucified Christ had just been removed from them.

The acolyte led Didi back to the theater. I was certain that a froth of whispers was already whipping through the auditorium, each worshipful fan concocting another morsel to add to the cocktail of the most intoxicating performance any of them had ever consumed. The myth of their drenched idol, the sodden, suffering Madonna, would grow. The wire services might pick up whatever item the local reviewer wrote about Didi's dramatic disappearance. In the end, she would probably get some national ink out of it.

Didi had won again.

My windshield was spangled with cottonwood leaves blown across it by the rainstorm. Each tender green leaf was a heart pressing against the glass. I flipped on the wipers. The blades shoved the leaves aside, then beat them to a chartreuse pulp.

Chapter Forty

I don't know how long I sat drinking on the West Mesa. Long enough to watch several carloads of teens get drunk, throw up, and leave me alone with the end of an extremely bad night. Long enough to wish I could claw out every single chip Didi had embedded in my brain. Long enough to realize that the peach daiquiris in a can that I was pouring down my throat as fast as I could tasted like hair conditioner and weren't fuzzing the hideous evening out. They were bringing it into sharper focus. The memory I most wanted to derail, yet returned to obsessively, was her saying *If you don't come tonight—*

"If I don't come tonight *what,* bitch?" I whispered to the black velvet painting outside my windshield. I didn't have to see the petroglyphs to know they were there, all those mysterious squiggles Didi and I had squatted among as she pledged to always have my back. "You'll kill yourself?" It was a comfort to spit out the words caroming inside my brain. To inject as much mocking scorn as I could into them. Didi would never kill herself. That would be one performance she absolutely wouldn't miss. That certainty was met with a crushing in my chest as a hard reality squeezed into me: If Didi kills herself, she will own you for the rest of your life. I could not allow that to happen. The one thing I absolutely had to do was to root Didi out of my life once and for all.

I headed back into town. Even the bars had closed by the time I drove down Central going east, going back in time, back to the university. Of course, Didi was staying at the Sculpture Garden, where all the visiting luminaries were lodged. I assumed that Didi, the star of that night, was even occupying the same bungalow as Guitos had. I parked and made my way through the grounds. The sculptures, charming during the day, were menacing at night. In the dark, the giant grasshoppers became ravenous predators from the Age of the Dinosaurs, the nail clippers weapons of destruction. The stone angels guarding the guest cottage were not the beneficent protectors they had been in daylight. They were stern, winged creatures on missions of revenge and atonement.

I stood for a moment beneath their rigid gaze and searched the bungalow on the other side of the gate. Not a single light was on. She was asleep. I was about to turn and leave when a small bubble of aggrieved righteousness burst inside of me. Why the hell was I skulking around, worried about disturbing Didi's precious sleep? How many nights of sleep had she cost me? More than she could, more than she *would* ever pay, but at least I could claim a few hours of slumber from her. Buoyed up, I unlatched the gate, stepped up to the door, and pounded heavily on it. When there was no answer, I pounded louder. I didn't care, I *hoped* I would rouse Didi from whatever substance-abused slumber or compromising sexual snarl she might have been entangled in. I pounded again, hard enough to rattle the curtained window at the door. I suppose I knew the door would be unlocked. That was so typically Didi, the unlocked door, the compromise waiting to be made.

The smell of leather that greeted me when Guitos occupied this bungalow had been replaced by the fragrance of candles and old roses. But there was another odor, deeply female, an estrous funk that forced an intimacy upon me I did not want. It was Didi's smell and I recoiled from it. I no longer wanted to wake her, engage her. In her own megalomaniacal way, by manipulating me into coming to her, Didi had won again. A laptop featuring Frida Kahlo's self-portrait as the screen saver provided what dim light there was. The panther bracelet gleamed in its glow. The bracelet was on my wrist before I had time to understand that the score between us would never be even. It didn't matter—an atavistic urge to take something, anything from her drove me to steal it. If I hadn't taken the bracelet, though, I wouldn't have moved into position to see her, a sliver of her anyway, through the bedroom door opened just a crack.

She was crumpled on the bed. In the dim glow of a small bedside lamp her face was bluish at the lips, pale as the sheets. Her body was floppy, boneless when I shook her. The creak of the bedsprings thundered in my head when I sat beside her. The sound subsided as I listened for breathing and heard only my own fractured gasps. Did I hesitate one second, two, three? It doesn't matter, I hesitated. For that speck of time, I willed her dead.

Then I pinched her nostrils, sealed her mouth shut with my own, and breathed. Two breaths and fifteen pumps a couple of inches below the nipples. I pressed the heels of my hands on her chest. The bed sagged beneath the pressure. I listened for breathing and wanted to hear it. I put my lips on hers and pushed air into her lungs. Tilted my ear to her face and felt for the dew of her respiration. Nothing came. Each breath I forced into her was a pact I didn't want to make. Every molecule of oxygen expelled a different accusation, a different memory.

I pressed my lips against Didi's and puffed air into her mouth again. They warmed beneath my own. A weak, hiccuping sigh formed either in her chest or in my imagination, my heart was thudding too loudly to tell.

"Didi, it's me, Rae," I whispered. "Breathe, okay?"

She didn't respond. Her chest didn't rise. It didn't move until, with my whole will, I breathed life into her mouth. I wanted her to live. Only then did her chest stutter, the muscles flinching and rippling. Her bluish lips brightened to a sickly mauve. She coughed, vomited, coughed. Breathed. I grabbed the phone, punched in 911, yelled between breaths. Didi inhaled. Didi exhaled. Minutes later, bullets of light strafed the room. A couple of EMT guys pushed me aside. While one of them worked on her, the other tucked his head to one side and spoke into the microphone on his shoulder. In answer to staticky questions about "substances," he picked empty bottles off the floor and read the labels out loud.

Shortly thereafter, a policeman barged in and asked me some questions. It took me a while to realize that he was trying to decide whether or not to arrest me. Whether or not I was a dealer or a murderer. He took my name and number and told me to make myself available. One of the techs brought in a gurney. They lifted Didi onto it, then slid her into the ambulance smooth as a loaf of bread going into the oven.

It was light by the time I walked back to the truck. Inside, I reached for the gear shift and the panther bracelet slid down my wrist onto my hand. The bracelet was all wrong on me. The panthers looked as if they were snaking around a fat, white radish, instead of the slender, tea-colored wrist they belonged on. I had believed I could hack Didi out of my life like an overgrowth of kudzu. Yet I now felt the twist of the vines twining about me more strongly than ever. They curled around my lungs and squeezed out the oxygen like a python suffocating its prey.

I touched the panthers on the bracelet, woven together until they were one animal, claw flowing into shoulder, tail into haunch, mouths breathing the same breath. I had the thought then that, maybe, the only thing keeping me upright all those years had been the vines.

Chapter Forty-one

I stood at the door of her room and discovered Didi's mother lying, asleep, in the bed. For a split second, Didi looked exactly like Mrs. Steinberg after Mr. Steinberg had died, pale, slack, a person haunting a body rather than inhabiting it. Probably exactly how Didi would look when she was old. If she lived to become old.

She was a mess. Her cheek and pillowcase were streaked black from the charcoal slurry they'd pumped into her stomach. Her right eye flamed red where a blood vessel had burst when she was throwing up. Her nose was greasy, ringed in the K-Y Jelly used to thread a tube into her stomach.

Behind me in the hall, a family passed by talking loudly enough that they woke Didi. Her lids fluttered up, then she worked to bring me into focus. "Rae." She exhaled my name on an exhalation so long she might have been holding it for all the months since she'd seen me last.

I lifted one hand in a *How, paleface* greeting but didn't step one foot closer.

"Rae." Her voice was a whispery wreck, so soft that I had no choice but to move forward. She shrugged and gestured at herself, the tubes coming out of her nose, her veins. The preemptive strike. It was what she always did, whenever she'd let me down, whenever she didn't do something she'd said she would. She'd always start by neutralizing any complaint I might have by detailing all her current dramas and misfortunes. This time she mimed the strike simply by presenting her pitiful condition. "You saved my life."

Only after I willed you dead. "Don't talk, okay? Save your voice."

"I have to talk. Rae, I did a horrible thing. I wasn't as good a friend as I should have been, but I wasn't as bad as you think." She shook her head, then chastised herself. "Cut the bullshit. Cut the bullshit. Here's the truth: I didn't take Tomás from you because you never really had him. Neither of us ever had him. No one ever will ever have him because Tomás does not have himself." Didi echoed the exact words Guitos had spoken to me.

"Rae, he's waiting for you. Up north. He wants you, he needs you to come and see his village. That's the only way you'll understand." Her eyelids drooped, then popped back open. She lifted a hand with an IV taped to the back of it. "Look, I'm zoning out here. I don't know what they're putting in my soup, but I gotta make this short. Go. Just go to him. Anyone in town can tell you where his cabin is." Her eyes rolled up and she laughed. "I told you. Told you I'd get him for you and I did." She was drifting off again. "I got him for you. Go get him. The name of the village is . . ."

Her eyes closed and I considered leaving, simply walking out while I still had a choice because I knew, once she told me the name, the choice would be gone. I hoped she was asleep. Her eyes and mouth twitched as if she were struggling to open them. She didn't open her eyes, but the name sighed as if of its own accord: "La Viuda."

Chapter Forty-two

The first map I picked up didn't even have La Viuda marked on it. I found the tiny village on a hiker's map, wobbly with topographical markings. Desire, identify my own heart's true desire and let it guide me, that was what my moment of *duende* had taught me. Desire? Tomás? Yes, I wanted him. I shouldn't, but I did. It was late afternoon by the time I finished teaching my beginners class and set out. I roared north on I-25, bypassed Santa Fe, then just outside of Pojoaque, I turned off onto the back road to Chimayo.

In the space of one curve, long enough for the big trucks on the highway to disappear from view, I was sucked back four centuries into a time when not only the heart but the body of New Mexico belonged to Spain. Last night's storm had torn through the fertile valley, leaving limbs from elephant-barked cottonwoods and droopy Navajo willows lining the winding road. A usually placid stream raged alongside the road churning with battered cattails, uprooted tamarisks, and, washed in by the downpour far to the north, the blackened stumps of trees burned in the forest fires. The smell of those fires, doused by the heavy rains, hung over the valley like incense.

The road bent north away from the stream and evidence of the fires. An adobe estate with a coyote fence of lashed-together cedar saplings presided over acres of apple and plum trees. Yellow, oblong mailboxes with NEW MEXICAN printed on them stood guard beside each gate. The names on the mailboxes, on campaign posters lashed to trees, became biblical, portentous, medievally Spanish: Balthazar Reyes, Cristo Oveido, Fidelina Chavez, Nazario Mascarena, Euphonia C de Baca.

In Rio Chiquito, a spindly old Hispano woman, her hair tucked into a shower cap, sprayed a trickle of water from a garden hose onto a leggy geranium planted in a lard can. Behind the frail woman, an airbrushed head of Christ floating amid a galactic swirl of stars and planets decorated one entire outer wall of her small house. A broken-down wringer washing machine leaked a trail of rust against the bottom of the epic mural.

The road climbed out of the lush orchards and adobe estates of the Espanola Valley and onto a piñon-freckled stretch of mesa, pink and gold in the late afternoon sunlight. A solitary windmill sliced the ceaseless currents that had eroded rock columns into lines of dancing cobras. Far overhead, the path of a circling hawk slashed the white contrail of a jet in a sky newly cleaned of smoke.

Truchas, Las Trampas, Peñasco, the villages hugging the hairpin turns I slewed around, splashing through puddles left by last night's rain, could have been transplanted from the Spanish Sierra Nevadas. If I stuck my arm out the window, I could touch the adobe houses I flew past. Beside each one stood a silver tank of butane, several cords of wood seasoning in ragged piles, and a beehive-shaped horno oven with a round opening at its front like a mouth frozen in a wail.

I screeched around a corner and slammed on the brakes, my tires slipping on the road still slick from the rain. An old man in a crumpled felt fedora and a white shirt buttoned up over the cords in his neck wandered down the center of the road ahead, oblivious of my presence. Houses crowded the road so tightly that I couldn't pass him and had to slow down to match his crabbed pace as he ambled down the street. I was close enough to see his shoulder blades raise bony wings on either side of the X where his suspenders crossed his back. He heard the engine and looked back, turning his entire upper torso, so that I saw the winged shoulder blades in profile. His eyes widened in surprise and he hopped like an injured bird across the frost-buckled road.

The motor labored on the steep uphill grade outside of town. Perched atop a ridge, the road was as thin as the backbone of a starved dog, ribs of erosion digging into its side. A few houses were tucked away in the green crotch of a deeply shadowed valley far below. Their tin roofs winked in the fading rays of the sun, sending silvered greetings from a world left behind hundreds of years ago.

Next to the road, strips of red ribbon bleached pink fluttered from a weather-grayed cross. CIPRIANO ARCHULETA. KILLED IN A CRASH, JAN. 6, 1969. In the distance an abandoned adobe chapel melted back into the earth it had sprung from. A scrap of dirty rag, once a curtain, blew out of the empty socket of a window where a congregation had once prayed amid the cold beauty their grandchildren would abandon.

A truck lumbering up the mountain blocked me for several miles on the narrow road. The truck spit bullets of wet gravel that pinged off the windshield. Each one jangled my nerves, caused my heart to accelerate. A stab of pain in my neck made me aware that I was gripping the steering wheel so tightly that my nails had dug deep grooves into the flesh of my palms.

I followed the directions on the hiker's map and turned off onto an unmarked gravel road. For a time, the cratered road aimed straight at Agua Fria Peak. One face of the peak was scorched black from the forest fire. The scarred crag shifted in and out of my vision as the road wobbled eastward.

I was nearly on top of the procession before I made myself understand that it was not a mirage. Gravel spattered as I jammed on the brakes. A priest in purple vestments led the windblown group. Behind him a stocky man, face as long and brown as a Tiki war god, fought the wind to keep a flapping white satin banner appliquéd in purple with INRI from being torn out of his callused hands. On the other side of the banner was a Sacred Heart wreathed in piercing thorns and stabbed through with a wooden cross. Perfect tears of crimson blood hung from the organ like plump fruits. Old women wearing head scarves and plastic shoes fingered rosaries. The cut-glass beads slipping between the women's fingers glinted in the harsh mountain sunlight as corrugated lips slid over the cycle of prayers. The road widened, giving the faithful enough room to allow me to pass.

"Gracias a Dios del cielo: porque es eterna su misericordia!" The priest, the youngest in the group by several decades, intoned a prayer of gratitude for God delivering his flock from the fires. His followers repeated his words.

The road rose higher and low-cropped piñon and sage gave way to tall ponderosa pines, their trunks reticulated like a herd of frozen giraffes. As I drew closer, then entered them, the mountains turned from dusty pine green to the cold blue of granite. I slid into a canyon that abruptly blocked out the sun. At the corner of my vision, a magpie cartwheeled high above, black then white, catching the bugs darting through the last flashes of sun.

The road was walled in by tall pines, their trunks banked with old, humped snow, black in the shadows. I downshifted when the tug of the engine grinding up the mountain became a groan. The lower gear engaged with a shudder that shimmied through the car body to the sensitive space between my legs. An artery of pain opened between my jaw and a soft spot behind my earlobe. I shifted my jaw from side to side, but the pressure didn't ease until I pinched my nostrils shut, blew, and swallowed. My ears crackled, popped, and cleared. I went higher.

Darkness had begun melding all the trees into one black shape by the time I found the final turnoff. The few dusty houses that composed La Viuda hugged the road even more tightly than those of other villages. The village had one store and it was boarded up. Its flaking sign read EL NORTEÑO, The Northerner. The name wasn't referring to the northern part of the state of the New Mexico. It was talking about the people who'd settled La Viuda and the south they were northerners to was Mexico. La Viuda was the last outpost of a fallen empire, the residents still commemorating the home in Mexico their ancestors had left to claim this territory for New Spain.

I drove past the houses of the descendants of the conquistadors. All were made of adobe, all were dissolving back into the earth. Jerky television light flickered in the windows. In the driveway of a house at the end of town, an old man was hunched over an engine working in the harsh illumination of a light hooked to the raised hood. The car he was working on was Doña Carlota's old Buick. The mechanic glanced up and raised a hand in greeting. It was Teófilo, Doña Carlota's brother-in-law.

I parked and approached. The old man greeted me in a mixture of English and Spanish of the archaic type that charmed visitors from Spain. The kind that must be like hearing backwoods Appalachians speak Elizabethan English. I told him I was trying to find Tomás's cabin and asked if he could give me directions.

At the mention of Tomás's name, Téofilo's friendliness vanished. He looked away and concentrated on wiping his hands. I thought he hadn't understood and repeated my question. In the silence that fell, I watched a nighthawk swoop down, diving after the bugs darting through the corona of illumination cast by the light hooked onto the raised hood. Far off, a coyote howled. The night fell completely silent again before the old man asked why I wanted to know where "Tomasito" lived.

I sorted through several answers. "Friend?" "Former girlfriend?" Finally I answered that we had toured together. I was a flamenco dancer.

He peered at me skeptically, and though he smiled, it was obvious I did not look like a flamenco dancer to him. All I looked like was one of the outsiders he and his *norteño* ancestors had been repelling for centuries. He shrugged and smiled a smile meant to deflect me and my question.

For several minutes the old man tightened bolts; then, with no warning, he said, "You're her. You're Rae."

"I am."

"He's waiting for you." He pointed to a light winking in the distance. "Tomasito," he confided, then asked me to wait a moment. If I was going up there, he wanted me to take something to his *sobrino*. He hobbled into his house. The air had turned cool, almost cold, and smelled of rain and doused fire.

Téofilo came back cradling a Mason jar wrapped in a dish towel, handed it to me, and explained that it was his special posole, made from his brother's, from Ernesto's, recipe. Tomasito had loved his posole since he was a little boy. He walked me to my car, pointed several more times to the light in the mountain above, rattled off descriptions of turns, estimations of mileage, then sent me on my way.

I drove slowly and only found the road by connecting what looked like a dirt path to the flicker of light that was Tomás's cabin. In places, pine branches had grown completely across the rutted road. They scraped the windshield and the sides of the car with shrieking sounds.

The cabin was a solitary lantern, glowing alone in the dark night. As I pulled up, a door opened and Tomás stepped onto the porch. The headlights illuminated the sparse calligraphy of dark hair that flicked around his clavicles, the bow of his upper lip, the clean slope of his nose. It etched every wrinkle on his face in dark shadow. He seemed tired, bruiseable as he walked to the car, more a stranger to me than he had been the night we'd met at the Ace High. I switched off the engine but didn't get out. The window beside me was open and he came to it.

Before he could speak, I said, "I didn't come for you. I came for myself."

My hand rested on the door. He put his next to it. His nails, the long nails on his right hand, the hand that played *rasgueos* and plucked *picado*, were gone, cut now as short as a surgeon's. He said, "I miss you."

If I had moved my hand one millimeter toward his, if I had so much as willed the epidermis to thicken in his direction, we would have flowed together like pools of mercury. As we'd done all those times when he'd returned to me smelling of another woman, I would have tried to retrace and eradicate the geometry of betrayal. Where Didi had put her hand. Where his mouth had gone. We'd have reconstructed a painstaking model of the entire affair just so that he could smash it to bits, repudiate it, tell me it meant nothing. That I was the one true god and he would have no other gods before me. Then he would build a cathedral to me on the site of the false idol's temple. We would have melted into a trembling clump and I would not have been able to identify which molecules were mine and which were his.

We would have done all that because melting back together was the true reason I was there. I had a hole in my brain and he was the key that fit it. I shoved the door open, pushing him away. I had to because he was what I desired most and must never have again. His cell phone was ringing as we entered. The ring tone was a sprightly *alegrías.*

"Are you going to answer that?"

He shook his head no.

"Maybe it's about . . ." I didn't have to say Didi's name. We both knew who it would be about.

"It's not. Don't worry. I've got Alma's number programmed to play *por siguiriyas.* She said she'd call. If there was any change."

The smell of the piñon fire burning in the fireplace and of the century of piñon fires before it drenched the old cabin. We sat in front of the fire on straight-backed, wooden chairs made by people who had been dead for a hundred years before either one of us had been born. I studied Tomás in the firelight and realized what had changed: he looked mortal.

He said, "I'm sorry."

And I answered, "We're not going to talk about that."

"It's not enough, I know. Nothing will ever be enough."

"You are who you are. Didi is who she is. Neither of you will change and you will devour me if I let you. I can't let you. Only one thing has ever really connected us, Doña Carlota's story. I am going to give it to you. Then we will be done." If, in all the time we were together, I'd ever looked into and seen the hunger I saw when I told him I was going to give him Doña Carlota's story, I'd have known we could be together. But I hadn't. I never would. Whatever we'd had was a spindly offshoot of a tree so massive it cast everything else, even Didi, into shadow.

He knew that revealing his hunger was a strategic mistake and said, "Rae, this is the beginning for us, not the end."

"Doña Carlota's stories, her lies, I used them as passwords to gain admission to your world. It's time to surrender them. You are their rightful owner. I don't have the entire story, but I will give you what I have."

Tomás barely breathed as I spoke. It was the first exchange we'd ever had that wasn't essentially sexual and it was stilted and formal. That was as it should have been. I was fulfilling an obligation akin to the ceremonial returning of bones to an ancestral burial ground.

Piñon is a fragrant wood, hard and long-burning. The logs blazed, then burned down to embers in the time it took me to tell Tomás that what he'd considered his birthright, the tale of Gypsy ancestors with the power to make the earth burn and poets weep, belonged to a servant girl named Rosa. He was rapt but not surprised by the details of his great-aunt's lonely and illustrious childhood, its abrupt end in the back room of a mansion in Granada, her flight with Rosa to Sevilla.

When I had told all that I knew, he was silent for a long time. His eyes twitched as if adjusting to a changing light. Finally he said, "I've heard all those stories before. I grew up with them. But my great-aunt was always the dirty little girl in the cave."

The obligation of dispatching my duty as well as I could bound me to say, "I think the next part of the story, the part she would have told me if she'd had the strength, was that Rosa might be your grandmother."

Tomás looked at the ceiling and shook his head, exasperated. "And I think that she chose to lose her strength at the point that best suited her. Rae, she made me who—what—I am. That's what I want you to understand. I want us to be together. Jesus, this is hard." He put his open hand on the top of his head as if he were trying to contain the thoughts burbling up. "I don't know how to start. Tía Carlota didn't like me to speak."

It struck me that that was the first time I'd heard Tomás speak the name of the woman who had raised him.

"When I asked for something to drink, she'd stick a guitar in my hand and tell me to make her feel my thirst. And to do it *en compás* the way a real Gypsy boy would. I grew up with stories of how her family had lived in a cave in Sacromonte. How she saved herself and her family from poverty with her dancing. She told me the stories of the sufferings of her people. Of *our* people. *My* people.

"I grew up like one of the Romanovs. Like I had hemophilia, something in my blood that made me special but was a curse. That was how I thought of flamenco. That I was doomed to flamenco because I was *gitano por cuatro costaos*. She told me that my real mother was a relative, a great-niece or the daughter of a cousin. The story changed. When I was old enough, she told me my mother had been a drug addict who didn't want her identity revealed. It didn't matter. What mattered was that I was *gitano por cuatro costaos* and that my mother had given me up on one condition: that I be raised as *un flamenco*. That I learn our people's art, flamenco, but *flamenco puro*.

"She stuck a guitar in my hands when I was three and told me that Sabicas had started when he was two and I was already behind. When I was hungry, she wouldn't feed me until I could make her feel my hunger. Play my hunger for her on the guitar. When I got tired, bored, she'd ask me what would have happened if our people, exiled from their home, wandering for centuries, for so long that they even forgot where home was, despised and persecuted wherever they went, what would have happened if they had given up?

"Flamenco was all I knew growing up. School was my reward. If my playing was going well enough, she allowed me to go to school. If not, no school. We didn't have a TV in the house, most of the books were in Spanish. Biographies of Carmen Amaya, of Sabicas. I didn't learn to speak English that well and the Spanish I learned from her and Tío Ernesto was like something out of another century. Something that made me an outsider to the other kids in Santa Fe. So I didn't have friends. I had flamenco.

"This." He stopped and looked around at the cabin, lantern light flickering across the thick, round logs that formed the walls. "This was my sanctuary and my salvation. Mine and Papi's. Papi, that's what I called Tío Ernesto when we came here. I never called him father back in Santa Fe. Never in front of her. But when we were here together, he was *mi papi*. Papi and I would come up here without her. Everyone was related to Papi and that made them all my cousins, *mis primos*. This was Anaya land. It was just far enough from Santa Fe and from Taos to escape being developed out of existence. The young people always left La Viuda. They had to. There was no way to survive up here. But they always came back at holidays and during the summer. Then we'd have huge *pachangas*. Lots of beer. Lots of food. The women would bring pots of posole, green chile stew, chicos, *calabacitas*. No Paco de Lucía. I got to listen to Duran Duran and Van Halen like a normal kid. *Mis primos* were my best friends, my only friends.

"When we left Santa Fe and came up here, Papi would always pack the guitar just like she ordered. But he'd leave it in the trunk of the car. No one in La Viuda cared about flamenco. To them a *compás* was something to help you find your way out of the forest. No one cared if I was *gitano por cuatro costaos,* if I had the 'blood of the pharaohs' flowing in my veins. Uncle Ernesto was *mi tío, mi papi,* and that was all they needed to know. In La Viuda, I was family. They loved my uncle and they loved me. I was part of a pack here, just one of the *primos,* one of the swarm of boys who would throw Black Cat firecrackers at the girls we liked, who'd sneak out to the *morada* and spy on the *penitentes'* secret ceremonies, who'd hike up into the foothills and hunt for musket balls left by the conquistadors, for arrowheads left by the Indians the Mexican soldiers had killed.

"When you're young, you don't question anything. You don't question the world you are born into, especially when you are allowed to see very little outside that world. Especially when you are the little prince of that world. It's hard to ask questions when you're a kid and a concert hall full of adults is standing up to applaud you. I was a tiny phenomenon in a tiny world. I was the great New World hope. I would be the one to show Sevilla, Madrid, Jerez that we colonials could do flamenco as well as anyone back in the Motherland.

"When Tío Ernesto died when I was nine, she really went crazy. School became a luxury then. I'd play and she'd dance for hours every day, drilling the *palos* into me until all she had to do was clap two beats, three, and I could follow anything she danced. She'd read that Paco de Lucía practiced eight hours a day so she made me practice nine because he was a *payo* and a 'real Gypsy boy' will always be better than a *payo* because flamenco is in our blood. That was my childhood. They saved me, *mis primos.* They were always there to take me away when I called. We were badasses together. Me and the *primos.* Drugs. A lot of drugs. Some of the people I love best in the world are in prison. Some are dead. They are the true flamencos. Not these kids at the university smoking imported cigarettes. Right here in this tiny village, in all the places like it where the dreams of the Spanish Empire died, here in New Mexico, this is the only place where the old lady could have made all her dreams come true. Because there weren't any Cities of Gold, right?"

He leaned forward and an excitement I'd never seen before, not when he'd played, not when we'd made love, animated his face as he preached a lesson that was more autobiography than it was history. "They came for the gold, right? All those Spaniards in their bloomers, up through Mexico they came. And all they ever found was this amazing land. So they settled it. They spread across it and made it their own. *Los norteños,* my people, didn't slaughter the natives and enslave the survivors. They married them. They didn't leave behind silver mines and sugar plantations. They left children, generations of children who called themselves Hispano. Children who would make their little corner of the earth the one place in America where the most Spanish of arts would be truly embraced.

"Secrets?" Tomás's laugh was odd, almost manic. "The old lady thought the Gypsies could keep a secret. Shit. There are families up here who've been lighting candles on Friday and never eating pork and saying prayers with words no one understands anymore and burying their dead under Stars of David for centuries. They've been doing it for so long they don't know why they do it anymore. They would be baffled if you said the word *crypto-Jew* to them. All they understand is that you keep your secrets in the family. They understood that when the government came in and tried to set up public schools and they refused. They understood that when rich Anglos appeared and built vacation homes that mysteriously burned down. They understood that when anthropologists and folklorists came to study them and they made up stories to tell the outsiders and kept the truth for themselves.

"This was the world *mi papi* came from, and that and his money made him exactly what the old lady was looking for, a rich man who believed in keeping secrets. I don't know why he fell in love with her. Maybe he had a thing for her fancy Castilian lisp. Whatever, once they were married, the old lady made certain that she and her new husband were the highest of High-spanic. They were married in the Santuario de Guadalupe and paid for a front-row pew at St. Francis Cathedral so at Sunday Mass, they could sit next to families who'd lived in Santa Fe for a dozen generations. She ordered her groceries at Kaune's on Washington, bought her shoes at Dendahl's on the plaza. And just like that, the flamenco dancer transformed herself into Doña Carlota Montenegro de Anaya, the perfect Santa Fe doyenne.

"Who knows why she wanted a child?" Tomás asked. "I grew up with one story. From *mis primos,* I heard another one. This story was about a girl who was fifteen and pregnant. The girl's devoutly Catholic parents were frantic. They talked to the one member in a family that sprawled across the state who had done exceedingly well, an elderly relative who was known for his generosity. They needed money to send the girl away. The relative and his fancy wife solved their problems by offering to pay for everything and to adopt the child on one condition: complete secrecy. The parents agreed and the girl was sent away to Las Esclavas del Divino Corazón de Jesús, the Slaves of the Divine Heart of Jesus, a home for unwed mothers in Guadalajara.

"When the time came, according to *mis primos'* story, my aunt told a few women of her acquaintance, not quite friends since I never knew her to have any true friends, that she was going to Spain to adopt the child of a distant relative. The mother was a heroin addict, disappeared after the birth, probably dead. Like so many of her people, the Gypsies. 'Gypsies?' the women had said. 'Why, we had no idea you were Gypsy.' 'No, of course not. Where I grew up, it was dangerous to be Gypsy.' My aunt swore the women to secrecy. But she was a connoisseur of secrets. She knew which ones would be kept and which ones would be spread. Always in confidence so strict the secret was immediately accepted as absolute truth.

"There was no trip to Spain. Instead, Tío Ernesto and my aunt went to Guadalajara, to Las Esclavas del Divino Corazón de Jesús. From there *mi papi* took home a son and my aunt procured an instant heritage. Funny story, huh?"

"Tomás, I saw your birth certificate. You were born in Spain. I think your mother is the daughter, granddaughter, of Doña Carlota's friend, Rosa."

Tomás sawed off a bitter rasp of laughter. "Ah, the birth certificate. Was it on the wall?"

"No, it was locked in a box."

"Locked in a box. Good. That's a good dramatic touch. Heighten the revelation, right? Rae, I grew up with that birth certificate hanging on the wall above my bed. It wasn't until I heard this other story that I had to ask, 'Who puts a child's birth certificate over his bed?' Someone who gives an answer so the question won't be asked, that's who. With my birth, she was reborn. As a Gypsy. As the real thing. I became the answer to the question she couldn't allow to be asked. And you know what the hell of it is? She honestly thought she was giving me a gift."

Tomás had told me his story. He offered it to me. If I accepted, I would serve his story, the story that was also Doña Carlota's, for the rest of my life. Instead I said, "You could have gotten a blood test."

"I was scared of what I'd find out."

"Scared you'd find out you weren't Gypsy and couldn't be the Great Brown Hope?" It was exhilarating to challenge him. Exhilarating and terrifying. I was resigning from his cheerleading squad. There would be no other place on the team for Cyndi Rae Hrncir.

"No, I was afraid I'd find out I was. One way I'd lose my professional identity; the other way I'd lose my soul. I guess I was scared of finding out which one mattered more to me. Rae, there is darkness in my life, there always will be. That's why I have to have you to light it. You're the only antidote to the darkness. Rae, I love you."

It was the truth. I saw it in his face. He needed me. He loved me. The door was open. All I had to do was walk through it. A *siguiriyas* began to play. Even coming tinny and shrill as the ring tone on Tomás's cell phone, the *palo* was unmistakable. He checked the number. "It's Alma."

"Answer."

Tomás's eyes held mine as he greeted Alma in Spanish. He walked to the nearest, window, switching to English and plugging his free ear as he said, "Alma, I can't hear you. You're breaking up. You're breaking up. I'm only getting every fourth or fifth word. Alma, who died? Alma, I can't hear you. Alma!"

He held the phone out as if I might be able to resolder the lost connection. "Rae, someone died." For a moment, his face made me think of the lonely, dutiful boy in the photographs in his aunt's living room.

I took the phone from his hand and snapped it closed. "We'd better go."

Chapter Forty-three

We walked like a dozen brides down the narrow aisle. I led the procession as it slowly approached the coffin placed in front of the altar. Ancient planks creaked beneath our feet. The full skirts of our floor-length black dresses swept against the sides of the pews filled with mourners. Each of us held a candle, globes of light in the darkened chapel. A doll-faced virgin, green-winged angels, and a variety of saints, all originally carved and painted a quarter of a millennium ago, measured our progress.

She had always planned every detail of every performance and, a diva to the end, her final one, this *misa flamenca,* flamenco Mass, was no exception. The coffin was plain, lid closed as she'd directed. The altar was blanketed in roses so red the ones in shadow appeared black. The name of the variety was Carmen. That had been specified as well.

The scent of roses blended with the incense curling from the priest's censer. At the altar, we divided into two. We placed our candles in standing holders and took seats on straight-backed chairs facing the congregation, six dancers on each side of the altar.

Tomás, seated in front of the banks of roses, looked up from his guitar, nodded to me, and I began *palmas,* clapping out the slow, sonorous beat for the *canto entrada.* He made it a song of mourning, of death. The other dancers, then most of the congregation, joined in and the sharp slap of practiced hands rang in flawless cadence through the chapel. Everyone in the chapel knew the code, the girls I had danced with for years, the guys who had played for us, those who'd sung, those who'd listened, those who'd watched. Most of the Spanish luminaries from the festival were there as well. Everyone was *enterao.* We had shared the pulse and it had bound us.

I accelerated the tempo. Blanca, steady, kind Blanca, picked up the beat and twined a counterrhythm through it. A volley of finger snaps popped through the new rhythms. Knuckles rapped on the back of pews. Fingernails clicked. The sound was the sound of a stream rippling over rocks, of water pattering from a fountain designed by thirsty people, desert people. By *gitanos*. By Andalusians. By Arabs. By Indians.

Tomás plucked an E chord that announced he would start on the sorrowing side of a *soleares por bulerías* and we fell silent. His *toque* was terse, elegantly dry, a hymn to the spaces in between. He played a dirge for what had been held and was lost, what had been reached for and was never grasped. Three rolling *rasgueados,* then a simple statement of the first *compás,* was all he needed to play to state this fact: he had loved her. In his own way. In spite of everything. He had loved her.

Guitos, who'd arrived late the night before, stood and began his *temple,* singing the *"Ay"* that warmed his voice and opened his soul. He had been scheduled to open *La Convocación* in Madrid, an austere gathering of flamenco legends that was held once a decade. Though it was *el arte*'s highest honor to perform for the convocation, he had canceled the instant Tomás called to tell him that she had requested he sing. Guitos's voice quavered, freighted with grief more than a thousand years old. He shed the tears Tomás couldn't and his *cante* grew even harsher. A burble of clapping flowed into the *silencio* when he stopped. I picked up the beat, stamping my heels, tilting my ear upward, allowing the rhythm to fill my head. Tomás followed my lead and increased the tempo.

I took four *compases* to stand, just as Doña Carlota had taught us. With each one, my memory of the old woman who raised Tomás became clearer. I felt her in my arms, in my blood as the sacred rhythms coursed through me in the same way they'd coursed through her. I deciphered the history encoded in each *compás*. Wisdom surged up from my feet and, for that moment, the space of four *compases,* I understood why the old lady had given her life, why she'd tried to give Tomás's, to *el arte*.

One by one, each of the other twelve *bailaoras* stood and joined me. Alma, the soul of the flamenco program; Liliana, the star from the class ahead of ours; Blanca, the sweet one; Yolanda; we all stood. Didi was the last. She was wobbly and gray as pavement. Her nose was still red where they had fed a tube into her stomach. She faltered and everyone in the chapel leaned forward to catch her. But she found her balance, took her place beside me. In unison, we twined our arms up, dragging up scoops of perfumed air up with each languid twirl.

Behind us Doña Carlota rested in her coffin as cold as Queen Isabel ever was lying beside Fernando and her mad daughter, Juana, in the chilly fastness of Granada's cathedral shadowed by the castle of vanished Arabs floating in the sun above the city.

Didi and I danced, side by side. We'd done these steps so many times that she didn't need to look at me. I didn't need to look at her. We followed the pulses Tomás strummed on the guitar as if they were pitons hammered into a wall of sound guiding our hands, our feet. We reached a hand up, grabbed for the next one, and lifted ourselves higher.

A choir sang from the loft above our heads, releasing an avalanche of crystalline sound.

> *Señor, Dios de la vida*
> *Concédele a mi alma*
> *Tu gracia divina*
>
> *Lord, God of life,*
> *grant my soul*
> *your divine grace*
>
> *Porque soy pecador*
> *Dios mío de mi alma*
> *Ay! Ten compasión!*
>
> *Because I am a sinner,*
> *God of my soul,*
> *Ay! Have compassion!*

Five guitarists fanned a ravishing guitar introduction to the Kyrie. They fell silent and Tomás plucked a series of *falsetas* so poignant and ethereal that they turned the small chapel in La Viuda into the grand cathedral in Granada. Guitos's *temple,* the plangent warble of *Ay,* transformed it into the *Judería,* the *Albaicín,* the Jewish, the Moorish neighborhoods echoing with the quavering voices of cantors, of muezzins, in the days before the Moors and Jews were expelled. He sang and made us all walk the dusty paths of Sacromonte.

> *Señor, ten piedad, Señor, ten piedad.*
> *Lord have mercy. Christ have mercy.*

Señor, ten piedad, Señor, ten piedad.
Lord have mercy. Christ have mercy.

Señor, ten piedad, Señor, ten piedad.
Lord have mercy. Christ have mercy.

I turned and faced Didi. It was astonishing how well we two had learned the code. Every flick of her wrist, every stamp of her heel, held meaning. I translated each dot, each dash. Didi hung back on the beat, allowing me to surge forward to take the lead in a dance that had no lead. All we had was the solitary promise flamenco ever makes, the promise of eternity if you can create one moment beautiful enough to be called true.

That moment the *compás* unlocked not the truth of my brain, but the truth buried in my bones. I remembered Didi with the tips of her hair dyed lime green. I remembered the first morning she picked me up in the Skankmobile. I remembered squatting next to her on the West Mesa above a puddle of my own tears while she forced me to say that Daddy would always be with me. I remembered and I danced my joy that she was alive. Behind the anger, disappointment, and betrayal, there was that truth to tell: I was happy that she still breathed. In the end, I had not wanted her dead.

Didi's dance was hectic, out of *compás*. A flurry of apologies, an atonement not for any of the things she'd done, but for being the person who'd had to do them. Behind the frenzy the truth Didi danced was that, in spite of everything, she loved me more than she loved herself. It was the imperfect love of a girl who had lived her life on the pitchfork of renown, who'd believed she wasn't there if no one was watching. It was the love she had to give. She gave it to me.

We twelve dancers twined about one another. Our skirts rose and fell in perfect time, forming a child's curlicue of breaking waves. The chorus joined Guitos and sang, "You are the voice of the way. The joy of life. The light of the world. The salt of the earth."

I danced my gratitude for all the doors Didi had opened and pulled me through. All the stuffy rooms she had dragged me out of. I danced for the four of us, Clementina and Rosa, Didi and me. We four had been girls who'd wanted real families, real mothers. What we had found was each other. And flamenco.

We raised our arms to honor Doña Carlota Clementina Montenegro de

Anaya's life. I honored it in all its manifestations. All its contradictions. I honored her fierceness. Her talent. I honored the truth she had told, the truth she had not been able to tell.

Tomas's head bent over his guitar. His *compases* were so sturdy that time itself danced on them. He sliced time in half, then thirds, then again, until each moment expanded in front of me and I had time enough for everything. Time to put *triples* on all the footwork. Time to understand. Tomás looked up from his playing and made the one request that flamenco makes: *Dame la verdad.* Give me the truth.

I waded again into the familiar sea of his *toque* and danced. It was time to tell my truth.

Chapter Forty-four

I walked out of that tiny chapel in northern New Mexico almost two years ago. The truth I'd finally told was that I had a hole in my brain and Tomás had the key and Didi had the key and, one way or another, we would all be locked together forever if I remained. I wanted to put an ocean between us, but the most I could afford was one international boundary. Vancouver has an unexpectedly vibrant flamenco scene. I found a teaching job the first week I was here. The studio pays me in cash since I don't have a work visa. My real job, though, is learning how to be the major player in my own life. I'd been a member of the supporting cast for so long that it was awkward at first. For the first few months, I let myself be guided by the question WWDD?—What would Didi do?—and extrapolated from the answers.

Since the first thing Didi would have done was find her own supporting cast, I started a dance troupe. We melded instantly: a pair of sisters from a Hong Kong banking family; a Ukranian guy with a blond braid thick as my wrist; a chunky Japanese girl who had studied flamenco in Tokyo since she was four; a belly dancer from Marrakech; an assortment of grunge kids with blond dreadlocks, tattoos of salmon, and multiple piercings; an African Canadian who can't stay en com-pás to save her life but has almost more stage presence than anyone I've ever seen. Almost. I tell her she reminds me of someone but don't tell her who. Didi's isn't a name I'm ready to start dropping. We make a good troupe, we flamenco misfits. We fight. We laugh. We dance. We're a tribe.

For the first year, I would come nearly every morning to watch the sunrise. It was a way to keep myself from answering Didi's letters, Tomás's phone calls. A way to keep from going back. I never hid from them. That would have been clinging and I was letting go.

I have careful conversations with my mother. I call once a week on Tuesday evening and we speak from precisely eight until eight-twenty. Safe within that cage of minutes, my mother feels free to expand. She tells me which quilt patterns are selling the best. She tells me who has become a "disruptive influence on the community." She tells me that they are doing well with the herbs, the radicchio, and organic blueberries they grow now to support "the work."

It is impossible not to keep up with Tomás and Didi. Tomás called his last CD El Norteño *and dedicated it to "La Viuda and the true people of my blood." The interviews that followed kicked up quite a storm. Tomás renounced all claims to Gypsy heritage, stating that he was "*Nuevo Mexicano por cuatro costaos.*" As a "New Mexican on four sides," Tomás was embraced even more wholeheartedly than he had ever been before. An entire continent, not just a rarefied clique of* aficionados, *saw him as their own. His story was irresistible. The story alone would have propelled him to regional fame. His talent and beauty guaranteed an ocean of national, then international, ink with its attendant adulation.*

Just last week, I read about Didi's latest triumph. Like all flamencos, *my knees and spine are starting to require attention and I have been seeing a chiropractor. With the aromatherapy machine wafting a soothing blend of lavender and bergamot around the reception area, I leafed through a pile of magazines, passing up* Runner's World *and* Yoga Journal *in favor of the current issue of* Frisson, The Magazine of Cultural Exploration.

It was a shock to find her staring at me from a full-page photo. Didi didn't seem as if she had aged so much, as she'd finally grown into the world-weariness she'd been born with. In the accompanying review, her latest production, Ofelia Unbound, *was called "a one-woman show that channeled Federico García Lorca, Carmen Amaya, and Judy Garland." The review went on to say that "in a vertiginous performance, La O teeters perilously close to the very edge of self-immolation."*

La O. It must be a promotion to move from being a one-name celebrity to a one-letter celebrity.

The evidence of Didi and Tomás's fame calms me. The world sees what I had always seen. Others are as captivated as I had been from the very first moment. I wasn't crazy. I was never crazy.

In a few minutes, at our regular time just after sunrise, Collin will join me. We'll walk along English Bay and throw sticks for the two big dogs we adopted from the pound. I'll see in his kind attention to them, in his joy in their progress from malnourished discards to sleek beauties, the good father he will be to the children he wants to have with me. The air will be cool and moist. We'll nod at other couples passing in the opposite direction. Collin and I will find a private piece of driftwood to sit on and watch the sun, a courteous and remote sun, rise unobtrusively. In the soft, morning light, Collin will gaze at me and I'll see the same grateful astonishment on his face that I used to beam onto Didi.

For Collin, I am as exotic and wild and free as Didi was for me. I've pulled him through more doors and out of more of the stuffy rooms where he made an early fortune with computers than he'd ever dreamed of. Collin will be wearing something fleecy, a vest, a jacket the color of moss, of a fawn. He never wears black. He will make his body into a cradle to hold me while we watch the end of the soft pink sunrise reflect off orange hulls of tankers from China, from Liberia, from the Netherlands. He will kiss my neck. He will say he wants our children to have my lips. I will say his eyes. He will lock his arms around me and ask where I want to go for coffee. Because Collin reminds me of all the good things about my father, I will suggest a bakery in a neighborhood off West Broadway where a lot of new immigrants from the Czech Republic have settled. I will buy kolaches filled with blueberries that are better than any I ever ate in Houdek and Collin will tease me about "my people, the pink people."

The waves roll in all the way from Asia and pound the shore just beyond my safe square of blanket. My mug of tea has gone cold. The glitter of phosphorescence fades as the sky lightens with a murky, opalescent glow announced by the barest tinge of rose at the edges. The soft pastel awakening suits me. This isn't the diamond-sharp morning of New Mexico, colors so bright they pierce your eyes. The sun, even fully risen on this misty day, is a whisper compared to that full-throated shout. Here, beside the ocean, in the milky light, a person is not forced to examine every detail. I can stop for a while, puzzling out whose story it was and what my part in it had been. For a moment, I can simply watch the gulls gliding above the sea, knifing in, then soaring back up.

In the light, there are other distractions to take my attention from the pounding of the waves. Bulbous-headed tubes of seaweed coil along the beach like dozing anacondas. Crabs skitter past, scratching wavering lines in the packed sand. An astounding bouquet of pulpy starfish in violet, mauve, ultramarine, coral, blossoms in a tidal pool. Starfish arms entwine comically like rubber-legged drunks holding each other up.

The pounding recedes. The waves slosh in.

I toss out the last of my cold tea. Memory is a luxury I only allow myself once a week. Twice at the most. I limit the time I spend asking why. I have already lost so many years, I can't afford to waste another moment looking back. All I care about now is what is ahead.

Some would say I settled, but they are wrong. I like my new life. I like the soft air, the pink sun. I like performing with my troupe. I like throwing sticks for the dogs and deciding where to have coffee. I like being the one sought after, the exotic, wild, free one. The one who loves a little less. Perhaps those who would say I've settled have never known the shadows. For me, being, not the tallest, but a tree tall enough to feel the sun on my leaves, has been worth everything.

Still, sometimes in my dreams, once again I follow Tomás through the night and he leads me into a hidden park where he plays falsetas *so beautiful that the leaves on the trees turn into hearts and the stars are silver smears across the sky. And all the vowels sing their names. They sing the A. The E. The I. The O. The U. And sometimes they sing the Y.*

ACKNOWLEDGMENTS

Juanito Truitt believes that his influence was "no more than a flea fart in the Grand Canyon." In fact, Juanito, extraordinary musician, teacher, and most humane of *flamencos,* was my guide deep into the Grand Canyon of flamenco in general and New Mexico flamenco in particular.

Eva Encinias-Sandoval, who gave flamenco its academic home in the New World, deserves an entire novel all to herself.

Because she is as generous as she is smart, Carol Dawson maintains that she didn't save this book. I know that she did.

My gratitude goes to all the dancers who patiently explained their art and to the incandescent teachers who allowed me to join or observe their classes: Carmen "La Chiqui" Linares, Leah Powell, Ramona Garduno, Joaquin Encinias, Marisol Encinias, Farruquito, Fenny Kuo, Sue Drean, Karen Richmond, Helena Melone, Lili del Castillo, Celeste Serna, and to the tireless staff of Festival Flamenco Internacional de Albuquerque.

I thank the astonishing guitarists who elucidated and inspired me: John Truitt, Calvin Hazen, Ellen Baca, Lorenzo and Gustavo Pimentel of Pimentel & Sons Guitars, Marija Temo, and Gabriel Bird-Jones.

Gianna LaMorte, Sophie Echeverria, Rubina Carmona, Kay Bird, Hannah Neal, Carmella Padilla, Emily Tracy-Haas, Yvonne Tocquiny, Kathleen Orillion, Judith Walker, Ixchel Rosal, Inez Russell, Rose Reyes, Jim Magnuson, and Steve Harrigan generously shared formative insights about flamenco, obsessive love, the soul of New Mexico, friendship, and how to write a novel.

I thank Bill and the rest of the extraordinary Bridgers family for helping me survive an Albuquerque adolescence.

My thanks to Hannah Neal for sharing the writing of her mother, dancer and dance critic Josie Neal.

I am indebted to the gifted writers who have captured flamenco on the page and recommend to readers who would like to explore *el arte* further Donn

Acknowledgments

Pohren, Paul Hecht, Walter Starkie, Jason Webster, Timothy Mitchell, Paco Sevilla, Gwynne Edwards, Ninotchka Bennahum, William Washabaugh, Barbara Thiel-Cramer, Dorien Ross, Will Kirkland, James Woodall, Robin Totton, Merrill F. McLane, Felix Grande, and dancer and dance critic Josie Neal.

Jocelyn Ajami's documentary about Carmen Amaya, *Queen of the Gypsies,* is a revelation. The films of Carlos Saura are indispensable.

Thank you, Kristine Dahl; no writer ever had better representation or a truer friend.

Publishing with Knopf is a novelist's dream and here is why: Gabriele Wilson designed a stunning jacket to wrap around Robert Olsson's handsome text package. Kathleen Fridella marshaled the long march toward literacy. Kathryn Zuckerman and Nina Bourne made book promotion an act of love. Millicent Bennett's enthusiasm and kindness were essential. Ann Close looked at a few patchy fragments, saw a novel, and kept seeing it even when I couldn't. This book is hers.

This book and all the best parts of my life wouldn't exist without George Jones and Gabriel Bird-Jones.

The Flamenco Academy

Sarah Bird

A READER'S GUIDE

Dancing to My Own Beat

The one subject I always knew I wanted to write about was an obsessive love affair I had that began when I was sixteen and fell in love at first sight with a deliriously handsome young man and remained so for the next seven years of our on-again, off-again romance. For years, I tried to capture this experience on paper, but it always came out as a suburban melodrama, until I put it in the world of flamenco.

Here's the story of how I first discovered *el arte*. When I was twenty and living with Beloved, I walked in on him in bed with a friend. Realizing that I had to put at least an ocean between us or I would never break free, I went to Europe. So, dazed and heartbroken, I hitchhiked and Eurailed for a year and a half. During that time I found a job as a tour guide in a botanical garden owned by white Russian émigrés on Spain's Costa Brava. One very late night, very early morning, in a tiny club outside of Barcelona, I saw an astonishing performance of what I would learn later was flamenco.

Flamenco was the first materialization I'd witnessed that mirrored my tumultuous inner landscape. Decades later, as I was struggling to make a novel convey the experience of obsessive love, I recalled that night. The passion and intensity of flamenco, its insistence upon revealing the unrevealable, fit the emotional truth of the story I wanted to tell.

I began a fumbling, stumbling study of flamenco and quickly discovered how dauntingly vast and impenetrably arcane the subject is. I live in Austin, Texas; not exactly a hotbed of flamenco activity. I was despairing of ever cracking the flamenco code when I learned that my alma mater, the University of New Mexico, was becoming the academic center of flamenco, that each summer the UNM flamenco program hosted a festival that drew every flamenco star in the world.

To kick off my research, I wrote an article for Oprah's magazine about being a fumble-footed, middle-aged matron trying to get my flamenco groove on. The "beginners" class I took was filled with professional dancers, owners of dance studios, and teachers, so it was hardly the beginning I needed. Interestingly, because of the response to the article generated, the festival has added a true beginner's class which, I hear, is an uproarious amount of fun. Hard as they were, it was only through submerging myself in classes and performances that I began to understand a bit about this art that reveals itself in the moment of performance.

The University of New Mexico's vibrant flamenco scene was a gift from the universe not only in terms of research but also in providing a setting for my young protagonists. Exactly the same setting where, thirty years earlier, I'd enacted my own drama. Flamenco's other great gift to me is that, as one of my characters puts it, "Flamenco is OCD with a beat." Flamenco dancers, guitarists, and singers are obsessive and do become compulsive about their art.

Possibly best of all is that flamenco demands the same sort of transformation that my obsessive love affair did. My heroine, Rae, goes through the flamenco dance program in order to transform herself into someone that Tomás, the object of her adoration, will fall in love with.

If I had known how complicated *el arte* is, I'm not certain that I would have chosen this world. I chose flamenco thinking that it was the embodiment of wild, anarchic abandonment built on unstructured improvisational outpourings, but learned that it is as strictly regimented as haiku. Every stomp of a foot, every strum of the guitar, must fall precisely within a certain rhythmic pattern called *el compás* and that there are probably fifty different styles, or *palos*. The other daunting fact that I learned about flamenco is that it is an insider's art. Experts, aficionados, and buffs abound and they all have very strict ideas about what is and is not *flamenco puro*.

For me to understand flamenco well enough to write about it required colossal, titanic, gargantuan amounts of research. I did all the live stuff in New Mexico, took classes, sat in on lectures, interviewed performers, and watched the world's best dancers, singers, and guitarists.

Speaking of guitarists, I have to send a shout-out to the one person most responsible for whatever understanding I have of flamenco, John

"Juanito" Truitt. Once I decided to attend the flamenco festival and take classes, I knew I would need something to keep my then thirteen-year-old son, Gabriel, occupied. He'd been studying guitar, so I signed him up for a beginners flamenco class. In the most amazing and necessary of coincidences, his teacher turned out to be an old friend of mine from high school, John Truitt, who generously allowed me to audit his class. I already knew that John is a lovely human being but quickly discovered that he is a brilliant musician and, possibly, the best teacher I've ever witnessed. He electrified and elucidated me and the entire class.

During long conversations, John shared the history of flamenco within New Mexico and helped me understand how a guitarist and dancer work together. Best of all, he taught Gabriel the rhythm structures so that later, back in Austin, he could break them down for his old ma.

Some of the other guitarists that I mentioned in my Acknowledgments shared both technical information and stories from their own lives about romances with fiery Gypsy dancers and the intricate hierarchy of the flamenco world.

I've been asked repeatedly if I went to Spain. No, Spain would not have helped unless I could have visited in a time machine. The parts of the novel that are set in Spain take place from, roughly, 1920 until the end of the Spanish Civil War. Though, if I did have that time machine, I would return to the Golden Age of Flamenco, around the turn of the last century when flamenco flowered in the *cafés cantantes,* the singing cafés, of Andalusia. That period entrances me. Maybe it's the gaslight.

Writing about flamenco, imagining all the insiders picking my work apart, was extremely intimidating. At the times, though, when I could manage to stop worrying about those battalions of experts and sort of channel the years of research, it was exhilarating to feel that, perhaps, I was putting on the page a distillation of both flamenco and obsessive love.

The other great challenge that this novel presented was finding the right voice to tell a story of an overwhelming first love affair. My default voice verges on the comic, so that is the mode I was originally in when I wrote the first draft. But it just absolutely did not work. I love humor. I love writing it, I love reading it, but a novel about obsessive love is not the place for it. Humor is a distancing mechanism. Mostly a good one, it lets us detach enough that we can talk about tragedy and taboos, fears and failings. But I could not have distance or detachment in this novel.

Maybe that's the reason that I would say that *The Flamenco Academy* is both my most autobiographical book and the least. The most in the sense that I reveal the utter irrationality and humiliating self-annihilation of my own obsessive love affair. The least in that none of the particulars of the love story correspond to my own other than that they both took place in New Mexico. Like most people, I have a semi-mythological relationship with the place where I came of age. In my case, it was along a fairly funky strip of Route 66. So, it was great fun for me to mythologize some of the landmarks from my teen years: the Aztec Motel, De Anza coffee shop, Pup 'n' Taco drive-through, my high school just a few blocks off the main drag, Frontier Restaurant, the divey motels that were the sites of many a teen bacchanal. And, like Rae, my protagonist, I ate a lot of chili cheeseburgers at the Frontier Restaurant!

Reading Group Questions and Topics for Discussion

1. When the novel opens, Cyndi Rae and Didi are described as polar opposites who bond over the loss of their fathers. What else draws them together and drives their intense, longtime friendship? What do they get from each other?

2. The two young women in the novel end up changing their names. What is significant about the names that they abandon, and the ones that they choose? How is Rae different from Cyndi Rae? How is Ofelia different from Didi?

3. When Rae first meets Tomás she says: "He was brown and fully formed. His black hair, brows, the black lashes shadowing his cheeks had an etched certainty missing in the tentative pastel fuzziness of the boys I knew" (73). Why do you think she is so taken by his coloring?

4. Tomás has clearly had his share of romantic encounters. Why does the fact that Rae is a virgin feel so important to him?

5. Rae learns that flamenco dancing is a series of contradictions. Technically, the rhythm of flamenco is highly structured, and adherence to that rhythm is of utmost importance. But the heart and soul of flamenco is spontaneous and wild. How do Rae and Didi fit into this dichotomy? Do their roles change at all over the course of the novel?

6. When Didi and Rae enroll at the Flamenco Academy, Doña Carlota becomes an inspiring figure in each of their lives. How would you describe each of their relationships with this legendary dance instructor?

7. In the novel, Sarah Bird alternates between two completely different worlds: a college campus in Albuquerque, New Mexico, and a Gypsy community in Andalusia, many years ago. What makes each of these settings so vivid?

8. Doña Carlota says that a true Gypsy singer's voice "is the sound a man makes when the world tries to choke him to death at birth and he sings anyway." When Rae auditions for Tomás, she says something similar: "This is what flamenco is, knowing you're alone, you're going to die, and dancing anyway" (267). Do you think Rae, with no Gypsy blood at all, becomes a true *bailora*?

9. Why does Doña Carlota feel compelled to tell the story of Rosa and Clementina to Rae? How is this story from long ago important to the novel?

10. Tomás says: "I grew up like one of the Romanovs. Like I had hemophilia, something in my blood that made me special but was a curse" (367). In what ways does flamenco continue to be both a blessing and a curse to him?

11. Tomás, Didi, and Rae are driven throughout the novel by intense obsessions, but Rae is the only one who really becomes freed from hers. What do you think gives her the power to overcome her obsession? Do Tomás and Didi have more in common with each other than either had with Rae?

12. Do you think, in the end, that Rae regrets her friendship with Didi? Have you ever had an intense friendship like the one shared by Didi and Rae? If so, is it still working, or did it fade or burn out over time?

PHOTO: MATT LANKES

SARAH BIRD is the author of five previous novels: *Virgin of the Rodeo, The Boyfriend School, Alamo House, The Mommy Club,* and *The Yokota Officers Club.* She lives in Austin, Texas, with her husband, George, and son, Gabriel.